A Field Guide to Murder

A Field Guide to Murder

A NOVEL

Michelle L. Cullen

CROOKED LANE
NEW YORK

Published in the United States by Crooked Lane Books, an imprint of The Quick Brown Fox & Company LLC.

Crooked Lane Books and its logo are trademarks of The Quick Brown Fox & Company LLC.

Library of Congress Catalog-in-Publication data available upon request.

ISBN (hardcover): 979-8-89242-462-2
ISBN (paperback): 979-8-89242-463-9
ISBN (ebook): 979-8-89242-464-6

Cover design by Mallory Heyer

Printed in the United States.

www.crookedlanebooks.com

Crooked Lane Books
34 West 27th St., 10th Floor
New York, NY 10001

First Edition: January 2026

The authorized representative in the EU for product safety and compliance is eucomply OÜPärnu mnt 139b-14, 11317 Tallinn, Estonia, hello@eucompliancepartner.com, +33757690241

10 9 8 7 6 5 4 3 2 1

This book is dedicated to my dad,
who introduced me to
Jessica Fletcher; my mom,
who has encouraged me throughout
my writing journey; and my sister,
who has cheered me along the way.

Act I

"Trust your instincts. Your brain picks up details about everything around you all the time. Unconscious information, or that which is outside of your conscious focus, is assembled and analyzed based on previous experiences. These seedlings of thoughts send signals to your body—an unsettled feeling in your gut, hair rising on the back of your neck in warning. Do not ignore these signals. Sometimes they can be wrong, but the more time you spend doing fieldwork, the more often they are not."

—from *Lessons from the Field* by Harry Lancaster, Ph.D.

Chapter One

A *thwack* against the dark sunroom window startled Harry back into the plush club chair, smacking the binoculars into his eyes. Pain surged through his left hip, and he blinked away stinging tears.

"Dagnabbit."

The propped-up iPad on the nearby end table chirped with a FaceTime call. He blindly poked at the screen to connect. The force of his jab sent the iPad tumbling over the table's edge. It hit the rug, bounced, then landed against his walker to face the bookshelves that lined the wall between the room's floor-to-ceiling windows.

"Dad. Dad." Ceci's voice called out from the iPad's glowing screen. "What's happening?"

"I'm fine," he grumbled, hoping the blow from the binoculars wouldn't leave him with two black eyes. No way he could explain himself out of that one.

Harry placed the binoculars on the end table and bent over to retrieve the iPad. His daughter's concerned face came into view, connecting his Sunday night in central Ohio with her Monday morning in India.

Ceci was the spitting image of her late mother: high cheekbones, cobalt eyes, and an impish grin—now replaced with a frown. Her chin-length jet-black hair, which seemed to change as frequently as the weather, was the only thing that differed from Margaret's, which had been steadfastly shoulder-length and honey-brown.

"What happened?" She was sitting in her office at the American Embassy in Delhi, where she was stationed for her State Department job. A lonely fern sat on a stand in the corner to her right. Behind her cluttered desk was a packed bookshelf, much like his own. Though proud of his daughter, who was following so closely in his shoes that she practically wore them, Harry wished Ceci and her family didn't live so far away.

"Something hit the window and made me knock over the iPad as I answered your call." It was close to the truth.

He looked out onto his dusky front yard. The hydrangea next to the window moved. A crow emerged and scampered a few steps. Its onyx eyes fixed on Harry. It stretched its iridescent wings, and with three powerful flaps, returned to the darkness.

"Just a bird." He propped the iPad on the end table and settled into the chair. "How was Evie's birthday party?"

Ceci beamed. "It started off sedate for five-year-old kids, then Evan joined, and you know how Evie gets with him. Within minutes, cake was flying everywhere, and the kids were laughing and covered in icing. Steve turned on the sprinklers so they could rinse off. Everyone left damp but happy."

He smiled, wishing that Margaret could have seen their grandchildren grow.

As if reading his mind, his daughter's tone grew somber. "You doing okay?" She cocked her head to the right, a trait she'd picked up from him.

Harry knew she was asking about more than his fractured hip. "I'm getting around better each day." He ignored the throb in his left side. "I've read three of the anthropology books you sent. Have to keep my analytical skills sharp." He glanced at the titles underneath the iPad: *Bog Bodies Uncovered*, *Age of Wild Ghosts*, and *Purity and Danger*.

"Did you get the binoculars? They should have arrived yesterday."

Heat warmed his cheeks. The Sharper Image binoculars she'd sent had impressive daytime *and* nighttime ranges thanks to built-in infrared lights. He'd been figuring out how to focus them when the crow had slammed into the window. "I did, thank you. They'll be perfect for birding."

"Please. We both know you'll use them to snoop on your neighbors. Your chair is already angled for a better view out the window."

He caught his daughter's contagious smile. "I don't snoop," he said with mock dignity. "I'm an anthropologist. I make observations."

"Sure," she made air quotes with her fingers, "observations."

"I never look into windows, but anything outside, I reckon is fair game."

Ceci started grumbling about office politics, and as the woes and seconds ticked by, his eyes reverted to the window. Though the light outside was dim, years of familiarity helped Harry make out the details of the nearby Craftsman-style patio homes and duplexes that sat loosely scattered around an oval pond. Next door at the Buchanans, an Ohio State banner wafted in the wind, cheering for the Buckeyes with each flap. At Diana Middleton's majestic abode, potted plants in Tuscan urns stood guard by the front-porch steps. On the far side of the lane, a high-end golf cart perched in the Patels' drive, a symbol of their love for tee time and nineteenth hole martinis.

A shadow glided along the pond's edge. Harry tracked it as it moved along the water. Bigger than a fox, smaller than a deer. It progressed eastward and vanished behind a towering oak.

"Can you believe she said that?" Ceci's indignation caused him to meet her eyes and shake his head.

The shape reappeared on the road near Rachel's condominium, heading in Harry's direction. When it skirted by the pale light dribbling from a Victorian lamppost, he saw the flicker of a silver bob.

Huh. His neighbor Sue Daniels.

His daughter's voice crescendoed. "And then she demanded I finish it by tonight." Harry shook his head again, pretending he'd been paying attention.

Was Sue out for a walk past 11 PM*?* Clad in black, she seemed a perfect target for a passing car. She was asking for trouble.

A rogue cloud cleared the moon, brightening the landscape. Harry glanced over to see Sue retreat through her side yard and behind her house.

"I don't think it's a good idea, do you?"

Harry flicked his attention back to his daughter and tried to piece together what she'd said. "I see your point."

"I knew you'd agree with me." She sounded relieved, and he felt guilty for tuning her out.

A low siren sounded in the distance, and as it grew louder, Harry tried to discern whether it was coming from the iPad or outside his house. He interrupted her litany. "Sounds like a police car. I think the cops have been called to the lane."

"Da-a-ad," she chided.

He picked up the binoculars and wiggled them at her. "You're the one who gave them to me."

Ceci rolled her eyes and smiled. "Love you."

"You too. Hug the kids for me." They ended the call as the siren's clamor grew.

Harry looked outside to see Sue's porch light flick on. She walked out into her yard and stood beside a clump of flourishing mums. Gautam Patel joined her from next door, a surprise given the late hour. Gautam and his wife Sakshi habitually were up and out before seven for an early round of golf.

He fiddled with the binocular's controls and the figures of Sue and Gautam sharpened. They chatted and gestured toward

Sue's condo. Gautam's lanky silhouette contrasted with Sue's stocky build. Both wore robes and slippers.

A police car squealed to a stop in front of Sue's drive. Garish red and blue streaks bounced off the homes of Lakeview Lane and the pond at its center. Then the car's flashing lights flicked off, and two uniformed officers got out. Gautam returned home. Sue and the policemen disappeared inside her house, with Harry's curiosity not far behind.

That's it, he decided. Despite needing a walker for now, that wasn't going to stop him seeing what was going on.

Harry plodded to the foyer closet for his coat, turned on the outdoor light, then clambered out onto the porch, careful not to catch his walker on the doorframe or on the brick walk that led to his drive.

The police car was still parked outside Sue's, and he inched forward, wary of the steep incline. The chilly night air clung to him with foreboding.

When he reached the bottom of his drive, Sue's front door opened, and the two officers came out and returned to their patrol car. Headlights illuminated the lane as the vehicle snaked around the pond toward his home.

His mind flashed back to the crow and the loud *thwack* against his window.

Blinding beams flashed across his face seconds later and the car stopped next to him. The driver rolled down the window, but his face remained a silhouette. "Everything okay, sir?"

"I saw the commotion and wanted to make sure Sue was all right."

"She's fine." The officer leaned his head out the window. His cherub face made Harry wonder if he was old enough to shave. "Would you like help getting back inside?"

Annoyance sparked in Harry. He wasn't feeble. "Thank you, but I can manage. What happened?"

"Nothing. False alarm." The officer's eyes shifted to the precipitous driveway behind him. He cracked open the car door and started to get out. "Better safe than sorry. We don't want you getting hurt."

"I'm fine." Harry spoke in a churlish tone not even appropriate for his granddaughter when she needed a nap. He softened his voice. "But I appreciate your kindness." He started up the drive to prove his point.

"If you say so. Be careful." The door closed, then the car continued on.

Perspiration slid down the back of his neck as Harry struggled up the incline. Had Sue accidentally set off her alarm? She'd bragged about its bells and whistles at the Patels' last cocktail party.

By the time he reached his front door, he was breathless and worn out.

Time for bed. He didn't want his new caregiver, who seemed to have more zeal than a cheerleader after three double-shot lattes, to find him haggard in the morning. His dignity had taken enough hits over the past few months—with doctors and nurses poking at him, tracking everything from his pulse to his lungs to his bowels.

Harry trudged to the sunroom to turn off the light, then back through the living room, around the glass coffee table, and across the silky oriental rug that he and Margaret had bought in Nepal. When the rug ended, his metal walker thudded as he moved across the hardwood floor. In his mind, each step echoed the sound of that crow slamming into the window.

Thwack. Thwack. Thwack.

He tried to put it out of his mind, but the crawling shiver up his spine wouldn't let him. In many cultures, a crow flying into a window foretold an unexpected death.

Chapter Two

Harry reckoned not many could say no to Emma Stockton's pretty-please smile. "We won't go far," his perky caregiver encouraged. "Just a stroll around the lane." Lit by the bright light pouring through the sunroom windows behind her, she was the picture of youth: glowing skin, vibrant emerald eyes, shiny copper hair.

He stood, cringing from the kink in his hip, and leaned on his walker. Emma had been nothing but kind since she'd started working for him a week ago, yet he'd remained distantly cordial. It wasn't that he disliked her. Rather, he loathed his need for her.

After a long career of helping others—delivering aid to refugee camps, providing relief in conflict zones, designing projects to protect the world's most vulnerable—Harry was now the one in need, thanks to a nasty fall four weeks ago. He wondered if all those he'd helped over the years resented their reliance on assistance as much as he did.

"That's the spirit." Emma ratcheted up the wattage of her smile. "The more you move, the quicker you'll heal. And the quicker you heal, the sooner I'll be out of your hair." She widened her arms in a *ta-da* motion that swung her ponytail.

It was a compelling point, and he picked up his pace toward the front door and an Emma-free future.

Minutes later, they plodded around Lakeview Lane. When Harry had first seen the cul-de-sac, it reminded him of the Maasai villages he once studied, with fenced-in circles of thatched houses surrounding a corral of cattle and goats. He knew that this design reinforced people's sense of belonging and protection, keeping those inside united and safe from the threats beyond.

He and his late wife Mags had gone for routine walks around the lane and down Lakeview Estates' wide treelined streets, past its swanky golf course and country club, to the nearby commercial main street that exuded New England charm. But today the pain in his hip was prickly and deep, and Harry dreaded even one loop of the lane. He said nothing, but Emma kept looking at him from the corner of her eyes.

The temperature felt closer to June than October. Heat built up under his cotton sweater and by the time they reached the house next door, drops of sweat trickled down his back.

"How did you fracture your hip?" Emma asked.

This was a topic he preferred to avoid, but he and his two brothers had been raised not be rude by his childhood nanny, Old Ironsides, who'd been British and invincible like the ship. "I tripped."

"I know *that*. At home?"

"No, the university."

"Which one?" Her voice spiked with surprise. "Were you taking classes?"

Heat flooded his face, and in his fluster, he misplaced a leg of his walker onto a stray rock. He lurched. Emma rushed to steady him, with an empathetic smile suitable for wobbling toddlers.

Flush from a cocktail of humiliation and pain, he imagined a voodoo doll in her effigy and a few sharp pins.

Then Old Ironsides' influence stepped in. *Emma was only trying to help.* Without her, he'd had to have stayed in the rehabilitation center until he could get by on his own. And while the rehab center had been a step up from the hospital, he had no desire to go back.

"I was a guest lecturer for an evening anthropology class at Westerly College." Harry didn't mention how excited he'd been to speak at the prestigious private university. The lecture had been his first professional engagement after Margaret's death.

He'd just begun socializing with neighbors again and going to events. And his talk on rituals of the Cargo Cults in the South Pacific had been a huge success . . . until he tumbled on the walk home, landing him back in his shell. Crumpled on uneven bricks, surrounded by concerned faces.

"I'm sorry. That must've been difficult."

Her pity made him wince. He had summited Mount Everest, hiked El Camino de Santiago, and scuba-dived the Great Barrier Reef when she'd been in nappies. As soon as they got home, he'd lose himself in his latest library book, *An Anthropology of Anthropology*.

A door flew open at the gray home ahead of them, and his neighbor Rachel Valucci—a Sophia Loren clone—stepped out. "Darling, you look as handsome as ever." She glided down her drive on dangerously high heels, swooping toward them like a bird to a fat worm. "Heard about your fall, but I knew that wouldn't keep a strong man like you down."

Her tawny eyes moved to Emma as she adjusted her silk scarf. "And you are?"

"Emma Stockton," Harry said, struggling to keep discomfiture from his voice, "my *temporary* caregiver." The ever-polished Rachel surveyed Emma's practical clothing—what his daughter would call "mom jeans" and a faded blue T-shirt.

Harry turned to Emma. "This is Rachel Valucci," he said. "She owns and runs La Conchessa, a clothing boutique near downtown Columbus. My late wife Margaret did her best to keep Rachel in business."

Rachel tittered and gave Harry's arm a pat. "Welcome to Lakeview Estates. We're one big happy family." Rachel flashed blindingly white teeth, adding in a mock whisper, "We've even got a black sheep."

Before Harry could inquire who that might be, Emma spoke. "It's a beautiful community." Her tone was wistful.

Rachel teetered over to her stacked stone mailbox, which reminded Harry of a pagan altar awaiting a sacrifice. Her chestnut hair danced in the wind. "Yes, it is," she said over her shoulder. She reached in, stiffened, then bent down to peer inside. Inhaling sharply, she took a step back, rocking on her heels.

"Everything okay?" Harry asked.

Rachel recovered her balance. "Yes." She pulled out a few envelopes, then seemed to push something farther inside. Her eyes were wide, her skin blanched, and her words bumped into each other as she retreated up her drive. "Have to go. My boutique won't run itself."

Harry's eyes locked on the mailbox. If Emma weren't with him, he'd be tempted to look inside to see what had caused his neighbor's reaction.

At the next house down the lane, muffled voices rose from Milo Czesiak's open garage. Harry's ears instinctively perked to make out the words, which, given Milo's years of working as a trucker before owning a trucking company, were likely colorful and creative.

Sue Daniels emerged from the garage and shouted back to Milo, "You'd better, or else." Instead of cutting through the grass to her front door, Sue clomped down Milo's drive. In her late fifties, Sue kept her cropped hair straight, her lips rouged, and her ever-present cardigans neutral-colored.

When she neared, she greeted Harry with a smile that bared her teeth. "Glad you're doing better. Diana mentioned your fall at the women's luncheon."

Of course she did. Diana Middleton, a church-going widow, doled out casseroles and gossip as frequently as the postman delivered mail.

Harry turned toward Emma. "This is Sue Daniels. She—"

"I've seen you before, haven't I?" Sue closed the distance between her and Emma.

Emma frowned slightly. "I don't think so. I'm Harry's nurse—" She gave her head a quick shake. "*Caregiver*, actually."

"I never forget a face." Sue persisted. She tapped a forefinger against her lips, which matched the russet color of her nails. "I'm sure I have."

A moment of silence passed. Emma blushed under Sue's increasingly intense scrutiny, which was beginning to give Harry an uneasy feeling. He stepped in to ease the moment. "So, Sue, how've you been?"

"Busy. Making the most out of living in Lakeview Estates." Her eyes flitted from him to Emma.

"That's good."

"It is." She flashed a smile that looked more menacing than kind, then her gaze returned to Emma. Sue's face lit with recognition. "I've definitely seen you before," she said with certainty and without elaboration.

Harry, while confident in his ability to assess people and their behavior, had always found Sue difficult to read. She donned more masks than a Greek theater troupe, a behavior that did not instill trust. "Are you going to—" he started.

"I've got errands to run." Sue's hands brushed back her bob, then she headed up her drive. A few steps in, she looked back at Emma and uttered a few staccato jabs: "I'll see you around."

Puzzled by the interaction, Harry watched Sue until she disappeared inside. Emma started walking, her ponytail swishing across her back in steady time like a metronome. He struggled to catch up as a niggling feeling squirmed in his gut . . . something on Lakeview Lane felt offbeat.

Chapter Three

The following day, Harry nested in his sunroom, blissfully lost in some light reading: *Witchcraft, Oracles and Magic Among the Azande*—a classic. He didn't believe in witchcraft per se, but he couldn't deny the power it could hold over people.

Emma walked in, carrying a wedding magazine and a frown. That morning, she'd shown up with a stack of bridal magazines and had planted them on the kitchen counter. Up to this point, she'd barely referenced her upcoming nuptials. But the ring on her finger was hard to miss.

Was he about to be pulled into the morass of Emma's wedding planning? Thinking back to Ceci's wedding, and the decisions and stress it had entailed, his first instinct was to flee.

"You've been sitting for too long," she said. "We should go for a walk."

Relief made him sink further into the chair.

"Come on," Emma prodded. "You need to get used to using the cane."

His doctor had told him yesterday that he was ready to trade his walker for a cane, but he was enjoying reading. He countered her offer. "Not now. How about in an hour?"

Emma nodded toward his book with a slight smile. "I'm only giving in so you don't put some sort of spell on me." She left the sunroom, probably back to her mountain of magazines.

A minute later, a shrill ring interrupted Harry. He placed the book on the end table and reached for the phone handset, knocking down the cane that rested up against his chair.

"Hello?" He bent over to pick up the cane. A jolt of pain zinged through his hip, and he paused.

"*Ha. Haa.*" The faint voice broke off.

"Hello?" There was some shuffling and what might have been a muffled cough. "Hello?" Probably a darn telemarketer.

"Harry." It was a wispy female voice, followed by heavy breathing. Not a telemarketer, a nut job. His left-hand fingers grasped the cane.

"*Help.*" The word came out in a frail sob.

Harry sat up alert and put the phone back to his ear. "Who is this?"

"Sss . . . Sue." Her breathing was fast and hard, as if she'd run a marathon at full speed.

"Do you need help? Did you call 911?"

"*Yesss.*" Another labored breath. "Not. Here."

"What's going on?"

"*Everyth* . . ."

"Sue, are you with me?"

"*Nnn*-nurse."

Harry jumped up from the chair, agony surging down his left side.

Sue's next words were jumbled, but he thought he heard, "Lunch. Something wrong."

"Emma!" he called, and gripped the cane in his left hand, while tightening his hold on the phone with his right.

Something clattered in the kitchen. Footsteps rushed toward him. He met Emma in the sunroom doorway.

She eyed him from head to toe. "What's wrong?"

"It's Sue. I think she's having an allergic reaction. Sounds like she can't breathe."

"I've got an emergency kit in my trunk. I'm on my way." Emma rushed over to the kitchen table to yank her purse off the back of a chair.

"*Po—poi—*." Sue's faint words faded into labored breathing. "*—snnnn.*"

Harry hustled to the front door as best he could. "I'm sending Emma over now. Is your door unlocked?"

The only response was jagged breaths. Harry opened his door, juggling the phone and cane.

Emma jogged toward him, her hand digging into the depths of her purse. She yanked out her car keys, then nearly tripped on the rug in the foyer.

"Run," he whispered as she headed out the front door.

He put the phone back to his ear. There was a loud crash. "Sue?"

The line went dead.

Harry's heartbeat doubled, and every nerve in his body twitched with the need to help. He got his walker from the living room corner, knowing he couldn't get all the way to Sue's with just the cane.

By the time he made it to the porch, Emma was pulling a white bag from the trunk of her car, then she shot toward Sue's house at full speed. Her ponytail flapped from side to side in time with the slaps of her tennis shoes as she flew around the lane.

He'd wished he'd grabbed his cell on the way out the door. He tightened his hold on the walker and increased his pace as his driveway flattened onto the street.

With each step, his jaw clenched and his hip protested. A crow mockingly cawed from a nearby tree.

Had he heard Sue correctly? Had her last word been "poison"? Maybe she accidentally ingested a pesticide or cleaning product, or had incorrectly taken medication?

Emma was nearly there. Beads of sweat formed along his brow despite the damp chill that cut through his cardigan. A siren rose in the distance.

Two steps later, his walker hit a wet spot in the road, and he stumbled as it slid sideward. For a suspended second, he fought for balance. Then the walker's grip caught. He slowed his steps. His pulse kept racing.

When he looked up, Emma was gone. Sue's door stood ajar.

The siren was closer, a street away. Harry navigated to the side of the lane as he neared the Patels so the ambulance could pass.

A moment later, it slammed to a stop in front of Sue's. An EMT in a black uniform jumped from the passenger seat with a medical kit and ran into Sue's house. The driver went to the rear of the ambulance to let out another EMT, and the two of them rushed a stretcher inside.

The last three hundred feet to Sue's porch felt like miles. Harry kept waiting for the EMTs to rush Sue outside. They didn't.

* * *

Emma was standing in the doorway when Harry climbed onto the porch. "What happened?" he asked. The look on her ashen face did not bode well.

"They're trying to revive Ms. Daniels with epinephrin so they can defibrillate, but . . ." She shook her head, then sat in a nearby woven patio chair. Harry's hip throbbed as he eased into the seat next to her.

On the low wooden table between them he saw a pair of glasses, a cup of coffee with lipstick on the rim, and some brochures. The brochure on top proclaimed: *The Hilltop Inn: Eastern Ohio's top-rated B&B, and only a short drive from Wayne National Forest!* It pictured a charming Victorian home nestled among green rolling hills.

Harry sighed to lessen the sadness constricting his chest. The idyllic vacation promised by the pamphlet wouldn't be taken. The coffee wouldn't be finished. And the glasses wouldn't be used for reading anymore.

Over the decades, he'd learned about grief rituals from around the world—sky burials, funeral pyres, tears parties, celebrations—but death still hit hard, reminding him of those he'd lost and yearned to see again.

Emma's gaze focused on her feet. Heaviness seemed settle around her.

"You did your best." He patted her shoulder, but she didn't respond.

Another siren blared in the distance. A cold gust carrying the smell of rotting leaves swept across the porch, penetrating Harry's wool cardigan and forming goosebumps on his arms.

"How's your hip?" Emma asked.

"Tender but fine."

Emma's expression told him she knew he was lying.

A police car pulled into Sue's drive. Two uniformed officers—a young male built like a towering redwood tree and an older, lean female—got out and headed toward the house.

The giant male officer went inside. The woman, whose curly brunette hair tried to escape her hat, introduced herself as Officer Jackson. Her pale, world-weary eyes and the deep lines that surrounded them seemed to contradict the suggested innocence from the freckles that sprinkled her face. She asked Harry and Emma who they were, then peppered them with questions.

In the middle of Harry's description of Sue's phone call, a vintage blue Ford Crown Victoria that screamed law enforcement pulled into the driveway next to the police cruiser. A tall, brawny man in a tan coat got out and headed toward the porch. With his determined bearing, he must be a detective, Harry thought. A crime scene van pulled up and parked on the street behind the ambulance.

The man stopped just outside Sue's front door and motioned for Officer Jackson to join him. They spoke in hushed tones.

"Wait here, please," Officer Jackson called to them, then the two went inside.

Harry turned to Emma—the word "poison" still lodged in his mind. "Was there anything odd about Sue when you found her?"

"Odd? Odd how?"

"With . . ." He dropped off when the man in the tan coat returned.

"I'm Detective Nate Bradford," he said in a James Earl Jones voice as he flashed a badge. The navy suit beneath his coat was in dire need of pressing. His brown hair was messy and his dark eyes sharp. He looked to be somewhere in his early thirties, with wizened creases likely earned from the difficulties of his job.

The detective waited while Harry and Emma introduced themselves, then asked about Sue's call to Harry.

"It was hard to understand her," Harry said. "Her breath was labored and she had trouble getting words out. I could tell she was in pain."

"What *exactly* did she say, Mr. Lancaster?"

"She asked for help." He leaned back trying to remember Sue's exact words. "I confirmed it was Sue, and that she'd already called 911. Then she said—" he closed his eyes to prompt his memory, "something was wrong with her lunch. I figured she was having an allergic reaction."

Detective Bradford jotted notes in an index card–sized notepad he'd pulled from a jacket pocket. "Did Ms. Daniels say anything else?"

Harry wasn't quite sure how to best proceed without sounding like a paranoid fool. "I might be wrong about this, but I think her last word was '*poison*.'"

Emma's eyes widened. "*What*?"

"You think Ms. Daniels said 'poison'?" the detective asked.

Harry nodded. There had been something in the tone of Sue's voice . . . Something that made him think not an accident, not an attempted suicide. But he had no idea how to explain this ominous feeling when he couldn't explain to himself why he felt it.

"And after that?"

"There was a crash, and the line went dead." Harry's chest tightened. His voice must have been one of the final things Sue had heard.

Detective Bradford tapped his pen on the notepad, then turned to Emma. "Ms. Stockton, I understand you are a nurse?" She nodded. "Could you describe what happened when you arrived at Ms. Daniels' house?"

Emma sat up straight and wiped emotion from her face. "When I got here, roughly three minutes after Ms. Daniels had called Harry, the front door was unlocked but not open. I rushed in and found Ms. Daniels on the kitchen floor, curled in a fetal position on her right side."

Her tone became even more clinical. "Ms. Daniels had no pulse, was without respiration, and her pupils were nonreactive. Her skin was cold to the touch and gray in pallor. She had a red bump, about an inch in width, on the left-hand side of her forehead. There was evidence of emesis around the kitchen sink where she'd been sick. I checked her airways and found no restriction. I administered CPR for about two minutes, then the paramedic and EMTs took over, confirming asystole."

Detective Bradford looked impressed, and so was Harry. He'd of course read Emma's résumé and checked her qualifications, but with her wearing jeans, a sweatshirt, and a disheveled ponytail, these were easy to forget.

"What's asystole?" Harry cut in.

"No heartbeat," Emma answered.

The detective scribbled in his notepad. "Did you notice anything odd in the kitchen?"

Emma blew out a puff of air. "Two of the kitchen chairs were knocked over, as was a glass vase on the kitchen table, which had spilled water and flowers off to the side. A box of chocolates had been overturned and . . ." She looked up and squinted as if the answer was written on the porch ceiling. "Three chocolates were on the floor. I thought this might have indicated that Ms. Daniels had convulsed, knocking things over. That would track with anaphylactic shock. Her cell phone was under the kitchen table, its screen cracked."

Harry eyed his caregiver with newfound respect. She was observant to boot.

"Oh, one more thing. There were four pill bottles lined up on the far counter by a stack of books, with the pharmacy instructions sitting next to them."

"Did you smell anything?" the detective asked.

Her nose crinkled. "Pine-Sol."

"That's specific," he said, looking up.

"It's the brand my mom uses. Grew up with it."

He nodded. "Did you hear anything?"

The question deflated her. "No. I kept hoping for a gasp of breath."

Harry patted her shoulder again in understanding. He was a Vietnam veteran and an aid worker who'd watched far too many suffer and die.

Detective Bradford's tone softened. "Witnessing death can be tough, no matter how many times you've seen it."

After a pause, Emma added, "I think the dishwasher may have just finished running. I could feel heat coming from it." The detective jotted another note, asked for their contact details, then slipped his notepad back into his suit pocket.

"Detectives aren't dispatched for run-of-the-mill 911 calls," Harry said. "Do you think Sue's death was an accident or potential suicide, or something more suspicious?"

"It's normal procedure to look into unnatural deaths."

Harry wondered what that meant.

Officer Jackson reappeared on the porch to return Emma's medical kit.

"Thank you both for your cooperation." The detective's gaze landed on Emma. "You did good today, regardless of the outcome." He and the officer disappeared into Sue's house.

Harry stared after them.

Less than an hour ago, Sue had been begging for his help. Now she was dead.

Chapter Four

Harry maneuvered around the police vehicles in Sue's drive, Emma following closely. He tried not to wince when he put weight on his left side. Heavy clouds darkened the sky.

Margaret's death had been sudden too. A stroke, after which she'd lingered for two gut-wrenching days. Harry had sat helplessly at her bedside, watching her slip away. He blinked back a surge of sorrow and sucked in the chilly air.

At the base of Sue's drive stood a group of neighbors: Milo Czesiak, Rachel Valucci, Diana Middleton, and Jimmy Chatimont. Milo's brusque voice rose above the group's hushed conversation when Harry and Emma neared. Harry stopped a good six feet from Milo, who reeked of stale cigars.

"What's going on?" Milo raised his thick black brows, a contrast with his mostly bald head. He wore his usual tight jeans, designer T-shirt, and braided gold chain around his neck—an ensemble perhaps chosen to remind people of his working-class beginnings.

Before Harry could respond, Diana Middleton cut in, "My lands, Harry, what's happened?" Her flint gray eyes studied his. Concern puckered her porcelain skin and emphasized her Southern twang.

"It's Sue. I'm afraid she's passed away."

The group gasped collectively, while Milo uttered, "*Whoa.*"

Rachel Valucci, who now stood at Milo's side, raised her manicured fingers to her perfectly lipsticked lips. "How awful." With her fur-trimmed ivory wrap, she looked ready for après-ski cocktails in a swanky Swiss chalet. "But Sue wasn't that old."

"Bless that poor soul." Diana bowed her head and clutched her elegant Burberry scarf.

Diana's platinum hair remained tightly coiffed despite the stiff breeze, but Jimmy Chatimont's shoulder-length white hair whipped in the wind. "Do they know what happened?" He tucked his hands into the pockets of his apron, worn over jeans and a sweater. As a retired chef and well-known local artist, it was hard to tell if Jimmy had rushed over from his kitchen or easel.

Harry kept his response vague. "They're trying to sort things out."

"Why the meat wagon and the bears?" Milo asked, drawing puzzled glances. Rachel slapped his upper arm, and he dropped the trucker lingo. "Why an ambulance *and* the police?"

"I think they're being thorough." To change the subject, Harry introduced Emma to Diana, Milo, and Jimmy.

"Nice ta meet cha." Diana shook Emma's hand. "Though I wish it coulda been under better circumstances."

Milo's panther-like gaze navigated up and down Emma, who bristled at his not-so-subtle inspection. Rachel noticed Milo's leer and slipped her arm through his. "Nice to see you again," she told Emma, and pulled Milo closer.

Jimmy focused on Officer Jackson and the EMT on Sue Daniels's porch. His round face looked dazed. "I can't believe Sue's dead."

"She seemed healthy to me," Milo said. "Wonder what happened. Heart attack?" He narrowed his eyes at Harry. "You must know something. You and Red were up on that porch for a while."

"We were. And now I need some rest. It's been a tough day."

Harry said goodbye to them all, then he and Emma headed toward his house.

He knew that as a critical care nurse, she'd have dealt with death on a regular basis. But this had apparently hit a nerve. "There was nothing you could have done to save her," he told Emma.

"I know."

Her tone made him feel like he'd made matters worse, and his fatherly instincts kicked in. He stopped to get her full attention. "Do you want to talk about it?"

Her face flew through a range of emotions, far too quick for him to catch. She landed on a look that wavered between misery and gratitude. "She was *your* neighbor. Are *you* all right?"

"I've seen a lot of death in my years, but it's never easy when it happens on your doorstep. To be honest, I didn't know Sue well and didn't always think of her kindly. Which makes it that much sadder that I was the last person to speak with her."

She squeezed his elbow, and they continued in silence. The walker felt twenty pounds heavier than it had an hour ago. Harry sporadically glanced to make sure Emma was okay. When they got back to his house, he stopped in the doorway and read the lines of strain around her eyes that hadn't been there that morning.

"Why don't you go home? It's been a heck of a day."

"Are you kidding?" she protested. "I'm not leaving you after what just happened. And I can tell you're in pain."

"My hip does hurt. I'm going to take some aspirin and a nap. Your shift ends in two hours, and with the way I feel now, I probably won't get up until tomorrow morning. I'll be fine."

Emma scanned his face, then nodded. "Advil Liqui-Gels will help with inflammation and kick in fast. I'll grab two and get you some water. Go lie down." She set off for the kitchen, and he shuffled to the comfort of his king-sized bed. He melted into the fluffy pillows and silky duvet, feeling his muscles and eyelids relax.

"Sure you're okay?"

His eyes popped open. Emma stood next to his bed with a glass of water and two green pills in her outstretched hand. He hadn't heard her come in.

"Positive." He sat up, then swallowed the pills with a long drink. "See you tomorrow."

"Yep." She remained by his side.

"Are you planning on standing there until I fall asleep?"

That earned a slight smile. "No. Stay sitting up for twenty more minutes, then you can lie down again. See you tomorrow."

Harry listened to Emma gather her coat and bag and close the door behind her. The deadlock clicked.

As he sat there, he thought about Sue. In the banal interactions he'd had with her since she'd moved to the lane three years ago, he'd sensed a hint of an ominous vein, like the flash of a fin in tranquil Cape Cod waters, hinting at a Great White that lurked below.

Then a conversation with Sue had made him think he'd pegged her all wrong. A few months before Mags died, they'd had a dinner party that Sue had attended. After the meal, Sue had disappeared. She hadn't been with Mags and Jimmy at the kitchen table, nor mingling in the sitting area with Diana and the Patels, nor laughing with the rest of his neighbors in the living room.

Harry had found her in the sunroom, ensconced in his favorite chair in the far corner, leafing through a photo album of a trip to Central America in the colorful light of Margaret's favorite Tiffany lamp, an empty wineglass on the table beside her.

Harry had joined her, and they'd ended up talking for almost an hour about the adventures they'd both had living and traveling around the world. He and Mags with aid work; Sue and her late husband, Ralph, with his State Department job, where she also had sporadically worked.

"I didn't realize we had so much in common," Harry had said, his words causing her face to shift into a sadness that he sensed was genuine.

"But we don't." Regret and wine slurred her words. "Your travels with Margaret only brought the two of you closer together. My travels with Ralph kept me trapped alone."

A pang of pity had shot through him, making him wonder if the unease he'd experienced around Sue had been due to the lonesomeness that plagued her. At the time, she would have been widowed three years. Now that Mags was gone, it was an isolation he knew well.

Sue Daniels's final words had been to Harry. A desperate plea for help, hinting that she'd been poisoned.

Had grief driven her to attempt to take her own life, and she'd changed her mind at the last minute? Had she by accident ingested something poisonous or overdosed on one of her medications? Emma had also mentioned anaphylactic shock.

Then a darker thought unfurled, one that had been skittering around the shadows of his brain all day. Could Sue have been murdered?

Chapter Five

Emma waited underneath the glaring artificial lights outside the entrance of the Riverside Heights Hospital emergency room where her fiancé, Blake, worked. The parking lot across the road was full and resonated with the hum of streetlights. She'd left three texts and one voice message for Blake to meet her here, but who knew when he'd be able to break away. From her four years of nursing in the Intensive Care Unit at a rival hospital, St. Joseph's, she knew the long hours, stress, and heartbreak Blake faced with each residency shift.

How did he do it? She hadn't been able to.

Finding Ms. Daniels dead brought back memories Emma didn't want to relive—jagged images that kept her outside in the cold evening air, cell phone in hand, instead of comfortably sitting in the warm reception area that smelled of fresh flowers and day-old coffee. A few people milled about inside the entrance. Still no sign of Blake.

Theirs had been a whirlwind romance worthy of the Hallmark movies her mother adored. Boy and girl grow up together, families close. Popular boy jock goes off to college, leaving awkward freshman girl behind. Thirteen years later, they reunite at a joint family dinner. Four months after that, they're engaged. It felt surreal, like being cast from a face in the crowd to a leading part.

The automatic doors whooshed open, and Blake stepped out, as if summoned by her thoughts. Despite six straight twelve-hour residency night shifts, his hazel eyes were bright, and his blond hair impeccably styled. His scrubs and lab coat looked pressed. "Hey, beautiful."

She clasped his hands and, in a rush, told him what had happened that afternoon. In the distance, an ambulance siren became audible. The agitating noise rose in sync with her distress.

"It was terrible. She was gone when I got there. I must have been a minute too late. I tried to revive her but . . ." her words faded as the blaring siren and flashing lights neared.

In the recesses of her mind, a thought about Sue's death glinted, but it was too quick and vague for her to latch on.

Blake guided Emma farther away from the entrance. "I'm sorry," he said, pulling her back to the moment. "You gonna be all right?"

The ambulance slammed to a stop. The back doors exploded open, and two EMTs jumped out. A nurse in scrubs ran out to meet the stretcher being pulled from the rear, bearing an old man, with pale skin, mussed silver hair, and fear emblazoned on his face. The EMTs spoke to the nurse in rapid tones, and the emergency responders and nurse wheeled the man inside.

Emma returned her gaze to Blake. "Yes," she said with forced conviction.

Her world had gone sideways two months ago when she'd decided to leave nursing. Four years of witnessing death as a critical care nurse had taken their toll. The unexpected death of an asthmatic pneumonia patient, who'd seemed to be coming around, had been her breaking point.

In the morning her patient had seemed fine. By dinner, he was dead, and his sweet ten-year-old daughter, Annie, had bawled uncontrollably, red pigtails jerking as she gasped for air.

In an instant, Emma had been transported back seventeen years to her father's death, to the sterile waiting room where she'd sat with her mom and two brothers and sister. They'd huddled, heads down. Around them, her dad's fellow firefighters paced, with their soot-smudged faces and apprehensive eyes and bunker gear that reeked of acrid smoke.

Each minute of waiting had been excruciating. When a doctor finally emerged through the trauma center's swinging doors, the look on her face had said it all. For one crushing moment, everyone paused, taking in the Stockton family's new reality. Then her mother let out a wail that still visited Emma in the middle of sleepless nights.

After the sudden death of Annie's father, despite weeks of counseling and self-care, Emma couldn't bring herself to continue with nursing. Caregiving for Harry, while not ideal, had provided a sense of normalcy. Until today.

"Earth to Emma." Blake freed a hand to secure a loose strand of her hair behind her ear.

"I'm going to be fine," she reassured him.

"You know, you won't have to work once we get married."

Something in his tone made her stand up straighter. She *needed* to work, wanted to help people. Altruism ran in her blood—nurse mother, social worker sister, teacher brothers, and fireman father, who'd paid the ultimate sacrifice while serving.

"I can work. Caregiving, or something else. I'm not going to waste all that training."

"All I'm saying is, we won't need the money if you can't."

His emphasis on *can't* burned in her chest. "Just because I left nursing doesn't mean I can't."

"That's not what I meant," he said in placating tones. "I'm doing a terrible job of telling you my big news." His eyes shifted away from hers.

She let go of his hand and took a step back so she could read his face. "Big news?"

A mother and son bundled in puffy coats and holding hands crossed the street. The boy sniffled and the mother cooed reassuring words. The automatic doors whirled again as they scurried inside.

"This isn't the best timing," Blake said. "But I can't wait to tell you. I got into Washington University's residency program for plastic surgery."

Her mind stuttered. *Plastic surgery? Washington University?*

"What?" she heard herself saying. Blake had spoken of specializing in something during his last years of residency when they'd started dating but hadn't brought it up since.

"I know, I can't believe it. It's a top program for plastic surgery. I applied on a whim. Total long shot. But since it's my alma mater—"

"When did you decide to focus on plastic surgery?" The night's air cut through her coat, and she shoved her hands into her pockets. Blake seemed immune to the cold.

"Been thinking about it for a while. The pay is incredible." Blake's tone shifted to what swooning nurses called his Maker's Mark voice. Like the bourbon, it was sweet and robust with an intoxicating kick to lessen the blow of bad news. "I'll be able to double my salary. Maybe triple. And they'll count my years of residency at River Heights. It's a no-brainer."

"Wow." Emma tried to sound upbeat. Why in the heck was he dumping this on her now? And why had he decided this without consulting her?

As if he'd heard her last thought, he said, "I thought about telling you earlier, but I didn't want to let you down in case I didn't get in. Now it's up to you."

"Up to me?"

"Yeah, if we go. We'll need to be there by January if I accept."

"January?" Her voice pitched, despite her attempt to control it. Less than three months from now.

He gave a husky chuckle. "Yes, to St. Louis. Look, I know this is unexpected, but we'll be happy there. We can live in my old stomping grounds."

She tried to process all this.

"I don't need a decision now, but I do have to notify them by Monday." *In five days.* "I'll email info on apartments. I found a couple I think you'd like."

He'd already been looking for apartments. *Was he asking her to help shape their future, or telling her what he'd already decided?*

They moved closer to the entrance and through the glass doors the hospital's PA system murmured in the background. "I'll try to call you later, babe. My shift runs until three in the morning, but I'm hoping I can get a break around eleven. Love you." Blake kissed her check and disappeared inside. Like Superman, he was off to save lives.

Emma walked slowly back toward her car, feeling numb. Over the past two months, her life had started to fall into place. Moving into a new apartment, starting caregiving, getting engaged. And now, things were changing again as if they were caught up in an ocean's wave. Another new place to live, another new job—both in a new city—with a man who, while they'd known each other since they were kids, she was still getting to know.

It seemed promising and exciting, but something stirred in her gut. *Was this right for her?* She weaved through rows of cars, searching for her beat-up Honda Accord. Wind tickled the back of her neck, and she undid her ponytail.

Emma shook loose her hair, as if it would shake free an answer.

Chapter Six

By eleven that night, Harry had spent over five hours in his sunroom club chair, looking to find something, anything, that would give him insight into Sue Daniels. He shifted in the seat, his throbbing hip telling him it was time to move.

Before diving into the Internet, he'd known that Sue had retired from a government job, taking various State Department administrative posts as her husband's work moved them around. Like he and Mags, Sue had moved to Westerly from Washington, DC. Yet despite hours of clicking, he didn't know much more. He hadn't found any social media accounts, and the only search mentions of Sue were public records related to the value of her home.

It was peculiar. No one flew that far under the radar these days, he thought—*unless they had a reason to.*

In his experience, most people who worked in DC flaunted their status, power, and connections. It was prominent on their LinkedIn profiles and plastered all over their social media feeds with name dropping and photos of VIP events. And with her husband having a prestigious job, Harry was surprised Sue didn't have a Facebook or Instagram account flooded with images of the couple attending galas and ceremonies or checking out tourist sites around the world.

When he'd talked to Sue about her travels with her husband and their careers, she'd been vague. And in DC, if someone had a nondescript job they avoided talking about, it generally meant one of two things: either you were ashamed about your low rank or title, or you couldn't talk about what you did for reasons of national security.

Curious about the reasons for her absent electronic footprint, Harry emailed friends who'd worked with the State Department and the US Agency for International Development to see if they'd heard of Sue Daniels or her late husband Ralph. It was worth a shot.

He also emailed his friend Geoff Jeffries, a former cop now working as a private investigator when not training police forces overseas. They'd worked together on a few community safety projects, and he'd found Geoff a crafty problem solver. His friend didn't just think outside the box, he thought outside the room the box was in. If anyone would have ideas on how to figure out who Sue was and what had happened, it'd be Geoff.

His iPad started chiming, and he clicked the green button to see Ceci at her office desk. "How's my favorite daughter?"

She flashed Margaret's lopsided grin. "As your only daughter, I should hope so. How are you doing?"

Harry knew better than to tell Ceci about the pain in his hip, and certainly wasn't going to mention Sue's death. Now that her mother was gone, worrying about him had become a hobby. "Nose deep in *Witchcraft Among the Azande*. Thanks for sending it. How'd you know I lost my copy?"

Her grin broadened. "Because I took it. Your notes in the margins are great."

"My daughter, the thief." He had spotted his book on the shelf above her left shoulder. "And you're not even a good one. The stolen item is directly behind you." This earned a giggle. "If you're going to break the law—which, by the way, I do not condone—be more cunning about it."

"Runs in the family. Evie's taking after me." An image of his chubby-cheeked granddaughter popped into his head as Ceci told him how Evie had snuck home a mermaid Barbie doll from daycare, prompting a lecture on ownership.

Car headlights flickered outside the sunroom window, drawing Harry's attention away from his daughter's animated face. A light-colored sedan slowly rolled by, stopping momentarily to put a package into David Dubois's mailbox.

With a jolt, he remembered he'd seen the same car do this twice before but hadn't thought anything of it. Three times was a pattern—an odd pattern given the drop-offs were only at night. He recalled Rachel's reaction when she'd retrieved her mail the other day, thinking on this as he listened to his daughter.

"Anyway, I told Evie she couldn't borrow something without asking," said Ceci.

"Hopefully she learns that lesson better than her mother." Ceci chuckled as he glanced back outside. "I just saw the oddest thing. Someone keeps leaving late-night packages in David's mailbox."

"Who's David?"

"David Dubois. He lives in the duplex next door, beside Jimmy Chatimont's. Works for the local government in planning and zoning. David's the one who takes me to university events."

David had been a courteous neighbor who'd attended his and Mags's dinner parties, and he'd become a friend after she passed. David had invited—and at times dragged—Harry to lectures at Westerly College. He'd even finagled tickets to a sold-out viewing at the Ohio Theater of *The City of God*, one of Harry's favorite anthropology films.

Ceci's lips quirked with mischief. "Oh, the tall, handsome, muscular guy? Always looking ready for the Tour de France or the Met Gala? Yeah, I remember David."

"David is more than a decade older than you and has been dating the same woman for years, so don't go thinking of dumping Steve."

The skin around her eyes crinkled as she laughed. "Oh, Dad."

After saying goodbye, Harry opened his favorite app, Libby, marveling that millions of e-books and audiobooks were just a fingertip away.

Sue's death would not stop niggling at him.

He needed more data to figure out why. Several searches later, he found what he'd been looking for: *So You Want to Be a Sleuth: Criminal Investigation for Beginners.* He checked it out, but before beginning to read the e-book, also ordered a physical copy from his local bookstore. Nothing beat holding a real book in hand.

By one AM, he was fighting drooping eyelids. His head bobbed, then sat askew with his chin on his chest.

Screeching tires jolted him awake.

He jerked his head upward. Through bleary eyes, he could make out the grandfather clock in the corner: 3:30. Outside the window, car lights illuminated his street as an engine accelerated. He turned off the nearby lamp to better see.

An older, dark-colored Ford Mustang shot by his house, then braked, slowing. Red lights brightened the scene unfolding before him. With the car still moving, the rear passenger door opened, and a body tumbled out.

Harry gasped and stood. The sudden movement shot pain through his side, and the book dropped to the floor.

The body rolled. Stopped when it hit the curb.

The car door closed. Then the engine roared as the vehicle ripped around the pond toward the lane's exit.

Not seeing his phone in its charger—once again his phone wasn't nearby when he needed it—Harry snatched his cane and hobbled as fast as he could to the front door.

By the time he got out onto his porch, he saw the Buchanans' teenage son, Conner, brushing himself off as he limped across their front yard. Harry navigated around the rocking chairs, his cane thumping with every other step. "Conner? Are you okay? Do you want an ambulance?"

The teen stopped and looked in Harry's direction. Then the Buchanans' door opened, creating a beam of light that captured Conner and his attention.

"Get inside, now," a deep voice gritted. Jack Buchanan stepped out on the doorstep, his linebacker frame blocking most of the escaping light. He gestured for his son to go in.

Head down, Conner trudged across the lawn. Once near enough, Jack reached out and yanked him inside. The door slammed, returning the yard to darkness.

Chapter Seven

Harry sat at the kitchen table the next morning, waiting for his cup of Earl Grey to cool, thinking about Conner Buchanan. Close to seventeen, the boy would soon be a man. He couldn't shake the idea that the perplexing events of last night were somehow connected to Sue.

Or perhaps it had been some reckless dare, the type that frequented the passage from boyhood to man. Like the land divers he'd breathlessly watched in Vanuatu, where boys and teens had climbed to the top of crude wooden towers and tied vines around their ankles. To show their courage and to help ensure fruitful yam crops, they'd jumped, plummeting toward the ground over one hundred feet below. A terrifying ancient precursor to bungee jumping.

"Ha." Emma sat across the table, her nose in a wedding magazine with a glossy cover that boasted: WEDDINGS YOU'LL NEVER FORGET.

Not necessarily a good thing, Harry thought.

"Here's an article suggesting carnival food and a bounce house at a wedding reception," Emma pointed out. "Can you imagine? My mom would have a heart attack."

The doorbell rang, sparing Harry from answering.

Emma lowered the magazine and stood, retying her green cardigan, which matched the hues of Caribbean waters. "Expecting anyone?"

"No." He trailed her into the foyer using his cane. His hip still ached from the rush to Sue's house, but he wanted to be done with the walker.

"Ms. Stockton," Detective Bradford said when Emma opened the door. "Mr. Lancaster, I have a few additional questions." Emma stepped back and almost bumped into Harry.

"Of course." Harry moved around Emma and motioned for the detective to enter. Rain glistened on the detective's scruffy hair. He paused one step in, careful to keep his wet raincoat from dripping outside the tiled entryway. He had good manners.

"I'll hang that for you." Emma extended her hand.

Harry led the detective through the living room, giving the linen wingback chairs and their toile accent cushions a glance. He needed something comfortable in case this turned into a lengthy discussion, so he settled into his club chair in the corner of the sunroom.

The detective headed for Mags's floral loveseat, which rested against the wall opposite the windows. He removed the jacket of his suit, which was the same brown as his eyes. Emma perched on an ottoman she'd pulled in from the living room.

"This shouldn't take long." Detective Bradford removed a notepad from his suit jacket's pocket, then set the coat on the cushion beside him. "We're gathering details on Ms. Daniels's life and what she did during her final days."

"You're considering Sue's death suspicious?" Harry asked.

"I didn't say that," the detective rebuked, "but we have ruled out an allergic reaction." Emma's nod made Harry think she'd arrived at the same conclusion. "Initial signs of death point to poisoning, likely either accidental ingestion or suicide with too-late second thoughts."

Harry leaned back in his chair and wondered why he thought neither scenario sounded right. He glanced at Emma, who was looking at the lawman with a slight furrow between her brows. Was she thinking the same thing?

For the next five minutes, Harry answered routine questions, mostly about Sue's state of mind. He shared what little he knew about her, including that he understood that her husband, Ralph, had died over five years ago, prompting Sue's move to Ohio from DC. He didn't think she'd had children.

Harry explained that he hadn't socialized much with his neighbors after Margaret died, so his information on the residents of Lakeview Lane was dated. Then he mentioned an email from the condominium's social committee, that the upcoming Columbus Day potluck would instead be a Celebration of Life event for Sue.

By the time Harry finished, Detective Bradford had rolled up his sleeves and loosened his tie. He'd also filled several pages in his notepad. Just when Harry was convinced the detective was going to rule Sue's death a suicide, the lawman threw him a curve.

"Have you seen anything odd or out of the ordinary related to Ms. Daniels?"

Harry pondered the change in direction. "I saw her out walking late the other night, but that's not exactly abnormal. You know about her house alarm going off?"

"Yes. Did any of your neighbors have disputes with or grudges against Ms. Daniels?"

He recalled Sue's argument with Milo. He didn't know the context and wasn't keen to inadvertently misdirect the detective, but he also didn't want to hold back facts. When he'd finished relaying what he'd seen and overheard, the previous night flashed through Harry's mind.

"There is something else. Last night, I saw the teenager who lives next door, Conner Buchanan, get thrown from a moving car."

Emma gasped.

The detective kept his tone measured. "Someone threw him out of a moving car?"

"Yes. Specifically, from an old dark Ford Mustang. I went out to check on him, but it sped away. By the time I got onto my porch, Conner was on his feet, brushing himself off. I offered to call an ambulance, but he ignored me. Jack, Conner's father, stepped outside a minute after it happened. If they needed an ambulance or the police, I assumed they'd call."

A cell phone rang from Detective Bradford's suit pocket, and he pulled the jacket onto his lap to get the phone. After a glance at the screen, he said, "I need to take this." He folded the notepad and pen into his jacket, set it aside, then stood. "Just a sec," he said into his phone as he strode from the room.

In the detective's rush to leave, the notepad had slipped out of his jacket onto the cushion.

Harry stared at it, wishing he had X-ray vision. If only he could take a quick look, it might put to rest whatever was bugging him about the circumstances of Sue's death.

His moral senses pushed back. That would be unethical . . . then again, if her death hadn't been suspicious, what would be the harm? The details would end up in the local news anyway. It was practically public information.

"I can't believe Ms. Daniels was—" Emma started.

Harry cut her off. "Can you hear what the detective is saying?"

"No." Her lips turned down in disapproval. "I don't eavesdrop."

"Where'd he go?" he whispered.

"What?"

"How far away is he?" He kept his voice soft.

"He's back by the door to the screened-in porch."

He cringed from her loud tone. "Shh. Is he still in deep conversation?"

"Why?" Her gaze grew wary.

"Let me know when he's coming." Before he changed his mind, he stood and snatched the detective's notepad from the loveseat, then returned to his chair.

"Are you crazy? What are you doing?"

Harry ignored her, rapidly paging through entries in handwriting so neat it almost looked typed. It appeared that the detective had spoken to Milo Czesiak first, which made sense. Milo's condo was connected to Sue's.

There were three bullets on Milo's page:

Didn't know SD well
Neighbors for 5 yrs
Smokes like a chimney

Apparently, Milo didn't mention the argument he'd had with Sue days before her death.

"Harry." Emma's whisper was fierce, like a mother disciplining a wayward child during a church service.

He looked up. "Is he coming?"

"No, but you've got to stop. He's going to catch you."

"Cough when he's done with his call." He returned to the notepad.

Detective Bradford had also interviewed Gautam and Sakshi Patel, who lived next door to Sue in a standalone patio home. Harry grinned when he read the detective's note: *Avid golf fans.* They definitely were. The couple golfed almost every day, and Sakshi regularly won contests at the local country club.

Then the notes said: *Grandson went to SD's for cookies. Gave SD healthy gift basket. Some gone.* So Vihaan had gone to Sue's after school for cookies. Odd, Sue didn't seem the nurturing type. And it sounded like the Patels had given Sue a gift basket, and some of whatever she'd been given had been consumed.

"You shouldn't be doing this," Emma hissed.

He turned the page.

Jimmy Chatimont and David Dubois, who each had a unit in the duplex next to Harry's standalone home, must not have been there when the detective had stopped by, as their pages were blank. The detective was methodically working his way around the lane.

After a quick glance at Emma and smiling at the terror on her face, Harry flipped back to earlier notes from the crime scene. From the detective's notations, it appeared that when Sue had called 911, she'd mentioned being poisoned but didn't know the source. She'd apparently been taking four medications: cephalosporin, ibuprofen, Enalapril, and Metformin. Harry recognized ibuprofen, but not the others. He tried to memorize their spelling.

There were also notes on the vegetable garden in Sue's backyard and her numerous books on foraging. He wondered if those had been the books Emma saw on the kitchen counter.

Then there was a list of apparent items of food and drink Sue had been given. The detective had ticked several with a question mark, indicating that he didn't know the giver, but reading through the entries, Harry did.

One note read: "$$$ wine crate, bow, pantry. Bottle missing, rinsed recycle bin. Who?" Despite his gruff exterior, Milo was a wine connoisseur.

Another note described a tuna casserole in the refrigerator with a typed heating instructions note taped to the lid. Diana had delivered the same casseroles and notes to him in the weeks after Mags died.

"Please, put it back." Emma's whisper was more emphatic.

He turned the page. *Card from Rachel Valucci. Flowers and chocolate?* The detective had underlined Rachel's name twice.

There was a note that Sue's birthday was March 23—so why had Sue received so many gifts in early October? Harry started to turn the page when Emma began coughing, loudly and in fits.

There wasn't time to stand up and return the notepad to the chair cushion, so Harry leaned over, tossed it underhand, and prayed that his aim hadn't deteriorated since the days he'd helped Ceci practice her softball swing.

Harry held his breath as the notepad arced through the air. Emma's cough was now so violent that her face was turning purple. The second the notepad landed on the cushion the detective turned the sunroom corner.

"You should get a glass of water, Ms. Stockton. You don't look well," he told her.

With an exaggerated nod, Emma rushed from the room.

The detective returned his notebook and pen to his pocket. "No need to bother you anymore, Mr. Lancaster. I can tell you that the ME identified the poison. It was death camas, a plant that looks a lot like a wild onion and grows in the same types of places. We found a clump of it in Ms. Daniels's compost bin outside. She likely picked it while foraging and mistook it for chives. A tragic accident."

"So that's it? You're closing the case?"

"That's it," Detective Bradford said with a certainty Harry did not feel. Between Sue's phone call and the oddities he was beginning to notice on Lakeview Lane, his instincts, well-honed over decades, told him that there was more to it than this.

Chapter Eight

That evening at dinner, Emma thought about Harry and the risks he'd taken to read Detective Bradford's notepad. Had he broken any laws? Should she have said something?

She'd have to keep a close eye on him. The old guy was full of surprises.

Her mother placed a half-full glass of cabernet sauvignon on the black and white checkered tablecloth, keeping a loose grip on the stem. The rain had stopped hours ago, but the remaining humidity made her mother's voluminous ringlets frizz—ringlets that Bridget Catherine kept in their original russet hues thanks to Clairol.

"How's the assignment going?" her mother asked. Harry was only Emma's second patient since becoming a professional caregiver two months ago, and she knew her mom wanted it to go well.

"Fine."

"You've got to get him walking and talking. If he sits all the time, he'll never heal." Sure, Emma had over four years of experience as a critical care nurse before switching to caregiving, but her mom had clocked in over thirty in various nursing roles. She knew her stuff.

"We walk twice a day and I try to talk to him, but he doesn't say much." Harry mostly kept himself planted in a chair and his nose buried in books.

"He'll warm up to you. You need to get to know him. Ask him about his hobbies."

Sulking in the sunroom seemed to be his favorite pastime, but she got her mom's point. "Good idea." Emma pulled out her cell phone. Google had an answer for everything.

"Now, we need to get planning." Her mom's voice shifted into the bubbly tones she reserved for weddings and babies. "You've been engaged for *two weeks*, and we've done nothing. So we formed a wedding task force: me, your sister, Blake's sisters, and Patricia, of course." Her mom giggled, as if giddy from champagne. But really, Emma thought, she was drunk off the fact that her daughter was marrying her best friend's son.

As her mom bubbled on, Emma scrolled through search results on various Harry Lancasters. She'd had to leave nursing; she'd do whatever it took to make caregiving work.

To her surprise, her Harry's LinkedIn profile was the second result. According to his online résumé, he'd done aid work overseas, focusing on conflict, natural disasters, and humanitarian crises in a list of countries longer than her arm. He had a Ph.D. in anthropology and had written several books and articles on ethnocentrism, semiotics, and proxemics—whatever those were. Impressive for an old man who seemed glued to his chair, and just possibly reasons why no one would voluntarily sit next to him at a dinner party.

"Oh, my gosh," Emma interrupted her mom's litany of wedding planning to-dos. "Harry speaks eight languages. Can you imagine?" Despite her hours of study and strong desire to sound foreign and exotic, the main thing she remembered from high school Spanish was "Me gusto queso."

"Dear, when I said to get to know him, I didn't mean in the middle of our conversation. Put that phone away. Now, what did you think of the caterers' menus I sent you?" Her mom raised her glass for another sip.

Emma fought to control a sigh, not that her mother would have heard it. Their normal table in the back corner of DaVinci's was anything but quiet. Next to them, eight tween girls shrieked with laughter as they crowded around a circular table. They seemed to be fresh from soccer practice or a game, with their green and yellow jerseys and muddy shoes.

Emma needed energy for this conversation. If only they sold Starbucks Nitro Cold Brew here. She glanced around the boisterous room in search of their absent waiter—she'd have to settle for a Coke. On the walls, picturesque photos of Italy and shelves of gleaming copper pots added vibrancy to the busy restaurant. There was no sign of the server.

"Sorry," Emma said, "I haven't got to the menus yet. I needed to go through the apartment listings Blake sent, and the police came to Harry's today."

"The police? What on earth for? Was someone robbed?"

Emma hadn't told her mother about Ms. Daniels. "One of Harry's neighbors passed away." She left out the fact that she'd been the person to discover the poor woman.

Harry had told her the police thought Ms. Daniels's death had been an accidental poisoning. That didn't seem right. *Why?* And what had she noticed that had made her sure it hadn't been an allergic reaction? She chewed on her bottom lip and got the same feeling as when she tried to solve algebraic equations.

"I'm sorry to hear that, dear." Worry lines formed around her mom's eyes, and she pushed back the rolled-up sleeves of her navy sweater. "I've been so excited about the wedding I didn't notice, but you do look green around the edges." Emma wouldn't have been surprised if her mom pulled out a tongue depressor and pulse oximeter on the spot.

"I'll look at the menus tomorrow."

"Good." Her mom patted her hand and gave her a lipstick-smudged smile that extended to her eyes and warmed Emma's heart.

The waiter delivered their much-anticipated pepperoni and pineapple pizza. Emma took a bite and savored the flavors. "Blake needs to know by Monday about St. Louis," she mumbled while chewing.

A dreamy looked floated over her mom's face. "He is the perfect man. Smart, respectful, kind. And to have a plastic surgeon in our family. He'll be such a wonderful provider." Emma ate as her mom waxed on about Blake. Finally she added, "I do hate the idea of you moving away, but this is a great opportunity. For you both. A fresh start."

Emma knew that wasn't meant as a dig, but she couldn't stop feeling like she'd let her mother down by abandoning nursing. She took another slice. "I don't know, Mom. There's so much to digest. Moving, planning the wedding, getting married, trying to figure out my career."

"Are you sure it's not the pizza you're having trouble digesting, dear? That's your third slice."

"My second," she corrected, wishing she had her mom's bird-like appetite. The woman could survive on olives, dark chocolate, and red wine.

"Em, I know you're worried about moving, but life involves change. You need to learn to embrace it." Then panic flashed across her mother's face. "Oh no. This means we'll have to plan the wedding before you go. That's less than three months. And it'll be over the holidays." She drained her wineglass, as if fortifying herself.

Emma's mom nibbled her slice, and Emma downed two more, spurred by tension mounting from a source she couldn't identify. Their server maneuvered around the table of giggling soccer girls, and Emma caught his eye and motioned for the check.

Her eyes floated to her Tiffany-style round cut 1.5 carat white gold engagement ring, which was worth about as much as her car. She'd thought it impractical. The money could have been used for a solid down payment on their first home or toward her student debt, not that Blake was responsible for that. But as her friends and family fawned over the ring, she'd come to see it as not just a symbol of their relationship but an investment in their future. A safety net if they ever hit hard times.

"I should head home. I've got to go through your emails and the apartment listings Blake sent." Emma reached for her purse and handed her credit card to the waiter who practically ran by their table, past the girls' deafening shrieks.

"Don't forget to read that article I emailed you on canapés," her mom called over the ruckus.. "A French-themed wedding would be lovely."

Emma had to concentrate to avoid rolling her eyes—neither of the two families had ties to anything or anyone French. If she didn't manage to squelch this idea, the whole wedding party might end up wearing berets.

Chapter Nine

Emma stifled a yawn and squirmed in her seat, trying to get comfortable. She had been driving for three hours. Harry, pensive in the passenger seat, gazed at the passing southeastern Ohio countryside. Bright-colored leaves exploded like fireworks across the rolling hills, which were sporadically dotted with farmhouses, barns, and harvested fields.

Thanks to the two iced coffees Emma had downed that morning, she desperately needed a bathroom.

"Not much longer," he said, likely noticing her growing discomfort.

She had stayed up late, combing through a bazillion apartment listings in St. Louis. When did Blake have time to find so many of them? Then she'd worked on coming up with alternatives to her mom's French-themed wedding, composed from assorted ideas her mother had pilfered from Pinterest.

Emma didn't mind the suggested simple, bohemian dress and accompanying ballet flats. Nor did she mind the traditional croquembouche for a wedding cake, a cone-shaped tower of cream puffs held together by caramel drizzle. But she drew the line at proposed centerpieces of miniature Eiffel Towers with French flags jutting from their tops. Fortunately, no berets had been suggested.

The windy two-lane country road narrowed as they climbed the next hill. Harry's gray BMW X5 SUV had ridiculously strong horsepower, and if she hit the gas too hard it launched them forward at light speed. She despised driving it, but his walker had been too hard to get in and out of her car's trunk. And they'd stuck with his car once he'd shifted to using a cane since the heated seats helped ease the pain in his hip.

They crested a peak, her stomach floated, and she jammed on the brakes.

"I have insurance for my car," Harry said, like she'd been voicing her fears out loud. "If anything happens while you're driving it, I'm covered. I double-checked."

"Why would you say that?"

He responded with an amused "Hmpf."

Where were they going? Emma thought. Harry had suggested they go on a drive but had been evasive about the destination, spouting occasional direction after consulting his cell phone.

"Can we turn around soon?" she asked.

Harry glanced at the phone's screen. "Almost there. We'll stop for a bathroom break and some lunch. My treat. Make a right at the intersection ahead."

She slowed at the sight of a speed limit sign as they entered Brightondale, a tiny town that hugged the road, with twenty or so brick buildings that had seen better days.

"Make a left once we pass through town," Harry added.

She snaked the car up a wooded gravel drive for several hundred feet. The trees parted to reveal a lush green clearing with a coral-colored Victorian home. Three hanging baskets overflowing with flowers dangled from the porch. Off to the side was a sign in elaborate script: The Hilltop Inn.

"Ooh, it's lovely." Her frustration dissipated. She toyed with snapping a picture to post on Instagram once they parked, but she hadn't been active on her account since she'd announced her engagement. Somehow she didn't want to draw attention to her new caregiver role. It felt like a self-induced demotion.

"I called ahead. They're expecting us." Harry snagged his cane and got out of the car. Emma had a sense of déjà vu but didn't know why.

Inside, the inn was equally charming. The paneled foyer had an antique hardwood floor. To the side, a pedestal table held a vase bursting with a rainbow of flowers. A wide staircase with a worn patterned runner climbed the rear wall. On the left was a wooden reception desk, stationed by a gangly teen bent over an iPhone, her hair falling forward to cover her face.

"Hello." Harry stepped up to the desk, which smelled of lemon Pledge.

The girl stood with a jolt, her gray eyes wide, then removed her wireless earbuds. She wore an orange Creamsicle-colored uniform with a name tag that read Sally. "Sorry. Didn't hear you come in. Need a room?"

An uncomfortable look flashed across Harry's face. "Goodness, no. I made reservations for afternoon tea."

"Oh, yeah. Ma mentioned you were coming. Follow me to the parlor."

"Where are your restrooms?" Emma interjected, feeling desperate. Sally pointed toward a door by the stairs, and she dashed off, leaving Harry chatting to the teen.

When she returned, Sally grabbed two paper menus and led them across the creaking wooden floor to a daffodil yellow room that occupied the inn's turret. A dormant pot-bellied stove bulged from the far wall and large potted ferns squatted in front of each window. Four bistro tables, each set for two, circled in the center. Sally let them pick out where to sit, handed them a menu, and left them to it.

Emma studied the page. There was a selection of sandwiches (pear and stilton, cucumber and cream cheese, egg salad), a range of desserts (Battenberg cake, lemon curd tartlets, fruit tart), plus scones with clotted cream and strawberry jam. Her stomach grumbled, and she couldn't wait to try them. "This looks great."

Harry was busy looking around. "Mmm? Yeah."

For a man who had dragged her hours into the countryside for this specific place, he didn't seem that excited about it.

When Sally asked for their tea orders, Emma ordered Darjeeling, and Harry asked for Assam. Within minutes, Sally returned with two ceramic pots and a tiered silver tray stacked with food. Emma eagerly ate as Harry questioned Sally about the inn: if they were open year-round, when they were busy, the types of guests who visited.

After Sally rattled off details, Harry said, "I told your mother that my neighbor, Sue Daniels, recommended your afternoon tea."

Emma choked on her fruit tart.

Harry gave her a quieting glare. "Your mom said she recognized the name. Do you remember Ms. Daniels?"

The girl shrugged one shoulder. "We get lots of guests when the leaves change. But I'm glad she enjoyed her stay."

Emma took another bite. *Was Harry was investigating his neighbor's death?* This was an interesting development, especially since the case was closed.

Harry went on. "Ms. Daniels stayed overnight?"

"Had to of. You all are the only folks we had in just for afternoon tea this year. Everybody else has stayed with us. We're pretty isolated. Not many people drive this far for tea."

"I think Ms. Daniels was here not long ago. A woman in her sixties with a silver bob? Wears bright lipstick, always in a cardigan. Would have been alone."

Sally shook her head, her hair's ends floating with the movement. "We haven't had anybody come stay here alone. But there was one woman who sort of looked like that 'bout a month ago." Pink tinted Sally's cheeks. "She sent back the sandwiches 'cause she didn't like the bread and made me change the sheets after they checked in 'cause she said they didn't look clean."

"She wasn't alone?" Harry leaned in. "Who was she with?"

"Sally." A woman with a heart-shaped face and short salt-and-pepper hair called from the doorway. Her eyes bore holes into her daughter. "You need to clean the dishes. We've got three couples checking in later and there isn't enough tableware for the supper setting."

"Yes, Ma." Sally scurried from the room.

"I swear, that girl. You all enjoying your meal?"

Harry picked up a cucumber sandwich. "Delicious."

Sally's mother laid the bill on the table. "Holler if you need more hot water. I'll be in the back."

After the woman left, Emma turned to Harry and whispered, "What do you think you're doing?"

He looked nonchalant. "I'm curious about the inn."

"I'm not an idiot." Emma flashed back to sitting on Ms. Daniels's front porch. *That's why this place looked familiar.* "Ms. Daniels didn't recommend this place to you. You saw the brochure on her porch table." She tried not to be insulted by his look of surprise. "The detective said Sue's death was accidental. So why are you asking around like you're trying to solve a murder?"

"I was the last person Sue spoke to. I didn't know her that well and now I feel obliged to learn more about her. That's all."

Harry looked earnest, but Emma didn't buy it.

* * *

No matter what aid project Harry had worked on, one of his initial steps in assessing a place and the needs of its people had been to identify a prolific gossip. Their information hadn't always been reliable, but it had been a good place to start. It told him what was important within a community and which individuals might not be trustworthy sources.

Diana Middleton was the lynchpin of information in Lakeview Estates. If anyone knew about Sue's close friends or dating life, why Conner was tossed from a car, or why Milo and Sue would have cause to argue, it would be her. *Time to orchestrate a meeting with Diana.*

After Emma parked in his driveway, Harry suggested they take a short walk to stretch their legs. As if he'd conjured the woman straight from his thoughts, Diana exited her house when they neared.

"What a lovely surprise," Diana called from her porch. They met halfway up her drive, next to her gold Jaguar. Her sleek coat perfectly matched her platinum hair. "Afternoon, Ellen."

Emma flushed and played with the zipper on her navy fleece vest. "It's Emma."

"Of course it is, my dear." She turned to Harry. "I imagine you're right pleased to put that walker aside."

"Yes, I—"

"Hate to say it, but I don't have time for a chat. I gotta skedaddle on over to the church." Diana's Southern drawl stretched out like warm peach taffy on a hot August day. "We're having a dinner for single moms and I'm responsible for setting up. I wanted to do the cooking, but Veronica insisted on bringing pulled-pork sandwiches."

She harrumphed and the sun momentarily peeked out from the clouds, making her diamond earrings sparkle. "It is downright shockin' about Sue."

Detective Bradford must have visited Diana too. "What did you—" he started. But Diana spoke before he could finish his sentence.

"The Patels thought she might have died from something related to her appendicitis back in the spring," Diana said, sipping in a breath, "'cause she had some sorta complication, but that detective said it was an accident. To be honest, I wondered if . . ." Her voice trailed off.

"Wondered what?" Emma asked, stepping into the conversation.

"If her death had been, well, something else." Diana leaned in. "Sue was always sticking her nose into trouble, ruffling feathers."

She counted on her ringed fingers. "She didn't get along with Milo. Nor Rachel. And Sakshi said she saw Sue arguing with Jimmy in the clubhouse. Sue didn't even get along with David, and that man could charm the habit off a nun."

Emma snorted, but Diana was right, Harry thought, David was charismatic.

Diana looked toward the Buchanans' house. "I even saw Sue arguing with Conner." She shook her head in disdain. "Picking a fight with someone's child. The nerve. Not to say that Conner's an angel. Getting home at all sorts of hours. Running around with God knows who. Doesn't say much about his mother."

Harry opened his mouth to ask if by "something else" she meant murder, but Diana wasn't done.

"I suppose Linda does have her hands full with her ailing mother-in-law," she conceded. "Grace has been fighting the Alzheimer's for years. Struck her in her late seventies."

Harry knew that with the demands of Linda's estate planning practice and Jack's accounting firm, both worked long hours. Before Mags died, she had visited Grace twice a week to help. Harry hadn't given a thought about how his wife's death might have affected the Buchanans. His heart pinched with shame; he'd been selfish in his grief.

"Who was Sue dating?" Harry asked, to refocus Diana's attention.

"Sue? Dating? That's news to me." She looked thoughtful, and he guessed she'd have the answer by the end of the week.

"Do you know who she was close friends with?"

Diana's eyes sharpened. He could almost see wheels spinning in her head. Then she checked her watch. "My lands. I gotta run." She tightened her coat's belt. "Busy schedule today. By tonight, I'll be ready to put my feet up. You attending the Celebration of Life event for Sue tomorrow?"

He nodded, wondering if Diana truly had to leave, or if she had thought of something and didn't want to share it.

"See you then. In the meantime, you holler if you need anything, you hear?" He nodded again. Diana charged to her car and waved as she backed down her drive.

"Wow," Emma said under her breath, as they trailed in Diana's wake. "She's—"

"A force of nature." Harry looked over to the Buchanans' house. He'd stop by to see Grace this week if she wasn't at the event for Sue. Mags would have wanted him to.

As they made their way around the lane, Emma told him about her fiancé's new residency in St. Louis and how they'd move once they were married. He barely listened.

Instead Harry thought about how he'd initially felt in Rwanda. He'd gone to work there four years after the 1994 genocide, where communities and neighbors had turned against each other, leaving almost a million dead in three months. When he first arrived, things appeared normal. People went about their daily lives. Men watched over inyambo cows, their elongated horns dotting the pastures. Kids in light blue uniforms giggled on their way to school. Women tended to the crops that spanned the country's rolling hills.

But behind each face were secrets, things kept private—some terrible atrocity related to how they'd suffered or what they'd done. Whether victim or killer or both, everyone carried the weight of having lived through something so horrific.

His first months there had been unsettling. Nothing was as it seemed, with torrents of guilt, hate, and distrust coursing beneath the surface.

Similar dark undercurrents seemed to be rising beneath the picture-perfect façade of Lakeview Lane.

Chapter Ten

Emma absently skimmed DaVinci's menu that evening, not in the least bit hungry. She was still full from the late lunch with Harry, and she'd been here with her mom last night.

"I'm starving." Blake's eyes remained on the menu.

She couldn't stop thinking about that afternoon. *Why did Harry doubt that Ms. Daniels's death had been an accidental poisoning? More to the point, why did she think he was right?*

"Know what you want?" Blake asked. "Let me guess, pepperoni and pineapple pizza?"

She absently nodded, not mentioning that it'd be the third time she'd had it this week. Given how frequently she'd visited DaVinci's, she was surprised their server hadn't greeted her with a hug.

He signaled the waiter and they ordered. When the server stepped away, Blake asked, "So, what do you think?" He reached across the black and white checkered tablecloth and clasped her hands. His thumb grazed her large diamond engagement ring. "Are we headed to St. Louis?"

Emma studied Blake's perfectly symmetrical face. The proposed move had cost her precious hours of sleep ever since he'd mentioned it. She wasn't sold on the idea, but if she was going to be his wife, she needed to support him.

"It's a great opportunity. Of course, we should move," she said, and wondered why her stomach felt leaden as she said it.

"Atta girl, I knew you'd come through for me. It'll be great. Promise." Blake broke eye contact for a second and withdrew his hands from hers. "I've arranged for some time off to go scout apartments. Get a sub for work and come with me. We'll head out Wednesday and come back Saturday."

"Wednesday? That's only four days away." She looked for the waiter, suddenly in need of a breadstick. Blake was good at tossing out surprises. She wasn't as good at handling them.

"I know. Not much of a heads-up, but I was able to move my shifts around. You'll come, right?" He shot her a crooked grin, which nearly always did the trick. And he'd worn his coppery-brown shirt, the one that flattered his hazel eyes. He was pulling out all the stops.

She wanted to help pick out the place where they'd start their married life together, but she couldn't neglect Harry. Weight descended on her shoulders. "Harry's doing well. I'd hate to leave and have him regress."

"It's only a couple of days. Besides, you've only got another month or so with him."

The waiter dropped off a basket of breadsticks. Emma picked up one and took a large bite. "How about you go do some early scouting and I join you Thursday night? That way I only miss two days of work."

"Great idea." He continued in his Maker's Mark voice, regaling her with the wonders of St. Louis and stories about the friends he had there and the places he'd take her.

What would she do for a job there? While she liked Harry, she wasn't sure about caregiving, and the thought of going back to critical care nursing made her nauseous.

Plus, all of her family lived within a thirty-minute drive from her current apartment. Once she moved to St. Louis, it'd be a six-hour drive. And what about friends—sure, she'd been out of touch with most of her friends since leaving nursing but figured her wedding would reunite them.

Then her apartment. She would have to break the lease. It'd be costly and she was already settled in. The waiter delivered their pizza, and in a final crushing blow, Emma realized there'd be no DaVinci's in St. Louis.

"You look worried." Blake's eyebrows knitted.

"I'm fine." She flashed what she hoped was sincerity, then took a slice. As her mom had said, change was uncomfortable, but that didn't mean it was bad. Maybe it would be good to start anew.

Blake shot her his best smile, the one that made babies stop crying and women's knees falter. The one that could melt an iceberg.

It sent her reeling back to her freshman prom. She'd been cold-shouldered by the popular cliques *Mean Girls*–style. As the dance had worn on and boys continued to pass her by, tears threatened to flow. Then senior hottie Homecoming King Blake had waltzed in with his winning smile and asked her to dance.

Blake had been there with Lisa Sterpinski, the Ms. Universe–worthy Homecoming Queen, of course—but he'd noticed Emma's isolation and distress. His kindness at the time had included only that one dance, but he'd been her vision of a knight in shining armor ever since.

And now they were getting married.

Of course she could make a few changes.

* * *

Harry brushed his teeth at the master bath sink, reflecting on the afternoon. *Sue had stayed at the inn with someone.* Whoever she'd been with, whether friend or romantic partner, would know more about her and potential reasons why she may have been killed.

Or they could be the killer.

He'd been impressed that Emma had also noticed the brochure. On the drive home, he'd asked her about herself. *Why had she left critical care nursing? What did she think of caregiving? How had she met Blake?* All of which she'd only vaguely answered. He'd even tried to talk to her about her upcoming wedding, but she'd changed the subject. He found her hesitation to talk about the wedding curious. When Ceci had been getting married, she'd been unable to talk about anything else.

Movement caught his eye through the mirror's reflection of the bathroom window. Someone was walking up the drive to the duplex next door. It was late for a visit, past ten PM.

Harry rinsed out his mouth, then turned off the bathroom light to better see. When he returned to the window, he saw it was Milo Czesiak.

Milo stood before David's door, his hands in the pockets of his leather coat. David's front light turned on, accentuating Milo's profile, then David's silhouette when he stepped outside. Milo began talking, leaning into the conversation, his tones audible but not his words. As the seconds ticked by, Milo's feet gravitated toward a boxer's stance, and his fists clenched by his sides.

Hmm, Harry thought. *Something was going on here.*

David's muscular build, complemented by his workout clothes, towered over Milo's lean frame. He stood with his arms crossed, propped against the door jamb, as casually as if waiting for a cappuccino in a coffee shop.

Harry saw Milo step forward and jab his finger into David's chest. Twice. Both times, David swatted away Milo's hand, causing Milo to step back.

The apparent rant, which lasted several minutes, reminded Harry of a study he'd conducted on Big Men in Papua New Guinea, where informal leaders tried to win influence through persuasion or coercion. No matter the country or culture, the games of power were the same.

Milo ended the argument with a final thrust of his hand, then turned and stormed away. David shook his head and went back inside. The porch went dark, ending the scene.

Harry crawled into bed and tried to clear his mind. His mounting thoughts wouldn't budge.

Neighborhood tensions were swirling. Too many odd things kept happening. And Sue's last words haunted him.

Logically, he knew nothing he or Emma could have done would have saved her. According to the research he'd done on the plant death camas, Sue's fate had been sealed by the time she had phoned him in midst of convulsions.

But there was something he could do. Deep in his gut, Harry knew the police were wrong. Her death hadn't been an accident. Nor had it been suicide.

Sue Daniels had been murdered.

His career had been dedicated to saving lives and restoring justice. Figuring out what had happened to Sue felt like his duty—a challenge Harry couldn't ignore.

Chapter Eleven

Enticing smells wafted from the back seat of Harry's BMW SUV, though Emma wasn't sure about trying Thai food. "What did you order?" she asked.

"Larb gai, gaeng keow wan gai, and khao phat," Harry said. "You'll like it. Despite Thai-rrific's terrible name, the restaurant has excellent, authentic cuisine." She could feel his gaze, the one that made her feel like she was under a microscope. "You've really never had Thai food before?"

She shook her head. "I'm not that adventurous with food. I stick to American: pizza, doughnuts, sandwiches."

"You know none of those are American, right? They're Italian, Dutch, British."

Sometimes Harry's knowledge base was annoying. *Like now.* She put her hands at ten and two on the steering wheel and slowed the car. The powerful SUV reminded her of a Thoroughbred anxious to race, and she felt like the jockey struggling to control it.

"I thought Thai would be appropriate," he said. "In the one meaningful conversation I had with Sue, she mentioned how much she loved Thailand." Harry paused. "You know, you don't have to go if you don't want to. I can get a neighbor to help."

It was the third time that day Harry had told her she didn't have to go with him to the memorial service for Sue. She moved her eyes away from the road to him. "I'm going. Your interest in Sue is more than you wanting to learn about her now that she's dead. I opened the box of books that was delivered this morning, remember? Criminal investigations, poisons, murder."

His face turned angelic. "Those? I just like to read." Her expression in response must have showed her doubtfulness because it made him laugh.

Two could play at the sleuthing game, she decided. Her eyes and ears were going to be wide open. Like Harry, for some reason she wasn't convinced Sue had died by accident.

They weaved through Harry's neighborhood, full of VIPs and the HGTV-worthy homes they lived in. Lakeview Estates wasn't for those caught up in the rat race, it was for the lucky few who'd already won. She found a parking spot not far from the clubhouse and got out to retrieve the food from the back seat.

"Harry." A somewhat nasally voice rang out from a slim, preppily dressed man who looked a bit younger than her mother. He strode toward the car with an eager smile, giving Harry an affectionate hug, being careful of Harry's cane. "Good to see you."

"You, too. It's been a while." Harry motioned to introduce her. "This is my caregiver, Emma Stockton. She used to be a critical care nurse. You may have already heard about her, she's the one who tried to save Sue."

The pride in his voice warmed Emma's heart.

"This," Harry went on, "is Gautam Patel. He and his wife, Sakshi, live in the patio home next to Sue's duplex. Before he retired, Gautam was the chief financial officer at Digital Phoenix, one of Columbus's rising tech firms."

The man looked awfully young to be retired, Emma thought. He must have been quite successful. "Nice to meet you." Emma shifted the plastic bags in her hands, which were starting to cut into her fingers.

"Allow me." The man took the bags, and she flexed her fingers in relief, nodding her thanks. "I'm glad we were able to convert our Columbus Day potluck into a service for Sue. The food and invites were already taken care of, but Sakshi and I still had a devil of a time trying to figure out what to do once everyone was gathered. We couldn't find anyone to eulogize her. No one on the lane seemed to know her that well."

"It's the thought that counts," Harry said. "I'm sure Sue's family will be touched."

Mr. Patel shook his head. "It's only folks from Lakeview Estates. Her family couldn't make it. Diana mentioned that Sue's sister would come to settle her estate, but it sounds like it'll be a while before she arrives. She lives in France, runs her own business there."

They walked up a topiary-lined, stone path to the navy-blue clubhouse with crisp white trim.

"A word of potluck advice," Mr. Patel said to Emma, conspiratorially. "You'll want to choose Diana's dishes first because they'll go fast. Her cooking is even better than Jimmy Chatimont's, and he's a former chef. You should pass on the broccoli casserole. Sakshi, my wife, is great at Indian food, but casseroles of any kind are not her forte." He chuckled good-naturedly.

When they entered the clubhouse, Emma stopped short, caught off guard by its beauty. Decorated in off-whites and navies, the clubhouse's focal point was an Italian fieldstone fireplace—the kind her mom dreamed of—flanked by two windows overlooking a landscaped patio and covered pool. Slate-colored leather chairs huddled around the hearth. Several wooden dining sets dotted the center. In a cubby off to the right sat the kitchen, with a granite-countertop island littered with dishes. She breathed in the aroma of a wood-burning fire and the hint of apple pie that chased it.

Mr. Patel raised the bags of Thai food. "I'll take these to the kitchen. Come find Sakshi and me later." Emma watched him walk off, thinking he was one of Harry's nicest neighbors.

A few faces in the room were familiar, and to Emma's dismay, most in attendance were dressed up in expensive-looking clothing.

She'd never been to a Celebration of Life event before, so had opted for a simple black sweater and pants. Whereas others looked fashionably somber in dark tailored suits and dresses, she felt secondhand-store bleak. She trailed Harry through the crowd, fidgeting with her ponytail, trying not to feel like hired help who should have entered through a rear staff entrance rather than the front door.

Then she noticed Harry's balding neighbor, the one who drove a red Ferrari and smelled like an ashtray. Milo something-or-other. He wore a black skin-tight Armani T-shirt and jeans. Emma inwardly smiled. Maybe she didn't stand out as much as she thought after all.

"Harry," a sensual voice hummed behind them. Emma turned to see Rachel Valucci. Her chestnut hair was pulled back in a loose chignon. Her charcoal cashmere sweater paired with pewter-colored pants and ankle-twisting high-heel boots was what Emma's sister would call "European posh." Fiona seemed to know the trendy styles before they hit the racks, and which stores offered the best knockoffs. Not Emma. When it came to fashion, she was clueless.

"You look as dashing as ever." Rachel blew kisses at each of Harry's cheeks. "But that gray isn't your best color." She fingered the collar of his shirt. "I have Battistoni dress shirts on sale until Friday in a wide range of more appropriate shades." She winked and her fingers lingered.

What a flirt, Emma thought.

Rachel's eyes slid to Emma. "My dear, you *must* stop by my boutique, La Conchessa. I'll find clothing that suits your flamboyant coloring and Rubenesque stature." She spied someone else on the other side of the room and with a yes-I-know-my-teeth-are-perfect smile, Rachel flitted off.

Heat burned Emma's cheeks. Flamboyant coloring? Was that a euphemism for red hair? And *Rubenesque*? Did Rachel just call her fat? Emma glanced down at her outfit and wished she could disappear.

Harry broke into her reverie. "You remember Diana Middleton?"

Emma looked up to see the tall, older woman, her dark Brooks Brothers suit highlighting her bright silver hair that seemed to be lacquered into place with hairspray.

"Evelyn, dear." Diana grasped both of Emma's hands in a two-handed handshake that felt as awkward as being addressed by the wrong name. Again. *Was this woman name-blind, or was this deliberate?*

"It's Emma," she said, struggling to free her hands.

"Of course it is." Diana moved a worn hand to her chest. "It's such a blessing that you're here to help poor Harry since Ceci dashed back to India." Her blandly pleasant look didn't mesh with her tone or her choice of words. Clearly she thought that Harry's daughter shouldn't have moved away.

If Harry was perturbed by the comment, he didn't show it. "Gautam said you brought a few pies and casseroles," he said pleasantly. "You've been busy since yesterday."

"Best not to have idle hands." Diana launched into a description of her work in the kitchen and the volunteering she'd done yesterday for her church, then leaned closer to Harry, lowering her voice. "And at my watercolor class last night with Jimmy, you'll never guess what I learned. Sue lost most of her retirement money in the spring from a bad investment. Such a shame, because I heard that Ralph left her with a very nice nest egg."

Harry tilted his head. "But didn't she buy a new Lexus in August?" he asked. "She had to have money coming in. Maybe Ralph's pension?"

A look that Emma couldn't interpret floated across Diana's face. "I wouldn't know about that." She straightened her skirt. "I asked around in class about who Sue had been dating, but nobody knew."

The sudden shift in topic from Ms. Daniels's source of money to her dating life made Emma wonder if Diana thought Ms. Daniels had been supported by a sugar daddy.

Mr. Patel called for Diana from a nearby table decorated with photos and a watercolor painting. He held a large vase of white lilies and gladioli. "Shall I put the flowers you brought on the table?"

"Yes, but they need rearranging first." Diana patted her impeccably arranged hair and looked back to Harry. "We've set up an In Remembrance table for Sue, make sure to sign the book." She strode off.

"Remember me?" A man's voice oozed from behind Emma. He winked when she turned. "Milo. Milo Czesiak." He looked at Harry and raised his wineglass. "I brought a 2012 Opus One Cabernet Sauvignon from Napa." He sniffed the wine's bouquet. "It has a powerful and seductive blend of berries and smoke."

"That was generous to share such a nice bottle," Harry said.

"Someone around here has to be civilized. I knew the Buchanans would bring beer, the Patels prefer martinis, and Diana is a teetotaler, despite the fact the Bible says that even Jesus drank wine."

"There you are." Rachel Valucci slid up behind Milo and hooked her arm through his. She batted her black feathery lashes and reached for his wine. "I see you saved me some." She took the glass and knocked back half. Milo's eyes bulged.

"I can't believe Sue is dead," Harry said, making Rachel cough, although that may have been from downing the wine so quickly. "Detective Bradford stopped by the other day. Did he question either of you?"

"Yeah. Not sure why." Milo's tone was dismissive. "I barely knew her."

Sue Daniels had lived next door to him, and Emma remembered seeing her storm out of Milo's garage. It'd been a pretty heated argument to have with a so-called stranger. But she wasn't about to say so.

Rachel emptied the rest of Milo's wineglass. "It's awful what's happened. But I don't know why that detective is asking *us* about

Sue. Her death was clearly an accident, or more likely, suicide. She seemed like such a sad sack."

Emma inwardly winced—*What an unkind thing to say, let alone about a neighbor who just died suddenly.*

Milo glanced at his empty glass and frowned. "I'm taking the last glass of good stuff so I don't get stuck with plonk." He left with Rachel on his arm.

"Let's get something to eat." Harry beelined toward the Thai food, but Emma chose vegetables and salad and steered clear of anything that looked delicious—Rachel's fat comment still stung.

Since Harry had his cane, Emma helped him with his plate and drink to a table with the Patels, who looked like Ralph Lauren models, successful and ready for cocktails, golf, or a sailing adventure. After Mr. Patel introduced his wife, Sakshi, and insisted Emma address them by their first names, the couple and Harry spoke in another language for a minute or two.

"My apologies," Harry said to her. "I enjoy practicing my Hindi when I get the chance."

Hindi? Emma couldn't master basic Spanish.

Sakshi smiled. "Harry's accent is better than mine. I grew up in London." Her British accent sounded sophisticated and smart.

As the three talked about life in London and Delhi, the angles of Harry's face softened with joy, an expression she'd seen in the pictures of him and his family on the living room and sunroom walls. Those showed him and his late wife raising their daughter and traveling the world, always smiling, and usually holding hands.

When his plate cleared, Harry stood. "I'm going back for seconds." She started to stand to help him, but he flashed his palm. "Please stay. I can manage alone."

Emma returned to her salad, wishing she'd added dressing.

Gautam raved about the Thai food, and was sporadically interrupted by Sakshi *mmm*-ing over a large serving of lasagna.

He finished his five-star review by adding, "My, Emma, what willpower you have. You've chosen rabbit food."

She looked down at her plate and wished that she didn't so often turn to food with each worry that plagued her.

Sakshi raised a mammoth bite, with strands of sumptuous-looking cheese flowing from the lasagna on her fork. "Diana's outdone herself. This is divine."

Ever the good husband, Gautam nibbled a bite of his wife's oddly brown broccoli casserole, which looked wilted and greasy. He seemed to be struggling to get it down.

"Ghastly news about Sue." Sakshi took a sip of her martini, festooned with five olives skewered with a plastic pink sword.

Her husband reached for his water. "We weren't really friends with her," Gautam said, almost apologetically. "Though we did do neighborly things, like keeping each other's keys, picking up mail, stuff like that."

"Can't say we ever socialized with her outside of community events." Sakshi turned to her husband. "Did we?"

"No. She wasn't a member at the club." Gautam added for Emma's benefit, "The Lakeview Estates Country Club. We golf there."

While the two waxed on about the club's golf course, Emma nibbled on a cucumber, hoping they'd say more about Sue.

"You know, I always thought she was a tad, well, 'dodgy,'" Sakshi said the word as if it had quote marks around it. "Not sure why. Don't get me wrong. Sue was also kind. She often checked in on Grace, Jack Buchanan's mother, who's battling Alzheimer's. Sue also gave sweets to our grandson, Vihaan, when he came over after school."

Gautam pulled out his wallet and passed her a picture of an adorable boy in soccer gear with brown hair and a big toothless grin. As they shared photos and stories of Vihaan, Emma watched the couple. Their closeness was touching—they were perfectly compatible. *Were she and Blake?* she suddenly wondered. While they'd grown up together, there was that thirteen-year gap of not seeing each other. And in their four months of dating, dates had been sporadic, with them squeezing in time together between her work and Blake's residency shifts.

How well did she really know him?

Disconcerted by the question, Emma excused herself and headed to the kitchen in search of dessert . . . and maybe, a smidgeon of lasagna.

* * *

Harry regarded Jimmy Chatimont as he stared out the clubhouse rear windows. "Like I told the police," Jimmy said, "I hardly knew Sue."

Jimmy had been a dear friend of Margaret's and had aged since Harry had last seen him. If he didn't know Jimmy was in his early sixties, he would have guessed at least a decade older. Normally composed with artistic confidence, the man now looked haunted. And his customarily chic long hair was pulled back in a messy ponytail.

"I lost touch with Sue. Well, everyone actually, after Mags died." Harry fought to keep his voice neutral, suddenly longing to see his wife mingling among the crowd in the room.

"I miss Margaret too." Jimmy's face flashed with pain, then it was gone so quickly, Harry wondered if he'd imagined it.

A memory of Mags and Jimmy laughing in the kitchen at a recipe gone awry came back to him. They'd once had to throw away an entire chicken dish. Too much paprika or something. But more often than naught, their cooking adventures had resulted in great meals, and Harry had been happy to enjoy the fruits of their labor.

"Mags and I didn't really socialize with Sue. Who was she friends with?"

Jimmy looked away and rubbed the scruff beginning to grow on his chin. "Sue attended some of my classes and talked to the other students, but I don't know if anyone considered Sue a friend."

"Why was that?"

"Because Sue was not a good person."

Harry was startled by Jimmy's bluntness. "What do you mean?"

Jimmy went on, in a low tone. "About two months ago, after one of my watercolor classes, there was this argument. I found Rachel and Sue quarreling outside the clubhouse. They hushed as soon as I walked outside, but then Sue leaned over to Rachel and whispered in her ear. Rachel stepped back, called her something profane, then actually slapped Sue across the face."

"Wow," Harry said, his surprise showing. "That's some disagreement. Do you have any idea what it was about?"

"No idea. But Sue would be friendly with a neighbor in class one week, then they'd ignore each other the next. She was tremendously unpopular. I can't imagine living with that many people hating me." Jimmy took a drink of coffee that had to have gone cold. "There was also the lawsuit."

"Lawsuit?"

"Sue was suing St. Joseph's Hospital."

"St. Joseph's? Why?" That's where Emma had worked, Harry remembered. Sue had said she thought she had seen Emma before—maybe from the hospital.

"Yeah. Sue had an emergency appendectomy back in May, and her wound got infected. She'd hired a team of lawyers to put together a malpractice suit against the hospital and all the attending physicians and nurses."

That was quite the bombshell, Harry thought, especially since it sounded initially that Jimmy thought Sue's death had been suicide. Now his comments were implying something darker. A lawsuit would upset people and potentially put careers and reputations at the hospital at risk. If the case had settled, that may have been how Sue got the money for her new car.

"Hiya, Jimmy." Linda Buchanan plopped into the empty chair. "Hey, Harry."

He greeted Linda and her husband, Jack, whose bulky frame filled the chair next to his petite wife. The couple contrasted each other in coloring as well as size: Linda fair with blonde hair and blue eyes; Jack was dark and shaggy. Both wore Buckeyes' jerseys, showing their love for the Scarlet and Gray. Harry remembered their game-day parties as being epic. Their yard and house served as a memorabilia shrine: OSU football flags and pennants, signed Buckeye football helmets, framed Buckeye jerseys, and posters of the OSU Rose Bowl–winning teams.

Jack set down a plate laden with meat and bread and a bowl filled with melted cheese. They'd brought their customary fondue dish. Harry remembered Conner's ordeal, and wanted to ask about their son, but he didn't want to upset the couple.

Linda leaned toward Jimmy. "Where can I buy one of those dry brushes we used in class last night?" She paused to take a bite. "Mmm, these quiches are delicious. Ham and cheese." She ribbed her husband with her elbow. "Jack, slow down. That fondue is for both of us."

Memories of estate planning sessions flashed through Harry's head: he and Mags patiently sitting while Linda completed their wills. While brilliant and methodical at work, Linda's social conversations rambled like tumbleweeds, moving in any direction on a whim.

Harry excused himself and headed for the kitchen, stopping by the In Remembrance table on his way. His heart sank when he saw the paltry display. The flowers Diana brought were lovely, but it saddened him to think Sue's life had been reduced to a rudimentary watercolor she'd painted in one of Jimmy's classes and four photos of her at various clubhouse events, none of which had her looking at the camera.

He flipped through the In Remembrance book Diana had provided for them to sign for Sue's family. The condolences were generic. No personal notes, no anecdotes, no message of meaning or warmth. His eyes scanned the room to see who seemed most troubled by the loss, and he caught sight of Grace Buchanan, Jack's mother, sitting by herself across in a far corner. He moved in that direction. Emma left the kitchen and met him halfway, carrying a plate with three brownies.

"Follow me." He led the way to Grace's table.

Grace's milky blue eyes looked befuddled when Harry sat in the leather chair beside her. Emma took the chair to his side. The older woman's gray hair piled in a crooked bun atop her head. Her clothing, a lime green cardigan over a pink housedress, looked authentic 1950s.

"Hi, Grace." He gave the older woman his best reassuring smile. "I'm Harry Lancaster, Margaret's husband. I live next door to you."

Grace's right hand slowly floated up to center her bun.

"You remember Margaret, don't you?" Harry asked. "She brought you raspberry pies."

Her wrinkled face shifted in puzzlement, and she spoke in a creaky voice. "Margaret? Linda told me she was dead."

The simple truth felt like a punch in the stomach. "Yes, she is. I'm Margaret's husband, Harry."

A childlike grin stretched across her time-worn face. "Harold. I remember you. Margaret's sweetheart." Her watery gaze moved to Emma. "Who are you?"

Harry introduced Emma, who raised the plate of brownies in greeting. Grace eyed Emma for a moment before turning back to him. "Watch out for her," she warned, then pointed a gnarled finger at Emma. "She's dangerous."

A nervous laugh escaped Emma's lips; a faint blush tinted her cheeks. "I'm a nurse, Grace. I help people." Emma offered her a brownie. Grace declined.

The older woman leaned toward Harry. "People with red hair are evil." She cowered back in her chair.

Harry gently grasped Grace's hand to reassure her. "How have you been?"

It took a moment for her gaze to land back on him. "I love raspberry pie, but I don't remember how to make it."

Her condition had rapidly deteriorated over the past two years. Mags had loved her conversations with Grace, who had had plenty of amusing stories about growing up in Pennsylvania. "I like raspberry pie too," Harry said. "How about I buy you one and bring it over later this week?"

"Would you?" Her eyes lit up. "Sue used to make me pies, but Linda said she's dead like Margaret."

"Sue made you pies?" Harry asked in disbelief. Sue didn't seem the altruistic kind, let alone someone who'd bake.

"She made good pies. I miss them. No one makes pies for me anymore." A burst of laughter across the room made Grace startle. Emma's eyes sharpened, and he figured she was assessing the older woman's condition.

"That was kind of Sue."

She nodded, her head wobbling. "Sue would bring me pie and talk to me. She told me secrets."

Harry's stomach twitched. "What secrets?"

Grace turned to examine the plate of brownies, which rested on Emma's knees. She reached out to pick one, changed her mind, and pulled her hand back.

"What secrets, Grace?" Harry prodded.

"Sue told me her secrets. Other people's secrets too. She collected them." Her eyes flitted back to the plate of brownies. She sucked in her lips. Harry thought she wouldn't say more, but she did.

"Secrets about David, secrets about Milo, secrets about Rachel. She knew secrets about everyone on the lane."

Chapter Twelve

After Harry's appointment with the physical therapist the next day, he suggested to Emma that they go out to lunch. She'd said she wasn't adventurous with food. He had every intention of changing her mind—there were too many tasty cuisines out there not to give some a try.

Mesob Ethiopian Restaurant would do the trick. The restaurant was in a rundown neighborhood and had an aged linoleum floor, plastic tables and chairs, with a slew of faded Ethiopian travel posters pinned to the wall, but the food was fantastic. Harry tried not to smile as he watched her study the menu.

"I haven't had Ethiopian food before." Emma's nose crinkled. "What do you recommend?"

"Ingera, of course. That's the spongey bread that comes with everything. One of my favorites is misir wat, a spicy lentil stew. If you like beef, you could try the tibs fitfit or the derek tibs, although that's pretty spicy."

"Hmm . . . I don't mind some spice."

"How about we get an order of lentils and one of beef, then share?"

Her face and tone remained unconvinced, but she said, "Sure."

Harry marveled as every emotion flashed across her face. "You should never play poker."

"Why not?" Her features shifted to bafflement, underscoring his point.

Before he could answer, their server—whose name tag read KITTEN—stepped to the table. Harry would have called her style Goth Steampunk Fairy. She had pale skin, heavy black eyeliner, soft pink curls, and retro-futuristic, nineteenth-century industrial garb paired with heavy, fuchsia boots. Not your average server, maybe, but Kitten knew the menu well and from her pronunciation of the dishes, Harry wondered if she spoke Amharic.

Emma sipped her water, looking around while Harry placed their order. When Kitten walked away, he asked, "So, are you getting ready for the move to St. Louis?" In the two times they'd briefly talked about it, she'd sounded uncertain.

"Blake's flying to St. Louis tomorrow. He's lined up a several places for us to view on Friday and Saturday. Plus, there are friends of his he wants me to meet."

"It'll be a whole new life. New city, new job, just married."

"Uh-huh."

Harry studied the furrow of her brow. It was clear that Emma wasn't entirely happy about this sudden upcoming move. "I'm sure your parents will miss you," he said, thinking of how much he missed Ceci.

Kitten refilled his water glass before Emma spoke. "My dad passed away when I was ten. He was a firefighter and died while rescuing two kids in a house fire. They survived. The little boy my dad saved is now a father. He named his son Patrick after my dad."

"I'm so sorry. It must have been hard growing up without him." Sympathy for Emma ballooned in Harry's chest. He had watched Ceci grow and thrive, even now from a distance.

"Mom did a great job raising us while she worked full time as a clinical nurse specialist and a nurse practitioner." Emma's tone was full of admiration. "She retired last year, but I think she's bored. Once she finishes planning the wedding, I wouldn't be surprised if she goes back to work."

It didn't slip by Harry that Emma had referred to her mom doing the wedding planning, and that she'd said "the wedding" instead of "my wedding."

"Do you miss nursing?"

Emma's features twisted into what could only be called anguished relief. "No. In intensive care, you see a lot of death. Including unexpected death. It got to me." She paused, and the air around them grew heavy. Harry thought of her father, and knew Emma was thinking of him too.

"Problem is," she continued, "I have this degree and all this training. I don't want to go back to nursing, and caregiving doesn't . . ." She seemed to realize she was talking to one of her patients, and stopped. "Well, it's okay for now, but it's not my future."

"You're young, you have your whole life ahead you." That made Harry wonder what the future held for him once his injury healed. In his email outreach to learn about Sue from his friends in DC, he'd discovered that several of them were still working. He missed having a purpose, missed making a difference, he realized. Likely the same would be true for Emma.

"What will you do in St. Louis?"

For one horrible second, Harry thought she would cry.

Kitten saved the day. She placed a large colorful platter between them, sparing Emma the need to answer.

Emma peered at the tray with interest. "Smells good." A bowl of steaming red lentil stew sat in the center of the round platter, which also featured succulent cutlets of beef with onion and green peppers, a fresh green salad, and ample rolls of ingera. As he pointed out the items, Emma checked the sides of her plate. "She forgot our silverware."

"Nope, it's here." He pulled off a piece of ingera and dipped it into the lentil stew. "You use the bread."

Emma's face shifted back to doubtful. Then she took a stamp-sized piece of ingera and dipped it into the stew.

He smiled as she gingerly moved it toward her mouth. But after she popped it in and chewed, her face lit with pleasure.

"Wow. This is great." She took a larger piece of ingera, grabbed some beef, and took a bite. Her eyes widened in delight. "This is even better."

While Emma enthusiastically ate, they talked about his work in Africa. As they chatted, Harry found himself transported back to Ethiopia: feeding hyenas in Harar Jegol, watching boys from the Hamer tribe jump over the backs of bulls to become men, studying various Omo Valley tribes to discover the significance of the white chalk paintings that covered their skin.

When the platter was cleared, Emma wore a huge grin.

Ethiopian food had been a hit. Harry was pleased.

His cell phone dinged, and he checked his email as Kitten totaled up the bill. He'd received an out of office message from his PI friend Geoff Jeffries—he was in Sudan and wouldn't have access to email for a week.

He must have frowned because Emma said, "Hit a wall in the investigation?"

Harry used every muscle in his face to hide his surprise. "What do you mean?"

"It would be impossible to miss your nosing around. We both know Ms. Daniels's death wasn't an accident . . . well, most likely wasn't an accident." She looked up to the ceiling and chewed on her bottom lip. "I'm not sure why I think it, other than my nursing instincts. Why do you think it wasn't an accidental poisoning?"

He paused, unsure if he wanted to involve her. Then the list of medications Sue took flashed through his head. And she had died from poison. Emma had a wealth of medical knowledge he lacked—and needed if he ever hoped to figure out what had happened to Sue.

"Stop holding back," she prodded.

"Okay. I give." Harry held up his hands in surrender. He shared everything he'd learned and considered so far, finally working his way around to her area of expertise.

"According to Detective Bradford's notes, Sue was taking cephadoporoltorin, ibuprofen, Enlaporatorl, and Metfora—something or other."

She chuckled with an ear-to-ear grin. "Wow. At least you got ibuprofen right."

"Enjoy your victory lap, then tell me what they do."

Emma sat up straight. "Cephalosporins treat bacterial infections and are antibiotics similar to penicillin. Didn't Diana mention something about Sue having an appendectomy and a subsequent infection?"

"Yes."

"Then Sue was probably on either cefazolin or cephalexin, which treat staph and strep infections. Prescription ibuprofen fights inflammation."

His respect for Emma shot up again. He had made the right decision to team up with her. "Jimmy said Sue was suing St. Joseph's Hospital because of the infection."

"Really? Huh." She rubbed her chin. "It's a sensitive topic, but I'll ask around and see if I can unearth more details about it. I still have friends there."

"And the other two medications?"

"Metformin is a first-line treatment for type 2 diabetes. Enalapril"—she clearly enunciated each syllable—"treats hypertension and is used to manage heart failure. Combined, these medications would have taken their toll on Sue's liver and made her more susceptible to plant toxicity. That said, we know she had been prescribed the medications, not that she was taking all of them. Some of those bottles may have been old."

He nodded, appreciating the deduction. They sat in silence for a few moments as Harry digested his meal and the information Emma had shared.

"So what's next?" she asked in eager tones.

"Well, after her husband's death and retiring from a State Department career, Sue moved to Ohio from DC, the heart of national security. She had zero presence on social media and, from photos I've seen of her, was camera shy. In every discussion I had with her, she was vague about her government career."

Emma leaned in in rapt attention, figuring out that he was building up to something. "And . . ."

"None of my government agency friends have heard of Sue, including those who worked with State," Harry said. "Grace said Sue collected secrets. The State Department is frequently used as a cover for someone in—"

"You think Sue was in the CIA," Emma concluded.

"Maybe. It's a career that pulls all these threads together. And I have a way for us find out."

Chapter Thirteen

The landline phone rang as Harry was leaving his bedroom early the next morning. Outside of Ceci, not many people called him besides telemarketers, but they didn't call before seven. He turned back and picked up the phone on his nightstand, which held his favorite photo of him and Margaret.

It captured them on a trip to Suffolk, where they'd attended a wedding at Hintlesham Hall. He'd felt like a country earl dressed to the nines in his black tuxedo, and Mags had looked like a Hollywood actress in a gold evening gown that matched her hair and made her luminescent blue eyes glow. The grandiose English manor loomed behind them in the background as they walked down the stairs, hand in hand.

When he answered, a deep, gravelly voice responded.

"Lancaster. Duke here. Got your email."

Duke Riley had served with Harry in Vietnam, and Harry tried to picture what the bald, ruddy-faced man would look like now. Duke had had a permanent cagey smile, set crooked by the cigarette forever glued to his lips.

"You're up early," Harry said, wondering if the trademark cigarette was still there or if his friend had kicked the habit.

"Up before Reveille every day. Meet me in Raven's Park in thirty."

"What? You're in Ohio?" The last Harry had heard, Duke lived in Virginia not far from Roanoke. "Raven's Park? You mean the one near me?" The park was less than a ten-minute walk away.

"Of course I mean the one near you. Catch up, Lancaster." *Click.*

Harry stared at the phone. *Duke. Down the street at Raven's Park.* If his email had drawn his old friend to travel this far overnight, something was up.

He hurried to the hall closet and put on his burgundy cashmere scarf and tan wool coat. He gathered a pair of suede gloves, his cell phone, then reluctantly, the walker. He was getting around pretty well with the cane, but there was no need to take chances, especially going that far.

The lane was quiet in the early morning light. Only the occasional car passed as he made his way toward the Lakeview Estates entrance, where the path to the park began. Most houses he passed were dark. A few had on a sole upstairs light, giving the appearance of the home winking. Although it was predicted to climb to sixty that afternoon, his breath came out in visible puffs.

Within minutes, he was on the park path, walking by a patch of soon-to-be-bare trees and a grassy soccer field. Birds chirped in cadence with the tapping of his walker. Clouds loomed in the distance, promising rain.

Two empty basketball courts sprawled on his left, and beyond that was a play area that his grandchildren Evie and Evan loved, with monkey bars, swings, a jungle gym, and slides. A lone brown Jeep sat in the parking lot.

Harry headed for the covered picnic area, where a bulky figure in a dark coat sat at a wooden table.

The man stood and looked his way. His face launched Harry back forty years to his time in Vietnam: the heart-wrenching loss, the abject fear, and the victories that had seemed to come too far between. Duke was still bald and his cheeks still ruddy, but a little bit wider with a lot more lines.

"What happened?" Duke nodded toward the walker. "If you're hurt, why didn't you drive?"

Harry had promised Ceci he wouldn't get behind the wheel until he got the doctor's approval to do so, but he wasn't about to explain that to his old war buddy. "Temporary setback. You're well?"

"Y-ep," Duke replied in two enthusiastic syllables. He pulled a red pack of Marlboro cigarettes from his pocket, extracted one, then lit it with a rusted Zippo lighter. He took a lingering inhale, as if sipping through a straw, then placed the pack and lighter on the table. On the concrete below him, Harry noticed a pile of ash. This cigarette wasn't his first.

Duke sat and motioned for Harry to join him. He slid onto the bench, conscious of his hip, while trying to figure out the best way to start the conversation. He'd always found Duke more informative when approached from the side. "Nice seeing you after so long."

"Some days Nam feels like it was a million years ago, and sometimes just yesterday."

"I hope you didn't take time off work to drive up here. Or have you retired?"

"You got that right, boyo. My sister, Gladys, she's at the cancer center downtown. Been in Columbus a week. Imagine my surprise hearing from you while I'm here. Figured we might as well meet in person, cloak and dagger style. You know, for old time's sake."

Harry chuckled. They chatted about Duke's sister, whose prognosis was good, and about Margaret and Ceci and the grandkids. Then they reminisced about the last time they'd seen each other: on an airstrip in Hanoi, where Harry had boarded a military plane to go home. Duke had saluted the plane as it taxied down the runway.

After leaving the service as the war wound down, the men had chosen different routes. Harry had gone on to get a Ph.D. in anthropology from Ohio State University, then a career focused on international aid and development.

Duke took a role with an unnamed "government agency" near Washington, DC—which Harry suspected likely benefited from Duke's cunning. During the war, he'd been nicknamed "Mr.," which stood for midnight requisition, because Duke wasn't above "acquiring" supplies from other units on late-night runs to keep theirs stocked and running no matter how fiercely the war raged around them.

Though Duke had never mentioned his role or employer, Harry was sure he worked within the intelligence community—most likely, the CIA. Duke's sporadic, out-of-the-blue calls to casually talk about the conflict-affected places where Harry had worked, were big clues.

It would have been easy for Duke to figure out that Harry had ended up working for the United States Agency for International Development, but not to know the precise villages or towns *where* he'd been working, but somehow Duke always knew. And Duke's questions during what he called "just-shooting-the-shit" conversations were specific, suggesting he'd been privy to insight gained on the ground.

While USAID kept its distance from the CIA, Harry had shared information with Duke when appropriate. He trusted his friend and had wanted Duke to have an accurate lay of the land in whatever war-torn place Harry had been working.

Ever blunt, Duke asked him, "What's up? You need some info?"

Harry hesitated. If Sue had been a spy, she would have blended in, not stood out as the neighborhood troublemaker. "I do. But now that I'm about to say it out loud, I realize how ridiculous it sounds. One of my neighbors, Sue Daniels, died under suspicious circumstances. Information I've learned about her has made me wonder if she was one of you."

"A ruggedly handsome fisherman?" Duke's lightness made Harry feel slightly less quixotic.

"A colleague," he clarified.

"And by suspicious circumstances you mean . . . ?"

"The police think her death was accidental. That she foraged and then ate the wrong plant. But her call to me before she died and a few other things are making me wonder."

Duke tapped the ash off his cigarette and nodded.

"Did you work with Sue?"

"No."

Harry nodded. "Figured it was a long shot."

Duke continued. "But I did work with her husband."

That brought him up short. "You knew Ralph?"

"Y-ep." Duke's response told Harry two things. If Ralph had worked for the CIA, he didn't retire under cover. And if Ralph hadn't worked for the CIA, he could have worked with them under joint operations with another agency in the intelligence community.

Duke could only say so much. Harry would have to carefully frame his questions. "Did you ever work directly with Ralph?"

His friend lit another cigarette, inhaled deeply, then exhaled a round puff. "From time to time."

"I see." Harry's mind raced as he formed his next question and the thrill of a quest surged through him. "At *your* headquarters, or in the field?"

Another inhale, then exhale. "Both."

If Ralph been working with Duke at CIA headquarters, he probably worked for the Agency too. "Analysis or collections?"

"Both."

So Sue's late husband had analyzed information that intelligence officers collected overseas and had also worked in the field—both an analyst and a spy.

Harry sat back. "What did you think of Ralph's work?"

"One of our best." Inhale, exhale. "I didn't trust him."

"Why?"

"Ralph would never betray our country. But he'd betray you."

Harry kept silent, watching the smoke plume.

Duke snuffed out the butt of his cigarette on the tabletop, started to get out another, stopped, and pushed it back in. He returned the pack and lighter to his coat pocket. He exhaled. "Ralph could make it seem like he was supporting you, but somehow he gained in the end—the best assignments, promotions, raises, you name it. Ralph always ended up on top."

Harry thought about how much Sue would have known about the work her husband had been involved in, what she would she have learned from him over the years.

"But you never met Sue?"

"Nope. Though I knew she existed. From what I heard, she kept a low profile, didn't mingle with the ex-pats outside of the office." Duke looked at Harry with a gaze so intense it felt like an X-ray. "You poking around for fun, Harry? Or did you become a private detective when you retired?"

"Long story, and I don't want to take up too much of your time. I'm sure you have things to do with your sister. But one final question. Do you think Sue knew what Ralph really did, that his job at State was a cover?"

Duke's barking laugh turned into a cough practically worthy of tuberculosis. "Ralph was cocky," he finally got out. "No way he didn't brag to her."

"Huh." *Maybe Sue picked up where Ralph left off*, Harry thought, but didn't say it. "You've been quite helpful. Thank you." He wondered if he'd ever see his war buddy again. The thought that he wouldn't formed an ache in his chest. "We should go fishing this spring."

"You got a deal, boyo." Duke's grin was deep and sincere. "Come on down to Smith Mountain Lake. You can tell me about what's going on, and I'll teach you to fish like the best of 'em."

"Sounds great."

"Just say when and I'll gas up the boat. Want a ride back to your place?" Duke asked as they stood.

His hip felt tender, but Harry wanted to walk. The movement might help stimulate his mind. "No, thank you. I need the fresh air."

"See ya in the spring." Duke saluted, then crossed the parking lot for his Jeep. Harry headed for the path that led to Lakeview Estates. Several steps later, the Jeep slowed as it passed him. Duke rolled down the window for a parting word.

"Watch your back, buddy. Watch your back."

* * *

Emma parked her Honda Accord in the departures bay of the John Glenn International Airport, wishing she'd had another hour of sleep. "I'll ring when I land," Blake said, shooting her his Prince Charming smile as his hand found the handle to open the passenger side door.

Anxiety fizzed in her chest, and she fought to keep it from her face. "Safe travels." But it wasn't his safe arrival in St. Louis that worried her.

He leaned over and gave her a warm kiss. "Love you."

"You too." Blake got out and retrieved his overnight bag from the back seat. Emma watched him walk away through the rain-speckled, passenger-side window, thinking about their discussion last night. They'd stayed up late talking about their future, in St. Louis and beyond. She was still processing the conversation that had tipped her world sideways and filled her stomach with something that felt like concrete.

One day, Blake envisioned them living in a gated golf club community like Harry's in Los Angeles or Miami. They'd be club members and have three kids who went to private school. Their large house would have plenty of room for family visits. He'd drive a Porsche 718 Spyder to help attract an elite clientele. She could work if she wanted or stay at home and focus on the house and the kids.

There wasn't anything wrong with that dream, but it wasn't how Emma envisioned their future, working together to help others. Maybe something overseas like Harry and his wife had done. She didn't want to try to keep up with elegant neighbors like

Rachel Valucci, didn't want to eat salad the rest of her life and buy haute couture and pay careful attention to her hair and skin.

She'd built Blake up in her mind as a selfless hero dedicated to saving lives, unconcerned with the trappings of the world. Someone like her father. But now she realized that wasn't the case, and the misalignment between her vision and reality was jarring. She was living both a dream and a lie.

The story she'd told herself about Blake and their relationship was worthy of a Disney ending, and Emma had fallen in love with a story, a fictional character, not the real man.

Her stomach sank another inch. What was she going to do? She couldn't imagine hurting Blake. He was kind-hearted and thoughtful and treated her well.

Oh God. What would she tell her mother?

Whack.

Emma jerked upward, making the seatbelt cut into her neck. A gesturing cop stood outside the driver's window. "You gotta move, lady."

She nodded, marshalling strength to pull herself together. *Pre-wedding nerves. That's all, right?* Typical doubts and fears that temporarily plagued all brides and grooms.

Her shaky hands found the steering wheel. She pulled into the exit lane and flicked her windshield wipers on high, trying to leave behind the airport and her ballooning unease. Rainwater pooled in low dips of the road, and she decided against taking the freeway to Harry's. After a few tense miles on back roads, the morning's downpour turned into a drizzle. Her shoulders lowered, and she loosened her grip on the wheel.

At a red light, her cell phone rang. She checked her caller ID and answered on speaker. "Hi, Mom."

"Are you on your way to work?"

"Yeah. Traffic's awful with this rain."

"Did Blake get off okay? I can't wait to see what apartments he finds for you two. I'll come down and help decorate."

Emma paused. The thought of mentioning her concerns made her stomach plummet. And she wasn't really sure what she was feeling.

Their conversation inevitably veered into wedding planning. "I've sent out an invite for the wedding task force to have dinner next week," her mom said.

"What day—"

"Fiona suggested a beach-themed wedding. What do you think?" Emma's younger sister had gotten married in South Carolina, a beautiful sunset service on the sand and the bride had showed off her sun-kissed tan in a strapless wedding dress.

"I burn and freckle. Plus we're getting married in Columbus."

"Don't be such a spoilsport. Patricia was pushing for Boho-chic." Emma fought back a groan. Blake's mom was a huge Stevie Nicks fan.

Her mother rambled on, and Emma tuned out. It *had* been exciting to brag about the news of her engagement, and part of her cringed at the thought. She'd plastered it all over Instagram and Facebook and spoke about nothing else at her high school class reunion in September. *Did she care more about what other people thought than she wanted?*

". . . with feathers and crystals in the centerpieces," her mom's voice cut in.

Feathers and crystals? "The Chain" by Fleetwood Mac began playing in her head.

Her mom's description of a bohemian-inspired reception made Emma reroute toward Perk Me Up, the coffee shop near Harry's. They had fantastic doughnuts.

"I gotta focus on driving, Mom," she finally cut in, and said goodbye.

Surely she'd feel better about the move and Blake once she visited St. Louis, Emma reassured herself. Two days with him would ease her mind. Surely.

Chapter Fourteen

Harry sat by the hearth in the kitchen sitting area that evening, the flames dancing in sync with his flickering thoughts. He picked up a notebook from the nearby end table and turned it over in his knobby, wrinkled hands. On some days, he couldn't believe these hands were his own. Where had the time gone?

Before losing himself in rumination over how much of his life was behind him, he shifted his thoughts back to Sue. He and Emma had spent the day discussing what they'd learned about her: the arguments with neighbors, a lawsuit, money problems, Grace's talk of secrets, and that her late husband had been a spy. Had Sue picked up Ralph's tricks of the trade to gather secrets about her neighbors and then blackmailed them for financial gain?

The thought made him shudder. So did the possibility that motives and murder suspects were likely close by.

Glancing up from his notebook, he caught a glimpse of movement through the rear windows. He hadn't closed the blinds after the sun had dropped below the horizon hours ago. He squinted, and a moment later, saw it again.

He turned off the nearby lamp, leaving the fire as the room's only source of light. As his eyes adjusted, dark figures materialized as they moved across his backyard.

Harry gripped his cane and moved to the window. Two silhouettes appeared against the tree line. Neither used a flashlight despite the darkness.

One stood with shoulders rolled forward and head down, while the other jittered from side to side, as if fending off the cold. They looked like boys, not men—maybe young Conner Buchanan and a friend.

The person on the left gestured toward the Buchanans' house. Harry figured that if he went out onto the cedar deck, the noise would send them scattering and perhaps diminish their chances of getting into trouble. He opened the rear door and stepped outside. A blast of cold air tensed his body. The two figures were gone.

Curious, he inched out farther, moving beyond the porch's overhang and into a drizzling rain that tickled his face. His cane thumped against the deck with each step as he navigated around the wicker chairs.

Probably he should call the police. But he didn't feel a twinge in his stomach, the one that warned him of impending danger. During the Vietnam War, he'd felt it twice minutes before his unit was ambushed. In southern Sudan, it had helped him avert the hijacking of his Land Cruiser. The last time he'd had it, it'd stopped him from crossing a field in Mozambique riddled with land mines.

Conner was a kid who got into trouble, but he wasn't a threat. Harry would tell the two boys to go home then head back inside. He walked to the end of his deck, wondering how they'd disappeared so quickly. He thought maybe they dropped below the low stone-walled garden along the screened-in porch.

The damp chill kneaded his spine. The smell of wet earth filled his nostrils. Perhaps a look from the yard . . .

When he stepped down from the deck's bottom stair, the bush beside him rustled.

Before he could turn his head, one of the intruders exploded into motion, jumping up to run, knocking into Harry. Hard.

The world slowed. Harry pitched forward. He released his cane before smacking the wet grass, using his knees and hands to brace his fall.

Whoosh. Air knocked out of his lungs when his chest slammed into the ground.

Stunned, he lay motionless. Two sets of running footfalls receded into the night.

Cold rain trickled down the back of his neck, and he fought to control his breath. Caught in a flashback of his fall in late August, Harry was afraid to move.

As he listened to his choppy exhalations, he forced his breathing to slow. Once he managed to control his thoughts and fear, he took a mental scan of his body.

Nothing felt broken. He rolled onto his right side. His hip seemed okay. Cautiously, he got onto to his hands and knees, which ached with the pressure of his weight. He searched for the cane in the slick, wet grass.

He found it and slowly stood. Step by step, he climbed onto the deck with the aid of the railing, then relied on his cane to get inside. He bolted the door behind him.

His body started to shake. Perhaps from the chill. Perhaps from shock.

Calling for an ambulance was out of the question. Diana Middleton would have a field day. Instead, he dialed Emma. She picked up on the second ring.

"Harry, what's wrong?" It was 10:30 PM. He never called this late.

"I fell again. Could you please come over and help?"

"Do you need an ambulance?"

"No," he said with force. "I'm just cold and rattled."

"I'm on my way." She clicked off.

He returned to his seat by the fire, leaving a trail of mud and grass across the kitchen's hardwood floor and the sitting area's oriental rug. He pulled a chenille blanket off the back of the chair and placed it around his shoulders to stop his shivering.

While his body processed the adrenalin from his scare, his mind became equally active.

Once unafraid to stand up to armed rebels, this time Harry had gone down without a fight. He'd been pushed over like a child by a wayward teen. Gloomy thoughts consumed him until Emma burst through his front door.

* * *

"Harry!" Emma rushed over, leaving the door ajar. He looked at the clock and cringed. She'd made it in twenty minutes—Mario Andretti time.

"What happened? How are you?" She turned on the lamp next to him. "Why are you wet and muddy?" Her rapid-fire questions matched the agitation on her face. She wore a tangled ponytail, an oversized OSU sweatshirt, and what looked like pajama bottoms. She hadn't wasted a second to get there.

After she closed the front door and turned on more lights, he did his best to tell her everything without sounding like a bumbling buffoon for going out alone at night not long after a suspicious death took place houses away.

Emma listened and made him a cup of tea. After he'd sipped from the warm mug and finished recounting the event, she examined him, paying close attention to his wrists and knees. While she agreed that no bones appeared to be broken, she disagreed about what to do.

"I want to stay home tonight and see how I feel in the morning."

Emma put her hands on her hips and raised her chin. "Absolutely not. We're going to the emergency room so you can have X-rays. We need to make sure you didn't reinjure your hip."

When he tried to argue, she held up her hand, then pointed toward his bedroom. The pitch of her voice plummeted along with its volume. "Go change into dry clothes." It was not a request.

He moved forward, and Emma stepped to his side to help him to his room. "I'll get the walker out of the garage. You'll be using it again for a while. Call if you need help getting changed."

He recognized her soft repentant tone to compensate for the harsh command. He'd used the same tone after he'd caught Ceci playing with a bow and arrow he'd received as a gift from a Waiaipi chief in the Amazon—an arrow that, besides being deadly sharp, had been regularly dipped into poison for hunting. It'd been cleaned, but if even the slightest trace had been left behind . . .

It was the angriest he'd ever been with his daughter, and when he'd finished scolding her, she'd said in a small voice, "I was pretending to be you." Then her face crumbled into sobs. It had shredded his heart. He'd ended up drying her tears, locking away the bow and arrow—which he should have done in the first place—and taking her out for a jumbo ice cream sundae.

When he reemerged, Emma had cleaned up the debris he'd tracked throughout the house and sat, ready to leave. They were silent the entire trip to the hospital. Once parked, Emma made him stay in the car until she could get a wheelchair to transport him into St. Joseph's ER waiting room.

If he hadn't acted so foolishly, he wouldn't be here. *Bloody hubris.*

She expertly navigated him toward the check-in window.

The pale-yellow room smelled of sickly sweet vanilla that didn't quite cover the pervasive odor of disinfectant. Over the hospital's PA system, a Dr. Miroux was called to the delivery ward. The message repeated. A new life was on its way.

Harry flashed back to when he and Mags had Ceci, near lifetimes ago. Those days had faded, and so, it would seem, had his independence. Emasculation ballooned alongside his rising years. As if reading his thoughts, Emma slowed the wheelchair and patted his shoulder.

"Emma, girl, how are you?" A tinny voice filtered out from behind the glass of the reception desk as they neared. A young brunette chewed on a piece of gum looking out at them, her pink top matching the hue of her cheeks. "How's that hot fiancé of yours?"

"Hi, Sheila. I need a doctor and a bed." Emma smiled weakly and pointed to him. "Harry is checking in for the night." She summarized his fall, and the injuries she'd observed so far, which primarily seemed to be minor lacerations on his hands and face and swollen knees.

Within five minutes, they'd filled out all the required forms and Harry was queued to see a doctor. While they waited, the fortysomething couple seated beside him were called back. A nearby girl of about ten started crying, her mother unable to staunch her tears.

Emma got out of her chair, had a quick word with the woman, then kneeled before the child. She spoke so softly Harry couldn't make out her words. But the cries slowly shifted to sniffling, and then a giggle. She gave the girl's knee a squeeze and returned to her seat, giving Harry an all-in-a-day's-work shrug.

At last they were summoned to an examining room down a forlorn-looking hall. After the doctor concurred with Emma's assessment, Harry was taken in for X-rays. Nothing new appeared to be broken, but the doctor wanted his orthopedic surgeon to review the screen before Harry went home, which meant staying overnight—just like Emma predicted. He was wheeled by a female orderly to a private room upstairs.

It looked out over the freeway, where streaks of red and white lights paraded in parallel paths. Raindrops hit the window and cascaded down the pane. A male nurse in scrubs, looking as muscular as a Samoan warrior, took over from the orderly and helped Harry move from the wheelchair to the bed. Once settled, exhaustion swept over him.

Emma, who'd stuck to his side the whole way, took a seat in the room's sole chair. The entire process—from the parking lot to his hospital bed—had taken less than an hour.

"You pulled some strings for me," he said once the nurse and orderly left. "That had to be the fastest check-in and processing ever."

Her faint smile didn't reach her eyes. "I have my ways." Reproach furrowed her brows. "What were you thinking going outside? We both think there's a murderer out there, for God's sake."

"I thought it was Conner and another teenage boy. I didn't feel threatened."

"If it was that kid. I'll throttle him." She rose from her chair, hands fisted. "I'm calling Detective Bradford."

"Why? Knocking me down was an accident, which is also what he thinks Sue's death was."

"We'll see about that." She charged from the room.

Harry slipped into emotional darkness. He'd been fit and healthy his entire life, up until recently. Six weeks ago, he'd been moving heavy boxes around the garage and climbing the ladder to clean the attic. And now he was in the hospital, again, immersed in loneliness and a lack of purpose that he'd felt since Mags died.

Ten minutes later, Emma reappeared. "Detective Bradford will drop by the house once you're home." She took another step toward him, her face creased with worry. "Get some sleep."

He remained silent, studying his hands.

She moved to his side. "I'll get you back to normal—wait, better than normal—in no time. We'll add more strength building to your physical therapy sessions. You'll be running laps around me."

Harry placed no confidence in her words. "See you in the morning."

After Emma left, he stared out the window, watching the world continue around him. The echoing beeps of his heart rate monitor set a steady tempo. Like a conductor waving a baton, they synchronized his thoughts of loss, of despair, of defeat.

Chapter Fifteen

Emma walked under dawn's dusty pink hues through St. Joseph's Hospital's parking lot. Inside the hospital's main entrance, elaborate flower arrangements bursting with purple and yellow brightened the reception area. The antiseptic smell spurred vivid memories, from her apprehensive days as a newly minted candy striper to the rewarding highs and at times abysmal lows of being a critical care nurse. Every day had been a battle to save lives, with too many battles lost.

The PA system crackled to life. "Dr. Baxter to Cardiology. Dr. Baxter to Cardiology." People in scrubs and white lab coats hurried this way and that, each on a critical mission.

Emma's tennis shoes squeaked on the clean linoleum floor, becoming louder when the PA system went silent. At the large bay of elevators she pressed the Up button.

"Emma?" A tentative female voice called. She turned to see Kathleen Monahue, whose kind smile reached her eyes. Kathleen's hair was secured away from her full face with bobby pins.

"Kathleen." Emma embraced her friend, while she struggled to remember when they'd last spoken. It'd been around the time Emma had left nursing. Kathleen had called. Emma, filled with shame, hadn't called back.

"Have you come back to work?" Kathleen's tone was unmistakably hopeful.

"I'm here for one of my caregiving patients. How are you?"

Emma had been glad when she'd shared shifts with Kathleen in the ICU. During the most terrifying crisis or tragic defeat, Kathleen had remained gentle, level-headed, and honest, even when delivering the worst news.

"Good. Tiffany's growing by leaps and bounds." She glowed with motherly pride. "You and Blake need to come over for dinner so you can see for yourself. She's starting to walk."

"The pictures of her on Instagram are adorable." Tiffany was a cherub-faced toddler who had a linebacker's build. "She's getting big."

"Yep. And a handful now that she's mobile." Kathleen transferred her weight to her opposite foot and rubbed her bloodshot eyes, evidence she'd just finished a night shift. "I heard you and Blake got engaged." Both women's eyes landed on Emma's large engagement ring.

"About three weeks ago. I know it's a bit fast, but we grew up together. Our families have known each other forever. I guess it's the classic love story." Emma laughed halfheartedly and wondered why she was explaining. "As you can expect, my mom is over the moon. Both of our families are, actually."

Kathleen's face shifted, and Emma recognized the look—the one Kathleen would give before she had to tell patients upsetting news. "I'm happy for you. You're a lovely, if unexpected, couple."

Emma pressed her lips together, thinking before she responded. When word had spread around the hospital that she was dating Blake, she knew there'd been talk among the nurses that he was out of Emma's league. Her cheeks flamed. She couldn't believe Kathleen felt that way too.

As if reading her thoughts, Kathleen put a comforting hand on Emma's shoulder, then patted it. "I don't think Blake is too good for you. If anything, you're out of his league. You two just seem so unalike, with different priorities and lifestyles. I'm glad you've found common ground."

Kathleen had worked with Blake for years at Riverside Heights before moving to St. Joseph's Intensive Care Unit. She had known Blake as an adult several years longer than Emma had, Emma realized. If someone else had noticed their stark differences—someone who knew them both well—the growing uncertainty she felt went beyond normal wedding jitters. Maybe she should start trusting her feelings.

"As long as you two are happy." Kathleen's voice sounded reedy and distant. She gave Emma's shoulder another squeeze. "You look faint. Are you okay?"

"Yeah." Emma didn't have time to digest this now. She had a job to do: to look after Harry. Her personal life could wait.

Kathleen didn't look convinced. "Are you enjoying caregiving?"

"That's why I'm here. My patient fell last night. He didn't injure himself physically, but I'm worried he might slide back into depression. Just when he was beginning to make progress." Her mom had warned her about patients who hadn't recovered, not because of physical limitations, but from limitations they'd set in their minds. She wouldn't let that happen to Harry.

"With your bedside manner, not a chance." Kathleen checked her watch. "I should go. I hate to miss breakfast with Tiffany. Great seeing you. Let me know when you and Blake want to come over for dinner." They hugged and promised to keep in touch.

While glad to see her friend, the run-in had been unsettling. Emma wanted to brush off Kathleen's remarks, but their barbs of truth clung to her.

The PA system called again, and she got into the elevator, bound for the sixth floor. On the way to Harry's room, she took in the sounds around her: the beeping of life-saving equipment, the shuffling of nurses' feet, the banging of metal meal carts.

Soft crying floated from a room down the hall, and Emma peered in when she passed. A heavyset nurse in scrubs held an old woman's fragile hand. Although the adjacent bed was empty, an unplugged heart rate monitor and IV stand were positioned nearby. Emma wondered if the woman's roommate had passed during the night. That part of nursing, she didn't miss.

She found Harry sleeping, so she went to freshen up and get caffeine. Three hours of sleep were hardly enough.

Emma stepped into the ladies' room and frowned at herself in the mirror. Purplish circles surrounded her eyes and her complexion looked pallid. Was it possible to age ten years in one night? And what was up with her hair?

After splashing cold water on her face, she added blush and mascara, then did her best to smooth out the rat's nest on her head. When she'd called the detective late last night to tell him how an intruder had shoved Harry to the ground, he'd sounded concerned.

When she'd told Blake about Harry's fall, he had suggested she get a sub so she could fly out to St. Louis that evening—when Harry needed her most. She'd told Blake no, but he'd taken it well.

Emma looked back into the mirror and added concealer, eyeliner, and lipstick to cover up her lack of sleep, anxiety, and growing doubt.

In the cafeteria, she purchased two large teas, added cream and sugar to both, then made her way back upstairs. This time, Harry was awake.

She pasted on a smile brighter than the sunshine pouring in through the window. "Morning. Got you a tea." She jiggled his cup.

Harry's skin paled against his dark eyes, and his thick gray hair matted to his head. He looked worse than she did.

"How ya doing?" She removed the cup's lid and placed it on the nearby tray table.

"Better." His tone belied him. "My orthopedic surgeon said the X-rays showed no new damage. The consensus is I'll be fine."

He would be, Emma thought, if she could make him believe it.

* * *

After they returned from the hospital, Harry regarded the iPad he'd propped up onto the nightstand under his bedroom window and sat in the nearby chair.

His daughter's blue eyes no longer sparked with joy but reflected her frustration. She'd also dyed her hair from jet black to a fiery red—appropriate given the heated conversation. He was glad Emma was in the other room.

"We should have chosen Agatha Hooper as your caregiver. Emma is too lax. Nurse Agatha suggested good protective rules."

Harry swallowed a frustrated sigh. When Ceci had learned of his initial fall, she'd rushed back from India, leaving behind her kids, husband, and job. She'd begged him to remain in the rehabilitation center where he'd spent two weeks after his week in the hospital, but Harry had wanted to be home.

Then they'd argued over caregivers. He'd preferred no one but conceded to the choice of Emma over the stern Agatha Hooper, who'd treated Harry like he was useless and feebleminded.

It hadn't been Harry's first battle with his daughter over his well-being, and it wouldn't be their last. He tried to evade the emotions Ceci's last visit had evoked: love tinged with humiliation, father now feeling like son.

"Emma wasn't here when I fell. It was in the evening." He strained to keep his voice gentle. "I went outside for some fresh air and I slipped given the rain." It wasn't a great cover story, but believable. Emma had agreed.

"Dad," Ceci's voice cracked, "I worry about you. It's hard being far away when things like this happen."

"Emma is here to help."

"Not all the time. What about getting an alert system? Something with a button you can push for help if you fall again."

There was a light knock at his bedroom door. "Harry? Detective Bradford is here." Emma's tone was apologetic.

"Ceci, I need to go."

"Promise me, Dad."

She had him cornered. "I promise, pumpkin. Love you." He ended the call before she chimed in about something else, then gripped his walker and went into the living room. He greeted Detective Bradford, who took a seat on the couch after Emma and Harry sat in the facing linen wingback chairs.

"Ms. Stockton told me about the intruders and your fall, Mr. Lancaster, but I want you to walk me through it." Harry was grateful for the detective's tone. It held no pity.

He recounted what happened and described the intruders as best he could, trying not to feel like a fool. "I was sure one of the boys was Conner. It was the way he carried himself. Conner's shoulders are usually hunched, and he hangs his head low. He walks with an awkward saunter."

"I'm going to talk to Conner and his parents as soon as I leave." From the tenor of the detective's voice, Harry guessed it would not be a pleasant afternoon for the Buchanans. "When I spoke to Conner earlier about being tossed out of a car, he said he was joking around with his friends and jumped out when it was barely moving."

Harry shook his head. "The car was not moving slowly, and he didn't jump out."

"I know. Don't worry, I'll get to the bottom of it." Detective Bradford started to stand, then glanced at Emma, back at Harry, then sat back down. "Why do I get the feeling there's something else?"

Emma's eyes widened, and after a pause she asked, "Are you sure Ms. Daniels's poisoning was accidental?" Harry met her gaze and subtly shook his head no. They had no real information to share, only hearsay and hunches.

Detective Bradford spoke firmly. "As I've said before that case is solved. Closed by professionals who know what they're doing. I don't want either of you entertaining fanciful ideas about detecting because you watch too much British television. There is nothing to investigate."

* * *

Emma led the detective to the door and slammed it behind him, hoping it bumped him along the way. *Serve him right.* He had been so rude and dismissive. And he was wrong. There was a killer lurking out there—she was sure of it.

For the rest of the day, she tamped down her frustration by focusing on Harry, trying everything to lure him out of the depression he'd slipped into since his fall. She made copious amounts of tea, served up BLTs with extra bacon (his favorite), speculated about Sue's death, and handed him several of the books he'd ordered on poisons, murder, and criminal investigation.

Harry didn't take any of the bait.

She was reluctant to leave that evening, but he repeatedly reassured her that he'd manage. Finally, he'd insisted, and since she was no longer flying to St. Louis, her mother had arranged appointments for her to try on wedding dresses. When she left, Emma told Harry she was just a phone call away.

* * *

Two hours later, Emma was decked in white in the middle of a swanky bridal boutique dressing room, trying to rally the strength to share her doubts about her upcoming marriage with her mom.

"Turn around," Emma's mother commanded. "Stand up straight. I can hardly tell the cut of the gown if you're slouching."

Emma straightened her spine, simultaneously wishing she'd grow one.

"It's perfect." Her mother clapped. Of the ten she'd donned, this was the fifth "perfect" one.

Emma glanced in the dressing room mirror. She had to admit, she looked good. The wedding dress had plunging V-necklines in the front and back, and rows of pearls and crystals around the waist. Its sequined underskirt was topped by a layer of tulle. She looked like a fairy princess, though perhaps one doubtful about her happily ever after.

"More perfect than the other ones?" she asked.

"Oh, it's so hard to tell. Every dress is lovely on you. That Blake Derrickson is one lucky man. Beauty and brains." Her mom clasped her hands. "I'm so happy for you. And for our families. You're the *perfect* couple."

Emma had never seen her mom so delighted. Emma's siblings' weddings and the birth of her grandchildren had brought her mother joy. But she was the last child to be married, and to the son of her best friend. It was impossible to top.

But Emma could not forever hold her peace.

"Mom—" Her mother dreamily looked at her, likely fantasizing Emma's white-picket-fence future. "I'm not sure . . ." She tried to muster the strength to continue.

"About the dress?" Her mom waved as if shooing away a pesky fly. "I know, lots of glitter and shine, which isn't typically you, but it's so lovely."

Emma bit her lip, then looked around to make sure they were alone. "I'm not sure about the move."

Her mom waved away her words. "You'll love St. Louis." Her mom had never been.

"It's more than that, actually." *Just spit it out.* "I'm not sure about the wedding. Blake and I seem pretty different."

Her mother met her eyes. "Don't be ridiculous."

"Something doesn't feel right."

"Pshaw. Blake is smart, respectful, handsome, and has a promising career ahead of him. You're getting cold feet, that's all."

"That's what I thought at first. But we have different ideas for our futures. I don't know him as well as I thought I did. He's—"

"That's what's wrong with your generation. Always thinking there's something *better* out there."

"That's not what—"

"You won't find better than Blake." Wrinkles around her mother's mouth deepened as she pressed her lips together. "And you don't want to end up alone like me. You saw how lonely I got without your father."

"I did." Emma gave her mom's shoulders a loving squeeze and couldn't help but notice her engagement ring—glinting under the dressing room lights, daring her to continue. *It didn't even look right on her finger, too big, too showy.*

"It feels like Blake and I are rushing things. Maybe now isn't the right time."

"Right time?" Her mom's voice raised in pitch and Emma withdrew her hands. The saleswoman's head popped around the corner, her black glasses, platinum bouffant bun, and fuchsia lipstick hard to miss. She caught Emma's this-is-a-private-discussion glare and retreated.

"Emma Bethann Stockton . . ."

Whenever her mother used this tone, and the expression associated with it, Emma and her siblings referred to their mom, Bridget Catherine, as BC. As in *Did she go all BC on you?* or *I got the wrath of BC*. She braced herself.

"You are one month away from being twenty-nine years old and not getting any younger. Your sister and brothers are all happily married with children. I'm sure they had hesitations, but they got past them. You will too. And now I have six beautiful grandkids. But I want more. My friend Mary Kate has eight."

Frustration kneaded Emma's chest. "It's not a competition, Mom."

"Hmph. You don't know Mary Kate." Her mom shook a stern finger at her. "Put aside your doubt. What you're feeling are normal jitters. Trust me, you're going to have a *wonderful* life being Mrs. Blake Derrickson."

The saleswoman walked another mother-daughter duo into the dressing area, her arms full of flowy white dresses. She said to Emma in a perky tone, "You look *stunning* in that dress." The newly arrived mother-daughter duo added their approvals, causing the saleswoman's face to shine.

Emma could almost see the sales commission fairies dancing around the saleswoman's head, frolicking from shoulder to shoulder. She envisioned squashing a few. "I need to think about it."

"You *need* to make a decision," her mom chided. "These dresses are selling fast. You're running out of time."

Her mother's words hit home. She *was* running out of time. If she was going to say something to Blake, she had to do it soon.

Emma sighed. Without saying a word, she returned to the dressing room to change into jeans and a sweatshirt.

While rehanging the delicate dress, its long train knocked over the dressing room's stool. Her purse and its contents splayed on the floor.

She swore under her breath and began retrieving her things. Gum, wallet, cell phone, pen (that no longer worked), two Starbursts (that came from who knows where). She needed to be more organized.

Something in her brain pinged. Righting the stool, she sat down to think.

An image of Ms. Daniels's kitchen flashed before her. The books on foraging stacked on the counter for easy consultation, as were the pharmacy instructions for each medication. Some people immediately threw the instructions away without even consulting them; Ms. Daniels had kept them right next to the pill bottles.

Would a woman that organized and careful—who stored books on foraging right there in the kitchen for easy reference—be haphazard enough to pick some random plant and eat it without being positive about what it was?

The answer hit her like a ton of bricks falling from the Rhodes State Office Tower downtown. *No.*

Emma pulled out her cell phone to call Harry. His home line rang and rang, and he didn't answer his cell. She sent several "Call me, ASAP" texts.

He didn't respond.

Chapter Sixteen

Thursday morning, Harry awoke tangled in his gray sheets, feeling like he'd been run over by a bus. Sleep had been elusive. Fears had haunted him all night. Fears of diminishing health, fears of increasing age, and fears of the resulting limitations.

After getting cleaned up, he was on his way to the kitchen with his walker when Emma burst in, barely stopping to close the door. Her hair was pulled back into a messy ponytail, and she wore the same jeans and sweater she'd worn yesterday, though it was hard to tell, her outfits looked interchangeable.

"Do you *ever* check your voicemail or cell phone?"

"Is something wrong?"

She rushed past him to the kitchen table and dumped her jacket and purse onto a chair, he followed slowly with his walker. "I called and called. Why didn't you call me back?" Her words tumbled over each other. "You are *never* going to believe this. I was shopping with my mom for wedding dresses—"

"You finally admitted your doubts about the wedding?"

"*What*?" Her mouth dropped open. "How did you—"

"Your facial expressions and body language when the topic came up made it clear, the way you redirected conversation, the fact that you haven't touched the wedding magazines in days . . ."

As soon as the words were out of his mouth, he wanted to take them back. He was beyond overstepping and braced for her response.

But instead of hurt or anger, Emma laughed. "I bet your daughter didn't get away with anything."

"Want to talk about it?"

"No." Her face flew through several emotions. "Maybe. I don't know. Not now."

"Sorry. I didn't mean—"

She waved away his apology. "Listen. I figured out why I believe Sue's death wasn't accidental." She explained her conclusions, and he had to admit, it was a solid deduction, but hardly proof.

"You must have been a fabulous critical care nurse. Think you'll ever go back to it?"

"Stop"—she air-quoted with a smirk—"redirecting conversation."

"The case is closed, remember."

She huffed and stepped past him. "I'm starving."

"Emma." She stopped to look back at him. "Listen to your gut about the wedding and the move. Only *you* know what you need and want."

With a nod, she retreated into the kitchen.

Soon after breakfast, Harry sat in the sunroom, pretending to read while he thought about his second fall. The doorbell rang. Dread balled in his gut. If Diana had gotten wind that he'd fallen again . . .

From his club chair, he watched Emma open the door, then step aside to let in Milo.

"Harry, old coot," Milo boomed as he strode into the sunroom, exuberating a chumminess they'd never shared. Under a black leather jacket, he wore his usual T-shirt, designer jeans, and gold chain. "Diana told me about your fall. Wanted to see how you're doing." Milo sat on the ottoman and stretched his legs out in front of him. He wore black Ferragamo loafers, paired with navy socks decorated with corks and corkscrews.

Harry's mind kicked into gear, puzzling out how Diana had found out so quickly. The detective had said he was going to talk to Conner Buchanan and his parents about sneaking around in Harry's backyard. One of Diana's kitchen windows faced the Buchanans' house, and since Diana spent most of her time cooking, she'd likely seen the detective stop by. The Buchanans' phone had probably rung by the time the front door closed when he left. He sighed. All of Lakeview Estates probably knew by now.

"What'd the doc say?" Milo asked.

"Minor setback." The metal walker to the side of Harry's chair mocked him, and he nudged it away with his foot.

Milo then rattled on about his trucking business, residents on the lane, the Buckeyes' winning streak, and then Sue Daniels, her nosiness, and her affinity for being a thorn in his side—though his exact words hadn't been as politely put.

"I thought you didn't know Sue," Harry cut in, while wondering why Milo had stopped by.

"I didn't. But the entire neighborhood is gossiping about it. From what I hear, Sue fought with everyone."

"Who's everyone?" Harry pushed back, his grumpiness starting to win out over his manners. "She didn't fight with me."

"Well, she fought with the rest of our neighbors: Diana, Jimmy, Conner, David."

"I saw you arguing with David the other night." Harry hadn't planned on bringing that up, but it just came out.

Milo uncrossed his legs, sitting up slightly straighter. "When?"

"A few nights ago, on David's porch."

"That was nothing." He waved it away.

"It was heated enough for you to storm off afterwards."

Milo's eyes narrowed to reptilian slits. "Mind your own business, old man." He stood. "I should go. You look tired." Harry moved as if to let him out, but Milo stopped him. "I can find my way."

Harry pondered the abrupt departure as Milo left. Something was going on between Milo and David, and his mind began to spin over possibilities.

Emma stuck her head around the corner. "What was that about?"

He shrugged as the phone rang. Harry picked it up and barked, "Hello."

"Heavens to Betsy, sounds like you're pitching a right fit. Why is that nurse of yours not answering your phone?" asked Diana. He tried to respond, but she continued. "Linda told me about your fall. How ya doing?"

The day kept getting worse. "I'm fine."

"Now, we both know that's not true. The ink isn't even dry on your hospital release papers. I'll be by later today with a batch of fresh-out-of-the-oven gingersnaps and to have a word with that nurse of yours." Diana hung up before he could argue. He slammed the phone down.

"Tea?" Emma asked.

He shook his head and sank deeper into his chair. He couldn't pick which emotion bugged him the most. Humiliation, frustration, or despair?

* * *

The doorbell rang as soon as Emma finished preparing a snack for Harry. He'd said he didn't want anything, but she figured he needed perking up.

He had been grumpy all day. If that hadn't been frustrating enough, Blake had texted to say he was extending his stay in St. Louis—he'd be back Tuesday instead of tomorrow. There were more apartments he wanted to check out. And she was busy trying to figure out how to voice her doubts about the life he was planning for them.

Emma opened the door to find Diana, and her exasperation rose. The woman could toss out backhanded compliments faster than a Vegas croupier could deal cards. "Hi, Ms. Middleton. Harry's not taking visitors. Said he wanted to be left alone."

"Nonsense." Diana pushed past her then handed her a plate of deliciously fragrant gingersnaps. "I baked these for Harry."

"I don't think—"

But Diana marched past her toward the sunroom. "Oh, Lordy. Harry, you look too weak to whip a gnat. What happened?" Emma walked to the kitchen table to set down the gingersnaps, then crossed her arms, her blood pressure rising.

She didn't hear his reply, but Diana's voice was crystal clear. "Now what on earth made you go outside at night? And in the *rain*? Do you not have a lick of sense? A man your age can't do such things."

Emma guessed Diana was Harry's age or older, yet the woman spoke to him as if he was ancient. She walked into the sunroom. "Would you like tea?"

"I'd prefer coffee." In less than two minutes, Diana had managed to push about four of Emma's buttons. That had to be a record.

She strode off to the kitchen. While the doors to the sunroom were open, Emma couldn't make out their conversation. She tapped her foot, waiting for the coffee to brew.

Five minutes later, Emma carried a tray of refreshments into the sunroom and joined them by sitting on the ottoman.

After her first sip, Diana returned to her lecture. "You need to be prudent, Harry. Back in June, there was a man at our church, 'bout five years younger than you, who fell. The doctors thought he was fine, but now he's on death's door."

Emma wondered how the fall was related to his demise, but Diana didn't elaborate.

"And my Aunt Madge, God rest her soul, fell when she was eighty-five. Never recovered. It took less than a month for her to die." Diana took another sip and puckered, likely from the coffee's strength—thanks to nursing school, Emma made it strong enough to fuel a rocket.

Sadly, this did not stop the older woman's litany. "Now, my younger brother, Vern, fell when he was sixty. He passed away three years ago. Granted, he died from a heart attack."

At least Diana caught this inconsistency. Emma was still trying to figure out how she thought the other people's falls caused their deaths. She glanced at Harry. He'd sunk deeper into his chair.

The older woman continued, seemingly not noticing her effect on Harry. "You've got both of your oars in the water. Stop actin' like you just got the one."

Time for an intervention. Emma stood. "Ms. Middleton, I think Harry's had enough visiting for the day. Thank you for stopping by. I'll get your purse and coat."

Not waiting for a response, she went to the closet and retrieved Diana's items. She waited in the foyer, holding Diana's belongings out to her.

"Well, I *never*." Diana stood and pointed her index finger at Harry. "Stop taking risks."

Emma's exhales became louder, like a huffing bull before it charged.

"Thank you," Diana said in a truculent tone when she accepted her coat and purse. Emma escorted the older woman out the door, then headed back to the sunroom.

Harry looked beaten and defeated.

"Diana is not a nurse. She has no idea what she is talking about." She tried to slow her breathing and calm her voice. "Yes, aging is an inevitable physical process. There will be limitations as you age. That's natural and to be expected. But there's a difference between physical limitations, and limits we set in our minds. You're smart enough to make the distinction."

"I've fallen twice now within months. Who's to say it won't keep happening? Maybe it is best for me to play it safe and stick with the walker."

His downtrodden tone made her emotions boil. "Poppycock!"

Harry blinked, then his lips formed a whisper of a smile. "Poppycock?" *Where had she pulled that word from, Mary Poppins?*

"You seem too refined for four-letter words. I wanted to say bullshit."

"That's eight letters."

"Stop trying to change the subject."

"I've heard explicative language before. I've even used it."

"That is exactly why I said poppycock. Who says explicative language?" She assumed her stern-nurse stance. "Regardless of what word I use, we're adding strength training to your physical therapy, and in a week, you're moving back to the cane."

His barely perceptible amusement faltered. She caught sight of a picture hanging on the wall behind him and suddenly knew how to bring him around.

"And don't forget you fell this time because you were *knocked down*. What would Margaret say about you wallowing in self-pity?"

Harry flinched.

"I bet she wouldn't put up with it for one minute."

"You're right," he conceded. "She'd have none of this."

"Good. Get your walker, we're taking a stroll around the lane. Your body will stiffen up if we don't keep you moving."

He stood, and she tried not to feel guilty about the look on his face. But her comment had pried him from the chair. Now she had to encourage him to keep him investigating. The police had closed the case, and she didn't want to try to solve it alone given the possibility that one of Harry's neighbors was a stone cold killer.

Chapter Seventeen

"Look, there's Milo." Emma pointed to the convertible Ferrari in the lane adjacent to Harry's SUV the following day.

Harry shrugged, his glum mood persisting.

The traffic light was still red, so she edged toward the sedan in front of them for a closer look. Milo's bald head glistened in the sun. Pungent, billowing smoke from his cigar filtered through the SUV's open windows. "Wonder where he's going?"

She got another shrug, and her concern for him verged toward irritation. Whether he liked it or not, she would get him out of his self-pity. Might as well start now.

"Let's follow him."

"What?"

"Out of all your neighbors, he's the roughest. If I had to guess, he's the one who killed Ms. Daniels. Let's follow him."

Harry turned in his seat. He didn't have to speak; his look said it all.

The light turned green, and as much as Emma was afraid of driving Harry's car, she committed to following Milo through the dense traffic. She didn't really think Milo would do anything suspicious or they would learn anything by following him, but she needed to get Harry out of his head.

Cars arced through the intersection from the freeway exit to the main thoroughfare. As soon as Milo completed the turn, he gunned it but didn't get far because of the truck in front of him. Emma switched to Milo's lane and kept about a hundred feet back.

They trailed Milo up Route 23, past gas stations, car lots, bargain stores, and fast-food chains. Instead of turning in the expected direction of Lakeview Estates, Milo continued straight. When they passed the turnoff, she could feel Harry looking at her.

Minutes later, Milo got tired of putzing along behind the truck, and in three quick maneuvers, hopscotched the Ferrari around it. The sleek car's engine roared with each move.

"Crap." She was going to lose him. Emma gunned Harry's car, which lurched them ahead and threw her stomach into her back.

Before them, a battered pickup with a "HONK IF SOMETHING FALLS OFF" bumper sticker trundled along as they zoomed in. Harry audibly gulped as they sped toward it. Every muscle in Emma's body tensed.

Harry's hands braced the dashboard. "You're not going to—"

"Oh yes, I am." Her heart kicked up a gear and she revved the engine to slide the SUV over into the congested neighboring lane, then punched the SUV forward to slip back into the right lane just in front of the lumbering pickup with barely a foot to spare.

The pickup's horn blared. A thrill surged through her. She was Angelina Jolie in *Salt*, not safe and plodding Emma.

"Are you crazy?" Harry's right hand gripped the roll handle above the passenger door.

"There he is." Emma left one car between Harry's SUV and Milo's Ferrari. She decelerated to match Milo's speed. Her heart slowed and dropped back down into her chest.

They continued down a commercial strip. Milo tossed the cigar butt into weeds on the side of the road, then darted into the left-hand turn lane and roared through the turn as the green arrow shifted to yellow.

Without missing a beat, Emma followed suit, screeching the tires of Harry's car as she sped through the light to make the left-hand turn on red.

"What are you doing?" Harry asked with exasperation. More progress; he hadn't responded with a shrug.

They snaked behind Milo's car through side streets that led to an upscale shopping district in Powell. A row of renovated, early twentieth-century brick and mortar buildings sprawled alongside the road under tall protective oaks. They passed a gourmet ice cream shop and glitzy-looking boutiques. Milo turned down a narrow alley.

"It leads to a parking lot," Harry said. "Go around the block. You can come into the lot from the side. That way you don't have to directly follow him."

She'd hooked him. She tried to mask a victorious smile. "Got it."

When they reached the gravel parking lot a minute later, Milo's car was nowhere to be seen. "Did we lose him?" she asked.

"He must still be in the alley. There are only two ways out of the lot, this lane and that alley." Harry pointed to a parking spot. "Park there."

Emma navigated Harry's SUV so the rear of his car was facing the alley and the back of the shops and restaurants that lined the main street. Through the rearview mirrors, they could see Milo standing in the alley next to his parked car, talking to a guy dressed in black. Milo was shaking his head, fingering the gold chain around his neck.

"Looks like they're disagreeing about something," Harry said when Milo started gesturing with both hands.

She rolled down the windows and strained to hear, but Milo and the man were too far away. The two kept conversing, then Milo looked up and down the alley, pulled out his wallet, and handed the guy money. The guy nodded, then descended through an open cellar door connected to the building, disappearing step by step.

"Wonder what that's about?"

"Don't know." Harry sounded genuinely interested. "I'm pretty sure that's the back of Valentina's. If you haven't been, they have the best arancini and cannoli outside of Sicily."

A hunger pang rippled through Emma's stomach, and she thought she caught a whiff of marinara sauce and fresh baked bread.

"If Milo was picking up food," Harry continued, "he would have used the main entrance. There were open parking spots in front when we drove by."

Minutes later, the man reappeared from the cellar stairs. He carried a large wooden crate. Both men looked furtively around, then Milo popped his truck for the man to put the crate into it.

The two men shook hands. Milo closed his trunk and got back behind the wheel. The huge guy vanished back into the cellar, closing the metal doors behind him with a clang. Emma turned on Harry's SUV at the same time Milo's car engine roared to life.

"What do you think was in the box?" she asked.

"Who knows? But they acted suspiciously about whatever it was."

"Let's see where he goes now." They followed Milo at a discreet distance, then through winding streets to the entrance of Lakeview Estates. Milo turned in, but Emma kept going.

"Now where are we off to?"

"To get Grace a raspberry pie. You promised, remember? The bakery is down the street and when we drop it off, maybe she'll have more to say about Sue's secrets. Besides, this little adventure has made me hungry."

* * *

Emma opened the door to the bakery, Tickled Pink, and the smell of vanilla, butter, and chocolate swept over her. Her shoulders relaxed as she breathed in deeply. She crossed the store's pink and white tiled floor to examine the glass case filled with cakes, pies, cookies, doughnuts, and pastries in enticing displays.

Minutes later, she returned to the car with a pink pie box and a small pink bag, proud she hadn't gone on a huge sugar spending spree—just a pie for Grace and two brownies. Five minutes later, she parked in Buchanans' drive so the visit would be easier for Harry. "I'll get your walker."

"You can drop off the pie. I'll stay in the car."

"The visit will do you good."

"I'd rather not."

"Then why don't you go home? Your house is right there. The walk next door will give you a bit more exercise."

"I'll wait here." And then, heaven help her, he gave her that blasted shrug.

"*Fine.* But I'll be there for a while. I want to get a better idea of Grace's mental state. I might have some recommendations for the Buchanans on full-time memory care when the time comes." She grabbed the pie box and headed for the Buchanans' front door.

After Emma rang the doorbell for the second time, Grace answered, wearing a retro patterned sack dress, which she'd probably bought when it was first in style. "You have red hair." Her craggy voice was full of suspicion.

"Yes, I'm Harold's caregiver. You know, the man who lives next door?" She held up the pink pie box. "I have a raspberry pie for you."

A slow smile spread across the woman's face. She looked from Emma's hair to the box, back to her hair, back to the box.

"Thank you." With the speed of a snapping turtle's bite, Grace snatched the pie and slammed the door in Emma's face, whacking her on the nose.

"Friggin' frack." Tears welled in her eyes from the pain, and she fought back a growl of irritation.

Harry didn't ask her why she returned so quickly and remained silent during the thirty-second drive to his house. While they waited for the garage door to open, a blue Crown Vic pulled up behind them. Emma parked in the garage, then retrieved her purse and the pink bag from the center console. "I'll get your walker."

Detective Bradford joined them as she opened the SUV's tailgate door. "Mr. Lancaster, Ms. Stockton." His suit had been replaced with faded jeans and a pine-green wool sweater that made Emma itch by looking at it.

She reached to get out the walker while juggling the bag and her purse. The detective stopped her. "I'll get that."

He set the walker down by Harry. "I wanted to give you an update on Conner. It was one of his friends who pushed you down. He didn't mean to hurt you. He just didn't want to get caught. Conner and his friend have been dealing marijuana at school and that night they were exchanging money and product. Conner had tried to stop, but his dealer convinced him to keep at it by tossing him out of a moving car. Minor misdemeanors and the first offense for both Conner and his friend. But they've been warned."

"Hopefully this will straighten Conner out," Harry said.

But Emma didn't pity the boy. "He could have refractured your hip. Or worse."

"Well, I don't think the boy will bother you anymore, Mr. Lancaster." The detective readied to go. "Have a good evening."

Without thinking, she shoved the pink bag in her left hand toward him, making her giant engagement ring glitter. "It looks like you could use a pick-me-up."

He peered inside. "Brownies, my favorite. Thank you." His expression teetered between gratitude and suspicion.

She hoped the treat would buy her and Harry some goodwill for when they eventually shared with him what they were learning about Ms. Daniels's death. Because Emma knew in her heart she and Harry were going to solve this case. It was just a matter of time.

* * *

Emma sat in her car that evening, staring at one of the ornate iron streetlamps that dotted Harry's neighborhood. She'd parked outside the circumference of its light on a street that paralleled part of Lakeview Lane. Through her open window, she could hear tree leaves rustle in the chilly breeze. Serenading crickets accompanied the clicking of her car's engine as it cooled.

This was crazy. Really crazy.

Despite Milo's odd behavior, Harry had been withdrawn all afternoon, with his nose buried in some academic book. She needed to reignite his curiosity about the murder.

She picked up her cell phone and reread Blake's last text: "Found the perfect place. Details tomorrow." She'd called him in hopes of having an discussion about her doubts, but he hadn't answered, and she didn't want to send him the dreaded *We need to talk* text. No one needed that.

Despite the crickets' peaceful song, she sighed. She thought about that pair of Nordstrom's shoes she'd worn to her older brother Michael's wedding. It had been a black-tie affair, and Emma had found the perfect sandals: elegant silver with a four-inch heel and a thin jeweled strap that ran across the top of her foot. Sexy, flattering, and sophisticated.

They had pinched a bit when Emma first put them on, but they looked fabulous and matched her dress. As the night wore on, with each step and passing hour, they'd rubbed uncomfortably. By the end of the night, she was barefoot and blistered, the shoes abandoned on the side of the dance floor. This is what her relationship with Blake felt like—like she was trying to wear shoes that looked pretty but didn't fit.

Cool, fresh air blew through the car window. She gathered her keys and cell phone, then saw the phone's battery was almost dead, so put back it into the center console. After rolling up the windows, she got out and propelled herself down the street, looking around to assure herself that no one was watching.

Cloud cover blocked the moon, obscuring her path, which was dimly lit by the streetlamps and light that trickled out from the windows of the charming homes she passed. She flipped up the hood of her dark gray sweatshirt, which she'd paired with matching yoga pants to help her blend into the night.

She slowed her steps a few homes down. The woods behind the houses were too thick to peer through, but she was pretty sure she was almost directly behind the duplex where Milo lived. Harry had lost interest in Milo's mysterious errand, but she hadn't. The exchange had looked suspicious, and if she could find some compelling evidence, he'd investigate again.

At the edge of the next yard was a line of strategically placed bushes to help provide cover. She slipped off the street and beelined for the trees. Her brain told her this was a fool's errand, but she kept her feet moving.

Ground cover was sparse at the edge of the woods. As she progressed, the brush got denser, the crunching of the leaves beneath her feet louder, and her surroundings darker.

Emma pushed on, wondering how far it could be to Milo's house. Concentrating, she looked for a light to reveal the homes on the other side.

Something jostled to her left, and she jumped sideways with a squeal.

Fortunately, she'd sounded like a wounded cat. Sweat formed on her palms, despite the nip in the air.

Then a branch ripped across her ankle. She yelped. Subtle as a marching band.

She swore under her breath and bent down to check it out. It would leave an angry lash. Lesson number one: when spying on people, thick jeans are a better choice than cropped yoga pants if traipsing through the woods.

When she tripped over a log that launched her headfirst into a nearby tree a minute later, she realized lesson number two: bring a flashlight or remember to charge your cell phone so it can light the way. She silently swore again and rubbed her forehead.

Light flickered through the trees in front of her. She retucked her hair under her hood and crept to the tree line, doing her best to keep the leaf crunching and twig cracking to a minimum. As she neared, she could make out two separate patios and two rear doors. *Bingo.*

Ms. Valucci and the Patels both lived in standalone homes, and if her bearings were right, this duplex between them was the one shared by Milo and Sue Daniels.

Light streamed from Milo's ground floor windows, where the blinds were wide open. Ms. Daniels's side remained dark. Although Milo's yard was about forty feet deep, Emma had a clear view of his living room and kitchen; Milo was nowhere to be seen.

A lone pine grew in the center of his yard. A perfect vantage point.

She checked his windows again. Not seeing anything, she raced across the well-manicured grass and ducked behind the tree, waiting for the outdoor light to flick on because she'd been seen.

But nothing changed. Emma settled into a comfortable stance with a view between the branches and peered.

And peered.

And peered.

An hour later, Emma restlessly shuffled from one foot to another. She needed to pee and was bored. Who knew spying could be so uninteresting?

Every now and then, Milo's head and torso would float between windows as lights turned off and on. But other than that, nothing. It had been a colossal waste of time.

What'd she been thinking? That he'd come out onto the back porch and confess into the night? Or laugh maniacally in front of a window while holding a bottle marked poison?

Emma blew out a horse-lipped sigh, tired, defeated, and ready to go home. When she turned to retrace her steps, light poured across the backyard.

Crap. Had she been seen?

She dropped to the ground and scurried under the pine tree's lowest limbs into the damp, cold earth. Her heart pounded against her chest. Something scratched her face, and despite her hood, her hair tangled in the branches.

Images of the insects that lived under the tree flashed through her head, and she could almost feel a spider skittering across her face. Her entire body shuddered, and she fought every urge to scream.

Milo stepped outside, puffing on a cigar. A cell phone was glued to his ear.

". . . uh-huh. I heard you."

As he listened to the caller, he began pacing across the small concrete patio, which allowed six to seven steps in each direction.

"I. Heard. You." The cigar's tip glowed orange as Milo inhaled. "I'm telling you, it's no longer a problem."

The pattern continued: pacing, puffing, and angry retorts. He reminded her of a tiger at the zoo. Trapped in a cage, muscles taut, ready to lash out.

Then Milo bent down and crushed the tip of the cigar into the concrete patio, violently snuffing it out. She burrowed farther into the ground.

"I'll make it crystal clear since you're an idiot." He turned toward the house, and though his back was to her, his voice got louder. "I took care of her. She's out of the picture. Permanently. *Capiche*?"

Emma felt her mouth drop open, then slammed it shut for fear of something crawling inside. *Was he admitting to killing Sue?*

He turned back in her direction, and she held her breath. Her heart pounded louder than horses' hooves hitting the racetrack at Scioto Downs.

In the dim light, she could make out the sneer on his face. His voice grew softer. "And if you're not careful, I'll take care of you too."

Chapter Eighteen

Harry was sitting in the sunroom the next morning, leafing through one of the recent books he'd purchased when a noise at the front door made him look up. Emma wasn't due for another hour but it was her, a jumble of excited energy, wildly looking around. "Harry? Harry?"

She caught sight of him, closed the door, and rushed over, pulling off her windbreaker along the way. "I know who killed Ms. Daniels."

Her hair was disheveled, and a thin red scratch ran across her face. While she'd never dressed up for the job, today she was even more casual in an oversized blue sweatshirt and black sweatpants. She reminded him of Ceci when he'd pick her up from summer camp: scraped, scruffy, and brimming with enthusiasm to tell him about her adventures.

"What are you talking about?"

Emma dropped her jacket and purse on the ottoman, the air around her jittering. "Last night I spied on Milo."

He wasn't sure he'd understood correctly. "What?"

She beamed. "I parked on Nightingale Drive, snuck through the woods, and hid behind a pine tree in Milo's backyard."

That explained the scratch. Harry nodded slowly, wondering what had come over her.

"I waited *forever* for something to happen," her words grew rapid, "but eventually Milo came outside while talking on his cell phone. He told whoever it was that he'd," she moved her fingers to air quote, "'taken care of things.'" Emma shuffled in place from one foot to another. "Then he said," she air quoted again, "'She's no longer a problem.'"

"Did he say anything else? Anything that would point directly to Sue?"

"No, but . . ."

"He could have been referring to any female. Maybe an employee."

"Pffft. Please." She gave him an eye roll that made Ceci's look tame. "He is *so* guilty. If Sue was blackmailing people, it'd likely be people she could easily keep an eye on. Which means the killer is someone on the lane. That someone is Milo."

"All we have is conjecture and hunches about a case that is closed." He stood and grabbed his walker, placing the book in his hand into the walker's basket. "I need some tea." He left the sunroom, suddenly irked, and not sure why.

"Hold on, I'll get it for you," Emma said in deflated tones.

In one swoop, Harry had crushed her joy. Regret settled on his shoulders. Feeling like a heel, he sat at the kitchen table and stewed.

Emma twitched and squirmed as she made breakfast. She couldn't seem to stand still. Minutes later, she brought over toast and a fruit bowl. When she placed it down, she jostled from foot to foot.

He studied her intently. She blinked, doing her best to look like nothing was wrong.

There was something she *wasn't* telling him about her trek through the woods.

Then it hit him. Evan had played in the surrounding woods when Ceci and her family came to visit this past summer. The poor little guy got the worst case of poison ivy Harry had ever seen. It was everywhere in the underbrush.

Despite his foul mood, he found himself smiling. "Anything else you want to tell me?"

She tried to feign confusion, while red dotted her cheeks. "Me, what? No." Her eyes doubled in size, reminding Harry of a frightened bush baby.

He took a bite of toast. In between bites, he added, "On the off chance you're interested, there's colloidal oatmeal and calamine lotion in the cabinet under the sink in the rear guest bedroom bath."

Her mouth opened, then closed. "How did you . . . ?"

"My grandson, Evan, an utter jumping bean after playing in the woods."

"I didn't have anything for poison ivy at home and rushed here this morning." She shot a longing glance toward the hallway off the sitting area that led to the guest rooms, then hustled in that direction. "I'll clean up the kitchen after I've taken an oatmeal bath."

Harry returned to his toast, amused. The book in his walker's basket caught his eye: *Bludgeonings, Poisonings, Stabbings, and Shootings: A Primer for Coroners on the Mechanics of Murder*. He picked it up to read while eating breakfast.

* * *

That night, Harry stood in the walk-in closet in his master bedroom, in front of the shelves where Mags had once kept her clothing. Now the area now housed other items Harry cherished: books.

As he read over the titles and tomes that had shaped his life and career, he thought about how many of his friends were working, and how much he still had to offer the world. Rather than sitting in self-pity—a state that Mags would have never tolerated—it was time to act. Tomorrow, he'd start applying for consulting jobs that interested him.

Feeling empowered, he thought about finding a way to encourage Emma to voice her concerns about her upcoming wedding. He doubted unsolicited fatherly advice would be appreciated. Heck, even Ceci resented it at times. Harry needed an unobtrusive way to get through to her.

He continued skimming book titles until an idea sparked. He broke into a slow grin. He selected a book, and when he passed through the foyer, left it on the hall table for Emma to find the next day.

That done, he returned to his chair in the sunroom and a half-eaten box of Tim Tams. The Patels had dropped off a get-well gift basket late that afternoon, with his favorite Australian cookies and his favorite Oolong tea. They'd promised to send their grandson Vihaan over for a visit after school one day this week because, they said, he was wonderful at evoking smiles.

Harry picked up a book about criminal law and prosecuting heinous crimes. It was fascinating, and despite the doubt and fear that had swept over him after his second fall, what Emma had overheard from Milo had piqued his interest. As did the mysterious wooden crate that Milo picked up in the alley behind Valentina's.

From the corner of his eye, he saw someone walking down the street and turned to get a better look. It was Diana, armed with a casserole and, most likely, the latest gossip.

He groaned. He wasn't in the mood. She meant well, but at times her words did knock him down rather than build him up.

To his surprise, she walked past his house. When she was no longer in view, he headed to his bedroom and the windows that looked off to the direction she'd gone. In his rush, he'd left the walker and instead grabbed the cane that Emma had placed near him in a not-so-subtle cue to leave the walker behind.

He pulled back his bedroom drapes to track Diana's path. She made her way up the drive to the duplex that held Jimmy's and David's units and knocked on Jimmy's door.

Once Diana went inside, Harry resumed his post in the sunroom. He caught sight of Diana heading home about forty-five minutes later, illuminated by headlights from a pale-colored sedan. The car pulled up to David's mailbox, put a parcel inside, then drove away.

Since Sue seemed to rub everyone the wrong way, Harry had assumed her death had been the result of something she had done. But there'd been strange things going on with David too: his argument with Milo and the mysterious parcels left in his mailbox.

Harry leaned back in his chair. Perhaps he and Emma were focusing on the wrong neighbor.

Chapter Nineteen

The next afternoon, Emma opened the door to a young boy with a big toothy grin and untamed black hair. "Hi, lady, I'm Vihaan." He carried a pink paper bag and was bundled in a red winter coat too heavy for the mild weather.

"Grandma and Grandpa Patel said Mr. Lancaster was sad, so they wanted me to bring him some cookies." He held up the bag. "They said I could have some too. I wanted double chocolate, but they got oatmeal raisin."

Emma was already smitten with the boy. "How nice of you. I'm Miss Emma. Let's go find Mr. Lancaster."

Inside, Harry sat ready at the kitchen table and greeted the boy while he took off his coat. When he smiled at Vihaan, he looked the epitome of a doting grandfather. Her kids, if she had them, would never know her father. The thought pierced her heart.

Vihaan handed her the bag, then climbed into a chair at the table. She went into the kitchen to get milk and put the cookies on a plate, deciding to heat them.

"Mr. Lancaster," Vihaan said as she placed the cookies into the microwave. "Grandma told me to tell you to feel better, so I'm doing it now in case I forget."

"Thank you. I hope you'll have some cookies with me." Vihaan nodded vigorously and looked Emma's way when the microwave dinged, his eyes brimming with anticipation.

Harry opened with the quintessential grandparent question. "How was school today?"

His face crumpled in distaste. "Can we talk about something else? I have homework and if we talk about it, you'll make me remember I gotta do it."

Emma agreed with his logic. When she approached the table with a tray of warm cookies and milk, his face lit up. She passed out plates as Harry passed out napkins.

"What would you like to talk about?" Harry asked.

"I really just came to eat cookies."

Harry chuckled and placed a cookie on Vihaan's plate "Then I think you'd better have one. So, what are you going to be for Halloween?"

"Either a superhero or a wizard." The boy picked up his cookie and took a bite.

"Tough choice," Harry said.

It'd been more than fifteen years since Emma had had to decide what to be for Halloween. Her last choice had been between dressing up as Avril Lavigne or the main character from *Black Swan*. She put a cookie on her plate.

"Yep, and—" Vihaan wiped his mouth with the back of his hand "—if I decide to be a superhero, I have to pick which one." This warranted a sigh, followed by a big swig of milk.

"Have you made your Christmas wish list yet?" she asked.

"Oh yeah, you got to do that early so Santa can get everything." She handed Vihaan a napkin to wipe off his milk mustache. The kid was adorable.

"These cookies are good, but I like the peanut butter and chocolate ones Ms. Daniels made better," Vihaan said in between bites, making Emma pause mid-chew. She'd forgotten the Patels had mentioned that.

Harry tilted his head. "You had snacks with Ms. Daniels?"

"Yup. Sometimes after school." His nose wrinkled. "Grandma and Grandpa's snacks are gross. Carrots and apples. But Grandma and Grandpa said Ms. Daniels is dead." Vihaan's bottom lip jutted out, but he kept eating. He was a boy after her own heart. She took another bite, relishing the cinnamon-oaty taste.

"Do you have toys like Ms. Daniels?" Vihaan asked. He didn't seem to mourn long.

Harry studied the boy. "What kind of toys?"

"Ms. Daniels had special glasses that let you see in the dark. And a pen that recorded things so you could play it back and hear it again. It was sooo cool."

Emma exchanged a glance with Harry.

"Did Ms. Daniels tell you why she had all those toys?" he asked.

Vihaan giggled. "To spy on people. Why else would you have spy tools?" He shook his head at the stupidity of grown-ups. "She also had toy boats and motorcycles. And some baby toys, but I'm too big for those."

"Toy boats and toy motorcycles?" Harry mumbled, half to himself.

"Yep. I asked if I could have a toy boat because it floated in water and was purple. That's my favorite color. But Ms. Daniels said she bought it for the motorcycle lady."

"Who's the motorcycle lady?" Emma asked.

"The old lady who lives next to Mister Seezak."

"Ms. Valucci?" Harry asked. "The woman with brown hair who lives in the gray house?"

"Yep." Vihaan nabbed another cookie.

Harry returned his cookie to his plate, without taking a bite. "Why did Ms. Daniels call her friend the motorcycle lady?" *And why would Sue get a toy boat for her?* Emma thought.

"Dunno. I asked Ms. Daniels if she could get Ms. Valchi to give me a motorcycle ride, but she said Ms. Valchi didn't have one anymore. Ms. Daniels said Ms. Valchi got rid of it when she got fancy and left where she grew up."

The boy nibbled his cookie, and for the next several minutes, Harry asked questions to figure out what Ms. Daniels had meant, but the boy didn't have any other useful information.

Several cookies later, Vihaan left, with Emma hoping he'd still be hungry for dinner.

She started cleaning up the kitchen table. "Why do you think Ms. Daniels called Rachel the motorcycle lady? And why did she have toys? I thought she didn't have kids."

"She didn't, as far as I know." He pulled his cell phone out of his cardigan pocket and started typing. "I'll see if I can find out where Rachel is from. If it's close, maybe we can take a trip there tomorrow."

The grandfather clock chimed four times. Emma's relief that Harry was interested in the case again was displaced by a fear of being late. "Oh, shoot. My mom and I are visiting possible reception venues tonight. Mind if I leave early?"

She'd convinced herself to try talking to her mom again about her wedding concerns. The cookies churned in her stomach, and she wished she hadn't eaten them.

"I don't mind at all." Harry's eyes remained on his phone.

Emma finished loading the dishwasher. "See you tomorrow." She waved, then went to collect her purse from the hall table and froze when the title of the book sitting under it registered.

She walked back toward the kitchen table and held up the book. "What in the *heck* are you reading?"

He seemed surprised by her question. "It's one of my favorite anthropological studies. Why?"

"Wha . . ." She couldn't finish a word, let alone a sentence. She looked again at the title. *Wombs and Alien Spirits*. "What is it about?" She was almost too afraid to ask.

"It examines the role and position of women in northern Sudan and how they can express their opinions and make demands in ways that are socially acceptable, despite the cultural constraints against them. Basically, it's about women finding their voice."

She scrutinized his all-too-innocent face, then returned the book to the hall table and walked out the door.

Act II

"People are never one thing. Every person is multifaceted and inherently complex, with identities, behaviors, and motivations that change depending on context. This has methodological implications for ethnographic fieldwork. You must observe individuals in an array of settings to understand how they navigate different roles. Additionally, engagement should be longitudinal and triangulated to help verify findings. Reflexivity is crucial: remain aware that how people present themselves to you is contextual; they may emphasize certain aspects of identity depending on how they perceive your role."—from *Lessons from the Field* by Harry Lancaster, Ph.D.

Act II

Chapter Twenty

Emma scarfed down breakfast the next morning: two eggs, bacon, toast, sausage, and half a grapefruit, while Harry sat on the other side of the kitchen table, barely nibbling a piece of toast, captivated by the printouts he was reading.

Stress increased her appetite. Blake's mom had joined her and her mother last night, so she hadn't had the intended chat with her mom. Nor had she gotten through to Blake on his cell phone, and what she had to say couldn't be relayed in a voicemail or a text. Everything was careening out of control.

Patricia had pulled some strings, and they were able to secure the Woodside Country Club for their reception. It was only five miles south of St. Francis Catholic church, which just happened to be available for their ceremony on their preferred date. The wedding task force had decided on a rustic, Italian-themed wedding and Valentina's, the posh Italian restaurant in Powell, would cater the food. Deposits were due soon.

Her mom and Patricia had designed save-the-date cards for the fast-approaching wedding. They'd be mailed within the week. And Blake had texted that morning to say he'd signed the lease to their new apartment—an apartment she hadn't seen—and was headed home.

"We should get going," Harry said, interrupting Emma's ruminations. "Rachel's hometown, Tiffin, is about an hour and a half from here. I've already called my physical therapist to tell them I can't make today's appointment."

She read the cover of the report in Harry's hand. "Why are you reading about health care in South Asia?"

"I like keeping up to date on things."

Was there a topic he wasn't interested in? She crammed the final bite of toast into her mouth so she could clear the table. Two hours later, they were driving down a tree-lined street with large, well-kept Victorian homes. The trees were at their height of changing color and the sky a crystal blue.

"What's your plan?" Emma slowed the car so she could enjoy the scenery.

"I thought we'd check out the downtown area. Rachel owns a fashionable boutique, so perhaps she did something similar before moving to Columbus."

"That's not exactly a plan. I thought you Googled her, so we'd have a place to start. I hope we didn't drive this far for nothing."

"I did Google her, but I didn't find much other than a couple newsletters from the Tiffin's Ladies' Auxiliary Club, where Rachel was featured in their 'Successful Women of Tiffin' column. Turn right up here. It'll take us to the commercial district."

The main street in historic Tiffin consisted of picturesque brick buildings and colorful shop signs, with a smattering of pedestrians milling about. After Emma anxiously parallel parked—a nerve-wracking endeavor in Harry's expensive car—they got out and started wandering.

There were six clothing boutiques in the four-block downtown area, and they decided to hit those first. Emma perused racks while Harry chatted with shopkeepers to see if they knew the woman from Tiffin who ran La Conchessa in downtown Columbus.

Shop after shop, they were told "No." On the second to the last clothing store, which mainly sold tunics, big jewelry, and leggings, they finally got a hit.

"You know Rachel Valucci?" Harry asked the sixtysomething shopkeeper. She gazed at him with wistful brown eyes highlighted with blue eye shadow. Emma pretended to keep browsing as she eavesdropped.

"Heard of her." The shopkeeper ruffled her yellow hair. Peach rouge dotted her cheeks, and she wore a leopard print tunic with black tights over her thin frame. Emma liked leopard print but didn't think she had the confidence to pull it off.

"My younger sister went to school with her," the shopkeeper continued with a smile. "But I think she had some other name at the time—Rachel, not my sister. And then, when my sister opened a beauty shop, Rachel worked for her for a while. Then she met some rich guy and left town—Rachel, not my sister. My sister still has the beauty shop."

"What's the name of the shop?" Harry upped her smile by adding a dash of charm.

"Betty Lou's Beauty Bar. It's next door." The shopkeeper turned to Emma. "You know, hon, I've got just the thing for you. Something to set off those pretty eyes and that shapely figure of yours." The woman examined her from head to toe. "Back in a tick."

The shopkeeper disappeared behind a rear door. Emma looked around at the tunics with dread. They looked great on tall, thin women, and while she was above average in height, she was also above average in weight.

"Here you go," the older woman said when she reappeared, then shoved a rose-colored peplum top and cream capri pants into Emma's hands. She placed her hand on Emma's back and gently pushed her toward the changing room. "Go on now."

On the other side of the dressing room curtain, the shopkeeper spoke to Harry. "You must be so proud of your daughter. She's lovely and seems so nice. I've got an eligible nephew if she's looking." Emma imagined the shopkeeper giving Harry a matchmaker's wink.

"Emma is lovely. More importantly, she's intelligent, kind, and compassionate. But your nephew will have to keep looking. She's engaged."

The shopkeeper cackled. "Worth a shot."

Emma changed from her jeans and sweatshirt, fighting back tears. Harry's comments were sweet, and they made her realize how much she missed her father and his loving support. Her mom supported her, in her own way, but her dad had always accepted Emma for who she was.

"Take these too." The shopkeeper shoved a pair of linen wedge shoes and a layered gold necklace through the curtain.

There was no way everything would fit. The woman hadn't asked her size, thankfully, since Harry was standing there. When Emma finished changing, she turned to face the mirror. The outfit was too dressy for her messy ponytail, but she had to admit, it was flattering. She stepped outside the curtain.

The shopkeeper whistled. "Wow. That's a loss for my nephew. It's perfect."

"The outfit does suit you," Harry said. "Let me get it for you? My treat. A thank-you for helping me out the other night." The shopkeeper grinned and offered to bag Emma's jeans and sweater so she could "show off her new duds."

Twenty minutes later, Emma wondered if Harry bought the outfit so she'd feel compelled to get a blowout and makeover at Betty Lou's Beauty Bar. "It's our main lead on Rachel," he'd said. "I can hardly go in and get that done myself."

So, while Harry drank tea at the café across the street, Emma sat in a salon chair, undergoing what Betty Lou had promised would be a "metamorphosis." She deserved a raise.

Emma yelled over the hair dryer as Betty Lou pulled on her locks, "Your sister said you know Ms. Valucci, the woman in Columbus who owns La Conchessa."

Betty Lou was a near twin of her shopkeeper sister, makeup and all, but an inch or two taller. Oddly enough, she wore a black top with leopard skin leggings, and Emma bet they'd coordinated it.

"Yeah, but she didn't go by Rachel back then," Betty Lou bellowed. "She changed her name to Rachel after that husband of hers died. We knew her as Rita Mae. Rita Mae Banaszynski."

Rita Mae? She hoped they were not pursuing the wrong woman. "Your sister said Rachel, I mean, Rita Mae, worked for you." Betty Lou tugged her head back.

"Yeah, but not for long. She was a fabulous stylist—that is, when she decided to come into work. Rita Mae was a partier, hung out with a biker gang from Toledo. Had her own purple Harley-Davidson Sportster 883 SuperLow and went to Sturgis every year. Don't think that woman owned anything but black leather."

Emma suppressed a sigh. This was definitely the wrong woman.

The enthusiastic hairdresser pulled on her hair again. "The next summer, Rita Mae went up to Cedar Point and met this rich Italian dude in the beer garden. She got all snobby after that. When they got hitched, she became Mrs. Valucci and moved to some chichi neighborhood in Cleveland."

The hair dryer lowered in speed, and Betty Lou continued. "I heard she offed her husband but beat the rap. He died in a boating accident, and for a while, the police thought his death was suspicious. But they couldn't prove anything. After that mess cleared, Rita Mae inherited the lot, and she changed her name and packed up and moved to Columbus. Set up that highfalutin clothing shop of hers as Ms. Rachel fancy-pants Valucci." She turned off the hairdryer and stepped aside so Emma could view the mirror.

"My hair . . ." Emma raised her hands to touch the shiny, flowing curls that stylishly fell across her shoulders and back. She was shocked. If only she could style her hair like this. "It's beautiful."

"I knew you'd like it." Betty Lou beamed.

Emma turned her head to catch her hair at different angles and noticed a four by six photo in the bottom corner of the mirror. There were four women with their arms around each other smiling at the camera. The woman on the far right wore black leather pants and a black leather bustier. She had spiked chestnut hair. There was something about her face that seemed familiar. Emma leaned closer.

It *was* Rachel Valucci.

"Now, you just need a touch of makeup." Betty Lou snared a bag of supplies and got to work. Emma could hardly sit still as Betty Lou worked her magic. When she finally finished, Emma barely glanced in the mirror.

"Looks great." She paid with Harry's credit card, then rushed out of the shop and across the street to the café, trying not to twist her ankle in her new wedges.

Once inside, Emma went straight to Harry's table. Predictably, a near-empty cup of tea sat next to an uneaten slice of peach pie.

He glanced up from his cell phone. "Wow. You look lovely."

"Thanks." She sat down and ignored the pie despite its calls to her. "You are not going to believe what I found out."

* * *

As Emma drove back to Lakeview Estates, Harry used his cell phone to do an online search for Rita Mae and what had happened to her husband in Cleveland. All Emma had supplied for her last name was Banana-ski, which clearly wasn't the correct spelling. He eventually got close enough, and numerous searched results popped up.

"Found it."

"Read it out loud," Emma begged, in a rare instance of looking away from the road.

Harry did a quick read to himself first, which was interrupted with at least six exclamations of "What?" from Emma. He began summarizing with the headline: "Man Dies While Boating. Accident or Foul Play?"

The ten-year-old article outlined how Rachel and her late husband Giovanni Patrizio Valucci had been boating one July afternoon on Lake Erie. It'd been a weekday with little traffic on the water. Around four PM, the US Coast Guard got a distress call from Rachel, saying her husband had tripped, knocked his head, and fallen overboard near Kelleys Island State Park. She hadn't been able to find him in the water.

After a boat and helicopter search by the Coast Guard and the Ohio Department of Natural Resources, Giovanni's body had been found. The County Coroner ruled the cause of death as drowning. However, according to the article, the police had questioned Rachel several times. In the end, her husband's death was ruled accidental.

"There's a photo," Harry said. "It's definitely the Rachel Valucci who lives on Lakeview Lane." In the image, a youthful Rachel stood outside a police station with her head held high. She wore a fitted white dress and high-heeled white sandals.

How had he not heard about this before? Since he hadn't, there was no way Diana Middleton knew.

"Talk about blackmail material," Emma said. "Gossip like this might stop wealthier clients from shopping at her boutique."

Harry sent the article from his phone to his printer at home, then printed five other articles on the boating accident. When the subject was exhausted, Emma changed the topic and started rambling about a diet she was thinking of trying.

"It involves a lot more kale than I'm used to eating, which is like none, but I want to start taking better care of myself. I need to stop stress eating and . . ."

He didn't think she needed to lose weight, but after living with Mags and Ceci, he knew that his reassurances on this topic would not be heard.

When they pulled up to his house, Detective Bradford's Ford Crown Vic was parked out front.

"Uh-oh." Harry's heart sank. Had someone else been murdered?

Emma's face turned pink. "I texted the detective before we left Tiffin. We need to tell him about Rachel and all the other things we've learned about Sue."

Harry rubbed his chin. He'd been thinking the same thing, but couldn't figure out what the best approach to that would be. Detective Bradford had already told them not to investigate a case that was closed.

Emma parked in the driveway and called, "Detective Bradford," when she got out of the car.

The detective, wearing yet another ill-fitting suit, greeted them, and Harry suggested they go inside. On the walk in, Harry noticed the detective couldn't take his eyes off Emma. She was a natural beauty, but with the new clothes, styled hair, and makeup, she was absolutely striking. Entertained, Harry slowed his pace to observe, falling behind by about twenty feet.

The detective spoke in a low voice likely not meant for Harry's ears, "You look really nice. Special occasion?"

"No." Emma remained oblivious to his admiration and went inside. Despite her prominent engagement ring, whether she realized it or not, Harry thought, Emma had an admirer.

Once they settled in the sunroom, the detective said, "So, Ms. Stockton, your text made it sound like there was something important you wanted to share."

"Yes. Well, something *we* want to share." She motioned between herself and Harry, ensuring that he would get hit by some of the condemnation that might come their way. "Over the past week we've been out and about in the neighborhood and talking to people and have learned a few things about Sue."

Detective Bradford's gaze landed on the pile of books on poisons and criminal investigations perched on the end table next to the floral loveseat Emma occupied. His eyes narrowed. "I see."

"We bring unique expertise to the table," Harry added, pulling some of the heat his way. "As you know, Emma was a critical care nurse for years, and I spent my career living and traveling around the world, studying people and their behavior."

The detective's voice was polite, but with a forceful edge. "So, despite me telling you the case was closed and that Ms. Daniels died from accidental poisoning, you've been poking around, convinced it was something else. Clearly, you think you found something worthwhile, so get to the point."

They told him about why Emma didn't think the death was accidental, the late-night packages in David's mailbox, Grace mentioning Sue collecting secrets, the lawsuit, and how most people didn't like her.

"I also overheard Milo on the phone." A nervous flush rose on Emma's cheeks, likely from not wanting to explain how she'd overheard it. "He said 'It's taken care of,' and then, 'She's no longer a problem.'"

Detective Bradford stretched his long legs out from the low ottoman. "I'm not going to ask how you heard this because I don't want to know. Anything else?"

They were already in for a penny, might as well be in for a pound. Harry jumped in, "Did you know Sue's late husband used to be a spy for the CIA?" he asked, causing the detective's head to swivel toward him at record speed.

"Yes."

Harry went on. "Also, Rachel Valucci, formerly known as Rita Mae Valucci of Cleveland, née Rita Mae Banaszynski, was a person of interest in her husband's suspicious death in a boating accident."

The detective's jaw clenched with a force that made Harry worry for his teeth. "I am aware of these things, because I was thorough before I closed the case. I know how to do my job." He leveled a fiery glare at them. "I'm not a watch-too-much-British-TV-wanna-be detective. *I'm* the real thing. Now, if you don't mind, I need to get back to work." He stood. "And you two need to find a different hobby."

Fire burned in Emma's eyes and flamed her face. She said nothing and wasted no time showing him the door.

Harry had known the talk wouldn't be comfortable, but it had turned out worse than he thought. Detective Bradford saw them as fools playing a game.

One person had already died. He prayed the "game" didn't get more deadly.

* * *

Emma waited in the queue of cars for passenger pickup at the Columbus airport. Blake was back from St. Louis and, from his text when he'd landed, very excited about the outcome of his trip. She was still steaming from her run-in with Detective Bradford. *The nerve.* She and Harry had found useful information, and he hadn't been grateful at all. He'd dismissed them entirely.

Blake's tall figure, clad in jeans and a brown leather bomber jacket, stood out from the crowd in the pickup bay. She pulled over and unlocked his door. The reality of her situation hit her. She had to say something. *Tonight.* Keeping these doubts and feelings bottled up was living a lie—not fair to her or to Blake.

He threw his olive-green duffel bag in the back and then got into the passenger seat. When he turned toward her, he paused, his hazel eyes drinking her in.

"Wow, you look gorgeous." His hand caressed her cheek, and he gave her a kiss, then sat back. "I appreciate you getting so dressed up for me."

Guilt pricked her. Emma had forgotten about her "metamorphosis" and had been dreading picking up Blake and hearing about the new life he'd planned for them.

She suggested a quiet night in at her place so they could talk, but he insisted on taking her out. They compromised on Umberto's, a casual restaurant in the Short North district, not far from her home.

The restaurant was hopping, and they struggled to hold a conversation over the noise. Blake showed her pictures of the place he'd found for them, and pictures of St. Louis, and pictures of the friends he'd visited, his excitement making her feel worse. She excused herself and fled to the bathroom.

"Sorry," he said, when she returned to the table. "I've been monopolizing the conversation all night." He put down his champagne glass and took her left hand, which had rested on the table by her nearly full plate of gnocchi arrabbiata.

"I can't get over how beautiful you look. I wish I hadn't agreed to pick up a residency shift tonight. I'm due in by ten."

"What?" The change in plans caught her off guard.

"Rawlings called while you were in the bathroom. His wife has the flu. He needs to stay home to take care of the baby." He checked his watch, then waved at a waiter for the bill. "We should leave now. Mind dropping me off at the hospital?"

"Sure." Emma forced a reluctant smile, simultaneously frustrated and relieved that she didn't have to tell him tonight.

But the clock was ticking. She would have to act soon.

Chapter Twenty-One

From the rocking chair on his front porch, Harry was enjoying the unseasonably warm morning and the soothing sound of the pond's fountain. Emma, who had been uncharacteristically quiet through breakfast, stepped outside to join him.

"What are you reading today?" She pointed to the book on the table beside him.

He held it up: *Claim Your Power* by Kip Mastin.

Her face morphed into a perfect combination of peeved and amused, then she sat down. "I saw the Lakeview Estates newsletter you left on the kitchen table. If you're planning to go to the condo board meeting tonight, I should go with you."

"Have you ever been to one? In general, people tend to avoid them. Watching paint dry is more exciting."

"Rachel might be there, and we might be able to learn something else about her, or about Ms. Daniels. Or maybe something about Milo." Her focus stayed on the pond. "Besides, my mom's pushing me to finalize the save-the-date cards so they can be mailed tomorrow. Given my options, the condo board meeting sounds fantastic."

Ah. The real reason. He debated about doling out advice, but he didn't want to seem overly intrusive. *What he needed was to find better book titles.*

They chitchatted and rocked for the next hour, enjoying the day. Then the temperature dropped and sent them inside just as the security company technicians arrived. Harry was following through on his promise to Ceci to install safety measures—he'd chosen a combination of an alert and security system.

The security crew mounted stadium-worthy bright lighting in the front and back yards and added sensors to each door and window. The package included an emergency button on a lanyard that Harry could wear around his neck. He felt ridiculous when he tried it on, so he decided to keep it on the nightstand instead.

The workmen finished in time for Harry and Emma to grab a quick bite before they walked to the condo board meeting at the clubhouse. The night was cloudy, the wind damp. Harry speedwalked to fend off the chill, noting that despite the speed, his hip wasn't hurting and he was moving well with the cane.

A phone rang from the depths of Emma's puffy coat. She ignored it. Minutes later, it rang again. She let it go to voicemail a second time. When it rang for a third time a minute later, he arched his eyebrows in question.

"I texted my mom and told her I couldn't finish the save-the-date cards after work because you needed my help. She's furious."

Harry slowed his pace. He couldn't hold back. "Emma, it's not my place to say anything, but you know what's right for you. If you're having doubts about Blake or the wedding, don't ignore them. Acting now is easier than later."

"I know. I haven't found the right time to talk to Blake about things, and he's working again tonight. I need to tell him before I tell anyone else."

Somewhat appeased, he let the topic drop.

When they walked into the clubhouse, a welcoming fire burned in the fireplace. Milo was perched on the hearth, making a show of opening a bottle of wine. David Dubois and Jimmy sat in nearby leather chairs. There were also some residents from

Lakeview Estates whom Harry didn't know. Rachel was nowhere to be seen.

Harry returned a wave from David, then continued to the kitchen. Sakshi was making coffee, and Gautam was placing store-bought chocolate chip cookies on a tray—gluten-free, according to the nearby box. Harry greeted the couple, who were dressed in similar Fair Isle sweaters and jeans. "Small group tonight."

"Fewer people come in the fall and winter," Gautam said.

"We've stopped having meetings in December." With Sakshi's dark hair pulled into a ponytail and her unwrinkled skin, she didn't look old enough to be a grandmother.

"I tried to get Sakshi to bring gulab jamun." Gautam glanced appreciatively at his wife. "But she was worried some people might hesitate to try it."

"Nonsense," Harry said, "with all that sugar, cardamom, and rose water, who couldn't love it?"

"Sounds delicious," Emma said.

"If I didn't know better, Harry, I'd think you were angling for a dinner invitation," Sakshi teased.

Harry felt his cheeks heat, but Gautam jumped in. "We know how much you love Indian food. Please come for dinner one evening." Gautam turned to Sakshi. "We've got openings on our calendar this month, right?"

Sakshi placed cream and sugar next to the brewed coffee. "We do, and we'd love to have you over. Is there anything special you're craving?"

"Anything you make will be delicious. Though I can't eat as much spicy food as I used to." As they discussed possible dates, Harry thought of the monthly dinners he and Mags had shared with the Patels.

In the two years Mags had been gone, outside of the Celebration of Life event for Sue, he realized he'd socialized with the Patels only three times: at his wife's funeral services, at a church service he'd attended with Diana, and at a cocktail party David had dragged him to. He'd gone home feeling lonely and bereft. After that, he'd withdrawn completely.

Once the attendees were well stocked with caffeine and sugar, Gautam and Sakshi herded everyone to the chairs arranged around the fireplace. Sakshi recorded attendance, then took notes while Gautam went through official community business: the budget, landscaping, and changing the neighborhood's color scheme.

Colors proved to be a controversial topic and caused a thirty-minute digression. From the look on Emma's face, she was finding it agonizing. But she'd been warned.

As the group discussed switching the development's neutral earthy shades to brighter mid-Victorian colors, he leaned over to her and whispered, "Listening to discussions about paint is more boring than watching it dry." She snickered, causing Jimmy's and David's heads to turn toward them. Harry ducked back in his chair.

Before closing the meeting, husband and wife whispered in a tête-à-tête. Sakshi nodded in encouragement, spurring Gautam to say, "There is one final item."

"Unfortunately, we can't decide on it tonight," Sakshi added, "because there are not enough of us in attendance to vote."

"But with Sue's death" Gautam continued, "and the rumors around it, we thought perhaps we should consider installing closed-circuit television, or CCTV, throughout Lakeview Estates."

A hushed silence filled in the room, accentuated by the crackling fire. Then several spoke at once.

"Good idea," said a thirtysomething brunette woman Harry didn't recognize.

"To hell with that," Milo jumped to his feet, which were decked in elegant, handmade shoes that clashed with his jeans and T-shirt.

A man from a neighboring street shouted, "Our HOA fees will skyrocket."

"Over my dead body," said David, with a cold force in his words. Given Sue's recent death, it wasn't exactly an appropriate comment. Nor was it characteristic of his normally warm demeanor.

During the tumult, Emma leaned over to Harry. "With you on Lakeview Lane, there's no need for CCTV. You don't miss a thing." His cheeks warmed, and he checked to see if anyone had overheard. Jimmy and David sat closest to them, but they were focused on Milo, whose objections were getting louder by the minute.

Gautam put his hands up in a surrendering motion. "I can see this isn't as popular as Sakshi and I thought it would be." He looked to his wife, and she patted his knee.

"We'll table the discussion for now." Sakshi put her notebook aside and the two adjourned the meeting.

As the neighbors dispersed, Harry made a beeline for Jimmy, catching him thirty feet from the door.

"How are you?" he asked. From Jimmy's rough appearance, he guessed not well. Instead of his normal polished look, Jimmy's white hair was scraggly, and his drab clothing rumpled and oversized.

"I'm fine." Jimmy's eyes roved around the room, landing briefly on David who stood nearby.

"Are you sure? You look—"

"I'm sorry, Harry," Jimmy cut him off. "It's been a long day. Let's catch up another time." He headed toward the clubhouse entrance.

Emma was helping the Patels clean up, so Harry moved on to David, who was reading his cell phone screen. In a stylish navy suit, pink button-up shirt, and striped tie, he'd probably come straight from work.

"Not many Lakeview residents agreed with the idea of CCTV," Harry said.

David shook his head. "It's the craziest thing I've ever heard. I don't want to feel like I live in a communist state where everything I do is monitored."

Harry wasn't sure how communism was tied to CCTV, but he wanted to draw David out. "It's intrusive, the thought of being recorded at all times."

"There are some in this neighborhood," David's eyes focused beyond Harry's shoulder, "who would hate that—a digital record of where they've been and when, and who's been visiting whom."

Harry tracked David's gaze. He seemed to be looking at Milo and Jimmy, now talking near the clubhouse front doors.

"Diana told me about your second fall, I'm glad you're recovering." David was a warm-hearted extrovert, and when he turned on his charm, conversations with him felt like basking in verbal sunshine. "Want some coffee? Sakshi told me it's decaf."

Harry nodded and followed David to the kitchen. Unlike most Americans, Harry preferred tea—everything from a grassy green to a citrusy Earl Grey or a brisk Assam. But sometimes you just needed to adapt to other people's customs.

David picked up the coffeepot and poured Harry a cup. "I'm glad you're out and about again. I've missed seeing you."

"Rather hard to stay in isolation with so much going on in the neighborhood these days."

"Yes, with Sue's death and all." David scowled after finishing a sip, whether from the topic of Sue's death or the taste of the coffee, Harry wasn't sure.

Harry took a drink of the acrid sludge and struggled to swallow. "According to the police, it was accidental poisoning."

"That's what that detective told me as well. To be honest, I'm sort of surprised it wasn't murder."

Harry blinked. "Why?'

"Sue was trouble." David's tone was low, and for a moment Harry thought he hadn't heard right.

"What does that mean?"

David shrugged. "You know."

"I don't," Harry said. "I haven't mingled with our neighbors in ages and have no idea what's going on anymore."

"I doubt that. Your finger is always on the pulse of Lakeview Lane."

"Not this time. I didn't really interact with Sue."

David shook off his comment. "Never mind. I was just joking around."

Harry looked at him closely. He knew that the things people blurted out were often what they really believed or wanted to get off their chest. He spoke gently. "Perhaps. But there had to be some reason why you think she may have been killed."

In the pause that followed, David exhibited the telltale signs that he was internally debating about what to say, if anything at all: fidgeting with his coffee cup, shifting his weight from foot to foot, pursing his lips.

Harry waited. Sometimes the best way to get answers was to not speak.

"She manipulated people," David finally added. "And you never knew she was pulling your strings until it was too late."

Harry shifted uncomfortably. It was something he did himself sometimes when conducting key informant interviews with stakeholders withholding information. "Manipulate how?"

David's brows flattened and his eyes roamed the room. "You know, just manipulate."

Harry remembered the late-night packages he'd seen left in David's mailbox. Though he hated to think ill of his friend, he wondered if they were somehow related to Sue's death. "Surely getting people to do things they may not have done on their own isn't grounds for murder?"

"No. It's not. But if someone had asked me who on the lane was most likely to get murdered, I would have said Sue." He gulped the rest of his coffee before adding, "Next up would be me."

"You? Good heavens, why?"

David placed the empty cup on the counter. "My work in city planning influences decisions about Columbus's future every day. These decisions have long-term consequences that don't always make people happy. I even got threatened at a restaurant the other night by some guy who claimed I ruined his business and his life. But that comes with the territory."

That piqued Harry's attention. "Must be—"

"Either of you want a cookie?" Emma stepped beside him, with a plate full of sweets in hand.

Harry fought back the frustration that perched on the tip of his tongue. He wanted to ask more questions about the threat and David's argument with Milo, maybe even get around to asking about those late-night packages. He declined the offer, then introduced Emma to David, who grabbed a cookie and thanked her.

"I should run. Nice chatting with you, Harry. Let's get dinner soon." David gave him a quick pat on the shoulder, then left to exit the front doors behind Milo. Jimmy was gone.

By the time he and Emma headed out to the car, the tree-lined street was empty except for two parked cars and the iron lampposts that cast fuzzy yellow circles through a hazy, descending mist. Vapor curled around them in chilly tendrils, like the growing doubts Harry had about his friends.

Chapter Twenty-Two

Harry stood in his kitchen, waiting for Diana, the Lakeview Lane crier, to answer the phone. He'd prominently placed *Off the Sidelines: Speak Up, Be Fearless, and Change Your World* on the kitchen counter so Emma couldn't miss it. His intent to help her find her own way was sincere, and the quest to find appropriate titles kept him busy.

After the third ring, he began to worry. Diana had missed the condo board meeting last night, and she rarely missed the chance to chat with neighbors. He walked over to an accent chair in his kitchen's sitting area and sank into the gray leather, enjoying its earthy smell.

Diana answered after the fourth ring with a worn-out "Hello."

"It's Harry. You missed the condo board meeting, and I wanted to check in on you."

"Bless your heart." Her Southern twang was in full force. "I felt dreadful yesterday. But thanks be to God, I'm doing better. Fit enough to go visit my sister this weekend. She's having problems with the gout. I tell her she needs to cut back on eating bacon and sardines, but does she listen?" She harrumphed.

"Sorry to hear about your sister."

"Well, I'm heading down to Athens on Saturday to run some errands for her, which sadly means I'm gonna miss the Sacred

Heart Pumpkin Festival. Such a shame after all the work I did to organize it."

"I'm sure your sister will be grateful." He wondered if her sister had asked for help, or if Diana was foisting herself upon her. "We missed you at the condo meeting. And your delicious gingersnaps."

Laughter crackled through the line. "Oh, Harry."

"It was a lively one. Gautam introduced two controversial topics: potentially changing our condos' color scheme and adding CCTV throughout the neighborhood."

"CCTV? In Lakeview Estates?" Her voice raised a decibel. "Well, I *never*."

Harry smiled. He wasn't keen on the idea either.

"And what's wrong with the colors we have? I swear, I think Gautam and Sakshi make stuff up to keep themselves busy. They both retired too young. Was Jimmy there? That poor soul has worked himself into a right tizzy over Sue's death."

"He was but didn't say much. Rachel wasn't there."

"Probably off with that Milo. Those two are thick as thieves. I see Milo heading over to Rachel's house at all hours of the night."

Harry had noticed that as well—but did she know about Rachel's history? "They're an odd couple. Rachel is refined, and Milo is rough around the edges."

"They go together like waffles and—" A loud buzzer dinged in the background. "That's my timer. My casserole's done. I have to go. Thanks for checking in."

"Least I can do. Why don't you drop by for a visit when you have time?" If he couldn't benefit from Diana's rumor spreading over the phone, he'd invite it into his home.

"What about Sunday afternoon? I can stop by after I'm finished with all my doings at church. 'Bout three?"

"Perfect. In the meantime, ring if you need anything." They said goodbye, and a second later, Emma charged in through the front door.

"Sorry I'm late." She bustled to the kitchen table and dropped her coat and purse on a chair. Her burst-in morning arrivals were becoming habit.

"I needed another oatmeal bath this morning because this dang poison ivy is driving me crazy."

"No worries."

Her eyes looked sunken, and her ponytail frazzled.

"Why are you looking at me like that?" Suspicion clouded her face.

"Like what?"

"Whenever you're analyzing something, you tilt your head." She cocked her head to the side, mimicking him. "The closer you get to a conclusion"—she tilted her head farther—"the sharper the angle. Stop analyzing me."

Though amused by her astute observation, his concern for her grew.

* * *

A car horn honked, making Emma focus on the evening rush hour traffic. She navigated her Honda down a side street in Columbus's trendy Short North neighborhood near her home. Its brick sidewalks were bustling with restaurant-goers and evening strollers. Behind the glass storefront windows, shoppers browsed, and lively crowds drank and dined.

Detective Bradford had told her and Harry not to investigate because there was no crime to solve. But she and Harry knew there was. And working on the case made Emma feel confident and daring, and she craved living differently than her usual staid existence. She'd gravitated toward nursing—*and* her relationship with Blake—partly because they were familiar. Until now, Emma hadn't ventured into anything outside her small and comfortable universe. Harry, and to an extent looking into Sue's death, had cracked the door to the world beyond.

On the passenger seat beside her, were one hundred bundled save-the-date postcards that her mom had asked her to mail that day. Despite her having passed three open post offices, they remained on the seat. Blake was working yet another night shift, and she couldn't do anything to stop the runaway train her life had become until she spoke to him.

The light turned green, and she inched ahead. According to the car's clock, Emma had enough time to visit La Conchessa before it closed. Since Rachel hadn't been at the condo board meeting, Emma decided to visit her boutique to see if she could learn anything more about her.

Given what she and Harry had learned about Rachel in Tiffin, it sounded like she was ripe for blackmail. Rachel thrived on presenting herself as a well-heeled, European-influenced beauty, who wouldn't want the truth to get out. Her name change from Rita Mae all but confirmed it.

And if she and Harry had been able to find out about Rachel's past, it was likely Ms. Daniels had too. What Emma needed was to find out if Ms. Daniels had been blackmailing Rachel. That would confirm motive.

Emma scored a parking spot in front of Rachel's boutique. The shop's large window featured mannequins dressed in chic ensembles of burgundy, chocolate, and cream. Across the top of the storefront, La Conchessa was scrolled in elegant scarlet letters that told Emma she couldn't afford anything inside.

A chime dinged when she walked in. Men's items were on the left, women's on the right. Clothing was organized in sections determined by color, each centered around artistic displays of silk ties or scarves. Italian lounge music played softly in the background. Emma definitely couldn't afford anything here.

"*Ciao,*" a warm voice called out from the back of the shop. A brunette with huge sable eyes moved toward her, exuding an effortless elegance straight from the pages of *Vogue*. She wore a fitted ivory wrap dress, layers of gold chains, and brown leather boots that might've cost as much as Emma's bedroom furniture.

"Sorry, I was in back taking stock. May I help you?" The saleswoman assessed Emma's generic jeans and sweater, her look suggesting, *Surely you've wandered into the wrong store.*

"Yes, I need a new style," Emma said, peering around her to see if Rachel was working.

The woman flashed a pitying smile. "Of course."

"Perhaps Rachel could help me? She's a friend of a friend and I hear she's great."

"She is, but she's not in this evening. I'm Natalia. I'll do what I can to help you. Follow me."

She turned and motioned with her French-manicured fingers, beckoning Emma along. Over her ballerina-esque shoulder she said, "With your coloring, greens and browns will be the most suitable for the season." Emma trailed the pencil-thin woman.

Natalia stopped in front of a circular rack of clothing, then with Vanna White gestures, showed Emma designs and fabrics. While Emma looked over the items, she and Natalia had an uncomfortable discussion on sizing. All the clothes in the shop were in European sizes, so Natalia had to translate.

"That's a lovely engagement ring. The diamond's cut is exquisite," Natalia said, handing Emma a pair of jeans with a waist that didn't look wide enough for her thigh.

An armful of clothing and scarves later, Natalia escorted Emma to a dressing room cordoned off with scarlet velvet curtains. "Let me know if you need different sizes." The door chimed, turning Natalia's head toward the entrance.

As Natalia walked away, Emma stepped inside and closed the curtains. She'd been hoping to ask Rachel some questions about her business and if Sue had been a customer. But without her working, Emma would have to improvise.

When she heard Natalia greet the new customers, she popped her head out for a quick look. To Emma's right was a door with a keypad that probably led to a stockroom and maybe an office. Those types of doors locked automatically, so she wasn't getting in there.

This little adventure might be a bust. She thought of Natalia's pitying smile, the pile of too-small clothes behind her, and the awkward size conversation. Correction: a humiliating bust.

She glanced toward the front of the store, readying to close the curtain. The checkout counter sat twenty feet away. It was empty, minus some hangers and a cherry red journal. Could it be Rachel's? The bold color matched Rachel's personality.

Natalia was chatting with two stylish, lanky teens near the front of the store.

Emma tugged on a dress, then slid out of the dressing room. Natalia and the two girls seemed engrossed in conversation as Emma inched toward the counter.

Two feet shy of her target, Natalia called out, "May I help you with something?"

Did the woman have eyes on the back of her head? "Um, I wanted to see what you thought of this dress." She walked past the counter so Natalia could get a better view.

One of the teens snorted. The other raised her hand to cover a grin.

Natalia's lips formed a delicate moue. "Hmm. I'm not sure it's for you. Perhaps try the Versace? I believe the cut will be more flattering."

Heat flared on her cheeks, and Emma retreated, swiping the leather journal off the counter on her walk of shame back to the dressing room. She closed the curtains and looked in the mirror.

She looked like a lumpy green sausage.

But a sausage that could work to solve a murder, she thought. She checked that the curtains were closed, then opened the journal. It was a day planner, with notes, and meetings were recorded in neat handwriting. There was no name in the front, but after seeing Milo's name listed numerous times, she could assume it belonged to Rachel.

She turned back to May and read closely, day by day. There were luncheons, notes on stock orders, dates with Milo, hair and nail appointments, as well as notes on bills and due dates. It all looked normal. There had to be something.

Minutes lapsed as she scoured the pages. "How's it coming?" Natalia's voice slinked through the curtain.

Emma simultaneously squeaked and jumped, her fingers barely catching the day planner before it fell from her hands. "Fine."

"Let me know if you need other sizes."

She felt her face flush again. "Sure." She stood still until Natalia's boots clicked away. She had to find something. Emma flipped through a few more pages.

Then a few more. And there it was.

Proof.

Chapter Twenty-Three

"Wow." Harry turned off the kitchen sink and set down the Staub kettle as Emma came in from the front door. She wore a sleeveless green blouse that complemented her coloring and brown pants that added to her height. The leather purse on her shoulder matched her shoes. Her long copper locks cascaded over her shoulders. "You look lovely."

Displeasure flickered across her face, and she stopped midstep. "Don't sound so surprised."

"New outfit?"

This brought back her momentum toward him, and she joined him in the kitchen. "Yes." She flashed a smile that extended to something beyond stylish clothing. "You're *never* going to believe what I found out at La Conchessa last night."

"You went on your own?" He tried not to sound like a nagging father. He'd left the book *Women of Courage* for her to find on the hall table and now wondered if that was a message that would encourage more rash behavior.

"Rachel wasn't there, don't worry. Now, do you want to know what I learned?"

"Of course. Let me get the morning tea going." He finished filling the kettle and put it on the stove, then pushed his Oxford shirt sleeves back and turned on the gas. "What'd you learn?"

Her lips formed an impish quirk. "It'll cost you four hundred and eighty dollars."

Harry whistled lightly. "Price of the outfit?"

Emma giggled and gave him a wave of her engagement-ringed hand. "Kidding. But seriously, who knew detecting could be so expensive? I had to buy something so I could sneak the day planner back to its place on the checkout counter."

"Day planner?"

"Yes. Rachel's day planner. You know, her shop isn't cheap. That four hundred and eighty dollars was with the pants and blouse being fifty percent off."

Harry whistled again. He knew how much Emma was being paid, and that this was a stretch for her. "You were saying something about a day planner?"

Emma leaned against the granite-topped island. "Yep. In which Rachel recorded how much and when she was paying Sue Daniels what had to be blackmail money."

"You're kidding."

"Nope." She retrieved her cell phone from her purse and tapped the screen. "Look."

He took the phone and scrolled through images of calendar pages. Under July 15 in neat handwriting, it read: *$800 SD*. The same entry appeared on August 15 and September 15. On October 15, it was scratched out.

"Impressive work. Detective Bradford will be recruiting you in no time."

She snorted. "He thinks we're foolish. He'd find another explanation and tell us we're chasing windmills."

The heavy cast iron kettle shrieked, and Harry poured steaming water into a ceramic teapot filled with loose-leaf Irish Breakfast tea. Emma gathered two cups and the cream and sugar and set them on the kitchen table, commenting on how well he was getting around. He was pleased about his healing too.

"Let's go through the suspects on the lane," she said when they sat down.

While Harry enjoyed the thrill this investigation gave him, he hated the growing distrust of neighbors whom he'd befriended for years. The same uncomfortableness had plagued him while working on an economic development project in Indonesia after he'd discovered a significant portion of project funds were missing. He'd collaborated closely with the regional team and couldn't have imagined any of them bilking money on the side. But someone had, his friend Dharma Hidayat—whose first name, ironically, meant "good deed."

"There's David Dubois," he replied, pushing aside his discomfort. "I couldn't find anything on him through online research that would make him vulnerable to blackmail, but someone keeps leaving packages in his mailbox."

"Still?"

"I know. It's odd. If Sue had been involved with that, however, it should have stopped." He poured them each a cup of tea and added cream and sugar to his. "Next is Milo. We saw him pick up that mysterious wooden crate, and you overheard him talking about taking care of someone. But we don't know what secrets may have made him vulnerable to blackmail."

Emma blew on her cup to cool the dissipating steam rising from it. "It looks like Conner Buchanan is in the clear, at least for Ms. Daniels's murder. Plant toxicity doesn't seem like a teenager's MO."

"I don't think Conner's parents are involved either. No one mentions Jack or Linda having run-ins with Sue, and I can't find anything scandalous about them online that would make them vulnerable to blackmail. Plus, they're so busy with Grace and juggling their jobs. I think they go on the suspect back burner."

"We never figured out who Ms. Daniels was with at the Hilltop Inn."

"No, we didn't. I've invited Diana over for a visit on Sunday. Hopefully she'll have heard something."

"What about her as a suspect?" Emma took a sip, then winced—the tea was still too hot.

"Diana a killer? No way. She and Jimmy are the least likely suspects. Diana helps everyone in need and Jimmy is well-loved because of his art and cooking classes."

"Which makes them the most obvious suspects. That's always the way it is on TV."

He hesitated. "I did see Diana deliver a casserole to Sue right before she died. But the police would have tested all the food and drink they found in Sue's house. If the poison's source was the tuna casserole Sue had in her refrigerator, which Diana surely gave her because she's given me the same one, they probably wouldn't have closed the case as accidental poisoning. You don't type instructions for heating up a casserole if you made it yourself. So it wasn't that."

"Maybe Diana gave Ms. Daniels something else too, something that she finished eating, so the police had nothing to find."

"Maybe." Guilt lodged in his chest for suspecting his kindly neighbor. She'd helped so much after Mags died. But Emma was right. It was possible, though it seemed unlikely. "There's a fundraiser at Diana's church tomorrow. We might be able to learn more about her there."

* * *

Harry and Emma sat in the Sacred Heart Church's parking lot the next afternoon beneath a canopy of maple trees, their fire-colored leaves blazing in the sun. The lot had been recently repaved and crisp white lines denoting parking spots contrasted sharply with the pristine blacktop. Adjacent to the lot sat a brick church, comprised of several attached buildings that marked the church's growth in wealth and congregation over the years.

"Are you sure you want to do this?" Emma removed the navy blue fleece vest she wore over a cream-colored sweater. The day had grown warm.

"Now's the best time to snoop. Diana's visiting her sister in Athens. Plus, it's beautiful outside." He looked down at his burgundy sweater and thick olive corduroy pants and wished he'd worn a lighter outfit.

"What if she finds out?"

"What—that we went to one of her church's fundraisers? Diana would be ecstatic."

"I mean, what if she found out we were asking around about her?"

He turned in the passenger seat to look at her. "I built my career on getting information out of people. I can do this in a way that will seem natural. Trust me."

While she said, "Okay," her tone said, "The mess you create will be your own." It made Harry immensely grateful he'd hired Emma over Nurse Agatha.

They got out of his SUV and zigzagged around the parked cars. A crowd milled on the church's side lawn, where three stalls featured a bake sale and other homemade goods. A blue-haired contingent of elderly parishioners ran each stall. Young parents congregated around four boisterous games of cornhole.

Behind them sat a pumpkin patch, where already picked pumpkins were strewn about for kids to choose from. Near the front was a face-painting station that was giving away colorful balloons. Throughout it all, children ran amok, most with faces painted like puppies or tigers. Their giggling and shrieks took a bittersweet bite at Harry's heart—it had been so long since Ceci had been this age, and he was missing this stage of childhood for Evan and Evie.

When they stepped onto the grass, Emma said, "Oooh. Look, there's a stall for gluten-free cookies, and another for sugar-free candy. I've been trying to eat healthier." She dashed off, dodging strollers and running children, her ponytail flipping behind her.

Harry looked around. When Mags was alive, they'd joined Diana for an Easter service, a newcomers' ice cream social, and a touching sermon before Christmas. He had met the senior pastor, Bill, and several of the deacons, of which Diana was one. Harry quickly spotted Bill's large frame near the face-painting station. His size made him stand out from the crowd—that and the baby blue suit he'd paired with an orange sherbet–colored tie.

Making his way across the lawn with his cane, Harry headed in the pastor's direction. As he neared, the man's face lit up with recognition. "Brother Harry," he said with a resonating baritone voice. He extended his hand for a firm handshake. "I'm glad to see you're up and about."

"Pastor Bill. Nice to see you again."

The man smiled, showing crooked teeth. "Diana's had us praying for you. I bet she alerted the prayer chain to pray for your recovery before you even hit the ground on the night you fell." He chuckled.

"Wonderful event. It's nice to see all these happy families."

"Yessir, it is. We have a good flock. You here for a pumpkin?"

"That and maybe some healthy sweets if there is such a thing. I think my caregiver might buy out your stock." Pastor Bill laughed again, and Harry sensed that he sincerely enjoyed people and his calling. "Diana had a hand in organizing this?"

"Of course. I swear, we couldn't run this church without Sister Diana. That woman's one of God's brightest gems."

"She helped quite a bit after Margaret passed."

"That does not surprise me one bit. I'm sure Diana's casseroles gave you strength for your heavy load during that time." Pastor Bill patted his protruding stomach.

"I normally don't care for tuna, but I like her tuna casserole," Harry said, remembering Diana's various dishes. "Her lasagna's the best."

"A veritable miracle worker, that one."

"She's been a real support to the lane through the tough time we're having now. You heard about Sue Daniels's passing?" Harry asked as a burst of laughter rose from the cornhole games.

Pastor Bill's face grew solemn. "Diana mentioned it. Bless Ms. Daniels, poor soul. Though from what Diana's said, it sounds like that woman had lost her way in her walk with the Lord."

Harry's curiosity spiked. But he needed to tread carefully, as if he knew what the pastor was talking about.

"Sue was a complex person," he said. "Kind to the infirm and children, yet didn't get along with many in our neighborhood."

"No wonder with her shenanigans. That woman truly upset Diana. She confided her troubles in me, and we prayed and prayed for resolution. It came, but at a high cost for Ms. Daniels."

"Yes." Harry desperately wanted to ask if Diana's troubles were related to being blackmailed by Sue, but the pastor would never betray Diana's confidence.

"Pastor Bill." A stout, fierce-looking woman in her forties charged toward them. Her hair stuck to her head, despite the breeze. She wore orange and brown plaid pants with a lime green sweater, an outfit that would make Rachel Valucci shudder.

"Pastor Bill. You're needed at the cornhole game. Two men are placing bets, and we can't have gambling here."

A resigned smile formed on the pastor's face. Harry guessed this wasn't the first time the woman had pointed out the sins of others. "Come on," she commanded with a wave of her arm and headed back toward the offenders.

"Brother Harry, it's been a joy. Please join us again." The pastor strode off. The crowd split to ease his way, like Moses parting the Red Sea.

Harry looked for Emma, whom he found strolling through the pumpkin patch. "Going to buy one?"

"Nah, too messy to carve. I saw you talking to that man. What did you learn?"

"Tell you in the car." Emma's hands held two bags. He pointed at them. "And those?"

"I did it for our investigation. You know, so we'd blend in."

He looked at her closely and grinned. "You have chocolate on the side of your mouth."

She sheepishly wiped her lips with the back of her hand, and they headed toward the car.

Once inside his SUV, Harry selected a buckeye. They were his favorite—the chocolate–peanut butter combo couldn't be beat. "Wow, this is pretty good to be sugar-free."

"Of course it's good. It's the real deal. I didn't like the sugar-free ones. The peanut butter fudge isn't sugar-free either."

Harry recapped his conversation with Pastor Bill as Emma nibbled on a piece of fudge.

When he finished, she said, "I know you don't want to think Diana's a killer, but given what the minister said—"

"Pastor," he corrected, earning him a grand eye roll.

"Given what that *pastor* said, we need to investigate Diana. Maybe being blackmailed caused her to murder Sue. Maybe in addition to the tuna casserole, she gave Ms. Daniels another dish that contained the death camas. Perhaps Ms. Daniels ate it for lunch, then put the dishes in the dishwasher—remember, I thought it had just finished running. That would have gotten rid of all traces of poison."

"Maybe," he acknowledged. "I did some more research this morning on my other neighbors. All I could find on Sakshi was that she's won numerous golf tournaments, and she's written a slew of journal articles. Her Ph.D. is in biological engineering."

"I've thought about going back to school. I'm not sure I want to stick with nursing or caregiving."

Harry stopping chewing the overly sweet fudge and looked at her. She seemed to have doubts about everything in her life at the moment. "You're thinking of going back to school?"

"I'm wondering, that's all." She chewed on a buckeye. When she finished, she wiped her hands on her jeans, then shoved the bags toward him. "I've already had three pieces of candy. Did you learn anything else?"

There was something important going on with Emma, and he wanted to find out what, but she motioned get-on-with-it by rolling her hands, so he pushed on. "There were a few stories about financial discrepancies at Digital Phoenix, where Gautam used to work as CFO. Some hints at embezzlement, but his name was never mentioned."

He closed the bag of buckeyes, as Emma put her purse in the center console.

"Oh my gosh." Her spine straightened, and she gripped his arm. "At the potluck, Gautam mentioned that they have keys to Ms. Daniels's house. He could have used them to go in and add poison to something in her kitchen."

Instead of narrowing the list of suspects, they were adding more each day. "I don't think—"

"If Sue found out Gautam had embezzled funds, she could have blackmailed him. That's motive. And they're awfully young to be retired."

Reluctantly, Harry conceded her point. As they drove back to Lakeview Estates, the sweets he'd eaten swirled in his stomach, while suspects swirled in his mind. Bleak clouds consumed the bright blue sky, hinting at the storm to come.

Chapter Twenty-Four

A whoosh of chilly air swept in when Emma opened Harry's front door the following afternoon. Goosebumps rose on her arms beneath her long-sleeved T-shirt. "Diana, please come in."

Diana stepped into the foyer, unbuttoning her Burberry jacket. "Thank you, Emmylou."

She held back a sigh. "It's Emma."

"Of course it is, dear. Sorry about that. I'm not the sharpest with remembering names." Diana handed Emma her coat, then smoothed her royal blue shift dress that was bedazzled with rows of pearls around the neckline. Emma once again marveled at the stiffness of her platinum hair.

"My, it smells divine. Someone's been busy in the kitchen. You must be spoiling Harry somethin' fierce."

"I'm trying a recipe for a high-fiber banana nut bread." She had been in the kitchen for hours, trying to quell the ball of anxiety bouncing around in her gut. Emma still hadn't talked to Blake. He'd worked nothing but second and third shift hours since he'd returned from St. Louis. The post office was closed since it was Sunday, and the save-the-date cards remained on the passenger seat of her Honda. She'd finally resorted to a "we need to talk" text, and he'd responded with proclamations of love and how he was missing her too.

Harry had been consumed with his iPad all day, researching his neighbors. Although the last time she'd walked by, he'd been reading something about Nepal. The man was interested in everything.

Not in the mood to make coffee, Emma didn't offer it to Diana. "I'm making tea. Do you prefer Earl Grey or English Breakfast?"

"Whatever Harry is having."

"Earl Grey. I'm some having too, so I'll make a pot."

Harry had already moved from the sitting area in the kitchen to the table. He greeted Diana and offered her a seat. "How was church today?"

"As inspiring as ever. No wonder with Pastor Bill. He mentioned y'all stopped by our fundraiser. You need to start joining me for church every Sunday." Diana waggled her index finger at him.

Emma moved into the kitchen and tuned out Diana's recitation of the morning service. She put the heavy cast iron Staub kettle on the stove, then gathered the ceramic pot for brewing.

A book had appeared on top of the wedding magazines she'd shoved into the corner: *#GIRLBOSS* by Sophia Amoruso. According to the book blurb, it was about women trusting their gut and not being afraid to go against societal rules. She caught Harry watching her out of the corner of his eye, his lips quirked.

When she joined the table with tea and slices of the fresh-baked banana bread, she gave Harry one of her best eyerolls. His response was an innocent look that she now knew meant anything but.

"It's unfortunate you missed the fundraiser yesterday," Harry said to Diana. "Pastor Bill gave you credit for organizing it. Admirable, especially with all that's been weighing on you lately."

Diana shifted in her chair. "What do you mean?"

Harry kept his response vague. "This Sue business. I know it's put you under a lot of strain."

The air around Diana stilled. Her eyes went wide. "We're all under strain. Sue's death has been hard on everyone."

"It has," Harry said in a reassuring tone. "You know, if you need help with anything, all you need to do is ask."

She looked around the room, as if readying to flee. "What else did Pastor Bill say?"

He tilted his head—a dead giveaway that he was supercharging his gray cells. "He couldn't stop praising your casseroles."

The topic change surprised Emma. Harry had been zeroing in. But when she saw the relief on Diana's face, she realized Harry might be trying to lull her into a false sense of security before he struck again. Emma had fallen for that trick before.

They chatted more about Diana's casseroles and the event's pumpkin patch and food stalls, before Harry circled back to Sue. "I didn't know Sue well," he said. "I'm not sure anyone did. She was an enigma."

Diana nodded. "It was hard figuring out who Sue was. She could be mean, but at the same time, she helped with Grace and spoiled little Vihaan."

"I only met her once," Emma added, "but I didn't get the feeling that she was the warm and fuzzy type."

"That's true," Diana said. "And frankly, she didn't seem the creative type either. I never understood why Sue attended Jimmy's classes. Sue wasn't artsy, and even though she seemed more suited for fancy restaurants than home cooking, she was at all three of the classes I took: one on pastries, another on airy soufflés, and one for layered cakes, which, frankly, I think I've mastered better than Jimmy."

"Aren't those advanced classes?" Harry asked.

"Not for me." She placed a hand on her chest, showing off a lustrous pearl ring. "But Jimmy's classes are too advanced for most." She glanced at Emma, who was doggedly resisting rolling her eyes. "Come to think of it, Sue didn't pay much attention in class. She spent most of the time trying to stir up gossip."

Diana's look of disapproval caused Emma to sputter her tea.

"You okay?" he asked.

"Yes, sorry. Wrong pipe."

Harry's gaze locked on Diana. It was fun watching him at work when she wasn't the object of his scrutiny. "There seem to be some rumors going around the neighborhood that Sue was murdered. I wonder why."

Diana's eyes rounded, like a deer in headlights "I wouldn't know about that. That kind policeman said it was an accident." She fidgeted with her teacup, clinking it against the table. "Jimmy said Sue's sister is coming to settle her estate. She's gonna put Sue's condo on the market within the month. She's asking nine hundred thousand dollars. That would do wonders for the value of our homes."

That was a good deal of money. It'd take Emma more than a decade to earn that.

"Sue's sister was her beneficiary?" Harry asked.

"According to Jimmy, but I don't know how he knows." Diana picked up a slice of banana bread and took a bite. "Emma, this is *delicious.*"

"Thank you." Emma was pleased Diana had gotten her name correct.

But just when she started to thaw toward the older woman, Diana added, "I can see why you've got meat on your bones."

Emma's cheeks heated, and she pushed her plate away.

Harry politely edged the conversation to another topic. "Can you believe the Patels think it's a good idea to install CCTV?"

"Sometimes I wonder where Gautam's elevator stops. I'm not worried about the monitoring 'cause I follow the straight and narrow, but the *cost.*"

Diana rambled on about CCTV, and Emma remembered seeing an app that helped track calories. She pulled her cell phone out, and her embarrassment shifted to panic when she saw the time.

"Crap," she blurted, interrupting Diana's diatribe. "There's a wedding task force meeting tonight to discuss bands for the reception." She stood and looked at Harry. "I've got to run. You set for dinner?"

"Yep. Enjoy time with your family."

Emma stifled a grimace and raced out the door.

* * *

As soon as the door closed, Diana said, "Goodness, does she often leave you in the lurch like that? How are you supposed to manage with your hip?"

Diana lost her husband a year before Mags passed. For that reason, he made allowances for her sometimes malicious tongue. But it wasn't always easy.

"Emma does a great job. My hip's much better, thanks to her." He took a slice of banana bread as a show of support.

With the topic of Emma off the table, Diana moved on. Had Harry heard about the scandal with Conner dealing drugs? Did he know Milo and Rachel were having an affair? Had he seen Bianca since her plastic surgery?

The answers were yes, yes, and no. In fact, he had no idea who Bianca was, though he hoped her new nose was to her liking. He asked if Diana had learned who Sue might have been dating, but she didn't know.

After twenty additional minutes about Lakeview Estates, Harry interrupted. "If you'll excuse me for a moment, I need to use the washroom." He stood, needing a break.

When he returned from his master bathroom, he found Diana in the sunroom. Her head snapped to attention when he appeared. She looked guilty.

"Is everything okay?"

"I, uh, wanted to see your view. Such a lovely little room." Diana stepped through the sunroom archway toward him. "It's been a hectic day. I should go." She hurried across the living room, passing him on the way. "Thanks for your hospitality." She yanked her purse and coat out from the closet.

"I appreciate you stopping by."

She pulled on her coat and stepped out onto his porch, then waved as she sped down his drive.

Puzzled, he watched her flee. Harry closed the door and returned to the sunroom.

The books on poisons and criminal psychology that he and Emma had been reading sat stacked on the end table, but their titles weren't visible from the angle where Diana had stood. He positioned himself exactly where she'd been standing—facing out the side window, near the shelf that held the printouts of information he had gathered on his neighbors.

The article on top was about the death of Rachel Valucci's husband. Harry thought for a moment. An article on Sakshi had been on the top earlier that day.

So Diana had rifled through the printouts, looking for something. Now Harry was convinced there was something to find on Diana that would make her vulnerable to blackmail. And given how fast she'd fled, it was something big.

Chapter Twenty-Five

Harry stood in his bedroom's walk-in closet the following night, searching the shelves for a new book title for Emma. She'd been moody and withdrawn all day. He feared that if she didn't say something soon, it'd get too close to the wedding, and then she'd feel forced to go through with it.

They'd spent an hour or so talking about the investigation over breakfast, but they'd uncovered so many suspects and motives, they weren't sure what to do next. So he'd ended up spending most of the day applying for consulting jobs, ignoring the fact that so far, he'd heard nothing but silence from his applications.

Outside a storm raged. Thunder cracked and rolled as it barreled across the sky. Deep reverberations hummed through his chest.

A thumping noise caused him to raise an ear to better hear. It stopped and he returned to skimming book titles.

Five titles later, the rhythmic knocking returned. Someone was at the door.

He wasn't expecting anyone. He gripped his cane, then to be safe, popped the emergency alert lanyard on his nightstand into his cardigan pocket.

When he opened the door, he found a drenched Jimmy Chatimont. His wet ponytail drooped, and the corners of his mouth angled downward. He seemed smaller than Harry remembered him to be, far below Harry's six-foot-two.

"You must be freezing. Please, come in." He motioned for Jimmy to enter.

"Sorry to bother you so late." Jimmy's bright yellow raincoat left a steady trail of raindrops when he stepped inside.

"Let me hang your jacket." Harry shook rain off the coat onto the foyer's tile and hung it in the closet. Jimmy slipped off his muddy boots, leaving them on the mat inside the door. His somber black top and jeans seemed to match his bleak mood.

What was so important that would make Jimmy brave heavy rain on a Monday night? "Are you all right?"

"With everything going on, I wanted to see how you were doing," Jimmy said with a faint smile. "And I supposed I wanted company. Diana and the Patels have been kind, but, frankly, I miss Margaret. She would have made things better. She always could make me laugh."

Harry's chest tightened. Mags would have made things better. Comforting others had been her superpower. "Would you like something to drink?"

"Sure. Maybe tea?"

He directed Jimmy to sit by the hearth in the kitchen sitting area, where he'd left a fire burning. "Go dry off. It'll take me just a few minutes."

Harry busied himself in the kitchen, watching Jimmy from the corner of his eye as he settled into a chair and lifted his feet toward the fire to help his socks dry. Halfway through the tea preparations, he caught Jimmy looking at the aid reports he'd left on the end table.

When the tea was ready, Harry left his cane in the kitchen and carefully carried their tea to the sitting area without incident. He'd have to tell Emma. With a pang, he realized he'd miss her company once they parted ways.

Jimmy took the Wedgewood blue cup and saucer from him. It'd been Mags's favorite china set. "Thank you. These cups make me think of her."

"Me too." Harry made room for his cup on the end table, then sat.

The hiss of the gas fire filled the room as something wriggled at the edge of Harry's thoughts. Though Jimmy had visited Mags almost weekly, he'd only stopped by once to pay his condolences after Margaret died. Mags and Jimmy had been close, while he and Harry had been friendly but not friends.

They talked about the tea Harry had chosen: a crisp decaf Orange Pekoe, which Jimmy liked. Then they reminisced about Mags and moved on to Jimmy's painting and cooking classes.

"Margaret's art supplies are upstairs. I can bring them to you when I'm done using a cane. I'm not ready for stairs yet."

Jimmy's face flickered with an unidentifiable emotion. "I couldn't."

"Don't be silly. Mags would be overjoyed to know you were using her old supplies to create new art."

His expression softened. "Sure."

Harry's eyes fell to his cup. The delicate blue contrasted sharply with the russet hue of the tea. He felt the same contrast with Jimmy, but he couldn't put his finger on why. "How are your classes going?"

"Five women have dropped out since Sue's death. We did some foraging as part of one of my cooking classes, so that's not a surprise." He flattened his lips. "Sue always had a way to ruin things."

A thunderclap roared, and Harry wondered about Jimmy's comment and the bitter force behind it. "Her death has shocked the lane."

"There's a rumor going around the neighborhood that Sue was murdered."

Harry tilted his head, scrutinizing Jimmy's face and posture. "I'm not one to pay attention to rumors. But I do wonder if there was more to Sue's death."

"That policeman talked to everyone on the lane. So if Sue was killed, he likely suspects someone on the lane—which is just crazy."

"People do all sorts of unexpected things if cornered under the right circumstances. From what I've heard, quite a few of our neighbors clashed with Sue."

"You got that right. A *lot*."

Harry was still pondering the purpose of Jimmy's visit. Perhaps he wanted to feel closer to Mags by talking to Harry and returning to her home. "Do you have a theory about why Sue didn't get along with others? I didn't really know her."

"Not really."

It felt like Margaret's old friend was holding something back, like he'd done at the potluck. Harry decided to be blunt—perhaps in a way that Mags might have frowned upon, given her close friendship with Jimmy. "Do you think people didn't like Sue because she was blackmailing them?"

Jimmy's teacup clinked against the saucer. With trembling hands, he placed his tea on the end table. "What would make you think that?"

Harry said nothing. Silence was his favorite tool to get mouths running.

Seconds ticked by before Jimmy relented. "Did Diana tell you that? I swear, that woman does more harm than good, running around tossing out casseroles and gossip. You know, you can't believe everything she says."

"Diana does prattle," Harry reassured, wanting to keep him talking.

Then his iPad rang from the sunroom. The moment broke. "Sorry. That's Ceci's ringtone. I'll tell her I'll call her back. Otherwise, she'll think I've fallen again and send in the cavalry."

After a brief exchange with Ceci, Harry returned to find Jimmy vacantly staring at the fire.

"Ceci wanted to organize dates for their trip back to Ohio in December." Excitement buoyed his heart. "When was the last time you saw Ceci?"

"At Margaret's funeral."

"Of course." Harry sat and picked up his cup. Jimmy stilled and watched him from the corner of his eyes.

As Harry moved to take a sip, a piercing crack of thunder jolted both men in their chairs. Tea spilt down the front of Harry's sweater, and lightning lit up the room through the half-closed blinds.

"Criminy." He brushed off the spot. "At least my cardigan's the same color." He returned his nearly empty cup to the table and looked up to find Jimmy eyeing him intensely. "Don't worry, it's an old sweater."

"It's getting late, and the storm is getting worse. I should go." Jimmy stood and dashed for the door.

Without his cane, Harry lagged behind him. By the time he joined Jimmy in the foyer, his neighbor had already put on his coat.

"I appreciate the chat." Jimmy slid on his boots, which squished with each foot.

"Anytime." Harry opened the door, puzzled over the man's odd behavior.

Jimmy bolted outside. Halfway across the porch, he turned back, looking washed-out and hollow. "I'll come back another time for Margaret's art supplies."

Then he rushed into the lashing rain, the darkness of Harry's yard slowly swallowing his yellow raincoat as he hurried away.

Chapter Twenty-Six

The next morning, Harry and Emma sat across from each other at a bistro table inside Perk Me Up, a Westerly College student hangout in the commercial district near Harry's house. The smell of coffee filled the air and warmed the coffee shop's cool industrial décor with exposed brick, hanging tin lanterns, and metal tables.

Emma took another bite of the overnight oats she'd ordered. They were better than she'd thought they'd be.

Harry's empty dish was pushed aside. ". . . and then Jimmy disappeared into the night," he said, ending his recount of the previous night's visitor.

"Sounds like he was up to something."

"It was strange," he agreed. "But Jimmy was one of Mags's dearest friends. Perhaps he thought I could help fill the friendship void Mags's death created."

"Everyone is behaving so suspiciously. Maybe Sue was blackmailing the entire lane."

He leveled his gaze at her. "She wasn't blackmailing me. You know, it's weird, despite all the time Jimmy spent in our house, goofing around in the kitchen with Mags, I don't know that much about his past other than he's from Èze."

Her confusion showed and he added, "It's a beautiful medieval village on the French Riviera. But I have no idea why, how, or when he came to this country."

"Did you ever wonder if Jimmy had fallen in love with Margaret?"

"There's no way he didn't."

She sat back in surprise; he seemed so matter of fact about it. "And you were okay with that?"

"How could I blame him? Mags was beautiful, on the inside and out. She had an infectious laugh and a heart of gold. On top of that, she was brilliant. Jimmy and I couldn't have been the only men who fell for her."

"That didn't bother you?"

"I knew nothing would come from any of it, other than broken hearts for the men who fell under her spell. Well, except me." Harry leaned forward, looking every bit the happy sage. "I never doubted Margaret's love. And I know she never doubted mine. From the moment I met her, I *knew*. And that belief only became stronger over time. Every day I fell in love with her all over again."

Emma leaned back in her chair, jealous of his certainty and wondering if she'd ever find anything like it. A pulse of guilt reverberated in her stomach. The longer she took to reveal her true feelings to Blake, the more painful it would be for them both. She had to tell him. Tonight.

She tried to calm the spasms in her gut as she watched Harry twirl his tea cup, mesmerized by its unfurling steam. He sucked in a gasp of air and sat up straight.

"Oh, my goodness." He pulled his cell phone from a cardigan pocket and typed.

"What?" Emma asked him.

He held up his free hand to quiet her, then put the phone to his ear.

A faint female voice from the phone rose above the coffee shop din. "Hilltop Inn."

"Sally?" Harry asked.

An espresso machine kicked on and Emma couldn't hear the response.

"This is Mr. Lancaster, you served afternoon tea to me and my friend Emma about a week ago."

Harry was shaking his head as he listened. "No, nothing like that. I was calling to ask a quick question about Ms. Sue Daniels. You remember, the woman who sent back the sandwiches because she didn't like the bread? Do you remember who she was with?"

He listened, then after a moment his face shifted into a triumphant smile.

"What?" Emma mouthed.

"That's right. An older man with white hair in a ponytail."

Emma felt her jaw drop.

There was another pause. Harry nodded. "Thanks so much, Sally. Emma and I will be back before the end of the year." He disconnected.

Emma put it together. "Jimmy Chatimont was the person at the inn with Sue?"

"He was. Sally said she hoped Ms. Daniels wouldn't come back, but, and I quote," Harry's voice perfectly mimicked Sally's southern Ohio accent: "I didn't mind the old artsy guy who was with Ms. Daniels 'cause he was nice. Gave Ma a recipe for some fancy rosemary shortbread cookies. Think he was a chef or something."

"Holy crap." Emma rested her elbow on the table and her chin on her hand. "Jimmy and Sue were dating?"

"Looks like it. Although just because they were there together doesn't mean they were dating. Could have been there as friends."

"I know that, but if they were dating, and it ended badly, Jimmy could have a motive to kill Sue."

"Whatever form of a relationship, platonic or romantic, Jimmy's been keeping it a secret," Harry said. "Think we should tell Detective Bradford?"

"What on earth for? Their affair is not proof of anything, and the detective is convinced the case is closed. The only way Sue's killer ends up behind bars is if we"—she motioned between them with her right hand—"figure out who did it."

* * *

Harry answered the door that evening dressed in corduroy chinos, a button-up green Oxford, and a tweed jacket.

"Sorry I'm late," David Dubois said, looking flushed. He wore an exquisitely tailored navy pin-striped suit. "The mailman left some of Jimmy's mail in my box, so I dropped it off when I got home from work. He invited me in for a quick drink, and I felt like I had to take him up on it. He seems pretty upset about Sue's passing."

"No worries. Jimmy popped by last night and asked me about Sue too. Must be making his rounds. I'm sure we won't have a problem getting a table for dinner. It's still early."

Outside the air was crisp and pleasant. Harry deftly used his cane as he and David strolled around Lakeview Lane and down the tree-lined streets of Lakeview Estates to the nearby commercial district. They discussed the weather, sports, Columbus politics, Harry's job search, and anything but Sue's death along the way.

On Main Street, the trees' golden leaves glowed in the setting sun, and sporadic stone urns bursting with burgundy mums lined the sidewalk. Groups of college students congregated around Perk Me Up's outside tables. A young mother in a loose polka-dot dress pushed a stroller with a sleeping baby while she chatted on her cell phone. Outside the ice cream shop, three young boys licked ice cream cones, enjoying the Indian summer day.

As they headed toward the restaurant, each storefront prompted Harry with another memory of Mags: the pink bakery, the antique shop, the florist who sold colorful blooms. The proximity of the commercial district had been one of the reasons why they'd chosen to move to Lakeview Estates. It was an idyllic place to retire.

Once they got to Chez Margot, a pretty blonde hostess with a coy smile led them to a rustic wooden table near the windows with a good view of the street. She handed them dinner menus, and with a twirl of her fluffy gold skirt, went back to the hostess stand.

Mags had loved this restaurant and its cream and blue décor. Its ambiance and delectable food magically transported diners to the south of France. Since it was Tuesday and close to five, instead of the busy norm, there were only two other occupied tables. Edith Piaf's "Je Ne Regrette Rien" warbled in the background.

David removed his suit jacket and hung it over the back of his chair. The crisp white button-up shirt he wore beneath it was so clean it had a neon glow. He picked up a menu. "I love this song."

"Me too." Harry and Mags had met in Nice, when their respective families were on summer holiday, before they shipped off to college. The first three weeks of their relationship had blossomed in chic French bistros under silky Mediterranean nights. Ever since, they'd loved all things *français*.

"I think it's great that you're trying to find consulting work," David said, his eyes still pinned to the menu.

"We'll see if anyone hires me. So far, I've not had any luck. I've applied for a few consulting jobs that would take me to South Asia. That way, I'd be close to Ceci, Steve, and the grandkids."

"That would be fantastic. With your expertise and background, I'm sure you'll find something soon." David's voice brimmed with an optimism Harry hoped wasn't unrealistic.

Their waiter, a fortysomething man with a stiff white shirt, black creased pants, and a gallic nose, came to the table to take their order. They both requested soupe à l'oignon for the first course, and for the main Harry went with coq au vin while David chose confit de canard and a Loire Valley Pinot Noir.

Over soup and a warm baguette that quickly melted the fresh butter, conversation stayed safe. Far away from the troubles of Lakeview Lane. The waiter cleared their bowls and delivered their entrees. David eagerly dug in, clearly savoring the duck.

"Looks like Emma is working out well," he said between mouthfuls.

"She is. I'm surprised by how much I enjoy having someone around the house. I didn't realize how empty it had become."

"I understand. It can get lonely being on your own all the time."

A flash of gratitude filled Harry's heart for all the love and joy he'd shared with Mags. He wanted that bliss for his friend. "You've been dating Victoria for years now. Have you two considered getting married? You seem to get along quite well."

David choked and averted his gaze. Harry immediately regretted adding his two cents. An uncomfortable moment stretched between them.

"I'm sorry." Harry hoped he hadn't ruined a lovely evening. "I've overstepped."

David loosened his silk tie and shook his head. "No, no. It's not that." He took in a deep breath. "I've royally screwed up. And frankly, I don't know what to do about it."

Harry put down his fork, giving his friend his full attention.

"When Victoria was promoted in March, I cheated on her." Discomfort pinched David's face. He squirmed in his chair. Harry waited, sensing there was more. "And if that wasn't bad enough, things got worse. Somehow Sue found out."

"So?" Harry didn't see the scandal. While he didn't approve of David's choices, Victoria and David weren't married and hearts roamed all the time.

"When Victoria was promoted, she became my boss. That's when I started seeing Charlotte, another colleague in my office, who also reports to Victoria."

"Oh." Harry winced at his friend's poor judgment. David held up his palms.

"I know. It's *beyond* stupid. If Victoria found out about Charlotte and me, she could fire us both on the spot."

"How did Sue find out?"

"No idea. Charlotte and I were careful not to be seen around town. And I told no one. I don't talk about my personal relationships, or anyone else's for that matter. They're private, as far as I'm concerned."

"So what did Sue do?"

"Held me over a barrel, that's what." David took a swig of wine.

"What do you mean?"

"It started with someone leaving packages in my mailbox that contained photos: pictures of me and Charlotte at dinner, of us out having drinks, or of Charlotte parking her car in my garage, where I had her park just in case Victoria ever unexpectedly stopped by."

An image of Rachel jumping back from her mailbox flashed through Harry's head. Had that been what Rachel had found, a threatening package from Sue? "Then what happened?"

"One day, Sue stopped by, and during our conversation, she got around to the topic of infidelity, and how painful and costly it could be. It was clear she was the one behind the photos."

"How much did she want?"

"She asked me how much I thought my job and reputation were worth." His voice became indignant as anger sparked his eyes. "Can you believe it? The nerve of that woman. Sure, it was my reckless behavior that got me into this mess, but I'd be damned if I was going to pay Sue for it."

David drained the rest of his wine and put the glass on the table with a solid clunk. "I told Sue to go ahead and tell the world. I didn't care. I've been thinking of moving anyway. I told her it'd be a cold day in hell before I gave her one cent." He sat back, his irritation fading as quickly as it had swelled. "Then all of a sudden, Sue's dead."

"So that was the end of it?"

"Not exactly. I guess Sue never gave the pictures to Victoria because Charlotte and I still have our jobs. But someone else must know because I got another package of photos in my mailbox the other day, *after* Sue died, with another demand for cash."

A sickening swirl twirled in Harry's stomach. There was another blackmailer. "How are you supposed to pay?"

"Cash in an envelope left in my mailbox. And it's for more than what Sue demanded."

"Oh dear." Harry's mind spun trying to figure out who could have picked up where Sue left off. "What are you going to do?"

David wiped his mouth, but the napkin failed to remove a subtle purple wine stain from his lips. "I'm not going to pay. I ended my relationship with Victoria *and* Charlotte yesterday. I didn't tell them about each other, I didn't think they needed to know. I just need some time to sort things out."

No longer hungry, Harry pushed his plate away. "I'll be honest, I do think Sue was murdered."

David nodded. "She was an awful person. I wouldn't be surprised if that's what happened. I told that detective about Sue blackmailing me. He needed to know."

"What did he say?"

"That it was an angle he was looking into."

Harry tilted his head. Could the detective be playing him and Emma, he wondered. Telling them the case was closed, when he really thought the death was suspicious. Is that why he'd been so angry with them for "poking around," because he was worried they would get in his way or do something to jeopardize his investigation?

Given all the clues he and Emma had unearthed, and the fact that the detective seemed quite bright, it made a lot more sense than his quick, closed-case ruling despite the mounting threads of evidence pointing otherwise.

David met Harry's eyes. "I hate to say it, but I'm not sorry Sue's dead. She was a master at lying and manipulation."

Or at least her husband Ralph had been, Harry thought. When Sue apparently had tried to follow Ralph's playbook, it hadn't worked out so well.

Chapter Twenty-Seven

Emma stood in front of the dumpster behind Billy's Burgers, Shakes, and Fries, the aroma of grilling beef and sour milk wafting through the air. Her palms were slick with sweat. Her stomach churned as if she was on the teacups ride at the Ohio State Fair.

Once she tossed the bundle in her hands over the side, there'd be no going back.

It was a drastic move, but she wanted to make sure she followed through this evening. That she wouldn't change her mind.

She thought of the book Harry had left for her that morning on the hall table: *The Art of Saying No.* Then she took a deep breath and with all her might, heaved the bag full of her and Blake's save-the-date cards over the side.

As it arced through the air, panic electrified her chest, driving her left hand out to snag it.

She missed.

When the bag thudded deep within the smelly cavern, Emma felt like for the first time in weeks she could finally breathe.

She brushed her hands together, as if wiping off dirt, then got back into her car and headed toward DaVinci's.

* * *

"What's wrong, Em?" Concern etched Blake's face. "You usually finish two slices of your favorite pizza before I finish one."

She poked at the slice of pizza on her plate. DaVinci's, Emma's comforting home away from home, was quiet. Only a third of the restaurant's tables were full. It was the perfect setup for sharing her feelings. She'd put this off long enough.

"I don't want to move."

"What?" Blake used his napkin to wipe his hands. Confusion knitted his brows.

"I don't want to move," she repeated with strength in her voice.

"I don't understand. You want me to go on my own? But you said you wanted to go."

"I did. But I've had time to think about it. And I'm sorry I didn't realize it sooner or admit I wasn't sure." She sat up straighter. "I don't want to go. I have no idea what I would do there, and, honestly, I'm bothered that you didn't consult me sooner. Why didn't you tell me you were applying for the residency? You had to have known about the possibility before we started dating."

Blake flinched and sat back in his chair. He hadn't seen this coming—and up until two weeks ago, neither had she. "We started dating before I applied. But I didn't want to tell you that I could be moving within months. You would have ended things."

"Is that why you proposed after four months of dating? Because you knew you might move?" She was surprised by the hint of anger in her voice, an anger that apparently jumped from her to Blake.

"I proposed because I love you. And you said yes. What's going on?"

Emma studied his handsome features. His strong clenched jaw. His hazel eyes now filled with hurt and confusion. "I guess I'm realizing that we don't know each other that well. In the few conversations we've had about our future, we don't see eye to eye on what we want that future to be."

"Why haven't you mentioned this before?" His response turned the heads of the couple dining across the room.

Her breathing became shallow. She didn't want to hurt him. Didn't want to destroy their friendship. Didn't want to destroy the relationship between their families. "Things have been moving so fast, I've barely had time to sort through what I feel."

"So what are you saying? You don't want to move, *and* you don't want to get married?" His pitch had raised, and another table started darting glances their way.

It'd been a terrible idea to have this discussion here. She lowered her voice and hoped he would follow her lead. "Let's go outside."

His lips flattened. He got out his wallet, flagged down the waiter, and handed their server cash to cover the bill. Then he grabbed his jacket and strode off for the entrance.

The two bites of pizza that Emma had eaten soured in her stomach. She gathered her purse, slipped on her fleece vest, and followed, her misery mounting with each step. She felt awful for doing this . . . and even worse for the underlying sense of relief that she'd finally spoken her mind.

Blake waited by the entrance, then silently escorted her to her car. Side by side, his six-foot-two frame towered over her five-six. The difference in height seemed to grow with each step.

He stopped at the trunk of her Honda Accord. In the clear, cold night, Emma could see her breath.

"So," he said, looking down at her, "you no longer want to get married. Is that what you're saying?"

Emma hated the suffering buried in his words. "I'm so sorry it's come to this. Maybe it'd be different if we had slowed things down. Took time to get to know each other."

"Know each other? Em, I've known you since you were six. That's over two decades." The sharpness of his voice revealed how deep she'd cut him.

Her courage wavered, and she leaned against the car. The cold metal bit through her jeans. "After you left for college, I had no contact with you for thirteen years. Now after four months of dating, I'm planning our wedding and a move. Uprooting my entire life."

"And you've *happily* gone along with everything. I haven't forced you to do anything."

Maybe not happily, thought Emma. *But she hadn't been honest with herself—sometimes that wasn't easy to do.*

A couple walked by arm in arm. Two giggling girls held hands and skipped behind them. A strong gust of wind blew through the parking lot, and the four scurried inside their nearby car. Their happy togetherness slammed against the fate unfolding between Emma and Blake, a stark reminder of a future that would never be.

Emma put her hands in her vest pockets and pressed on, despite the viselike grip crushing her heart. She didn't want to hurt him. "I know. But you asked me to move, to leave my job and family, on short notice. You applied for the residency without consulting me. You planned the trip to St. Louis and told me only days before leaving, and you started looking at apartments before even telling me about the move. It's like I'm along for the ride, not helping choose the direction we take."

Blake gulped in the frigid air. "Our relationship has always felt natural to me. I can't help but wonder if what you're upset about is something else, like the state of your career, and that's making you second-guess us."

It felt like there was an insult in his words. "You're right. Since I left nursing, I have been unsure about what to do. Nursing isn't a great fit, and neither is caregiving. But over the past month, I've gained clarity."

"Have you?" Patronization seeped into those two words. "Because from where I'm standing, you've been acting erratically." He placed his hands on her shoulders. "I miss the way things were when we started dating."

Of course he did. For the first three months of their relationship, Emma had fawned over him and stared at him with puppy-dog eyes, awestruck by the fact that *she* was dating Blake Derrickson. "So you're happy with me when I'm willing to do whatever you want?"

"That's not what I said." He dropped his hands. "My last relationship was nothing but struggle. Daphne and I fought over everything: who should lighten their work schedule so we could squeeze in a date, whose family we should visit over the holidays, whose career was more important. I don't want another relationship like that."

A sudden memory of the previous Christmas floated through Emma's mind. Blake's mom had lamented the absence of her son over the punchbowl in Emma's mother's kitchen. Blake and his high-powered lawyer girlfriend were visiting her family in California and would not be passing through Columbus.

"I'm offering you a great life, Em. I'll earn a ton of money. Money that will enable us to live in a beautiful house, belong to a country club, take care of our mothers, go on European vacations, drive fancy cars. Isn't that what all women want?"

"I'm not all women. I want to help people. To live a life of purpose, like my dad."

"And look what good that did him."

His words hit her with the ferocity of a sucker punch. She took a step back. Any vacillation she'd felt before was gone. "I don't think we're a good match, Blake. We want different things out of life."

"I seriously can't believe *you* are second-guessing *me*."

Pain and fury exploded in Emma's chest. She moved to jerk her hands out of her vest pockets. Her right hand freed, but the left remained. Her engagement ring had snagged on the pocket's lining. *Crap.*

She tugged at it with more force.

Blake's tone chilled. "Daphne is going to be *thrilled* to hear that you and I have broken up. I saw her in St. Louis, and she went on and on about how much she misses me."

Now thoroughly ticked off, Emma yanked her left hand again with all her might.

"What are you doing?"

"Trying to give you back that *blasted* engagement ring." Emma used her right hand to unzip her vest, struggled to remove her right arm, then slid the vest down her left arm to take it off.

"Emma . . ." He reached to help her. Her eyes fired warning shots for him to stop, a glare she'd picked up from her mother's arsenal.

The two stood in the freezing cold as Emma twisted and pulled the engagement ring. After a long, glacial moment that felt like a polar night, the ring slid off her finger but remained stuck inside the vest pocket.

"Here." Emma shoved the ring and vest at him. "May you and Daphne live happily ever after." Then she stomped to her car door as Blake stormed off.

She froze. Her car keys were in her right vest pocket. She swore under her breath, "Son of a . . ."

"Blake." She ran after him, her cheeks hot, her chest burning. "My keys are in the other pocket."

Without a word, he turned back, removed the keys, and tossed them to her. They hit the pavement near her feet with a final, deafening clatter that brought searing tears to her eyes.

Chapter Twenty-Eight

After Harry got home from dinner with David, he showed off for Ceci. With the iPad in his right hand, he walked around the house going short distances without his cane as they chatted via FaceTime.

"Dad, if you fall again, I'm moving you into an assisted living facility," she joked, her laughter crinkling the skin around her eyes. Her hair had gone back to his favorite style for her: jet black and tousled.

"Don't jest about such things. Did you and Steve confirm dates for your trip back?"

"Our flights are booked for December eighth. We'll be there for about a month." She sounded as excited as he felt. Soon he could start buying the kids Christmas gifts. Their wish lists were typically long.

"I'm so glad you're getting around better. I promised the kids we'll go see the lights at the zoo." The Columbus Zoo and Aquarium's Festival of Lights at Christmastime was a holiday tradition.

"Sounds great. I had dinner tonight with David at Chez Margot and told him how excited I am to see you all."

"Mom loved that place." She paused and softened her voice. "I put all of Mom's CDs, including all those French ones, in the cupboard next to the fireplace if you want to play them sometime."

There'd been a time when Mags had listened to nothing but Edith Piaf. He smiled at the memory and decided to give one of Mags's Edith Piaf CDs to David. He'd never properly thanked David for being a friend when Harry had needed one. He checked the clock—not yet eight thirty. Early enough to do that this evening.

Minutes later, after he said goodbye to Ceci, he picked up his cane and the CD he wanted, then headed outside.

The temperature had drastically dropped since dinner and when he got to the bottom of his drive, he regretted not putting on a coat. He smiled at the black and white CD cover and started humming "La Vie en Rose." The clicking of his cane and the pond's gurgling fountain providing accompaniment.

A stiff wind whipped up leaves. Clouds obscured the moon. Goosebumps rose on his arms as he climbed his friend's drive. None of David's lights were on, and Harry hoped he hadn't already gone to bed.

When he stepped onto the porch, Harry lowered his humming and knocked in beat to the tune. The door creaked inward.

The hairs on the back of Harry's neck stood, one by one.

"David? It's Harry."

No response.

Using his shoulder, he pushed the door inward, careful not to touch the door handle, and careful not to think about the instinct that told him not to.

He stepped into the foyer. He hadn't been inside David's house before, so didn't know the layout. Perhaps David was down in the basement or up in the attic. "David?"

The resounding silence made Harry's heart thunder, each beat a reverberating strike on a bass drum. He wanted to flee, but instead took another step in, feeling like an intruder defiling sacred ground.

Given the conversation at dinner, perhaps David had gone to see Victoria and, in his haste, hadn't fully closed the door. Had David's car been in the drive or the garage when they'd left for Chez Margot?

Harry reached to turn on the lights, then stopped himself, not wanting to smudge any potential fingerprints. He cursed the thought and took another step forward.

"David, it's Harry."

Moonlight trickled in through the foyer and living room windows, providing Harry with enough visibility to move around. A coatrack in the corner held three jackets. A bicycle helmet and stacks of mail sat on a nearby hall stand. He ignored the stairs to his right, which led up to a pitch-black second floor. He cracked the door in front of him to find a closet.

To his left, nothing appeared out of order in David's living room. A huge, widescreen television sat atop a modern console that faced a leather lounge set. There was a click from a neighboring room, followed by the gentle hum of a distant appliance.

Each of Harry's steps became slower, heavier, as if resisting what was to inevitably come. The adjoining room was darker, and Harry could barely make out a circular glass table with uncomfortable-looking chairs.

He moved into the dining room and his heart stopped. A metallic taste filled his mouth, accompanied by an unmistakable smell. His heart resumed beating, then tripled in speed and clawed its way up into his throat. He moved through the dining room toward the next doorway, dreading what he knew he'd find beyond it.

Harry knew violent death. He'd seen it in active combat and war-torn countries and under the conditions that sparked the brutalities of men. But he never thought he'd see it this close to home.

The kitchen was illuminated with a green glow from the oven and microwave clocks. Dishes were stacked by the sink. A skillet and pot sat on the stovetop. Everything looked normal, but the iron smell of blood was overwhelming.

He looked down. A dapper-shoed foot and a suit-pant-clad leg protruded from the other side of the kitchen island. The CD slipped from Harry's hand and clattered on the tile floor.

"Oh no!" Harry rushed around the island with his cane.

David sat slumped against the island in the same clothes he'd worn to dinner. His legs were awkwardly angled in front of him, his hands covering a dark mass that spread across the white shirt below his suit jacket. Blood pooled between David's legs and off to the right side of his body.

Harry maneuvered around the puddle of blood, then leaned down to check for a pulse on David's neck. He pressed up and down his friend's clammy skin.

"No. No . . ."

Then he felt it. A faint beat.

David was alive.

He dropped his cane and scrambled for the kitchen phone to call 911.

* * *

The next twenty minutes were a blur . . . trying to staunch the wound . . . begging David to hang on . . . being pushed away from his friend's body when the EMTs arrived.

Harry sat on David's couch, studying the blood that soaked his clothes and hands. He fought to push back the immense fear and sadness that overwhelmed him.

The ambulance had screamed away, with EMTs intense and David holding on. Police now flooded the living room, which was awash in beams of red and blue lights that burst through the windows.

A uniformed officer with the build of the Incredible Hulk approached him. "Sir, could you please stand and raise your hands," in an incongruous high-pitched voice. It was the same officer who'd been on the scene when Sue's body was found. "I need to make sure you're not armed."

Harry stood and held his hands out, palms up, as if carrying an invisible tray. "Will David be okay?"

"I'm afraid I don't know, sir."

As the officer finished patting Harry down, a deep voice called from the foyer, "Mr. Lancaster." Detective Bradford rushed into the room. "Thanks, Clark. I've got this." With a nod, he dismissed the giant, who joined the fray of lawmen in the kitchen. "What happened?"

Harry explained—he realized, incoherently in an anachronistic fashion—dinner with David and how he'd found David bleeding on the kitchen floor.

"I must have dropped the CD. It's somewhere in there." He pointed toward the dining room and the crime scene beyond. His shoulders hunched as memories of David washed over him.

Detective Bradford touched Harry's elbow. "Mr. Lancaster, are you with me?"

He'd missed what the detective had been saying. "What?" He refocused his gaze.

"Let's get you home. I'll have Officer Clark escort you while I check out the crime scene."

* * *

An hour later, Detective Bradford sat in the accent chair next to Harry in front of the kitchen sitting area fireplace. Harry had washed up, changed clothes, and settled under a blanket, consumed by worry for his friend. He'd called the nearby hospital three times; no one would divulge any information.

"Do you know how David is doing?" Harry asked, afraid of the answer.

"When I last checked, he was still in surgery in critical condition."

Harry nodded and sent up a silent prayer. Then, feeling oddly betrayed, he turned to study the detective. "Did you really close Sue's case, or have you been investigating her death all this time?"

Bradford's expression changed slightly, and he moved in his seat before speaking. "Technically, it was closed after the ME ruled it an accidental death from poisoning. But whatever you and Emma picked up on at the scene, I also noticed, and it stuck in my craw. Too many abnormal events in the neighborhood, too many people didn't like Sue Daniels. And there were some oddities in her bank records."

"So why did you tell me and Emma otherwise?"

"I didn't want you two under my feet—or putting yourselves in danger. Perhaps I should have handled it differently." He scrubbed his face with his hands. "I want this killer behind bars before anyone else gets hurt. What else have you learned that I should know?"

"You know about David cheating on his girlfriend, and how Sue had been blackmailing him because of it?"

"Yes. Mr. Dubois told me about that, and mentioned the blackmail hadn't stopped. I—"

Harry cut him off. "You need to look for someone in a light-colored sedan. That's who's still leaving packages in David's mailbox.

Detective Bradford pulled out his pen and notepad. "What's the make and model?"

"I'm not sure. It wasn't distinctive. Perhaps something by Chrysler? It was an older, boxy model."

He nodded and wrote it down. "Maybe Sue hired someone to follow David, help gather blackmail material, take photos, that sort of thing. And that person has now taken over. Did you ever meet Victoria or Charlotte?"

"No. But David mentioned he'd broken off his relationship with them both."

"That's another angle to explore. Although, given Sue's death, it seems unlikely. You're sure you didn't see or hear anything before heading over to David's that might help?"

Harry shook his head. "You don't know how sorry I am for not following my normal routine of sitting in the sunroom tonight. If I'd been by the window, perhaps I could have seen something. Or if I'd gone over earlier, maybe I could have prevented this."

Guilt pummeled his chest. He'd been joking with Ceci while his friend inched toward death next door.

"If you'd gone over earlier, I might have two people at the hospital fighting for their lives, or worse, on their way to the morgue." Detective Bradford checked his watch. "It's almost midnight. I need to get back to the crime scene. Try to rest despite the circumstances." They moved to the foyer.

Harry noticed deeper wrinkles on the detective's face. "Thank you, Detective Bradford. Lakeview Lane has you working around the clock."

Detective Bradford stepped out onto the porch, then turned back, buttoning his trench coat to fight back the frosty air. "I'll stop by tomorrow in case you recall anything else."

As he battened down the hatches for the night, fatigue battered Harry with the force of Drake Passage waves, though he knew sleep would be elusive.

David was a good friend. Always there for him with a warm smile and a ready ear after Mags had passed. This time, David had been in need, telling Harry, albeit in a roundabout way, that he feared for his life. A life that now hung in the balance.

Chapter Twenty-Nine

The doorbell woke Harry at nine the next morning. Groggy from a nearly sleepless night, he pulled on his robe, snatched his cane, and started toward the door. Emma must have misplaced her key.

The doorbell rang again, followed by heaving pounding. *Thump. Thump. Thump.*

He stepped into the foyer and opened the door to find not Emma but an irate Agatha Hooper: the nurse with coal pellet eyes, a thin face, and an elongated pointy nose. She wore drab clothes and an imposing glower.

Stunned, Harry stood frozen, mouth agape.

"Step back." Nurse Agatha ordered. "It's cold out here. Do you sleep all day? You won't get better if you're in bed all the time. Now go get dressed and I'll make you breakfast."

He didn't move.

"I said *go*," she commanded in drill-sergeant tones. The precision of her steely bun and the purse of her lips were ample evidence that she'd brook no argument.

Harry let her in and fled to his room. Where in the blazes was Emma? Nurse Agatha was more intimidating than Old Ironsides.

When he found his cell phone, he saw Emma had left a message that morning. He needed to stop keeping the phone on silent.

He listened to his voicemail. Emma sounded miserable, apologetic, and distraught.

"Hi, Harry. I have personal things I need to do today. I called the agency to send in a replacement. I'm sorry for the late notice. See you tomorrow at my normal time."

He'd been looking forward to Emma's nurturing smile, but she had problems of her own. His paternal instincts kicked in, and he started to call her back to check in on her, then thought better of it, not wanting to be overly intrusive. If she wanted to talk to him about what was going on, she'd call.

He dillydallied as he got cleaned up and dressed. The less time with Nurse Agatha, the better. When he finally exited his bedroom, he found a bowl of tepid oatmeal waiting for him on the kitchen table, next to a cup of coffee.

Nurse Agatha stood by the kitchen counter. She reminded him of a Victorian era schoolmarm—not that he was *that* old.

"You took your time," she harped. "After breakfast, you can rest. We'll go for a brisk walk at noon. I found a can of tomato soup in the pantry for your lunch. Then you can rest for an hour before we go to your physical therapy appointment."

He sat at the table, then turned to Nurse Agatha, who'd moved to the kitchen sink. "I drink tea, not coffee. Could you please put the kettle on for me?"

"Nonsense. The antioxidants in coffee are good for you, and the caffeine will make your mind sharp." She busied herself with cleaning dishes.

Harry finished the gooey oatmeal, leaving the coffee untouched. As soon as she left the kitchen, he'd brew some tea. He mentioned laundry that needed to be done to divert her to the mudroom. When she left, he rushed in to make a pot of Earl Grey.

She caught him as the kettle whistled. Her voice was equally as shrill. "What are you doing? You shouldn't be messing with boiling water."

"I'm making tea," he said defiantly, embarrassed that he felt this way in his own home. "And I'm perfectly capable of boiling water. I'll let you finish preparing it. You can bring it to me by the fireplace."

She curtly motioned him out of her way, and he retreated to the kitchen's sitting area before she changed her mind. When the tea was ready, she plopped it down on the end table beside him. He sighed in exasperation. He liked it with cream and sugar, but this was not a battle worth fighting.

He picked up the cup and took solace from the steam caressing his face. He used the remote to turn on the gas fire, but the heat couldn't rid him of the shock of finding David. Using his iPad, he tried to focus on completing another online job application. When that didn't work, he reviewed reports about current trends in international aid. The letters blurred, repeatedly displaced by images from the night before.

The doorbell rang, and he heard Nurse Agatha dislodge from her perch on a kitchen stool. Harry turned to watch her open the door.

It was a surprised male voice. "I'm Detective Bradford. I'm here to speak with Mr. Lancaster."

"He's recovering from a fractured hip and can't be bothered by visitors." She went to slam the door in the detective's face, but Harry, who despised raising his voice, called out to stop her.

"Nurse Agatha, I've been expecting the detective." He stood and motioned for the man to join him.

"I'll let you go about your business, but keep it short." She stepped aside so the detective could pass, then settled in a living room chair where she could eavesdrop.

The detective wore jeans, a Patagonia jacket, and the strain from Lakeview Lane's spate of violence on his face. It looked like he needed a haircut, a shave, and a week of sleep. "Where's Emma?" he asked as he neared.

"She got tied up today, so she called in a sub. She'll be back tomorrow. Any more news on David? The hospital won't share any information with me because I'm not family."

The detective looked sympathetic and pulled a notepad from his jacket. "I checked first thing this morning. David sustained damage to his stomach and small intestine from the gunshot wound. He was in surgery for more than eight hours last night. He's in critical condition."

"He's in the ICU?"

"Yes, and probably will be for a while. He hasn't regained consciousness yet. But he's in good hands." The detective readied his pen. "Are you up to answering a few more questions?"

"Sure."

"Do you remember anything else that might be helpful, from last night or over the past few weeks."

"There is one thing I forgot to tell you. Emma and I found out that Sue and Jimmy went on a trip together. And Jimmy told me that he didn't know Sue well."

"Hmm. He told me that too. Were they dating?"

"I don't know. But if they were, and it ended badly—"

"Jimmy would have motive." The detective made a rapid note. "How did you find out?"

Harry stretched the truth a bit. "I was at an inn where Sue and Jimmy had stayed for a weekend, and it came up in conversation with the inn's staff."

"Really? You just happened to be there, and it just happened to come up?" The detective didn't press the point. "Jimmy Chatimont lives in the unit attached to David Dubois's home, right?" Harry nodded. "I didn't see him come outside to check out the commotion last night. Did you?"

"No." Harry stilled. That seemed odd, but maybe Jimmy hadn't been home. Then another thought popped into his head. "I'm not sure if it's relevant or not, but late one night about a week ago, I saw Milo Czesiak and David arguing on David's porch. It lasted about five minutes, then Milo went home."

"Any idea what it was about?"

"If I had to guess, something related to zoning and Rachel Valucci's boutique downtown."

The detective's dark eyebrows bunched.

"Rachel and Milo are having an affair," Harry clarified. "While zoning may not affect Milo's trucking company, it would affect Rachel's business. David has substantial power in terms of urban development. While the zoning board makes final decisions, his opinions carry significant weight with the other members."

"We'll look into that. I'm sure there are more people who have been angered by city zoning decisions."

"True," Harry conceded. "One more thing . . . at the last condo board meeting, David and I were talking about Sue's murder. He said if he had to guess who in the neighborhood would be a murder victim, Sue would've been his first bet. Then he said the second person would've been him."

"That's odd. Did he say why?"

"Something to do with zoning, but he wasn't specific about any one thing."

"I'll have the team go back and cross-check for ways that David's and Sue's lives intersected."

"It would seem to be a rather big coincidence, two unconnected violent acts in a small community in such a short time."

"Yeah. Anything else?"

Harry shook his head.

Detective Bradford closed his notepad and slipped it back into his pocket. "You okay?"

"I will be. It'll take a few days to deal with the shock. You'll keep me posted on David?"

The detective nodded, then rose, prompting Harry to follow. "I've requested a squad car to drive around the lane several times a day and each night. I'm also telling this to all your neighbors, so hopefully future violence will be discouraged by an increased police presence. Now I've got others to interview, Mr. Lancaster. Hopefully, someone saw something that will lead to an arrest soon."

"Thank you. And you should call me Harry."

The detective's smile was tired. He glanced in Nurse Agatha's direction and whispered, "Good luck." Harry watched Nurse Agatha let him out, her scowl readily at hand.

Once the detective left, she refocused on Harry. "We should take your walk now before other visitors barge in to disturb you." He reluctantly stood, clasped his cane, and fetched his coat from the closet. This was another battle not worth fighting.

Outside, the day was bleak. Cold and gray and dreary. He and Nurse Agatha made their way down his drive, as Detective Bradford walked up to Jimmy's. Nurse Agatha moved around the lane at a brisk march. Harry focused on the ground to ensure safe placement of his cane and tried to match her gait. When they neared Rachel's, a door slammed. She scurried down her drive toward them, her tan leather boots clattering with each step.

"Oh, Harry. Diana told me about David. This is so awful. What's happening to our lane?" Rachel grabbed his free hand. He could smell her perfume, a pleasant blend of musk and vanilla. Her brown eyes pleaded with him to fix things.

As Rachel stepped back and adjusted her fur wrap, she must have noticed it was not Emma by his side. "Who are you?"

"I'm Mr. Lancaster's nurse. Agatha Hooper. Be careful with him. You could throw him off balance."

By the look on Rachel's face, Harry could tell that she'd already dismissed Agatha as irrelevant. Judgment made, Rachel turned back to him. "Where's Emma?"

"She's taking a day off. She'll be back tomorrow." For the umpteenth time that day, he prayed this was true.

Rachel fingered his knit scarf. "I have lovely cashmere scarves that would complement your coloring. This shade of red isn't for you. You *and* Emma need to visit."

"Speaking of your boutique, was David about to make a zoning decision that would affect your store?"

Rachel lips formed a delicate circle. "Well, yes, but how did you find out? David hadn't finalized things. He went back and forth between making the street behind my store residential or adding commercial storefronts."

Her gaze flitted toward Milo's house. "Milo spoke with David to outline the pros associated with making it residential. I think David would have done the right thing and limited the number of stores in the area. There really aren't enough homes in the Short North with walkability." Rachel eyed him with sincerity, a look she'd mastered.

He was about to ask another question when Nurse Agatha interrupted. "Mr. Lancaster, we need to keep you moving. You shouldn't be standing in this cold."

With a deep sigh, he pushed down the frustration rising in his chest. "It was good to see you, Rachel. I hope the zoning decision is made in your favor."

Rachel gave his elbow a squeeze. "Thank you." Then she flashed Nurse Agatha a crocodile grin and retreated up her drive. Halfway up, she called over her shoulder. "Be careful."

* * *

That evening at a quarter to six, Harry left his house. Nature had served up a stunning sunset. Streaks of pink, orange, and purple flared across billowing clouds. As he strolled around the lane, he used his free hand to fidget with his scarf so it blocked his neck from the biting wind.

With David's attempted murder and Emma's absence, he felt an urgent need to connect with those around him, and he was looking forward to dinner with the Patels. Life was short.

Mags would not want him squandering the time he had left. He could almost hear her now: "No sense in losing the present to the past."

He rang the Patels' doorbell, and a minute later, Gautam answered, smiling broadly, wearing chinos and a navy argyle sweater. Gautam patted Harry on the shoulder as he stepped in. "Come in, come in."

"Namaste, Gautam. Pleasure to be here."

Gautam hung up Harry's coat and scarf, and they headed toward the back of the house, the smell of turmeric and smoky cumin enticing them down the hallway. When Harry entered the pumpkin-colored dining room, he could almost see Mags sitting at the antique walnut table, commenting on the striking London cityscapes that filled the walls.

Harry greeted Sakshi, who'd paused in setting the table. "Namaste, aap kaisee hain?"

"Namaste. Main achchhi hoon." She beamed, her peach sweater complementing her coloring.

Harry caught another aromatic wave from the kitchen, and his stomach rumbled. "It smells wonderful. I've been looking forward to this all day." Nurse Agatha's disappointing breakfast and equally lackluster lunch had well prepared him.

After catching up over a predinner martini, Sakshi excused herself to get their meal from the kitchen. They began with daal tadka, a lentil soup that brought back cherished memories. It'd been Ceci's favorite when they'd lived in Delhi. For their main course, Sakshi served murg tikka masala along with homemade naan and raita.

Harry savored every bite, feeling the food and the friendship nourish his soul. He shouldn't have waited so long to reconnect with the cheerful couple.

"Remember the time Margaret made beef vindaloo?" He reached for more naan.

Sakshi chortled. "Do I? I think of her every time I make that dish now. Hers turned out so spicy we couldn't eat it, no matter how much raita we added."

"The look on your face with your first bite," Gautam could barely get his words out in between fits of laughter. "You must have downed a pint of milk trying to cool your mouth."

"I couldn't tell if you were crying from laughing or because of the spice." Sakshi picked up her martini glass. "But her saag paneer was divine." She gave Harry an affectionate smile. "I'm so glad you've come. We've missed having you at our table."

"Cheers to that." Gautam picked up his drink, and they toasted.

Conversation shifted, and they reminisced about India: the hot humid nights before monsoon season, the chaotic traffic often redirected by a wandering cow, and the vibrant atmosphere, brimming with people and color.

The discussion slowed, and Sakshi asked, "Would you like more raita? The tikka masala is spicier than normal." She looked pleased that Harry was eating with such vigor.

"Kripya." He held out his plate out. Once she heaped a spoonful onto his plate, he replied "Dhanyawaad," thanking her for her generosity.

When the plates neared empty, Harry decided to finally address the topic they'd avoided all night. The topic that weighted his heart. The topic that sat with them like a six-ton elephant in the room.

"I can't believe someone tried to kill David."

Sakshi put her fork down. "We've been in shock all day. It's surreal. Any more news about his condition? Last I heard he was stable but still in the ICU."

Harry nodded. "Detective Bradford sent a text late this afternoon stating that there'd been no change in his condition. A bit worrying because he still hasn't woken up."

"Oh dear," Sakshi's hand rose to her chest.

"Sue's death has to be related, don't you think?" Gautam asked.

"Seems likely," Harry said.

"That detective came back today asking questions," Sakshi said, "like he thinks someone on the lane is responsible for all of it. But it can't be one of us. I just don't see it."

"Perhaps you're right," Harry conceded. But deep down, he knew the killer was close. It was one of their neighbors, one of their friends.

"I think it makes sense that the police are interested in people on the lane," Gautam contradicted. "Sue fought with almost everyone: Milo, Rachel, David. I think Diana was her only friend."

"Not quite, dear," Sakshi corrected. "I know we have that landscaping service, but I enjoy fussing over our garden most afternoons. And I remember seeing both Diana and Jimmy taking dishes to Sue before she died."

Harry cocked his head and focused on Sakshi. "Both of them?"

"Yes. In fact, the two of them often dropped food off for Sue."

Harry sat back in his chair. The two murder suspects he'd deemed the most unlikely were looking guiltier with each passing day.

Chapter Thirty

"That's right, Nurse Agatha," Harry said, over the telephone, grateful he'd caught the caregiver before she arrived on his doorstep the next morning. "I won't need your services today." He half paid attention to her warnings about the risks of being alone as his mind revisited what Sakshi had said last night.

He put the cast iron kettle on the stovetop to boil water, rolled back the sleeves of his robe, then turned on the gas. "I'll be fine."

"I insist."

Nurse Agatha's tone was firm, but Harry's was firmer. "I appreciate your concern, but Emma has reassured me that she'll be back tomorrow, and I have neighbors nearby if I need anything today. Thanks for your help." He disconnected before Nurse Agatha could respond and replaced the phone in its charger on the kitchen counter.

The garbled message Emma had left late last night concerned him. It had not gone well with Blake. She sounded miserable, and he wondered if he should call to check in on her. But when did caring cross over into obtrusive?

Eager for caffeine, he added tea to a ceramic pot. The phone rang and he prayed it wasn't Nurse Agatha calling back.

A rumbly male voice spoke as soon as he picked up. "Lancaster, it's Geoff Jeffries."

It'd been so long since Harry had sent the email, he'd forgotten that he'd emailed his tall and gangly PI friend. With his deep-brown disc eyes, large nose, huge ears, and spikey brown hair, Geoff could blend in with roaming giraffe on any African savanna.

"Geoff, Good to hear from you."

"Apologies for the delay. Had to run some security training courses in Sudan, and then caught an unexpected two-day gig in Uganda. But you know how that goes."

Harry wished he did. Yesterday, he'd received three rejections from consulting applications. "No worries. You're doing well?" In the background, Harry could hear conversation and soft music.

"Things are great, but busy. My schedule has gotten crazier in retirement." Geoff chuckled, clearly happy about the situation. "I'm sorry about Margaret. She was a lovely woman."

"She was." To Harry's astonishment, instead of the usual weight that came with the mention of Mags's death, gratitude for having spent five decades with the woman he loved surged through him. He paused, reveling in the moment.

The kettle whistled, and Harry poured steaming water into the ceramic teapot. Across the line, he could hear an airport PA system call a flight. When it finished, Harry spoke. "I'm sure you're busy, so I won't take up too much of your time."

"Take as much time as you need. You saved my hide with on-the-ground insight too many times to count. Besides, I'm stuck in Delta's SkyLounge in Frankfurt. My flight home got delayed."

"Were you able to learn anything about that list of neighbors I sent?" He envisioned Geoff at a table with empty coffee cups and his possessions scattered about. Geoff was as messy as he was smart and ran on coffee as thick as tar.

There was some rustling before Geoff responded. "Yep. I found some gems with Lexis Nexis and Thomas Reuters' Clear, so I tapped some of my police connections to dig deeper. But the real gold mine came from social media, once I knew what to look for."

"Gold mine?" Harry turned up the volume on his cell phone, not wanting to miss one word. "What'd you find?"

"First off, the only thing I learned about Diana Middleton is that she gives a significant amount of money to her church and charities that support unwed mothers and orphans."

"I could've sworn she was hiding something." Harry poured a cup of the freshly brewed tea, then added cream and sugar.

"Just because I couldn't find a big secret doesn't mean one doesn't exist. Same with Gautam Patel. There'd been embezzlement at the firm where he used to work, but the police focused their investigations on the IT department and arrested the CIO."

"I didn't know that." Harry maneuvered to the kitchen table with his cup.

"That doesn't clear Gautam. The police could have been wrong. Anyway, Diana and the Patels are wealthy, so that would give a blackmailer incentive." There was an explosion of laughter in the background. "One sec. A tour group walked in. Let me see if I can find a different table. You need to hear this."

There was shuffling, more voices, and the PA system called another flight. Harry sipped his tea as seconds turned into minutes. His anticipation grew. A gold mine meant something big.

Geoff returned. "Sorry about that. Took a while to find a quieter place. Now, let's see . . . Jimmy Chatimont worked as a chef in a five-star restaurant, the Green Palm, in Miami for years before moving to Ohio. Thing is, his salary couldn't explain his lifestyle, especially the swanky home where he'd lived. So I made some calls to friends in France, where Jimmy is originally from.

He's part of a powerful and uber-wealthy family. My guess is they subsidize his way of life."

"Jimmy's family is rich?"

"Looks like it. I couldn't find a motive for blackmail, but he has enough dough to be ripe picking for a blackmailer. His family is worth several hundred million. And that's in euros, not US dollars."

Harry whistled. "That is a lot of money." Jimmy Chatimont's suave clothing pointed to considerable means, but he'd never been snobbish.

"That said, I didn't find a scandal associated with him. Then there's Rachel Valucci and her husband's death—"

"The suspicious boating accident."

"Oh. You knew about that?"

"Yes. Learned about it a few days ago."

"Well,"—Geoff raised his voice to be heard over the rising airport lounge din—"then I should get to the jackpot."

Harry tightened his grip on the phone. "Go on."

"So, your buddy Milo Czesiak," Geoff paused, milking the moment, "isn't Milo Czesiak."

"What?" Harry stood in shock, knocking over his chair and sloshing tea onto the table. He stumbled for a second before he found solid footing. "What do you mean?"

"I mean, he's not *the real* Milo Czesiak. The real Milo Czesiak is in a mental institution in upstate New York and has been for over ten years."

"Holy smokes." Harry expelled a breath of air and started pacing around the kitchen table. "Wait, maybe the two men have the same name."

"Two men named Milo Przemyslaw Czesiak born on March 3, 1955, in Pittock, Pennsylvania? The odds are better that I'll get remarried, and after wife number five dumped me, trust me, that ain't gonna happen."

There was more background noise on the line before Geoff continued. "After confirming Milo's birthplace, I called in a favor with a retired buddy of mine who worked for the Pittsburgh PD. He's four months into retirement and bored so was happy to help."

"A favor to do what?"

"Go down to Pittock to poke around."

"And?"

"By buttering up some of the town's pensioners—granted, you and I now fall into that category—with several rounds at the local drinking hole, he found out Milo's family had attended the local Catholic church. So, he buddied up to the priest, who let him go through boxes of decades-old parish newsletters, where he found a blurb about Milo. The real Milo."

"What'd it say?"

"The newsletter referenced a fundraiser to help pay for Milo's long-term care, but they didn't get specific about what kind of care that was. There was also a reference to some trouble that the real Milo had gotten into years ago."

The airport PA system crackled, and Geoff waited for it to subside.

"The priest hadn't been there when the Czesiak family were part of the parish, but the choir director, who happened to drop by, had." Geoff chuckled. "The Lord works in mysterious ways."

Harry swallowed his eagerness. "He does. What did the choir director say?"

"He told my buddy that the real Milo beat up his mother back in 2003, but she didn't press charges because he'd had mental issues his whole adult life. Come to find out, he's got schizophrenia, so the church has been helping raise money to keep Milo in an institution in upstate New York."

"Maybe they found the right medication and he got released."

"I called. The real Milo's still there. And here's the clincher: my buddy faxed me a copy of the church newsletter that featured photos of Milo—the real Milo—over the years. The two men's facial features look nothing alike. Very different jaws, eyes, and noses."

"How'd you get a picture of my Milo? It's not on his company's website, and I didn't find any social accounts for him."

"Give me some credit. I found his photo compliments of Rachel Valucci's Facebook feed. On Valentine's Day, she posted a photo of her and her love Milo enjoying a romantic dinner. So touching," he said with heavy sarcasm.

"Wait, Emma and I checked Rachel's Facebook page. It only shows four or five photos of her and her shop. Most of her account is private."

"Not for someone who knows how to hack it."

"You *are* good." Harry found himself smiling, marveling at how Milo and Rachel were the perfect couple. Neither were who they claimed to be.

Rachel's transformation had been more convincing, or maybe her flirting covered the gaps. Milo had adopted some Hollywood stereotype of a blue-collar worker: jeans, T-shirt, gold chain. But his feet had never matched, Harry realized. His fancy shoes and viniculture-related socks told a different story.

"So who is my Milo?"

"Beats me. The two share the same height, build, eye color, and hair color, but your Milo is now practically bald. Maybe the other guy is balding too, who knows? That's beside the point."

"How did the police here not catch this?"

"They would have run a background check through the NCIC, the National Crime Information Center, on Milo Czesiak with his date of birth and seen the alignment of his age, height, etc., and that he didn't have any current records. Again, the real Milo's mother didn't press charges. And it's not like the real Milo is getting into trouble or running up bad credit while institutionalized. They wouldn't have run the fake Milo's prints unless they had probable cause or an arrest warrant."

The PA system blared another announcement. "I gotta go. They're boarding my flight."

Harry heard shuffling and guessed Geoff was gathering his belongings. "One last thing. Your Milo must have paid handsomely for the real Milo's identity because it's a pretty good fit. Your Milo—the fake one—is definitely on the run from something."

Chapter Thirty-One

Emma stood in her IKEA bedroom assessing the distance between her pine bed and the floor. No way she'd be able to hide under it, she'd never fit.

She trudged toward the incessant pounding at her front door, passing the dining room table she'd assembled. Her bright and airy apartment typically brought her great joy. It was her first time living by herself, having left behind a group house of critical care nurses two months prior. But even home sweet home couldn't provide comfort today.

Her strategy of avoiding telling her mother about her decision was showing its flaws. She should have done it after telling Blake and done so over the phone. It would have been better to have the conversation with distance between her and her mom.

The empty pizza box on her coffee table from dinner last night caught her attention. She moved it to the kitchen counter, straightened her day-old sweatshirt, and opened the door.

Her petite mother somehow filled the doorframe, hands on hips, legs astride, steam streaming from her ears. Combined with her green skirt and blazer and functional brown boots, she looked like an aging Girl Scout assassin.

"Emma. Bethann. Stockton. What have you done?" Her mom's tone was controlled, which made the question and the use of her middle name even more menacing.

"Hi, Mom. I guess Blake must have told his mother about our conversation." She stepped aside to let her mom in, but the older woman didn't budge.

"No." She blustered. "He did not. Blake told Ethan, and Ethan told Matthew, and Matthew told me. *I* had to tell Patricia." Her heavy emphasis on "I" made Emma cringe.

Great. Now Ethan and Matthew and Patricia were all involved. "Why don't you come in?" Emma made a sweeping motion toward her living room. "No need to bring my neighbors into this too."

Her mother's eyes tossed flaming daggers. "Do not get smart with me, missy. I am in no mood." She hadn't used any contractions. That was never a good sign.

Two steps into her living room, her mom stopped. "What *is* that smell?" She scrutinized Emma's clothing. "You have pizza sauce on the sleeve of your sweatshirt. Did you have pizza for breakfast?"

Heat rose in Emma's cheeks. She scratched the back of her neck and waited for her mom to go for her jugular. She knew there'd be fallout from her decision but hoped they would understand—or at least respect her decision.

"I just had lunch with Patricia. We're both so upset that neither of us could eat a thing." Not that her mother ever ate much. "Why didn't you tell me? Why did I have to hear this from your brother? Your brother!"

"I tried to tell you when we were shop—"

"Do you know how many hours the wedding task force has slaved over planning your wedding? Do you?" It was a rhetorical question, and Emma was smart enough to remain silent.

"And after all of our hard work," she gestured with her hands to underscore how laborious that work had been, "neither you nor

Blake had the courtesy to tell your mothers that the wedding has been called off."

Emma sat on the couch, pushing aside the wadded blanket next to her. Her mom sat in the opposing chair and pinned Emma's attention with her steely eyes. "This marriage would have been the *perfect* union, of you and Blake as a couple, and of our families."

She could see hurt and disappointment burbling beneath her mom's indignation. She chose her words carefully. "Everything was moving so fast. As Blake and I talked about our future, it became clear that we want different things out of life. It took me a while to figure it out, and then I wanted to be sure about what I was doing."

"Blake is smart and kind and respectful." Her mom stressed each adjective. "He would have been a great provider, for you and your children." She leaned forward. "You *do not* toss someone like that aside—"

"Blake is a wonderful man," Emma interrupted with force in her voice that caused a stupefied look on her mother's face. She thought of Harry, and how he would have handled the situation, and tempered her tone. "But he's not *my* wonderful man. I know you understand what I mean. I want what you had with Dad. And I know deep down you want that for me too."

It was hard to convey something amorphous. Things with Blake just seemed *wrong*. A gap between them suddenly emerged, and within weeks stretched to a chasm. Harry no doubt, would have some inspiring but difficult to grasp Obi-Wan Kenobi explanation. But she wanted, no, needed, her mom to understand. "Mom—" Her mother held up a hand to stop her from saying more.

"I want you to have what I had with your father too. I think Blake *is* that man for you." Her mom's lips pinched and her eyes filled with regret. Or was it pain? "But your waffling has made you miss your chance. Blake and Daphne are already back together."

"What?" But somehow, this didn't surprise Emma.

Her mom moved to the couch. "Ethan told Matthew that Blake was flying to St. Louis tonight so he could sort things out with Daphne in person."

After a moment, Emma let out a bark that was halfway between an exclamation and a bitter laugh. If she had needed something to convince herself that she'd made the right decision, this was it. Blake could never have been in love with her if he'd simply plugged Daphne into the "wife" slot that had been planned for her. Or had it been the other way around all along, and she'd been plugged into Daphne's slot?

She put her head in her hands and coughed out a few sharp laughs, and when her laughter morphed into hard tears, her mom gently rubbed her back.

Emma knew she had done the right thing—a bit later than she should have—but it hurt, more than she thought it would.

* * *

That night, Harry tried phoning Detective Bradford again, to relay what he'd learned about Milo. His fifth call, like the previous four, went straight through to voicemail. He wasn't sure how to relay urgency without telling the detective in a message that he'd asked a PI to help investigate Sue's murder, so he simply asked him to call him back ASAP.

He'd spent the day in the sunroom, watching Milo's house with the aid of his binoculars and the phone nearby. But Detective Bradford hadn't returned his call, and there'd been no sign of Milo. He was contemplating yet another pot of tea when his security alarm shrieked.

Rrrrr. Rrrrr. Rrrrr. Rrrrr.

From his spot in the sunroom, he could see part of the living room and the full foyer. Nothing seemed out of place. He stood.

What to do?

Harry turned off the nearby lamp, throwing the room into darkness.

The security company would call the police if he didn't enter his access code within sixty seconds. If he could hang on for five or so minutes, help would arrive.

Harry stepped away from the sunroom windows, placing his back to the wall. With each passing second, the alarm seemed to crescendo: *danger, danger, danger, danger.*

Images of David's bleeding body flashed through his head. He tried to slow his breathing. Panic would get him killed.

He needed to find out where the breach occurred and to turn off the alarm so he could hear if someone was in the house. Forty long feet lay between him and the security panel. He'd have to cross the sunroom, living room, and foyer, standing out for most of it like a prairie dog popping out of its hole.

When he got to the sunroom doorway, he realized he'd forgotten his cane by the chair. *Blast.* He could have used it as a weapon.

Nothing looked out of place in the open space of his ground floor, so he crept forward. He paused two steps out, waiting for a gunshot to shatter the night. To shatter his muscles and bones. To shatter his chances of seeing his family again.

Seconds ticked by, and he continued forward. Twenty feet to go.

The alarm kept wailing.

In the dim light, Harry's foot hit a coffee table leg and he stumbled. He caught his balance with the couch's arm. He propelled himself into the foyer and jumped the last few feet to the security panel and the safety of the wall.

According to the faintly lit panel, a sensor was set off in the back of the house. If the intruder was inside, they'd be coming from that direction. He turned off the screeching alarm to listen.

Blood rushed through his ears, as he tried to adjust to the quiet. His eyes scoured the room for movement. Every shadow became the enemy. Every sound became a threat.

After surveying the room, he caught sight of his cell phone on the hallway table. He slid over and picked it up to call Detective Bradford. This time, he answered on the second ring.

"Detective, it's Harry." He tried to keep his voice low and wondered if the detective could hear it over his hammering heart. "My alarm went off. Someone's breaking in."

"Do you hear anyone inside?" The detective's voice remained calm.

Harry shook his head, then said, "No."

"Go to the nearest closet or bathroom and lock yourself in. I'm on my way. A squad car should be arriving soon."

The line went dead. Harry pocketed the phone, then stepped toward the hall closet to hide until help arrived. Or until the killer found him.

As he pushed coats and jackets out of the way to make room, he thought about the intruder knocking him over in his backyard. He thought about David, now struggling for life. He thought about the fear that now pervaded Lakeview Lane.

Fury replaced his fright. He was not the type of man who would cower when danger emerged. Instead of seeking shelter, Harry found his Callaway graphite golf clubs and wrapped his hand around a heavy driver. The clubs had been a gift from Mags, who'd hoped he'd pick up the sport so they could golf with the Patels.

He quietly closed the closet door and moved away from the wall, tightening his grip on the club. Outlines of his furniture were visible in the murky darkness. No movement.

When he reached the rear of the house and the wide spans of windows across the back wall, he peered out onto his screened-in porch. Nothing looked amiss.

His breathing and heartbeat began to slow, and he lowered the club.

A vibration from his cardigan pocket made him jump. His cell phone. He fumbled to answer while juggling the driver.

"Harry, what's going on?" The frantic voice belonged to Linda Buchanan. "Jack was out walking Baxter, and he thought he heard an alarm coming from inside your house."

"Something set it off, but I don't think anyone is inside."

"Oh, thank God. Jack started to head over with his shotgun in case you were in trouble, but I stopped him. I didn't want the police shooting him, thinking he was the intruder."

Terror shot through Harry as he envisioned the scenario. "Keep Jack inside. I'm not in danger, and I hear the police sirens now."

"I will. Call us if you need anything."

He hung up and put his cell back in his pocket. His home phone started ringing. It was the security company saying the police were on their way.

A minute later, Harry opened the door to let in the officers running up his drive. He explained what happened, and as the two officers searched inside his house to confirm no one had gotten in, he made a pot of tea. A second squad car arrived, and those two officers examined the outside of the house. They soon found the breach. Someone had started to pry open a window on the screened-in porch, but likely stopped when the alarm blared.

Harry shuddered when he thought about what might have happened if he hadn't installed the security system. If it hadn't been for Conner lurking in his yard . . .

When Detective Bradford arrived, he briefly spoke with his officers, then joined Harry by the fire, picking up the cup of tea Harry had left for him. Stubble covered the man's cheeks and chin; dark circles underlined his eyes. His clothes were more rumpled than normal.

"You gave me quite a scare. I'll have a squad car stay in the neighborhood for the rest of the night. I'll tell them to park in front of your house first."

Harry's adrenalin rush was waning, and he felt as drained as the detective looked. "Thanks. I've been trying to reach you all day. Milo Czesiak isn't really Milo."

The detective's brows furrowed. "What are you talking about?"

Harry rubbed the back of his neck. "A friend of mine is a PI. As a favor to me, he investigated my neighbors' pasts." He could tell the detective wasn't pleased with this news. Before he could admonish Harry for his actions, Harry explained what Geoff had found out: that Milo was operating under an assumed identity.

"I should have guessed it," Harry said. He'd read a criminal psychology book that discussed inconsistencies in a person's identity. "Milo's socks and shoes were all wrong. And then there was the wine."

"I'm not following."

"Milo wears expensive, handmade Italian leather shoes and his socks always have images related to wine."

"And?"

"His outfits are the same every day: jeans, T-shirt, and a gold chain. It's like he got lazy with his new identity and created a uniform of sorts for what he thought a former trucker would wear. But he forgot to extend that image to his feet. They never fit the body."

Detective Bradford looked unconvinced.

"Plus, the entire time I've known Milo, he's been a wine aficionado. Don't get me wrong, anyone can appreciate fine wines, but with Milo's in-depth knowledge, you'd think he was a sommelier. My guess is that at one time, he worked in viniculture. You should look for a fugitive who fits his age and physical description, who's wanted for white-collar crimes in states that can grow wine."

The detective's expression shifted to a mixture of annoyance and admiration. "I know how to do my job."

"Of course you do. Look, I've been watching Milo's house all day and he hasn't left. I think he's home."

"We'll check it out." He rounded up the four officers, and they huddled for a moment in the foyer. The officers left, but before joining them, the detective warned Harry with a hard tone that was full of concern. "Stop playing detective. You're going to get yourself killed if you don't."

"Understood."

Harry locked up behind him, re-armed the alarm, turned off the lights, and closed the blinds to all his windows except the sunroom window next to his club chair.

Despite his sheer exhaustion, Harry used his night vision binoculars to watch as the police entered Milo's house. He was anxious for them to take Milo in for questioning. Seeing Milo's apprehension might bring some comfort or feeling of resolution.

But minutes turned to an hour, and nothing happened. Milo Czesiak wasn't home.

Act III

"Safety first. You must consider how your work could expose other people to harm or put yourself at risk. Risk management is critical during fieldwork for the researcher, participants, and other involved stakeholders, as health concerns, social risks, political instability, privacy issues, and/or other unintentional adverse impacts may arise. Always keep an eye out for potential dangers or changes in the environment, and don't hesitate to seek guidance or help if you need it."—from *Lessons from the Field* by Harry Lancaster, Ph.D.

Chapter Thirty-Two

"I can't believe all that happened in two days." Emma shook her head in disbelief, wishing she had been there when Harry had needed her. She was in his kitchen, making English Breakfast tea and whole wheat toast with Irish butter and a drizzle of lavender honey. Or at least she was trying to. She'd been hanging on every one of Harry's words, so the process was taking longer than it should.

Harry sat on a stool on the other side of the kitchen island, fiddling with a now empty teacup. His recap of the drama of Lakeview Lane helped shift Emma's mind from Blake and her personal life, which had gone up in flames.

Their mothers were fighting, their brothers had almost come to blows, and their sisters were no longer talking. The one thing everyone could agree on was that Emma was to blame. She'd tossed the match that had ignited the blaze.

It seemed to occur to no one except her that if Blake had moved on from her in ten minutes flat, it couldn't have been the match of the century.

Yet after she'd arrived at Harry's that morning, it had dawned on her that everything would work out. Eventually. Perhaps because Harry had been through so much in life and had persevered. Or because he didn't expect anything from her, other than her doing what made her happy. Or because he accepted her for who she was, and in a way was teaching her to do the same.

When they moved to the table to eat, Emma examined the sadness on Harry's face. "I'm really sorry about David. Any updates on how he's doing? Want me to call and see if I can get some info?"

"The detective texted me earlier this morning. David's in a coma, his condition is still critical." He cleared his throat when his voice cracked. "The good news is the doctors are no longer worried about perotno—."

"Peritonitis. An infection that can result from a puncture in the stomach or intestines. That is good news."

"Maybe. But being in a coma—"

"While not normal, it's possible to become comatose after serious injury. Do you know if the coma was induced?"

"No."

Harry looked miserable; he needed a subject change. She took a bite of toast and continued with her mouth full. "Do you think it was Milo trying to break in?"

"Perhaps. When he came to visit me after my second fall, he did say I was as nosy as Sue. Maybe he thinks I know something. The police didn't find him at home, and I assume they haven't found him yet. Detective Bradford said he'd call when they had him in custody." He pushed a piece of toast across his plate.

"Eat." She pointed to his breakfast, now going cold. "I'm glad you told the detective everything. It's too dangerous for us to be involved now."

"I keep thinking about Valentina's and Milo getting that wooden crate. I bet he was buying stolen wines. If he goes on the run, he might take some with him."

"Did you mention that to the detective?" She took another bite. "Where did you get this honey? It's delicious."

He looked up at her. "What? Oh, I forgot. I mean, about telling Detective Bradford. The honey came from a shop on Main

Street." He moved to the kitchen counter for his cell phone. "I'll call him." She finished her toast as he waited for the detective to answer.

"Detective, it's Harry. I've got an idea of where Milo might be. Ring me as soon as you can." Harry ended the call, then slipped his cell phone into his cardigan pocket. The marled gray sweater was so nice it could have been knitted for British royalty. Or was it English? She didn't remember.

"Come on," he commanded, striding toward the mudroom that led to the garage.

"Come where?" She wiped her mouth and picked up her plate and cup. "Where are you going?"

He turned back. "Valentina's."

"Don't be ridiculous."

"We'll just see if Milo's car is in the lot."

"No," she insisted. There'd been one murder and an attempted murder. Harry seemed intent on making himself next in line. "Detective Bradford can take care of this. It's too risky."

"Look, I have to do something. If you don't go with me, I'll drive there myself."

She searched his face. He was serious. He exited into the mudroom, and she let the dishes clatter to the table. Grabbing her purse, she followed, her pulse picking up speed as she trailed him.

* * *

Twenty minutes later, they pulled into the parking lot behind Valentina's. They circled around once, looking for Milo's car. His red Ferrari was nowhere in sight. Emma parked in a spot where they had a partial view of the alley, then sighed with relief at Milo's absence. Her relief only lasted half an hour.

"He's here." Harry pointed to the car nosing down the alley to park by a dumpster. Milo jumped out, clad in jeans and a black leather jacket, then quickly disappeared down Valentina's cellar stairs. "Call the detective and tell him we've found Milo. I'll go stall him."

"Are you friggin' nuts?" Emma's heart began thumping against her chest. "The man is a killer. This is a matter for the police."

Harry leveled his gaze. "Call now." Then he opened the door and charged straight toward the alley with his cane.

Emma cursed under her breath. She fumbled for the cell phone in her purse. After she finally found it, and Bradford in her contacts, she hit the button to call, then looked for Harry. He was almost to the alley. Milo hadn't yet reappeared.

Her call went straight to voicemail. "This is Detective Nate Bradford, please leave a message. If your call is urgent, dial 911."

Finally, she got the beep. "It's Emma. Harry has found Milo and that fool is bent on stalling him until you get here. So, get here. *Now.*" She rattled off the address, hung up, then called 911. She told the operator that a potential violent crime may be about to happen, and the police were needed immediately. The operator asked her to stay on the call, but she wanted to be with Harry, who was now standing in front of Milo's Ferrari.

She hung up and jumped out of the car as Milo's head emerged from Valentina's cellar entrance. He was carrying a large wooden crate. Harry met him with a wave, looking calm and cool, as if Milo wasn't someone who may have killed in cold blood.

She jogged toward Harry, gravel crunching under her feet. *What was he doing?*

Milo said something to Harry, who then took the keys dangling from Milo's hand and popped open the trunk. Bottles clinked as Milo loaded the crate. She stopped next to Harry, and he glowered at her with a head jerk toward his SUV.

"Emma, I told you I could pick up our lunch order. I'll never be independent if I keep relying on you." Harry grinned at Milo, who seemed preoccupied. "Go back to the car. I promise I won't fracture another hip." He chuckled, as if he didn't have a care in the world.

Perspiration broke out across her hairline. "I'm paid to follow you." She tried to act nonchalant. Sweat trickled down her back.

"You can follow me anytime you want, Red." Milo turned to Harry. "I've got to get another crate. Watch my car." When he walked by, Emma caught a strong whiff of Milo's ever-present cigar smoke before he disappeared into the cellar.

"What in the hell are you doing?" she whispered, barely able to contain her anger. "Let's get out of here while he's gone. You have his keys."

"No, he doesn't suspect anything, I want to keep him here until the police arrive. You go. I don't want you to get hurt."

She clenched her fists. "I'm not leaving without you. And if we stay, you'd better hope that Milo kills me, because if he doesn't, I'm going to throttle *you* for taking stupid risks."

Clamoring footfalls rose from the metal cellar stairs. Milo's bald head appeared.

"We're debating the Valentina's menu," Harry said to Milo. "I want to go for the gnocchi, but Emma is bent on pizza. What do you recommend?"

"It's all good." Milo carefully loaded the crate, then closed the trunk. "Now, if you two don't mind, I'm off."

"Sure. Enjoy your wine." Harry turned to exit the alley, and Emma fell in step beside him. They got three steps away before Milo called out.

"You're going senile, Harry. I need my car keys."

Harry stopped and turned around. He straightened his spine and grew an inch. "I'm afraid I can't give those back."

"What?" The casual smile on Milo's face faltered, and he seemed more nervous than hostile. "Stop joking around. I need to get a move on."

"Sorry. I can't."

Milo's eyes narrowed into threatening slits, like a panther readying to pounce and rip apart its prey. "Give back my keys, or I'll take them."

"No." Harry stepped in front of Emma, then lifted his cane, ready to defend them.

Emma placed a hand on her chest, hoping it would hold in her out-of-control heart.

"And what do you plan on doing with that?" Milo asked with a derisive snort.

She glanced around Harry to see Milo reach into the pocket of his leather jacket. He pulled out a handgun and raised his arm to point it at them.

Her nerves exploded like fireworks. Her legs turned into jelly.

"Never bring a cane to a gunfight, Gramps. Give me the keys."

Harry moved again so she was directly behind him. "No." There was no trace of fear in his voice.

Milo slid something forward on the gun, then pointed it at Harry. "Give. Me. The. Keys."

Panic zapped through her, electrifying every inch of her body. She stepped to the side, pulling on Harry's elbow to emphasize her plea. "Give him the keys. Give him the keys."

Harry took three more steps, closing the distance between him and Milo's gun. "No."

Emma sucked in a gasp of air. The scene around her whirled.

The gun clicked.

Her world went black.

* * *

From the corner of his eye, Harry saw Emma go limp and fall to the gravel with a soft crunch. The gun hadn't fired. She must have fainted.

Milo's eyes popped wide, and he took a step back, lowering the gun in confusion. "What the—"

"Give up, Milo. The police are on the way." As if on cue, a siren became audible in the distance.

"I don't want to shoot you, but I will. This is your final warning. Hand over my keys!"

"No." Harry shifted his body, so he faced Milo side on, left foot forward. He assumed an en garde position, raising his left hand. Eight years of fencing lessons as a child were finally going to pay off.

Like a scene from the movies, Milo raised the gun again, holding it sideways.

There was a second click.

But the gun didn't fire.

Milo was surprised. Harry wasn't. He slid his left foot forward and brought the cane down hard on Milo's wrist.

Milo yelped. The gun dropped and skidded across the gravel, landing between them.

With another quick step forward, Harry used the cane to knock the gun under the nearby dumpster. Then he thanked Old Ironsides for making him and his brothers play ice hockey on the frozen pond in their yard every winter.

The police siren blared closer.

For a tense minute, Milo and Harry stared at each other. Harry could tell Milo was debating tackling him. While Harry was a decade older than Milo, he was also five inches taller and outweighed Milo's thin build by about forty or fifty pounds.

He readied the cane to strike again.

Milo swore profusely, then ran down the alley and disappeared into the parking lot. Harry turned his attention to Emma, who was now softly moaning.

"Emma?" He knelt beside her, ignoring the pain in his hip and his tender knees, which were still healing from his second fall.

Her eyes blinked open. "Where was I shot?"

"You fainted." He gave her hand a quick squeeze. "Did you break anything?"

Color started to return to her cheeks. "I don't think so." Her fingers probed the back of her head, and she let out a prolonged, "Owww."

A police car squealed to a stop at the base of the alley and two officers rushed toward them. Harry left his cane on the ground, raised his hands to show they held no weapon. He briefly explained what had happened and pointed in the direction Milo had fled. The young male officer, greyhound lean, sprinted off to find his quarry.

The older male officer, with his basset-hound cheeks and droopy eyes, remained with Harry and asked questions while Harry tried to help Emma sit up.

"My head hurts." She winced with each move.

"That was quite a fall." He turned to the doleful officer. "Is an ambulance on the way? She needs to be checked for a concussion."

The officer consulted his two-way radio, then said in a syrupy voice, "ETA three minutes."

Harry pointed to the dumpster. "I knocked the perpetrator's gun under that." The officer lumbered back to his cruiser and reappeared with a clear evidence bag.

"Did Milo get away?" Emma grimaced as she readied to stand.

A police vehicle and a Ford Crown Vic raced in and skidded to a stop in the gravel parking lot, stirring up a cloud of dust. Police radios squawked as the officers jumped out of their cars.

"He went that way," Harry yelled, pointing in the direction Milo had disappeared. Detective Bradford conferred with the two policemen who ran in opposite directions, then he strode toward them. Harry could feel the detective's anger twenty feet away.

Harry reached out to help Emma stand, but she slapped his hand away. "You fool." He was glad to see her wits had returned. "Were you trying to get yourself killed?"

"That's a good question. What happened here?" Detective Bradford demanded as he reached down to pull Emma up.

After Harry explained his run-in with Milo, the detective's voice vibrated with rage, and he put an arm around Emma's shoulder. "I told you not to get involved and you did it anyway. Milo could have killed you. He could have killed you both."

"No, he couldn't have," Harry contradicted. "His gun jammed."

"How could you *possibly* have known that?" The detective boomed, making Emma wince and pull away, her hand on her head.

"He's right," the basset-hound officer called, as he lifted a clear bag with the gun he'd retrieved from under the dumpster. "The slide got stuck."

"If you remember, Detective, I served in Vietnam. I can tell when a man doesn't know how to handle a weapon." Harry pointed at the bag. "Specifically, a Luger. On top of that, Milo held it sideways, like bad guys do on TV. And he rode the slide forward instead of letting it go. I could tell the gun would malfunction. The slide was locked back, hanging over his hand. The chamber was open and the barrel was sticking out from under the slide."

The fury on the detective's face dissipated. "Wait—" He turned to the older officer. "It's not a .22 caliber wheel gun?"

"No, sir. It's a nine-mil semi."

Harry realized what the exchange meant. "David was shot with a .22?" That gave him a boost of hope for David—a .22 bullet had less energy and momentum than the 9 millimeter, thus potentially inflicting less damage.

Detective Bradford glared at him. "See that Ms. Stockton is taken care of," he ordered. "And don't think this is over. I'll be by your house later this afternoon." He squeezed Emma's shoulder, then stormed down the alley to where the other officers had dispersed.

The ambulance stopped in the parking lot. Harry helped Emma toward it with a gentle hand on her back. "I'm sorry you got hurt. How are you feeling?"

She fingered a spot on the back of her head and flinched. "Like I deserve a raise."

Harry laughed. "Done."

Chapter Thirty-Three

Three hours later, Emma sat with Harry at his kitchen table. The EMTs had reassured them that she didn't have a concussion. To make amends for playing Dirty Harry and scaring the bejesus out of her, Harry had purchased her favorite from DaVinci's. Per her request, he'd altered it a bit: the normal pineapple but with a cauliflower crust and turkey pepperoni.

The table was littered with food: the pizza, two cans of Coke, a bottle of water, two salads, and a foil-covered quiche from Diana, which had been waiting for them on the porch when they got back.

"I'm glad the whole ordeal is over." Emma selected a slice, enjoying this healthier version of her go-to stress food.

Harry tilted his head as he toyed with his salad, uninterested in giving the pizza a try. "I don't know."

"What do you mean you don't know? Milo must be the murderer." She took a bite, then with a full mouth added, "I basically heard him admit to killing Sue. He's been living under a stolen identity. He pulled a gun on us. What other proof do you need?"

Harry pushed his plate away. "Poison doesn't seem like Milo's style. And the gun Milo pulled today isn't the gun used to shoot David. The detective mentioned David was shot with a .22 revolver. Milo had a Luger semi-automatic."

"So, he has more than one gun. Admit it, I'm right. Milo's our guy."

"Hmm." He sounded unconvinced.

She finished the slice, debated over trying the quiche, but turned to her salad instead. Two bites in, the doorbell rang.

"I'll get it."

Harry made it to the door without his cane, and a sudden sadness filled Emma's chest. He wouldn't need her much longer. And now that she wasn't engaged, she had no game plan other than another caregiving gig. She couldn't imagine enjoying it as much as her stint with Harry.

"Mr. Lancaster," Detective Bradford said when Harry opened the door. The detective looked desperate for a shower, a sleep, and a change of clothes.

She pushed away her salad plate with her bare left hand. Her engagement ring hadn't been there long, but it'd take a while to get used to not seeing it there. The detective's gaze lingered on the food strewn across the table. "It's not all for me," she blurted.

A confused look crossed his face. "Okay. How's your head?"

"Sore, but no concussion. We were celebrating that over pizza. Want a slice?"

"What kind is it?"

"Pineapple and turkey pepperoni on a cauliflower crust."

"I'll pass." He sounded like she'd suggested pizza topped with sardines and marshmallows. Emma ignored Harry's smirk.

"Your loss." She closed the pizza box to protect her beloved favorite from Detective Bradford's and Harry's disapproval. *Philistines.*

The detective's all-business demeanor returned as he faced Harry. "I want to make this clear, *again*. Stop playing detective. You both could have been hurt today. And I don't want to see either of you on the coroner's slab."

"You have the murderer in custody," Emma said. "It's a moot point."

"We're not sure if Pomeroy murdered Daniels *or* shot Dubois," the detective said, his tone brittle.

"Who's Pomeroy?" Emma asked, making the detective's tired eyes close.

"You know who Milo really is?" Harry's face lit up. "Did you get a hit on his prints in AFIS?"

"AFIS?" Emma thought she'd heard the term before on *NCIS* but couldn't remember what it meant.

"The Automated Fingerprint Identification System," Harry clarified. "So who is Milo? I bet he had something to do with wine. He's from California, isn't he?"

For a second, Emma thought there was going to be another death on Lakeview Lane when the detective strangled Harry.

To defuse the situation, she stood, picked up a Coke, and moved in between the men. "Here." She handed it to the detective. "Looks like you could use some energy."

His shoulders drooped, and he took the can, popping it open for a drink. She was as curious as Harry, but thought a different approach was needed. "Sounds like you already know a lot about this fake Milo."

"I could deny it, but you two are going to poke your nose in anyway, so I might as well save us all some time. According to AFIS, Milo is really Reeve Preston Pomeroy the third. From Sonoma County, California, where he ran a vineyard. He's wanted for tax evasion and embezzlement and, when he realized the authorities were on to him for these crimes, he left his wife and grown daughter to deal with the crumbling business. That is, after draining all their bank accounts to open a trucking company here—a type of business that can be used to launder ill-gotten gains. Not exactly husband or father of the year."

"What a loser," she interjected.

"Yeah. Pomeroy, aka Milo, has admitted to buying stolen rare wines in the alley behind Valentina's. But he denies murdering Sue Daniels and shooting David Dubois. And frankly, I'm not convinced he's the killer."

"Why not?" Harry asked.

"No more." Detective Bradford held up a hand. "That tidbit of information was to satisfy your curiosity so you two will stay out of my case." His voice hardened. "I mean it, stop playing around. David Dubois was shot twice and it's still not clear if he'll make it. And Sue Daniels's poisoning—"

"Oh my gosh, the quiche." Emma eyed the foil-covered plate on the table as if it had turned into a copperhead ready to strike.

Harry and the detective looked at her with perplexed expressions.

"When we got back from Valentina's," she said, "we found a covered dish on the porch table with a typed note from Diana—it was a chives and cheddar quiche. What if it's poisoned? Doesn't death camas look like chives and is confused with wild onions?"

The detective pulled a glove out of his pocket, pulled it on, and picked up the dish and the note beside it. "I'll get these to the lab and test them to be safe. For now, don't eat anything that you don't make yourself."

Harry cleared his throat. "There is one more thing you should know . . . There's a pot-luck dinner tomorrow night at the clubhouse."

"Why would anyone think that's a good idea?" Detective Bradford ran a hand through his already unruly hair, making it stand in different directions.

"I told the Patels they should cancel it," Harry reasoned. "It originally was supposed to be a Halloween party, but now it's just a get-together so neighbors can feel united during this difficult time. They thought it would be okay since Milo is in custody."

"Does anyone understand how serious this is?" The detective's eyes shifted between Harry and Emma, unsure of whom to blame. "Are you both planning on going?" Their nods elicited a few, as Harry would say, explicatives. "What time? I'll make sure a car is stationed outside the clubhouse."

"Five o'clock," Harry said.

The detective grumbled some more while his anger ebbed. "You both have my cell number. Call me if there's a problem." He exchanged a warning look between her and Harry. "Or call the second you sense there might be one."

Chapter Thirty-Four

The next day, Emma pulled a pan of whole grain chocolate zucchini cake from Harry's stainless steel Sub-Zero oven and took a comforting whiff. The lower-calorie pumpkin pie that had been baking alongside it had twenty minutes left on the timer. She placed the cake on a wire cooling rack and, not for the first time, wished her kitchen had half the features of Harry's.

Harry was reading by the hearth when the phone rang. "I'll get it," he called. He'd been anxiously waiting to hear from Detective Bradford with an update on David and if Milo had confessed. Her ears perked to eavesdrop.

"Hi, Diana," he said, and Emma knew there wouldn't be much to hear. Harry wouldn't be able to get a word in.

She eyed the cake, hoping the healthier option was as tasty as her normal brownies.

"Yes, we're going to the potluck. I told Gautam and Sakshi we should hold off, but they're keen to bring the community together." Harry fell quiet again. "Sure."

Emma's cell phone dinged from her purse, which hung on the back of a kitchen table chair. She debated checking the message, then decided against it. Everyone was still angry, but now the ire was split along family lines. Her family was upset that Blake had moved on so quickly, his family that Emma had supposedly driven him to it.

"You mean Emma?" Harry emphasized her name, and she guessed Diana had gotten her name wrong, again. "We'd be happy to."

Emma acknowledged his offer with an unladylike grunt.

"I will, see you later." Harry ended the call then turned in the chair so he could better see her. "Diana's outdone herself with baked goods. I said we'd help get it all over to the clubhouse."

"What did she call me this time?"

"Ethel."

Emma laughed. "I knew I brought the perfect book for you today." She tried to stifle her grin as she retrieved and rifled through her purse. She moved to the sitting area to show Harry the title: *In Search of Respect*.

His lips toyed with a smile, then he grew solemn. "Are you sure you want to go tonight? It could be dangerous. I'd rather you not come."

"If you think it'll be dangerous, then why don't you stay home?"

"I should be there in case something goes wrong."

"You're being overdramatic. And if something does go wrong, I need to be there for you. For everyone, actually. Remember, I'm a nurse." He opened his mouth, likely to argue, but she held up a hand to stop him. "It's not negotiable. I'm going."

As they were leaving for the potluck an hour later, the detective phoned. Harry put his cell phone on speaker so Emma could hear.

The detective's raspy voice made it clear he was running on fumes. "Pomeroy, aka Milo, still denies killing Sue Daniels and shooting David Dubois."

"He'll confess eventually," Emma piped in.

The detective hmmed, and Harry shrugged.

"How is David?" Harry asked.

Detective Bradford's voice remained grim. "Still in a coma and in critical condition. His vitals won't remain stable."

Emma furrowed her brows, wishing she could see David's chart to better understand what was going on.

"So you know," the detective continued, "the quiche wasn't poisonous. And Officer Jackson is already parked in front of the clubhouse. Can I convince you two not to go?"

"No," Harry and Emma said in unison.

"Please be careful," he said. "If there's even a hint of a problem, call."

Harry disconnected, and she asked, "Ready?" With a grave nod, he picked up the pumpkin pie, and she trailed behind him with the cake.

On their short drive, rain lashed the car windows, gushing from a menacing sky. Harry's concern was palpable. With Milo in custody, Emma couldn't understand why he was so grim. "Nothing's going to happen."

"Something's not right. I feel it in my waters."

She tried to lighten the mood. "As a nurse, I'm pretty familiar with human anatomy, and waters aren't part of it." He didn't respond.

They parked outside the clubhouse next to the patrol car. Emma gave Officer Jackson a wave as they retrieved the baked goods and rushed the forty feet to the door. She kept an eye on Harry with his cane.

After they placed the cake and pie on the kitchen island, Emma turned to Harry. "I'll go to help Diana. It's pouring down rain and slick outside, and you can't carry much with your cane."

Harry shook his head and moved toward the door in protest. Emma rested a hand on his elbow to stop him.

"Don't ridiculous. I'm not letting you go out in this rain and risk falling."

"There's a murderer out there. You are not going by yourself."

He would slow her down, and Emma was confident Milo was the guy, despite Harry's and the detective's hesitations. So she sprinted to the car with a farewell grin, knowing Harry had no way to follow.

"Doggonit, Emma," she heard as she dashed out the door.

Minutes later, Emma stepped onto Diana's porch and rang the bell. It was raining harder than before, and she was drenched. Her wet clothes clung to her.

Diana opened the heavy door wearing an elegant ebony dress with shoes that likely cost more than a month of Emma's pay. As usual, her hair was perfectly styled. Her platinum helmet told the world that while Diana was aging, she wouldn't go down without a civilized fight.

"My lands, it's a gully washer. C'mon back." Diana motioned for Emma to enter with a regal swoop of her arm. She closed the door behind them and led the way from the marble-tiled foyer down a maroon hall, her sensible but stylish heels clicking with each step. Emma wiped her feet on the doormat and followed. Evenly spaced pictures hung on the walls, depicting various stages of Diana's life.

"I think the Patels are right fools for having this dinner," Diana said, as Emma watched the older woman grow younger with each photo. "But you can't argue with those two. It's like fighting mules over a turnip."

Did mules like turnips? Emma didn't know. She wasn't sure she'd ever tasted a turnip. In the kitchen, the table and counters were packed with pies, cookies, and casseroles that emitted a heavenly smell.

"I'll be ready in two ticks. I just need to drum up some sacks to carry this all." Diana disappeared into a walk-in pantry and Emma looked around.

The kitchen was refined and functional, like Diana. Yellow walls were grounded by green Corian countertops and cherry-colored cabinets that matched the hardwood floors. It reminded Emma of a bountiful valley.

Along the back wall, a window box contained a potted plant with long, spikey leaves and delicate white and yellow flowers that clustered in a ball. "Your kitchen is beautiful. Those flowers are a nice touch." Emma pointed to the window.

"What's that?" Diana stepped out of the pantry. "Oh, aren't those sweet? They add a bit of sparkle." They loaded the bags and took the first round to the car, then both returned to the kitchen for the remaining items.

"Is that everything?" Emma had no plans of coming back out in this weather if something had been left behind.

Diana remained still, staring at the kitchen sink and the window box behind it. Her eyes went wide, her mouth opened.

"Ms. Middleton?"

The older woman seemed to be in a trance.

"Ms. Middleton, is everything okay?"

She snapped out of it. "What? Yes. I was making sure we got everything. C'mon now." Strain creased Diana's face as she shepherded Emma out of the kitchen.

Emma glanced in the direction where Diana had been looking. She couldn't see what might have bothered her. The window box contained cookbooks, the flowering plant, and a baby's bootie that probably belonged to a grandchild. Had someone passed by the window?

By the time Emma stepped onto the clubhouse porch, she was dripping wet. Miraculously, not one hair was out of place on Diana's head. Was her hairspray water-repellent?

Harry waited for them by the door, relief mingling with anger on his face. Emma was half surprised he hadn't sent Officer Jackson after her.

"See, I'm fine," she said, passing him with an armful of goods and Diana in tow. More people had arrived, and she wove her way through the crowd to the kitchen to place her load on the island.

After bringing in the last lot, she peeled off her dripping-wet jacket and headed for the women's room to fix her hair and makeup. Turning the corner once inside, she stopped short before running into Rachel, who stood before the full-length mirror, primping.

Black-leathered Rita Mae had made one heck of a transformation from her Tiffin days. Rachel wore a casual yet elegant Prussian blue dress that cinched her waist. A colorful scarf of navy, cream, and burnt orange loosely wrapped around her neck.

"Emma, darling, how are you?" Her words were slightly slurred. Rachel must have had some wine before coming to the party.

Rachel eyed Emma's outfit: dark, wet leggings and a marmalade-colored tunic now splotchy and clingy from the water that had seeped through her jacket. "My dear, you *must* stop by La Conchessa. After my magic, *no one* will recognize you."

Emma ignored the inferred insult, not wanting confrontation. For all she knew, Rachel was in on it with Milo. They both had devious pasts and secret identities. They were the perfect duplicitous couple. One could have killed Sue and the other shot David.

"I don't have a lot of money, but tips on how to polish my image would be helpful."

Pleased with her deft artwork, the older woman smiled at herself in the mirror. "It can be as simple as adding a scarf." Rachel turned to face her, took off her scarf, and held it up against Emma's outfit.

"You know—" she teetered on her four-inch heels "—once your shirt dries off, this will perfectly match what you're wearing." Rachel wrapped the scarf around Emma's neck and turned her toward the mirror. "What do you think?"

Emma's mascara was smeared, and her hair hung in tangled, droopy ringlets. The scarf matched her tunic, but it bunched around her neck, making her shoulders look broad. "It's a bit . . . poufy."

In the mirror, Rachel's lips twisted. "You're right." She spun Emma around and fiddled with the scarf. "Your shoulders are *much* broader than mine."

Emma pushed aside the urge to poke her. "I hear the police picked up Milo as a murder suspect."

Rachel stiffened, then continued with the scarf, adjusting the loop around her neck so the ends could hang longer. "Milo didn't kill anyone or shoot David," she said with confidence, then pulled on the ends of the scarf to decrease the size of the loop.

Was Rachel so certain that Milo was innocent because *she* was the killer? Emma's nerves twitched. At one time, the police had thought Rachel could have murdered her late husband.

The scarf tightened around her neck. Then it tightened some more.

Was the woman crazy enough to strangle her with a room full of people just on the other side of the door? Emma stuck two fingers in the loop around her neck to loosen it.

Rachel pulled down on the scarf's ends with force. "I wonder how you know Milo's in custody?"

"Word gets around . . ." Emma's voice had gone up in pitch, whether from fear or constriction from the scarf, she didn't know.

"Does that include words about *me*?"

Emma's pulse raced.

Rachel sneered. Menace filled her eyes. "Whatever you think you know about me, Emma dear, you *don't*."

They stood, eyes locked.

A scream formed in the back of Emma's throat. Would she be able to make any sound? Using both hands, she wedged her fingers under the scarf and tried to loosen the noose.

With the blink of an eye, the malice that had twisted Rachel's face slipped away. She released the scarf's ends and turned Emma around to face the mirror.

"See, that scarf looks fantastic with your coloring," she continued in her normal tone, like they hadn't had this bizarre exchange and near-assault.

"You're welcome to wear it for the rest of the night." Then, with a snarling-dog smile to Emma in the mirror, Rachel picked up her empty wineglass and left without looking back.

Emma gazed at herself, unsure of what had happened. Had that been a denial or a threat?

* * *

A wafting scent of Diana's lasagna pulled Harry to the kitchen. Rachel slinked by and she twiddled her fingers before linking arms with a handsome gentleman in his sixties whom Harry didn't know. Milo was being replaced.

Someone tapped Harry's shoulder from behind, stopping his progress. Jimmy's all-black outfit made his white hair glow. "It's good to see you getting involved again."

"It's good to be back," Harry said, and meant it. "It hasn't been easy moving on since Mags passed, but I'm starting to." He studied Jimmy's gingerbread-colored eyes. "How are you?"

"Relieved this ordeal is over. You've heard about Milo?"

"I heard. I hope you're right, and that it really is over."

"You don't sound convinced."

"Probably just being paranoid," Harry said, trying to quiet his instincts as his gut screamed back that his instincts were right.

Jimmy's expression turned sheepish. "Sorry about running off the other night. I guess everything just got to me." He shuffled his feet, then continued. "You mentioned Margaret's art supplies . . . How about I stop by sometime this week to pick them up? I was thinking I could use them to create a series of paintings in her honor."

Harry's shoulders dropped, and he blinked back the tears that filled his eyes. "That's a wonderful idea, Jimmy. I'd love that, and

I know Mags would have too. Just ring before you pop over to make sure I'm home. Emma can help since I'm not yet able to take the stairs."

"Speaking of art," Jimmy swiveled his head to survey the room, "I need to find Linda to talk about Wednesday's watercolor class. I'll be in touch." Then he waded into the crowd. Harry watched his back, feeling comforted—the exchange reminded him of why Mags and Jimmy had been such fast friends.

When Harry got to the kitchen island, he saw several dishes but no lasagna.

"I'm sure you're looking for your favorite. It's in the oven." Diana stepped from the corner workspace, with a white apron tied over her dress. "It'll be ten more minutes, so pick out an appetizer or two." She pointed a finger at him. "But you leave room for my cooking, you hear?"

"Your cooking is the main attraction." She beamed, then went back to fussing over a cookie tray. He chose a few carrots and some hors d'oeuvres to tide him over until the lasagna was ready and set off across the room toward Emma, who sat with Grace near the stone hearth.

Emma had spiffed up since her run to help Diana. A stylish scarf looped around her neck, adding elegance to her simple outfit. Grace wore a long-sleeved black wool dress with pearl earrings. A raspberry-colored shawl draped across her shoulders.

He offered each of them an appetizer. Grace looked at his plate, scrunched her nose, then returned her gaze to the low-burning blaze in the fireplace.

"Where did you get the scarf?" he asked as Emma chose a carrot and skipped the accompanying dip. She told him about her unsettling run-in with Rachel.

Harry looked over to see Rachel standing with a group of people, a half-finished glass of wine in her hand. Each day, it increasingly seemed like he didn't know his neighbors at all. Secret after secret emerged.

"It's incredible how many lives Sue was ruining," he said. "She was slowly poisoning Lakeview Lane, destroying one person at a time."

Emma stopped midchew, an odd expression crossed her face. Her gaze grew distant.

"What is it?"

Her attention returned. "What is what?"

"It seemed like you'd realized something."

"Something you said triggered a thought, but it's gone already. I hate when that happens."

He tapped Grace's hand and tried again to offer her an appetizer. She looked at him, this time with recognition.

"Harold, the raspberry pie you bought for me was delicious. Thank you." Her watery eyes floated from him to her lap. She smoothed the creases in her dress with her heavily wrinkled hands. Her attention then shifted to a nearby table's white lily centerpiece. "I like flowers too. Next time, you could bring me some of those with another pie."

"I'd be happy to, Grace. What kind of flowers do you like?"

"Red ones and purple ones, but yellow ones are my favorite."

"What kind of yellow flowers?" Harry figured they could go out tomorrow and buy a bouquet. "Let's see, in late fall we might be able to find sunflowers, maybe yellow roses. Do you—"

"Oh my God," Emma exclaimed, startling Grace in her seat.

"What?" He asked as he gave Grace's shoulder a calming pat.

"Death camas." Excited tension sharpened her words. "The poison Detective Bradford said Sue died from." She lowered her voice. "The plant was mentioned in one of your books on poisons. When it flowers, it has these delicate white and yellow buds. I just saw the same flower in Diana's kitchen window."

"What?" Diana couldn't be the killer. "Are you sure?"

"Pretty sure. I mean I'm not a botanist, but it looked similar. I told Diana I liked the flower and a minute later she got this weird look on her face, like she realized her mistake." Emma grasped his forearm. "If Diana poisoned Sue, she probably shot David."

He sat back, stunned. Grace stared at the fire, paying them no attention. "I did see Diana deliver a dish to Sue before she died, but if the police found poison in it, surely they would have arrested her."

"It has to be her." Her whisper was urgent. Her emerald eyes were wide.

"Let's see what Detective Bradford has to say. Call him from the women's changing room. There's no need for others to overhear."

She nodded and left. Harry looked around for Diana, wondering if he should be worried about the food being served.

"Grace," he touched her arm, "I'm going to the kitchen for a moment to see Diana."

She looked at him with a vacant smile. "Are you returning Diana's secret? Sue took it."

A warning twinge spread through his stomach. "What secret is that, Grace?"

"Sue took it. Diana wanted it back." Her gaze returned to the fire.

Seeing the Patels at the next table, he waved them over. "Could you two please sit with Grace while I run to the kitchen for a moment?" They moved over to join the older woman, who unsurprisingly, started telling them about her love for raspberry pie.

Harry hurried toward the kitchen where Diana was busy with food preparations. "Emma said you brought quite the haul. What did you bring?" he asked when he entered. He hoped he didn't sound as nervous as he felt.

Looking around, he made note of the dishes on the island, those set aside on the counter, and which ones were being heated.

Death camas was mistaken for chives or wild onion, so he focused on the savory items. Had Diana used any of those recipes to poison Sue? She wouldn't have reason to poison anyone here . . . would she?

"Yesterday I made those gingersnaps and those pies." She pointed to a raspberry and apple pie on the counter. "Then I made a tuna casserole and lasagna. Both are about ready to come out of the oven."

"You've been busy," he said as he tried to figure out the best approach to confront her.

Diana solved the problem for him. She stepped closer and dropped her voice, despite no one being near. "I've been so upset lately." She rested a hand on her heart. "With Sue and David and all. Cooking helps calm me."

He was glad she'd opened the conversational door to the recent tragedies—so he charged right through. "I know Sue blackmailed several of our neighbors. Was she by any chance also blackmailing you? Is that why you've been so upset?"

She pulled her head back as if he'd slapped her, then raised her chin with indignation. "How could you think such a thing?"

Harry decided to let her think he'd been blackmailed too. "I'm not judging, Diana. We've all made mistakes. Sue had a penchant for finding our biggest blunders, then using them against us."

Several emotions flew across her face, and she took a cautious step forward. "You too?"

Instead of responding—he didn't want to actually lie—he placed a comforting hand on her shoulder. The gesture disarmed her. Tears clouded her eyes, and she pulled a monogramed handkerchief from her dress pocket. She fled into the nearby pantry so she couldn't be seen from the main room.

He followed her, remaining at the pantry door. Diana faced the side wall so that Harry could only see her profile, her head down, like a penitent ready to confess.

"Oh, Harry," she cried into her handkerchief.

"What happened? Pastor Bill said Sue upset you about something."

"I can't. I just can't"

"Diana, you've been a good friend to me over the years. Let me be a friend to you."

She gave a low sob, and her shoulders shuddered. Harry glanced at the food to make sure no one was eating anything she'd brought.

"It's okay, Diana." He patted her shoulder again and waited. "I'm here for you."

Three sniffles later, she opened up. "Before I met my late husband, I dated a boy my high school senior year. He was forever in trouble, and it wasn't long before he got me into trouble too. Two days before graduation, I found out I was in a family way." Her voice choked. "I was terrified. If my parents found out, they'd've disowned me."

Muted sounds from the crowded room behind him filled her pause, and she went on. "I told my family I was going upstate to volunteer for a shelter for wayward women as soon as I graduated. They were so proud. No one knew that I was one of those women myself."

Tears trickled down her face. She wiped them away and blew her nose, struggling to maintain composure. "I worked there for 'bout eight months. Stayed till my baby girl was adopted."

Harry's chest grew heavy. As a parent, he couldn't imagine how difficult it must have been for her. "I'm so sorry. That must have been terrible."

"I've spent my entire life trying to make amends. I do everything I can for my church and local women's shelters. I even hope to help fund an orphanage one day."

"How did Sue find out?"

"I don't know." Diana turned to face him but stayed in the pantry, hidden from the eyes and judgment of others. "One day I came home and found a baby's bootie in my mailbox. I had no idea where it had come from, so I put it in my window box thinking the owner might come looking for it. Later that week, I found a rattle, then pictures of babies and the shelter where I gave birth decades ago." Her eyes dropped to her handkerchief.

"How did you know they were from Sue?"

"She dropped by with a pie she baked for one of my fundraisers for the women's shelter. Then she got to talking about unwed mothers and asked why I was so generous to their cause."

Anger surged in his chest. Sue had been so brutally cruel.

Diana dabbed her eyes. "She said if I didn't want the world to know my secret, I had to pay her twelve hundred dollars in cash each month. I tried to reason with her, to bribe her with my cooking and niceties, but nothing would soften that woman's heart."

"I am so sorry."

"Oh, it's my own doing. And if I wasn't so proud, I'd have never been vulnerable to her evil ploy." She looked away. "So, I did what I had to do."

"And what was that?" He whispered, terrified of what she was going to say.

She recoiled when she read his expression. "Pay her, of course. Oh, dear Lord, please don't tell me you thought . . . I didn't kill her," she whispered fervently. "And in case you're wondering, I didn't shoot David either."

He studied her wringing hands, her anguished face, her red-rimmed eyes. He believed her. *But if Diana wasn't the killer, why did she have the death camas plant in her kitchen*?

"Why did you stare at your window box when Emma was there?"

A blush rose on Diana's cheeks. "I was afraid she'd seen the baby bootie Sue had left for me. Everyone knows I haven't been blessed with children, let alone grandchildren."

"What about the flowers in your kitchen window? Where did you get them?"

She wiped her nose. "What? What does that have to do with the price of tea in China?"

"Please, it's important. Where did you get the flowers?"

"You mean the pretty, little white and yellow ones?" He nodded. "Funny you should mention them. I found them on my porch this morning with an unsigned thank-you card. But I recognized the handwriting. They were a gift from Jimmy."

Chapter Thirty-Five

The world slowed. Harry's focus tunneled. Pieces of the puzzle fell into place. He turned around and scanned the room for Emma and Jimmy.

"What's going on?" Diana stepped from the pantry to stand beside the oven. "First, you think I'm a murderer, then you're going on about flowers, and now you look like you're about to jump out of your skin."

"I have to find Emma and Jimmy." He turned to leave, but she caught his elbow before he could step away.

"What in tarnation is going on?" Her elevated voice pinned him in place; he did not want to draw attention.

Moving closer, Harry whispered in her ear. "Don't go anywhere with Jimmy. I've got to find Emma and call the police."

"What?" Diana pulled back, horror on her face as she guessed what Harry was thinking. "Jimmy wouldn't—"

"I'm pretty sure he would. Look, go ahead and serve the main meal. Remain calm and say nothing to anyone. The last thing we want is to create a panic. Got it?"

She straightened. "Understood." For a second, he thought she was going to salute.

He found Emma first, sitting in a deep leather chair by the fireplace, staring at her phone.

"Did you get through to Detective Bradford?" he asked.

"Not yet. What did Diana say?"

Harry motioned for her to lower her voice. "It's not her."

"What? It has to be."

"Jimmy gave Diana the plant." Harry looked around to make sure they were not being overheard. "Remember at the condo board meeting when you joked about me seeing everything in the community? Jimmy must have overheard. Plus, Mags used to tease me about watching our neighbors all the time, and I'm sure she did so in front of him. I bet Jimmy stopped by the other night to see if I suspected him."

"Holy crap." Emma's frightened eyes looked around the room, scoping for the killer in their midst.

"Call Detective Bradford again and get Officer Jackson. Better ask for an ambulance just in case. I'll find Jimmy and keep him engaged in conversation until help arrives."

"No—" she started to protest, but he cut in.

"Go, I'll be fine. We need to divide to conquer."

"Fine. Be careful." Emma sped off, busily tapping at her phone.

Harry spotted Jimmy sitting with Grace Buchanan at a table in the back corner near the rear door. The image of David's crumpled body flashed before him, and Harry was more than ever determined not to let the culprit get away.

He moved in that direction, doing his best to remain calm, and show no sign that would tip Jimmy off. On his way he was stopped by Sakshi and Gautam, who were dining with Jack and Linda Buchanan.

Sakshi waved him down as Gautam said, "Where's your food, old pal? Grab some appetizers and join us. Or are you staying on your feet so you can beat us all to Diana's lasagna?"

The table erupted into laughter. Harry did his best to play along, knowing his smile looked forced and hollow. From the corner of his eye, he saw Jimmy's head turn their way.

"You know me," Harry said, trying to edge around Gautam's pulled-back chair.

After another careful step, Jack rose to his feet. His large frame blocked Harry's view of the corner where Jimmy sat. "I wanted to apologize for Conner's friend knocking you down. As soon as Conner is no longer grounded, I'll send him over to apologize in person." Jack extended his meaty hand for a shake. "No hard feelings?"

"None." Harry shook his hand and inched further toward the rear of the room. "Back in a minute." He stepped past Jack, trying not to snag his cane on one of the chairs. He glanced at the entrance.

Where were Emma and Officer Jackson?

When he turned back to find Grace and Jimmy, Jimmy was no longer there.

Harry felt the sharp breeze before noticing the door next to the fireplace was ajar. Without a thought, he plowed toward it, then plunged into the relentless rain, onto the puddle-ridden concrete patio, confident that Emma and Officer Jackson would not be far behind.

The chill drilled into his bones. Rain slicked off the end of his nose, and he made a futile effort to wipe it. His eyes struggled to adjust to the darkness. A distant streetlamp cast billowing shadows and provided the only light.

The nearby pool was covered with a black tarp that bent from the weight of the water pooling within it. Raindrops rapidly rippled across the surface, accompanied by quick hollow thuds as each drop hit.

A blurry apparition materialized on the other side of the pool, Jimmy's white hair giving him away.

"Why?" Harry yelled.

Lightning struck and illuminated Jimmy's face as he glanced back. Disgust smeared his features. He no longer looked like the cheerful man who'd joked with Mags in the kitchen, the artistic man who painted enchanted landscapes, the endearing man who befriended every neighbor.

Harry moved forward, navigating around chaise longues left abandoned at summer's end. To his surprise, Jimmy halted.

"Of course it's you!" His bellow reverberated down Harry's spine. "Always standing in my way."

Jimmy's searing hatred evaporated the distance between them, and Harry finally understood. Jimmy had desperately wanted Mags, and now desperately wanted to get away. In both cases, Harry blocked him.

If he could just detain Jimmy until the police came outside. "Why shoot David? He did nothing to you."

"I didn't have a choice. He knew too much."

"David knew about you and Sue?" The question caused Jimmy to take a step back. Harry inched forward.

"He was my neighbor, he saw when she came over late at night. And that detective kept coming back and asking questions. Then David saw the death camas plant in my window when he dropped off my mail. It was only a matter of time before he figured it out."

The cruel twist of fate constricted Harry's chest. If it hadn't been for a few envelopes left in the wrong mailbox, David wouldn't have gotten shot.

Harry stopped twenty feet shy of Jimmy and took stock of his surroundings: the covered pool six feet to his left, a row of boxwood bushes four feet to his right, three chaise longues behind him.

"Why Sue?" Somehow he sounded calm, despite the fear ballooning in his chest.

Jimmy barked an angry laugh.

"Sue not only broke my heart when she dumped me, she used me to get dirt on my friends. I thought all her questions about my classes and students were because she was interested in me, impressed by my talent. The whole time she was drumming up material to blackmail me and *everyone* I cared about."

A thunderclap reverberated around them. *Where were the police?* Harry's pulse quickened.

"I was such a fool," Jimmy continued bitterly. "When I figured out what Sue was doing and confronted her, she *laughed* at me. Laughed. Said I was the perfect mark."

This time, Jimmy moved forward, jamming his hands into his coat pockets. "I loved Sue. Not as much as Margaret, but Sue helped me move on. I had . . . hope." His face crumpled. "But she never wanted me. All Sue wanted was my money and the information she could pull from me about my friends."

The storm snuffed out the world around them. Harry tightened his fingers around the cane, trying to predict Jimmy's next move. Every muscle in his body tensed.

"So I killed her." Jimmy raised his chin. Another bolt of lightning carved the sky. "Just like I'm going to kill you." He pulled out a gun. "You won't stand in my way anymore."

Harry's heart skidded.

A deafening thunderclap roared. Jimmy raised the gun and aimed.

A resonating blast.

Harry pitched backwards. Then two more shots pierced the night, followed by an anguished cry.

As he fell, images of Mags and Ceci and Steve and the grandkids swirled through his head. His body crashed into the chaise longue behind him. His head jerked, shooting pain through his neck. He slammed into the chair's wooden frame, and a starburst of agony exploded in his back.

His lungs emptied in one large puff, and he closed his eyes. Rain pellets stung his face.

After a few stunned seconds, he rolled onto his side. Gulping in air, his hands frantically searching for the wound, for the warm blood that would mark his hands.

But he found none. Jimmy had missed.

Harry struggled to his feet. Relief coursed through him as he regained control of his breathing.

Someone yelled for a paramedic from the clubhouse doorway. Looking over, he saw Officer Jackson standing in the rain, draped in shadows. She bent over a crumpled pile on the patio, obscuring his view.

Harry moved forward and tried to make sense of the scene.

The patio light flicked on, and he blinked in the harsh light. Two EMTs rushed outside with a medical kit and a stretcher.

He moved closer. Each step heavier than the last.

The EMTs sprang into action, checking vital signs, pulling out bandages, and inserting an IV. Between their kneeling figures, Harry could see patches of orange and red, then a deathly pale face.

Pain ripped through his chest. He struggled to breathe.

"Oh God, no . . ."

Emma.

Chapter Thirty-Six

Harry's knees weakened. The EMT's urgent voices melded together. He couldn't make out their words.

He forced air into his lungs trying to expand the vise that gripped them. "Will she . . ." His voice faded. He took another breath. "Where was she hit?" His voice sounded distant, foreign.

The EMTs ignored him, instead focusing on lifting Emma's limp body onto the waiting stretcher.

He took a step forward. Her eyes fluttered, then they wheeled her away in a flurry that filled him with terror. Harry stared at the spot where Emma had fallen. Rain was already rinsing away her blood.

Emma was here, and involved in this investigation, because of him.

Officer Jackson stepped over, concern in her eyes. "Sir? Should I call an ambulance for you?"

"I'm fine." He waved her off. "What about Emma? I couldn't make out what the EMTs were saying."

She hesitated.

"I'm a vet, Officer. This isn't the first gunshot wound I've seen. But I couldn't tell where she was hit. It looked like the chest." His last word felt heavy, portentous.

"I'm not sure. But she did get immediate medical attention. That's good."

He nodded, fervently praying for a miracle. "Someone should let Detective Bradford know what happened."

"Already done. He's on his way." Officer Jackson took Harry by the elbow and began to guide him inside, away from the relentless downpour. "Let's go sit by the fire. Detective Bradford will have questions for you."

Harry lifted his elbow from her light grasp. "No. I'm going to the hospital to see how Emma is doing. The detective can find me there."

"But, sir—"

"I *have* to be there for her." He started walking around the side of the clubhouse toward the front, then stopped. Emma had his car keys.

He had to find someone who could give him a ride.

Officer Jackson followed, and as if reading his thoughts, said, "I'll find a patrolman to take you to the hospital. I need to stay here at the scene." From the tone of her voice, he couldn't tell if it was an offer of kindness or a way to keep him from driving.

Within minutes, which felt like hours, Harry sat in the back of a police car as it whisked away from the clubhouse. Rain streaked across the windows. Anguish filled his heart.

* * *

Harry woke with a start, instantly aware of a dull ache in his neck and back. He couldn't remember why he was waking up in a chapel.

Then it flooded back to him with a razor-sharp slash: discovering Jimmy was the killer, their confrontation, Emma shot.

Once he'd arrived at St. Joseph's Hospital with the policeman, he had tracked Emma from the ER to surgery to the ICU, moving from waiting room to sitting area to standing outside of nurses' stations. The policeman who had escorted him had been steadfast at Harry's side until midnight, when Detective Bradford had cornered Harry for questions.

After refusing the detective's offer of a ride home, Harry had found refuge in the hospital's chapel, where he'd tried not to think about the last time he'd been there, pleading with God to save Mags.

He needed to see how Emma was doing. It wasn't yet six AM and visiting hours didn't start until eleven. He'd harass the nurses until they'd give him an update.

The last he'd heard was Emma's condition was stable. The doctors had told him she'd been lucky—if you could call getting shot that—because the bullet had gone straight through three inches below her left shoulder, just missing her left lung, left ribs, left clavicle, and an artery. The damage appeared limited. They'd done their best to clean the bullet track to help prevent infection. All that was left was waiting.

Numb with physical and emotional pain, Harry wandered through the maze of disinfectant-scented halls. His steps were awkward, and he was sure his face and hair were more bedraggled than his clothes. At the ICU nurses' station, monitors beeped and screens showed sleeping patients. The attending fortysomething nurse was dressed in scrubs that she'd garnished with a tight bun and a firm scowl.

"I'm checking in on the status of Emma Stockton?" he said in the politest tone he could muster.

Her glower deepened. "And you are?"

Another voice answered from behind him. "Mr. Lancaster?"

He turned to see a distressed female in her late fifties emerge from the vestibule to the side. The etched wrinkles on her face and clothing were testament to her rough night as well. She had Emma's striking red hair and green eyes. Had to be her mother.

"Yes." Guilt churned in his gut. *How do you apologize for getting someone's daughter shot?*

She rushed over to embrace him, her voice trembling. "I'm so glad you're all right. From what the police said, you were on the patio with Emma." Tears fell down her cheeks, which she wiped away with a heavily worn tissue. She pulled back and gasped. "Oh dear, I forgot about your hip. Did you lose your cane?"

"You must be Emma's mother," he extended his hand in greeting. He struggled to recall her name, realizing he didn't know it.

"Bridget." She shook his hand lightly. "Bridget Catherine."

"How is she?" He braced himself.

"The same, recovering, stable. But she's not yet regained consciousness. I've been here all night." A faint smile appeared. "A benefit from being a former nurse is not getting kicked out when it's family."

Harry remembered he had an Irish linen handkerchief in his jacket pocket, a long-ago birthday gift from Mags. He handed it to Emma's mother.

"Thank you." Bridget dabbed the corners of her eyes. "The doctors are optimistic. I know her surgeon and the attending nurses. She's in good hands. I've read her chart, and it looks like she's recovering well." Her features started to crumple, and she buried her face in his handkerchief to choke back a grateful sob.

With a surge of relief, Harry swayed. Bridget reached out to steady him and motioned for him to join her in the vestibule. The two sat across from each other in pink plastic chairs.

"Emma speaks so highly of you. Says you're the smartest person she's ever met." She broke into a genuine smile, and he knew where Emma had gotten hers, along with her natural beauty. "You're getting around without your cane."

He vaguely remembered dropping it by the pool. "I guess I lost it in the chaos last night."

"It's so terrifying. To think a madman could show up to a community event. And in Lakeview Estates of all places."

"I feel terrible about it." He looked down to his lap, his voice grew shaky. "Emma's here because of me."

Bridget's hands encased his, drawing his gaze. "Don't be ridiculous. She's here because of the crazy man who shot her."

A pretty woman with auburn hair stepped into the small space. "Mom, how is she?"

A tall man with ginger hair came to rest behind her. They each wore different college sweatshirts, but their similar eyes and facial structure put them both on Team Stockton.

Emma's mom stood and embraced her daughter and then her son. "She's going to be okay." This brought on tears from all three, who huddled in a hug.

Bridget stepped back and checked her watch. "Blake's gone downstairs to get coffee. The cafeteria opened ten minutes ago."

Instantly, Harry felt he was an interloper, cutting in on familial bonds. He stood. "Bridget, please keep me posted on Emma. If she wakes up, I'll come back during visiting hours."

He shared his cell phone number and told Bridget to call at any time if there was an update, then headed to the elevator. On his way, he passed who he guessed was Blake. The tall, sandy-haired young man carried a tray of coffees, and though wearing a preppy rugby shirt and jeans, walked with the air of someone comfortable in hospitals.

Unsure of where else to go, Harry headed for the cafeteria. He didn't want to go far in case Emma woke up. He bought a cup of tea, then retreated to an empty vinyl booth.

After an hour of stewing in his thoughts and staring at his phone for updates, a tired voice roused him. "Thought I'd find you here."

Detective Bradford looked like he hadn't slept much either. He wore the same disheveled clothing from the night before.

"Have you caught Jimmy?" Harry wanted this nightmare to end.

"Yes. It took hours, but we found him holed up in Sue Daniels's condo, crying at the kitchen table. We're holding him in custody. How's Emma?"

"Things look good, considering. The bullet passed straight through, below her left shoulder. She's in the ICU, but they expect a full recovery."

"Thank God." The detective rubbed his chin. "I need a cup of coffee, then I want to go over your story again. Tea?"

"Please."

When the detective returned, Harry walked him through what had happened with more detail than he'd shared last night, when his thoughts had been consumed with Emma. As they talked, the hum of conversation in the cafeteria rose as men and women in lab coats and scrubs ate breakfast.

Detective Bradford took notes and asked only the odd question. When Harry finished, the detective paused, flicking through the notepad pages, avoiding Harry's eyes.

Something was wrong.

"Is David okay?" David was recovering in Riverside Heights Hospital, roughly twenty minutes away. Harry had forgotten to check on his status with everything going on.

The detective met Harry's gaze. "His condition hasn't changed. Not better, but also not worse."

"So what's the problem?"

"Mr. Chatimont's story is different from yours. He said he stepped outside for fresh air, and you followed him out, then charged at him with your cane. He said he shot at you in self-defense because he thought you killed Sue Daniels and shot David Dubois. He said shooting Emma was an accident."

"*What*? You can't believe—"

"I don't. It's a ridiculous story." The detective's frustration was evident in his tone. "First off, he ran away after the shooting. Second, he didn't call 911 after he saw Emma was shot. Third, he didn't have the gun when we found him. Said he dropped it in a panic and has no idea where it is."

"Have you found anything that would implicate him for Sue's murder and David's attempted murder?"

"Not yet. My men are still looking for evidence and the gun. You said there were three shots?"

"Yes. I think he fired once, missed me, then I tripped over the chaise longue, sparing me from the next two rounds."

"Lucky you. If only Emma hadn't been caught in the fray."

The comment squeezed Harry's heart, and guilt came coursing from it.

"We haven't found any bullets, but we did find a mark on the fireplace where a bullet may have ricocheted. That said, my men were looking at night and in the rain. We'll try again this morning. We also didn't find any casings, just like at David Dubois's house. Maybe it was the same gun. And a .22 would be consistent with Emma's wound."

"So what does this mean?" Anger began to grow.

The detective let out a heavy sigh. "Jimmy Chatimont lawyered up after making a brief statement. Called one of the top criminal defense lawyers in the state, who will be at my office," he consulted his watch, "in less than three hours. There's a chance he could get out on bail. He's got no criminal record, and it'd be hard to present him as a threat to the community. He's a diminutive, polite man in his fifties who teaches painting and cooking. No one's going to see him as the next Jeffrey Dahmer."

Harry stared at him in disbelief. "Jimmy's family has endless cash. If he gets out on bail, he'll disappear in the wind. He can go anywhere in the world."

"I'm doing everything I can. We will argue that Mr. Chatimont is a flight risk." Harry could see the man was struggling with this as much as he was.

Officer Jackson walked up to the table. Her brunette ringlets were tightly secured under her hat. "I can take you home, Mr. Lancaster," she said, signaling the interview was over.

The detective leveled his eyes at Harry. "You need some rest, Harry. Go home. You could have gotten killed last night, and Emma is in a hospital bed. *Stay out of this* and let me do my job."

Chapter Thirty-Seven

Harry lowered the binoculars, keen for the last patrol car to leave. The police had been crawling all over Lakeview Lane since Officer Jackson dropped him off from the hospital that morning. Fourteen hours later, they were wrapping things up at Jimmy's house.

He had called Detective Bradford four times throughout the day to see if they'd found any evidence. The first three calls had been ignored. He answered Harry's last call to say they'd identified and picked up the second blackmailer—a down-and-out PI whom Sue had hired to stalk David and gather incriminating photos of his affair. He'd opportunistically tried to take over where Sue had left off.

Then in response to Harry's questions about finding the gun, bullets, or enough evidence to keep Jimmy in custody without bail, the detective had snarled, "I'm working on it," and hung up.

Which meant no.

According to Harry's research on legal procedures, Jimmy would come up for arraignment within forty-eight hours of arrest, and since a day had passed, that meant he'd likely be in court tomorrow. If his defense attorney did his job well, he'd get out on bail. He doubted anyone would ever see Jimmy again.

There'd been equally dismal news about Emma. When he'd called Bridget that afternoon, she'd sobbed. Emma was stable but hadn't regained consciousness—just like David. Bridget's cries had pierced Harry's heart and made his choice clear. He *had* to take action.

Margaret had minded Jimmy's plants when he'd traveled, which meant somewhere in the house, there was a key. It'd taken forty minutes of searching, and a painful climb upstairs to his office and Mags's art studio, to find it in a drawer, nestled among a slew of watercolor brushes. An acrylic "J" was painted on the handle. As soon as the police left Jimmy's house, Harry would see if the key still worked.

He knew it was unlikely that he'd find evidence the police had missed, but there had to be something to tie Jimmy to the crimes: bullets, the gun, a discarded death camas plant, financial records, mementos of Jimmy and Sue's relationship. Something.

At half past eleven, the last two officers exited Jimmy's house. After securing the front door with yellow crime scene tape, they drove away. Harry used the night vision binoculars to make sure the police were gone, then slipped on a black coat over his dark clothing and put thin leather gloves in his pocket.

Harry left his house via his rear screened-in porch, and instead of crossing the long, bare stretch of yard between his house and the duplex next door, he ventured into the rear woods.

Less than ten feet into the trees, he snagged his foot on a gnarled root. He shot his hands out to halt his pitch forward, ripping the skin of his left palm on the tree's trunk, barely catching his balance before tumbling into the mud. If only he had his cane.

It lay by the clubhouse pool where it had fallen the previous night. His heart seized with the memory, which propelled his feet forward.

Wispy clouds formed shifting shadows in the moonlight that did little to help gauge his footing. He wouldn't use the

Imalent SR32 flashlight in his front jacket pocket. He'd brought that to use inside, with its 20,000 lumens and narrow cone of light.

Not in all of his sixty-nine years had he broken the law except for speeding a few times: rushing Mags to the hospital when Ceci was born, scuttling through Maoist territory in Nepal on his way to Nepalgunj, and that time he'd been late for an anthropology lecture featuring Margaret Mead *and* her daughter Mary Catherine Bateson. But never more than nine miles per hour above the speed limit. Certainly nothing that could land him in jail.

The storm from the night before had left the ground soggy with leaves that smelled of decay. With each step, Harry sank into the soft earth, which suctioned his feet and threatened to steal his loafers. An impractical choice in his rush. He should have worn his Merrells. The sturdy ones he'd worn to trek the Inca Trail.

His foot sank even deeper on his next step, and he struggled to pull it free.

Impulse had driven him here. Caution—no, doubt—bloomed in his chest. He slowed, deliberated, then pressed on.

A frigid autumn wind ruffled his hair. The woods finally thinned, revealing the back of the house he'd been looking for. It sat dark, with no movement in any of the windows. The police officers who'd flooded his lane all day had finally cleared out. He checked the surrounding yards. Nothing.

Harry was the only fool out on such a miserable night. A night that could get a lot more miserable if he was caught.

Another shuddering gust warned him not to proceed. But he wouldn't be here, taking such a monumental risk, if he wasn't desperate.

From what he'd read this afternoon in a book on criminal law, this technically wasn't breaking and entering because Jimmy had given him and Mags a key and had never asked for it back. Yet he wasn't positive his interpretation of the law was correct.

On top of that, he wasn't sure that if he found incriminating evidence, it could be used. While the "fruit of the poisonous tree" doctrine applied only to government actors, evidence found by him could be called into question by a good defense attorney, thereby getting it thrown out.

But he had to try. Jimmy couldn't get away. He had to do this for Sue. For David. For Emma.

His hands trembled when he tried to insert the key into Jimmy's back door. In the dim light, it took several attempts to get the key into the lock. When it finally slid in, he unlocked the door with a loud, heart-stopping click.

He pushed the door open, its creaking hinges making him cringe. Remembering the mud on his trek there, he slipped off his shoes, set them on the back step, pulled on his gloves, then clicked on the flashlight.

He'd never been in Jimmy's house before. His gourmet French-country kitchen, with specialty appliances lining the granite counters, looked like it had been lovingly used, marred only by marks of a police visit. Drawers and cupboards were partially askew, while some had been dusted for fingerprints.

What was he doing? If the police couldn't find anything, it was unlikely he could. And he didn't know what he was looking for.

But he had to do this.

His search of the kitchen yielded nothing. Nor did he find anything in the dining room, first-floor bathroom, mudroom, or garage. When he moved into the living room, with its wide front-facing windows, he turned off his flashlight, closed the blinds, then turned it back on.

Like the rest of Jimmy's home, the room was neat, minimalist, and orderly. His bookshelves held vibrant-colored books on art and cooking and a large flat-screen TV. Decorated in muted shades of yellow, blue, and green, the room was cheery. Nothing like the home of a murderer. In a sudden rush of realization, Harry felt sorry for Jimmy and the ugly turns his life had taken.

Sue had been cruel, likely seducing Jimmy in hopes of finding some hidden dark secret she could use to blackmail him. His family had bottomless pockets. And when she didn't find anything on him, she'd taken advantage of Jimmy's friendships and closest connections, of the relationships he'd held dear.

Harry could imagine Jimmy's pain and betrayal. Through his love of art and cooking, the man had nurtured ties and built a beloved community, one that Sue had threatened to destroy.

He looked at each knickknack, painting, and piece of furniture. After finding nothing upstairs thirty minutes later, he admitted defeat.

On his way out, his flashlight flitted over the front hall closet. He'd missed it on his search of the first floor. Without holding much hope, he opened the door. The closet was about double the size of his and contained a jumble of coats, aprons, boots, umbrellas, hats, gloves, an easel, and in the far corner, a plastic crate full of discarded VHS video boxes. In other words, nothing.

After shutting the closet door, he made his way through the living room, his flashlight's beam splashing over the shelves around the television.

Something niggled in his brain. He stopped and trained the light on the shelves to examine them more closely. There was no VHS player.

That didn't necessarily mean anything. Jimmy could have gotten rid of it. He restarted toward the back door, then stopped again, thinking of the movie titles.

His breathing slowed. He traced his way back to the closet and pulled the crate out, aiming the light to read each one: *Blood and Wine*, *Double Jeopardy*, *Baby M*, and *The Seven Year Itch*.

Rocking back on his heels, he stood. He'd found the information Sue had gathered to blackmail his friends.

"Freeze." A baritone voice bellowed from the dining room doorway.

Harry's heart stumbled. His hands shot up, throwing the flashlight's glare to the ceiling. His feet remained glued to the floor.

Commotion at the front door behind him turned Harry's head as another officer stormed inside.

The overhead light flicked on, and Harry found himself staring down the barrels of two guns. One held by Detective Bradford and another by Officer Jackson.

"Are you trying to get your head blown off?" The detective screamed, then lowered his gun in disgust and motioned for Officer Jackson to follow. "What are you doing here? How did you get inside?"

"Jimmy gave Margaret and me a key, so technically, I didn't break in." Harry raised his hands higher. "And I wore gloves. Plus, you've probably already taken crime scene photos, so you'll know I haven't planted anything."

The detective's nostrils flared. "*Technically*, I can arrest you for interfering with a crime scene." He huffed again and seemed to be swallowing some likely not so polite words. "Officer Jackson has been doing hourly sweeps of the lane for the past six nights. Did you really think we wouldn't notice light flickering through the blinds?" He noticed Harry's sock clad feet. "Why aren't you wearing shoes?"

"I didn't want to muddy the floors. They're just outside the back door. Do you want to know what I found, or do you want to yell at me some more?"

"You found something?"

Harry pointed toward the crate of video boxes. "I'm pretty sure Jimmy took those VHS boxes from Sue's house after he killed Sue. I think each box contains the info Sue found on the people she was blackmailing. I bet you'll find Sue's and Jimmy's fingerprints all over them."

Officer Jackson and the detective exchanged a glance, then slipped on latex gloves. They each picked up a few of the VHS boxes, then moved to the dining room, splaying their bounty across it. Officer Jackson turned on the chandelier so they could better see.

Detective Bradford opened the first case: *Blood and Wine*, a thriller about a philandering wine merchant who tried to steal from his clients. This case was for Milo—it contained copies of the church newsletter Geoff Jeffries had mentioned and images of the real Milo Czesiak.

The case for *Double Jeopardy*, a movie about a husband who dies while out boating with his wife, held information about Rachel. There were scores of folded newspaper articles, testimony from neighbors, a miniature toy boat and motorcycle, and a copy of the police report. How she got the latter, Harry didn't know.

In the case for *Baby M* there was evidence about Diana's secret. Adoption records, a knitted baby's bootie, and files on the boy who'd gotten her into trouble. *The Seven Year Itch* contained photos of David and Charlotte, prompting Harry to remember that David and Victoria had dated for more than six years.

Harry's mouth went dry. A psychopath had lived under his nose. A psychopath who had tormented one of Mags's dear friends so much that it'd driven him to murder.

"I wish every criminal kept incriminating evidence like this," the detective said. "Would make my job a lot easier."

"My guess is," Harry said, "that blackmail was a game to Sue, these"—he waved at the boxes—"were just the pieces she used to play it. Think about it, Sue left items related to her victims' secrets in their mailboxes as a way to goad them into paying her, into getting them involved in her game." He pointed to the baby bootie and miniature toys in the open cases. "Vihaan, the Patels' grandson, mentioned that Sue had a toy motorcycle and boat. Diana told me she found a rattle and a baby's bootie in her mailbox."

"That's sick," Officer Jackson said. "To think someone could be that cruel."

"It's a good find. But I still want the gun." Detective Bradford pulled out a two-way radio and called in the crime scene unit.

Harry blocked out the detective and Officer Jackson, feverishly trying to put the last pieces of the puzzle in place. He strained to remember interactions with Jimmy over the years. Where would he hide a weapon?

Did his watercolors hold a clue? A location he favored?

Thinking back to Jimmy's works, he recalled they were bucolic landscapes or beach scenes. None were local. He wouldn't have had time to go far.

He remembered Jimmy and Mags cooking. Jimmy always had a new recipe for them to try. Though there'd been all sorts of dishes, he specialized in Asian and French cuisine. He'd favored sweets, despite staying trim.

Snatches of memories flashed through Harry's head, like the bulbs of a snap-happy paparazzo. Him reading by the fireplace, Mags and Jimmy in the kitchen, joking around as they filled the house with mouth-watering aromas: spring rolls, quiche, chicken satay, beef bourguignon, chocolate soufflé, pain au chocolat, macarons, tarte tatin, crème caramel . . .

Then it came to him. "I've got it."

"What?" The detective pulled the radio away from his ear.

"When you found Jimmy, he was in Sue's kitchen, right?"

"Yeah."

Harry shot out of Jimmy's dining room, dodging Officer Jackson on his way to the front door.

"Where are you going?" Detective Bradford trailed after Harry.

"Sue's." Harry quickened his pace to match the speed of his heart as he stepped out onto Jimmy's porch and into the windy night.

"Wait. You don't have shoes on." The detective ran around the side of house toward the back.

Harry's adrenalin surged, making him numb to the night's chill and the rough concrete beneath his stocking feet.

Seconds later, the detective caught up with him, Harry's shoes in hand. "I'm pretty sure you shouldn't be jogging, especially without shoes. Where's your cane?"

As if to underscore Detective Bradford's point, a dull pain throbbed in Harry's left hip. He slowed. The gun wasn't going anywhere. "I lost it on the clubhouse patio, but I didn't want to break through the crime scene tape to get it."

With that, the detective laughed. "Stop already and slip these on." He handed Harry his shoes. "Be right back." Then the younger man took off running with a pace Harry envied. The contents of the detective's pockets noisily clanked as he sped into the night, cutting through a neighbor's yard.

Detective Bradford joined Harry on Sue's porch minutes later, struggling to catch his breath. He held out Harry's cane. He'd run all the way to the clubhouse to retrieve it.

The detective pulled a ring of keys from his pocket to open Sue's door, and once inside, turned on the lights. Sue's condo had a modern interior, decorated in creams and whites with sleek modern furniture that looked uncomfortable. The air was stale. There were signs of a police search everywhere Harry looked.

Guessing the kitchen was in the rear, Harry walked down the hall, his shoes and cane clomping on the shiny white tile, now marred by his muddied steps. Staying true to the theme, the kitchen had glossy white cupboards and pearlescent countertops clear of any items. Stainless steel appliances gleamed in the bright kitchen lights. It was an elegant but cold showroom that revealed nothing about its owner. It matched Sue well.

Harry went to open a cabinet, and the detective's hand shot out to stop him. "No touching."

"I'm wearing gloves."

"*I'll* look for it, after you tell me what to look for."

"We need to find the sugar."

"Sugar?"

"Yes, sugar." Harry's hands itched to open cupboard doors and begin searching.

As Detective Bradford opened door after door, Harry tried not to guess where on the floor Sue had died.

"I think I found it." He pulled out a heavy green ceramic canister from a cupboard by the stove, then flipped it open and looked inside.

"Flour." He set it aside, then reached back to pull out a slightly smaller canister and opened it. "Sugar." The detective looked at Harry expectantly.

"Dump it on the counter."

With a quizzical arch of his brows, Detective Bradford turned the canister upside down over the countertop. Fine sugar grains tumbled out, accompanied by a loud *thunk*.

The detective moved the canister aside to reveal a .22 caliber revolver.

"How in the hell did you know that?"

Proud of his deduction, Harry did his best to sound humble. "When Mags and Jimmy were baking in the kitchen, Jimmy repeated the same phrase whenever they made desserts: 'Sugar makes everything better.'"

The detective looked at Harry like he'd turned water into wine. "If you ever want a job, give me a call."

Harry grinned. At least someone was interested in hiring him.

Chapter Thirty-Eight

Emma awoke, stiff and confused. Where was she?

Her right hand felt warm and constricted. Steady beeping filled her ears. She fluttered her eyes. Though her vision was blurry, she knew the ceiling wasn't hers. Someone was next to her, holding her hand.

"Hi, beautiful." The voice was familiar.

Emma turned and her eyesight sharpened. Blake.

"What happened?" Her voice was raspy. Her throat burned.

"Welcome back." He stood and stroked her forehead with his free hand's thumb. "Your vitals have been good for almost a day, but you've been in and out. Your mom was beside herself with worry, so I made Fiona and Matthew take her home. They all needed sleep."

"Don't remember," she eked out, yearning for ice chips to ease her raw throat. It felt like she'd been intubated.

"You were shot." He gave her hand a squeeze as emotion swept over his face. "Left shoulder. Fortunately, the bullet went clean through."

Her chest constricted with terror. "Harry?"

Blake shushed her. "He's fine. Been worried about you, like the rest of us. I think he's called your mom twenty times since you've been in here."

Despite her pain and discomfort, Emma found herself smiling.

A gray-haired, rosy-cheeked, plump nurse popped in to check on Emma. Blake left the room to call her mother with the news that she'd come around. Emma pleaded with the nurse to help her freshen up.

"He's quite the catch," the nurse said, stepping inside the bathroom to retrieve some toiletries. "Been at your side since you were wheeled up to the ICU. He's helped your mom cope, dried your sister's tears, and made your brothers eat. You're one lucky gal." She gave Emma a wink. "And he ain't bad looking either." Emma frowned, and stopped herself from explaining that they had broken up and Blake was with someone else now. In fact, why was he here?

Twenty minutes later, Emma had her face cleaned, teeth brushed, and hair unjumbled. She listened to her heart rate monitor and took stock of her life, and how close she'd been to losing it.

Blake returned ten minutes later with a well-wrapped, rectangular silver package in his hand. Even after an all-nighter, he looked rested: blond hair styled, hazel eyes clear. His khaki pants were pressed, his white button-up Oxford crisp, and his navy blazer perfectly tailored.

"Your mom was already on her way. She'll be here soon." Blake rested the box on her lap. "This is for you."

Emma stared at him, then moved to open the box. A stab of pain ripped through her left shoulder. "Oww."

"Sorry. Wasn't thinking. I'll open it." Blake lifted the present and removed the big loopy bow, then delicately peeled back the tape so the wrapping didn't tear. He gave her a tender smile, lifted the lid, and flipped back the tissue paper.

It was her navy fleece vest. For a confusing split second, Emma wondered if the engagement ring was still inside the pocket.

"It took some careful cutting, but I was able to remove the ring. I had it cleaned too. The vest, not the ring."

Her chest surged with emotion. Her voice was weak. "I'm sorry for the way things ended. If I hadn't survived—"

"Em, no need to apologize. I'm sorry for the way things ended too." He placed the box and vest on the chair and took her right hand.

"I didn't mean to hurt you . . ." Her words faded from the pain in her throat.

"I know. But you were right." He let her hand go. "We're not suited for each other. You're a beautiful, smart, and caring woman. But I realize now that I rushed things with us because I was hurting over Daphne. I guess I was trying to fill the void in my life."

His admission stung, but she appreciated his honesty.

"You know, after we broke up, I flew to St. Louis to see Daphne," he admitted. "We're giving it another try. I have you to thank for it."

It was what Emma had wanted. An amicable end. But it stung. Surprisingly, a lot.

A tearful Bridget Catherine burst into the room, saving Emma from the awkwardness of the moment. Her mom raced to her side and planted a big kiss on her forehead, like the kisses she'd planted on Emma at bedtime over twenty years ago.

The next hour was a parade of visitors: Emma's sister and two brothers and their families, and most of Blake's family. Anger between the groups had been replaced with goodwill. The excitement and commotion wore Emma out, and she fell asleep.

She woke hours later to the uplifting smell of roses and waning sunlight. Her friend Kathleen stood at the window, depositing a large vase of coral roses on the sill.

"Hi," she croaked.

"Sorry. I didn't mean to wake you." Kathleen gave her an affectionate look that felt like a hug.

The two women chatted about Kathleen's fast-growing toddler, the challenges of nursing, and then, Emma poured out her heart. The investigation with Harry, how she got shot, how she'd ended things with Blake, and how he'd already moved on.

"I did the right thing, ending the relationship." Emma's throat ached from all the talking. "But it still feels awful."

"It's only natural." Kathleen rested a hard-working hand on Emma's arm. "Most people's ego would have been hit by an ex moving on so quickly. Or knowing their ex never let go of their last love. You'll find someone better suited for you. Promise."

"My entire life is up in the air. I'm no longer engaged, not moving, and my caregiving assignment with Harry is over. I can't take care of him. Now I'm the one who needs physical therapy."

Kathleen's face shifted to the look she gave patients before sharing good news, a benevolent genie about to grant a wish.

"Funny you should mention the future because I have an idea for you for when you're recovered. A friend of mine from church asked if I wanted to do a medical mission to Peru with an international volunteer group that places medical professionals. It's not for long, about a month, and while I'd love to do it, I can't leave my daughter. But it'd be ideal for you."

Emma's heart skipped. After meeting Harry, she'd been dreaming of doing something like this. "I'd love to. But with my shoulder—"

"There's no rush. Applications are open, you can volunteer anytime. There's always a need." Kathleen explained the program in detail. Each nugget of information gave Emma hope. A plan for her future was forming. One that felt right.

In the dwindling visitors' hours after Kathleen left, Emma looked anxiously at the door, hoping the next person to enter would be Harry or Detective Bradford with details on what she'd missed. Neither man appeared.

Chapter Thirty-Nine

Early the next day, Harry left for the hospital, hoping to be Emma's first visitor. Bridget had called to tell him Emma had regained consciousness and had been moved out of the ICU. He'd held off visiting so far, not wanting to intrude on her family. But he'd stayed away long enough.

At the hospital, the halls were busy with candy stripers, food carts, nurses in scrubs, and teams of doctors with sleek laptops on wheeled metal stands. The PA system repeatedly summoned doctors and specialists.

When he found the right floor and unit, Harry picked up his pace toward Emma's room. He'd brought a fresh flower arrangement and a bag of treats, some healthy, some not. Best to cover all bases. He poked his head around the door, making sure he wasn't interrupting a visit.

The room contained two beds. The bed nearest the door sat empty. Emma occupied the bed by the window, which offered a drab view of the parking lot.

She sat propped up, reading a magazine, her thick hair pulled back in a messy bun that hung near the nape of her neck. Her heart rate monitor beeped in steady time.

He stood for a moment, watching her, sending up another round of gratitude. She turned a page, then scowled, clearly not liking whatever she was reading. "Pffft. As if."

He entered the room, joy sweeping over him. "Emma."

She let the magazine fall in her lap. "Where have you been? I've been dying to know what happened. Detective Bradford sent some random officer to interview me, and she wouldn't tell me *anything*." Her complexion was back to its normal peaches-and-cream.

Harry stood by her side. "First things first. How are you?"

"I'm going light on the painkillers, so my shoulder really hurts, but otherwise things are good." She sounded surprisingly upbeat.

"Good? You've been shot."

"I know, but it's worked out well." She gave him a crooked grin. "No one's mad at me anymore. Not even Mom. Everyone's just glad I'm alive."

"That's good, though I would have preferred you not getting shot." Harry broke eye contact, focusing on the flowers and bag in his hands. "I'm sorry I got you into this mess. I—"

She cut him off, her tone making his eyes return to hers. "Don't be ridiculous. It's the most excitement I've ever had. And you didn't pull the trigger."

"But—"

"But nothing. I'm the one who walked outside. Jimmy's the one who shot me." She eyed the flowers in his hand. "I assume those are for me, or are you carrying them around for some other reason?"

And in an instant, the guilt that had lodged in his chest since a bullet had entered hers dissolved. "Smart aleck." He set the vase down on the windowsill to join numerous others. "Nice collection."

"What's in the bag?" She sniffed hopefully. "Chocolate? And hopefully something healthy too."

"A book, of course, some double-chocolate brownies from Diana, and some sugar-free oatmeal cookies from the pink bakery you love."

She eagerly grabbed the loot with her right hand and placed it in her lap. "Diana's gingersnaps are amazing. Her brownies?"

"Even better."

Emma's grin spanned ear to ear, and she reached inside to pull out the book he'd purchased for her yesterday: *You Are a Badass: How to Stop Doubting Your Greatness and Start Living an Awesome Life.*

She snorted a laugh, then cried, "Oww. Shouldn't laugh yet. It's perfect, thank you." Placing the book aside, her hand went back in for a treat.

"I wasn't sure if you were allowed to have sweets, but I brought some in case."

"One or two won't hurt me. Remember, I'm a nurse, I should know. Now, pull up a chair and fill me in."

While Emma snacked, Harry told her all about how the police had captured Jimmy in Sue's house, about what Jimmy had initially told the police, about his high-powered criminal defense lawyer, and how he had helped the police find the gun and the information Sue had gathered to blackmail his neighbors. "I didn't get to speak with Detective Bradford yesterday, so I have no idea what's happened since then."

"Then I timed my visit perfectly." The detective's Thor-like physique filled the doorway. He wore a navy suit and was clean shaven and well rested. He stepped in and hovered at the end of the hospital bed. His eyes met Emma's. "You gave us quite a scare." Emma turned a lovely shade of pink.

Harry motioned for Detective Bradford to take the plastic chair next to him. "Looks like you got some sleep."

"Yep, a much-needed five hours. I'd love to get eight, but this case isn't over, and we caught another homicide on the east side this morning—"

"What's happened with Jimmy?" Emma interrupted.

"I can't say much now that the case is with the DA. But I think we have the evidence we need to prevent Jimmy from getting out on bail and to prosecute him for one count of murder and three counts of attempted murder." He leaned back in his chair, then asked Harry, "How's your hip?"

"Oh, come on." Emma looked like she was going to chuck the book *and* the bag of treats at him. "I've taken a slug for this case. I deserve at least *some* details, Detective Bradford."

The comment, and the look on Emma's face, made Harry realize how much he'd missed her these past few days.

The detective grinned. "At this point, I think you both can drop *Detective* and just call me Nate."

She gave a little grin. "Okay, Nate, fill us in."

"Give me one of the brownies I smell and promise that none of what I say will leave the room."

"Deal." Emma tossed him the bag. As he reached inside, she added, "Take as many as you'd like."

Nate removed a brownie and took a bite, then spoke while he chewed. "Jimmy Chatimont confessed to killing Sue Daniels, shooting David Dubois, and shooting at both of you."

"What?" Harry was surprised. "But his lawyer—"

"There's no more lawyer, and no funds for bail. When we confronted Mr. Chatimont and his lawyer with the evidence, things quickly unraveled for him. I guess word got back to his family about what happened, and wanting to avoid the public shame and scandal, they left Mr. Chatimont high and dry. Withdrew all their financial support. And they'd financed his house, so he now has a public defender."

"Didn't see that coming," Harry said. Nor did he expect to feel sorry for Jimmy after he'd shot David and Emma, but he did. Had unrequited love warped Jimmy? Harry couldn't stop picturing the jovial man he and Mags had spent time with.

"How did you get him to confess?" Emma leaned forward.

"I convinced him that confessing was his one shot for some leniency. Eventually he spit it out. Said he was tired of keeping everything bottled up inside. He'd felt so guilty betraying his friends, I guess he wanted forgiveness more than anything else."

A female candy striper with dark curly hair walked into the room, carrying a turquoise tray that smelled of boiled eggs. "Ready for breakfast, Ms. Stockton?"

"No, thank you." Emma looked thoroughly relieved she'd had a brownie and cookie instead. With a nod, the candy striper left.

Emma prompted Nate to continue. "So how did Jimmy kill Sue?"

"It started the day before Sue died. Jimmy gave Sue a Cambodian dish called amok."

"Margaret made that for me once." Harry winced at the memory. "Hated the stuff, full of onions and fish. Though I can see why in his mind he saw it as an appropriate way to poison Sue. The main ingredient is catfish, an opportunistic bottom feeder."

"Huh. That's funny," said Emma, and both men turned to her. "I mean not funny-ha-ha, but funny-interesting. In social media, like on Instagram or X, a catfish is a person who pretends to be something they're not. Ms. Daniels was that too."

The detective started on a second brownie. "Anyway, Sue must have had the amok for lunch on Tuesday, then put the dish in the dishwasher and turned it on. Evidence of the poison was gone, but the blue dish we found in Sue's dishwasher is a match to Jimmy's tableware. We figure Sue died not long after eating it. Once Sue was dead, Jimmy did all he could to not get caught, including"—Nate pointed at Harry—"visiting you. He was convinced you suspected him and poisoned your tea with a vial of antifreeze when he came for that late night visit."

"My goodness," Harry said. "A clap of thunder startled me, and I spilt the tea down the front of my sweater."

"Lucky you," Nate continued. "And when that attempt failed, he tried to break into your house days later with the goal of shooting you."

Emma's right hand rose to her mouth. "Oh, Harry."

"I owe Conner. If it hadn't been for him and my consequent fall, I'd have never installed a security system."

"What's weird is that Mr. Chatimont shot David Dubois with Sue Daniels's gun," Nate said.

"How did Jimmy get her gun?" Emma asked.

"He convinced Sakshi to give him the key and security codes. Said Sue had some of his art supplies, and he didn't want them mixed up with Sue's estate. That's when he found, and took, the VHS movie boxes that contained Sue's blackmail materials. He'd tried to break into her house to steal the blackmail materials, but her alarm stopped him. That failure made him decide to kill her."

"Why on earth would Jimmy hold on to that information?" To Harry, it made no sense to keep something so incriminating.

A look of pity crossed the detective's face. "It was symbolic. Mr. Chatimont said he'd given his friends' secrets away, and he kept the boxes to remind himself of how far he'd gone to get those secrets back."

"What did he have to say about David?" Harry braced himself for the answer.

"Jimmy was convinced David would put the pieces together—Sue's visits, the death camas plant David would have seen in his home. So he went to David's when he saw him come home from dinner with you. Told David he needed to borrow a cup of sugar, and when David led him into the kitchen, he shot him point blank."

Emma looked at Harry, her eyes full of concern. "That could have been you."

"By the way"—the detective focused on Emma—"Jimmy said he was aiming all three shots at Harry. He was sorry that he'd hit you."

She lifted her arm a few inches and winced. "Apology not accepted." Then she asked in a tentative tone, "How is David?"

Harry's spirit buoyed. "I got word last night that he's out of the coma and no longer in critical condition. He's still not out of the woods, but because he was so fit, the doctors are hopeful. I should be able to visit him in the hospital in a few days."

"That's great news," she said and clearly meant it.

Harry leaned back in his chair, relieved life seemed to be returning to a version of normal. "I'm glad Jimmy didn't know about Sakshi."

"The Patel woman?" Nate asked. "What does she have to do with this?"

"Sakshi saw Jimmy deliver a dish to Sue right before she died."

Nate blew out a sigh of relief.

Emma undid her bun, spilling her locks onto the pillow. "Sakshi is a beautiful name."

"It is," Harry said. "In Hindi, it means witness."

"You're kidding?" Emma asked.

"Nope. And it gets more bizarre. This morning, while getting dressed, I remembered what Jimmy's last name translates to in English. In French, châtiment means punishment."

* * *

Minutes later, Harry stepped into the hall to take a call that had lit up his face after glancing at his cell phone's screen. Now alone with the detective, Emma shifted in the hospital bed, adjusting her flimsy green gown.

Heat from sunrays pouring through the windows raised the room's temperature. Or perhaps the room had grown warmer from the smile Nate was giving her.

"Great work on the case," Emma said. "Sounds like everything is pretty much wrapped up."

"It is. Thanks in part to you and Harry, though I'll never admit that again. You two don't need any more encouragement. So now what? Looks like your assignment with Harry is over."

"Yeah. I'll miss him." A weight formed in her chest as she realized how much. "I'm not sure what's next, to be honest. There's a lot of change in my life."

"Speaking of change, I see you're not wearing your engagement ring. Worried someone will steal it from you while you're in the hospital?" He'd asked in a joking tone, but she sensed he really wanted to know.

The tempo of her heartbeat monitor quickened. "Blake and I are no longer engaged."

"I'm sorry. It's hard to lose someone you love." Remnants of suffering hung in his voice, and she wondered who he had lost, and how.

Then he stood and moved to the end of her bed. "You're an intelligent, talented, brave woman, who will have a cool scar from a gunshot wound. I'm sure you'll be snatched up soon." She watched as he left the room.

Chapter Forty

Early winter flurries danced in the wind as Harry traipsed down the sidewalk away from his parked SUV. He carefully watched each step sans cane; he wanted to keep it that way.

Emma's apartment was in an area of downtown Columbus experiencing gentrification, not far from the Short North neighborhood. Run-down and occasionally vacant buildings sat between sleek, modern apartments and trendy shops, creating a chaotic energy. He studied the changing environment in the frigid two blocks to her building.

At the entrance, he jostled brown paper bags and a DaVinci's pizza box as he pushed buttons on the intercom. He hadn't seen Emma in nearly a month. Somewhere along the line, she'd come to feel like a second daughter.

The intercom clicked. "It's Harry." A buzzer rang, and he opened the glass doors to go inside. The airy lobby had glass walls that opened to the street and a woodlike laminate floor. Conversation groupings of russet and leafy green chairs scattered across a golden accent rug, and intricate lights shaped like dandelions hung from the ceiling. It conveyed an earthy liveliness that suited Emma well.

He took the elevator bank to the third floor, then quickened his pace along the thick gray carpet in the corridor as a bag started tearing. When he got to her door, Emma pulled it open before he knocked.

"I'm starving. What took you so long?" Her rosy glow was back in full force, as was her smile. Emma wore her customary jeans and a ponytail, but instead of a sweater, she sported an extra-large OSU sweatshirt that likely had to accommodate some sort of wrap that, combined with the mint green sling, limited her shoulder's mobility while she healed.

"Hello to you too." He foisted the bags toward her. "Take them from the bottom, one's about to break."

She deftly grabbed them with her right hand and led him into the apartment. Expansive windows made up the far wall. In a sitting area, a sage green couch faced a flat-screen television and an overworn tan chair. Magazines and books were strewn across the coffee table, and framed photos cluttered the end table and TV console. The adjoining dining room featured a pale table and chairs with a large ceramic bowl full of fruit at the center.

Emma set the bags on the table, where she'd already placed a jumble of silverware, napkins, and plates. "Is the pizza warm?"

"Warm, yes. Piping hot, no."

As soon as he placed the pizza on the table, she nabbed a slice. Her left arm remained pinned to her side, and he hoped it wouldn't be a permanent limitation.

"I've been waiting for this *all day.*"

"It's not yet noon."

She sat, took a bite, and in between chews said, "A person needs their energy to recover from a gunshot wound."

"And your doctor recommends pizza?"

"Ha, ha. So, what's up in Lakeview Estates?"

"Sue's sister put her house on the market, and Jimmy's family put his up for sale too." He finished unpacking the bags, which contained salads, dressing, and two bottles of water, then he took the chair opposite her.

"I figured that," she said, or at least that's what he thought she'd said, given she'd spoken midbite through a chunk of crust. He pushed a plate, napkin, and silverware in her direction. With a grin, she set the slice down and wiped her mouth before diving back in.

"David is recovering well. Still in rehab but hopes to be back biking in the spring. Rachel's already dating someone else."

"No surprise there. If the guy has a lot of life insurance, he'd better watch his back." She smushed the remaining crust into her mouth and chewed, cheeks full like a chipmunk. She'd lost weight, too much in his opinion, and he was glad her healthy appetite had returned.

"Linda said Conner is applying to universities and wants to focus on computer programming. Jack thinks he's turned around."

She grunted. "Yeah, right."

"And"—he'd saved the biggest news for last—"Diana is trying to find out what happened to the daughter she gave up for adoption."

"Nuh-uh. Next you're gonna tell me she's stopped gossiping."

He'd missed their exchanges, even her mammoth eyerolls. "Well, now that you mention it, when we had Thanksgiving dinner together—the Patels, Diana, the Buchanans, and I—Diana didn't have one bit of news to spread."

"So things are better than normal in Lakeview Estates?"

"They're changing. Those of us left are bonding. All the tragedy has made us closer." Outside Emma's large window, Harry noticed the snowfall had intensified.

Emma wiped off a smudge of pizza sauce from her chin. "I'm glad to hear it. When's Ceci coming?" She tried to open a bottle of water but fumbled.

"Do you need help with—" The lid snapped open, and she took a sip.

"Ceci, Steve, and the kids get in tomorrow. I can't wait. But enough about me and Lakeview Estates. How are you?"

"Fine."

"That's hardly an answer. How are you really?"

"Getting shot's been annoying. My shoulder's healing slower than I expected. And physical therapy has been a pain. On the plus side, there are no hard feelings between my family and Blake's."

"That's good."

Emma bit into a new slice, prompting him to try the pineapple and pepperoni concoction. It wasn't that bad.

"And things with Blake?"

She broke eye contact and her glee slightly ebbed. She replaced her slice of pizza on the plate. "He's back together with his ex, Daphne."

"How do you feel about that?"

"It was a blow to my ego, that's for sure. But I know I did the right thing. We're not a great fit. I want to find someone who is." Her gaze flitted to the Christmas cards on the windowsill, and Harry guessed one was from Detective Bradford.

"So, what's next?" He took another bite. The odd pizza combo was growing on him.

"I don't know." Frustration edged into her voice. "I can't do anything weight-bearing with my left arm and my mobility is limited, so a medical mission is out, at least for a while. Regardless, it would only be a short-term fix to a long-term problem, like caregiving was. I don't want to go back to nursing." She pushed her plate away. "All those years of study and training were for nothing. Time totally wasted."

Harry tilted his head. Emma thought leaving her role as a critical care nurse had negated the good she'd done while she was there. He put down his slice and wiped his hands. "How did the nurses treat after you were shot?"

She gave him a quizzical look. "They were great. Did all they could to make me feel comfortable, they answered all my questions, checked in on me, and made sure I understood what was going on."

"And how did they make you feel?"

"Safe," she said without hesitation. "I knew they were going to do everything they could to help me get better."

Nodding, he waited for her to follow, wanting her to understand what she'd provided as a nurse now that she'd experienced it from the patient perspective.

"Oh." Emma's hand floated to her mouth.

"It wasn't time wasted, Emma. You did a lot of good along the way." He let her sit with the realization and went back to his pizza. A minute later, he could feel her scrutinizing him.

"You have that innocent look on your face, which means you're up to something."

"I am." He finished the slice before continuing. "I've accepted a consulting position with Aid First International, a nonprofit that focuses on improving health care around the world. It starts in early February and will last until late April."

"That's wonderful." She clapped awkwardly, trying not to jar her shoulder. "I'm so happy for you." When he didn't elaborate, she asked, "Why do I sense there's more?"

He wiped his hands on a napkin. "Because there is. I've been asked to evaluate various health care systems in South Asia and to propose affordable updates and revisions."

"So that's why you were reading all those reports."

Harry nodded. "I've completed these types of projects before and have already worked in each of the targeted countries, but I stopped working on health care projects back in 2000 to focus on infrastructure. The knowledge I have is dated."

He took a sip of water, realizing how much he wanted her to agree to what he was about to propose. "In fact, I need a health care expert to help me. I was thinking of you."

Her head pulled back, and she pointed to her chest. "Me?"

"I need a recently trained specialist who has work experience in health care delivered formally within the medical system and informally within the home. That's you."

"But what about me going on a medical mission?"

"Think of this as training for that. You said they had rolling applications."

"Hmm." She looked unconvinced. "What would it entail?"

"It would be a three-month assignment that would require travel to Sri Lanka, India, and Nepal. Once back in the States, we'd write a report on our findings."

This time, her "Hmm" seemed more thoughtful.

"Your pay would be almost triple what you earn as a professional caregiver."

That earned an enthusiastic "Really?"

"Yes. But you'd be self-employed, so no benefits. All travel expenses—per diem, airfare, hotel, taxis, etc.—would be covered while we're overseas. And while we're in Delhi, we can stay with Ceci and her family." He cocked his head and tried to tamp down the hope budding in his chest. "What do you think?"

A crease formed on her forehead. "I don't speak any of the languages."

"English is relatively wide-spoken, and where it's not, I can translate. It'd mean that for your first international adventure, you'd have a seasoned professional by your side. And, it'd give you a better grasp of the issues and realities you'd face on a medical mission."

"I suppose." Emma picked up her napkin and wiped her mouth. "But I've already told everyone I want to do a medical mission. I don't want to flake on something else, *again*."

His eyes held hers. "Despite years of medical training and your mom being a nurse, you had the fortitude to admit it wasn't right for you. Despite the pressures from your family and Blake's family being so close, you had the courage to call off your wedding. Knowing when something isn't right for you and changing course isn't flaking. It's being self-aware and courageous."

The napkin twisted back and forth in her hands, as if each move represented a pro and a con. Outside, the snowfall had lightened, and he hoped traffic wasn't bad. Harry didn't relish the idea of a messy drive home. But he wanted an answer before going.

"All you'll need is a passport and a suitcase. Aid First International will handle our visas. I'll provide all the materials we need to read in advance."

"I guess it would solve my income problem and help me figure out if I really want to do a medical mission."

He held back his mounting optimism.

"My shoulder might be sore. I'm not sure how much I'll be able to do."

"Our main job will be to listen, observe, and take notes, then analyze the data and report our findings. You were shot in the left shoulder. You're right-handed, you can still write and type, albeit slowly."

A car honked, and he got up to go look out the window and check the road conditions below.

She moved to stand beside him, shoulder to injured shoulder. The pace of the large, fluffy flakes had slowed. "I don't think we're going to get the four inches they predicted," she said.

He shifted his gaze from the slush-covered street below to the horizon. Above the billboards and brick buildings, a faint arc etched across the pale gray sky.

Emma gasped in delight when she noticed it. "It's a rainbow. I didn't know you could get them with snow."

Harry admired the sparkling, white-tipped urban landscape as the sun broke through the clouds. "In many cultures—Nordic, Polynesian, Hawaiian—rainbows are seen as paths or bridges, linking one world to the next. In others, they're perceived as a herald of good luck."

She turned to him, her high-voltage smile lighting her face. "With a sign like that, count me in."

Joy swelled his chest. "I promise it'll be a grand adventure."

"My only concern is how long we're gone. Three months seems like a lot."

He patted her back. "Before you know it, we'll be at my kitchen table writing reports, relishing the peace and quiet of Lakeview Lane."

Emma glanced at her sling and laughed. Harry couldn't help but join her.

Acknowledgments

They say it takes a village. And in the case of writing this book, it certainly did.

If it weren't for encouragement from Tiffany Yates Martin, I'd never have finished writing this book after receiving (brutally accurate) feedback on my first few chapters. Her brother, William Yates, helped with several police procedural questions. If I've made any mistakes along those lines, they are mine, not his.

Celeste Connally, thank you for being my first author friend and by my side each and every step of the way. Heather Harper Ellett, I cannot tell you how much I have benefited from your great advice on voice. Dana Isaacson, I'd have lost the plot, literally, without you. L. A. Chandlar, you made me feel part of the mystery writing community from the second I sat at your Malice Domestic table. Connie Berry, Sherry Harris, Mariah Fredericks, Mindy Quigley, and Kate Young, each of you provided the right type of support that I needed at just the right time.

Thank you, Meg Gardiner, who, after overhearing me talk about giving up on this book after querying only a few agents, talked me off the ledge by telling me that was like hitting the ejector seat button while my plane was still on the runway. And here's to you, May Cobb, for helping me write a killer query that turned everything around.

Acknowledgments

Hank Phillippi Ryan, E. A. Aymar, Greer Macallister, Jessica Strawser, Brian Andrews, and Don Bentley, each of you have provided sage advice to guide my journey. Meghan Leigh Paulk and Kat Caputo, thank you for your treasured friendship over the years! I know in my heart you are next.

I'm also grateful to my beta readers, who put up with early versions of this novel and gave me great feedback to improve it. The Writers League of Texas, Mystery Writers of America, Sisters in Crime, International Thriller Writers, and Margie Lawson all provided classes that have helped me learn the craft and business of writing. And a special thanks to the mystery writing community, which is incredibly kind—at my first Bouchercon, I knew I'd found my tribe.

Finally, my sincerest gratitude goes out to my dream team: my formidable editor, Sara J. Henry, whose eagle eyes and bestseller talent made this novel shine; the Crooked Lane Books team, who turned my dream into reality; and my lovely and amazing agent, Paula Munier, who put her faith in me and knows the writing industry inside and out.

I am eternally grateful to you all.